THE
LUCKY
ONE

BOOKS BY JESSICA PAYNE

Make Me Disappear

THE
LUCKY
ONE

JESSICA PAYNE

bookouture

Published by Bookouture in 2022

An imprint of Storyfire Ltd.
Carmelite House
50 Victoria Embankment
London EC4Y 0DZ

www.bookouture.com

ISBN: 978-1-80314-659-1
eBook ISBN: 978-1-80314-658-4

To my husband, who can keep up

PROLOGUE

TEN YEARS AGO

He's still there.

Still watching me with a hunger that makes me shiver.

A dark shadow of a man standing at the door of a decrepit cabin. A bird chirps nearby. The damp ground sucks at my feet.

Dawn breaks through the trees—enough light to see, enough light to escape.

I face forward again, inhale, exhale, as if Death is not at my back.

I have to get away. I have to *run*, but not yet. Not when he can still see me.

"I'll miss you," he calls. His voice startles me, and I steady myself with another breath before responding.

"I'll miss you, too." A lie. Not the first one.

One more step. One more glance. He's not following me. Not chasing me. Death is watching, not pursuing.

Two steps, then five, through the damp undergrowth, my thoughts racing.

Why would he let you live? You know what he's done. You're a witness. He won't let you live.

The answer comes just as fast.

He believed you. He thinks you like him. Maybe love *him. It worked. Just keep walking.*

A shudder rattles through me. My heart pounds against my ribs.

I count one, two, three, turning a corner on the trail, putting me behind a thick grove where he can no longer see me. Ahead, the forest path spreads out, the sunlight streaming between branches.

I hazard one last glance—no masked figure, showing nothing but dark eyes.

I'm not only leaving him. I'm leaving my friend August behind, cold and dead on that cabin floor.

But I'm leaving with a will to survive.

I break into a run.

I barely escaped being the victim tonight. Though I can barely think with the terror pounding through me, I know one thing.

I'll never be anyone's victim again.

ONE

According to my former therapist, the chance of falling victim to a serial killer is .00039 percent. The chance of being the victim of a serial killer *twice* is so small as to be... nearly impossible.

I repeat this to myself as I enter my apartment building and take the stairs to the fifth floor. I don't understand why anyone would lock themselves in a minuscule room—an elevator—with a complete stranger. Bad things happen in tiny spaces with strangers.

My therapist can help me process my trauma all she wants —she doesn't know what it's like to stare into the eyes of someone who enjoys, no, *relishes*—the thought of killing you.

My apartment is small, but upgrading to a house means windows and doors on the ground floor, and with my hours, I'm never home anyway. I'm always with Rob, at the gym. This is just a place to close my eyes at night. A fifth-floor apartment with one access point.

I unlock the two deadbolts. Push open the door. Listen.

My gym bag goes on the floor by the front door, and I check every room, every window, turning on lights as I go, until the once dark apartment blazes with lamplight. Only then, when I'm sure I'm alone, do I relock the deadbolts and let myself breathe.

My phone beeps, but I ignore it. I have a bag to pack. A flight to book. A trip home for the first time in a decade to plan. But then it rings, a special ring, and I forget all that. My heart leaps as I scramble to pick it up, slide the green bar to answer, and hear my best friend on the other line.

"Norah, are you okay?"

"Janie." Some of the tension leaves my body, just hearing her voice.

"I just heard. Do you know what happened?" she asks. "How he died?"

I got the call two hours ago at work. The police officer said they received an anonymous tip to check on my father. No one had come when they knocked on the door at his house, but through the windows, they'd seen him—seen his body, gray and still and dead.

"Probably a day or two," the cop said. "The anonymous call was strange, but he appears to have died of natural causes. Let me give you the name of the funeral home he'll go to once the autopsy is done."

I'd scribbled details, facing the corner of the gym, sweat trickling down my shoulders, Behind me, one of my athletes waited to resume their training.

"I don't know," I finally say to Janie. "I don't know how he died. But I'll be there tomorrow."

"I'm so sorry he's gone, Norah. I'm here to help with whatever you need."

We disconnect, and I stare at the wall in a daze.

My father is dead. Probably drank himself to death, knowing him. *Serves him right.*

I swipe a tear away—a tear he didn't earn—and go to microwave a sponsor-provided meal. I ignore the grief bubbling up in my chest. Stare at Instagram on my phone to distract my mind. Push thoughts of him away and focus on the present. Life is better that way.

I was on the brink of the big time as an MMA fighter when I realized fame was the last thing I wanted. So, I took a step back and became a coach, helping other fighters find glory. Beyond the obvious benefit of peak fitness and knowing how to kick ass, I get other things, too. Free meals. Free equipment. Occasionally, a sponsored trip.

I snap a photo when the microwave dings, post it to social media, tagging the sponsor, and pour a half glass of red wine. It's what I do every night.

But tonight is different. Tonight, my father is dead.

A ping, a text from Rob.

I'm sorry, Norah. You're right. You should go to Kansas City. I'll cover the gym.

He'd been irritable when I announced I had to fly home. *Dead is dead, Norah—what's the rush?*

But I shake it off and text him back, *No worries.*

Rob is my boss, but he's also family. He's the one who found me when I came to L.A., the one who kept me out of the street-fighting circuit and trained me to be dangerous. We squabble, because that's what family does. And then we forgive each other.

I run a bath, glass of wine almost gone, when someone knocks on the front door.

Another rule of survival: don't tell anyone where you live. Especially not when your face has been on television and you have a small army of superfans who hang on your every Instagram post. Despite my efforts to avoid it, I've become semi-famous through my athletes. I have to be careful how much of my life I let the public see. They don't get the dark and twisty pieces.

I stare at the door. It might be a Girl Scout selling cookies.

Or it might be *him*, returned from wherever he disappeared to a decade ago.

I gulp the rest of the wine. The roar of the bathtub behind me keeps me from being able to hear anything more than a second knock—this time harder, louder. *Rap-rap-rap*.

I take a breath and unlock the door.

TWO

Whoever knocked is gone.

In their place is a box. It's innocent enough. Brown card-board, a shipping label. I do a sweep of the hall anyway. Like I said, no one knows where I live—at least, no one I wouldn't trust with my life. Janie. Rob. Well, that's it. Janie and Rob.

I crouch to inspect it. It's addressed to me, but it's the return address that leaves my hands shaking: APPLETREE BOOK PUBLISHING, NEW YORK.

My breath comes out in one long hiss, followed by a curse. Our gym manager, Cher, has been on us about the cursing—with our athletes more and more often in the spotlight, she's asked we tone it down to PG-13. Then again, what's in this box was her idea, too, and I already know how that turned out.

Too many bourbons, a handsome writer with gentle eyes and a kind smile who knew just what to say to make everything I said seem *so interesting*. We'd built up a rapport through a month of emailing, but an intimate dinner sealed the deal. I bite back tears again and stand, kicking the box inside. He played me. He saw a woman who trusted no one and wormed his way into my life. Gained my trust, one email, text message, and kind smile at a time. I thought we were going somewhere. Somewhere real, somewhere serious.

And he knew he was blurring the lines between a reporter wanting an interview and a personal relationship. A one-hour interview around a meal and an intimate evening that continued into the next morning. The next *several* mornings.

Like most of my attempts at a love life, it didn't end well. Well, actually, it ended with what's in this box.

I refill my wineglass and sprinkle lavender bath salts into the tub. They are labeled SERENITY and CALMING, and I could use some of both right now. More texts come through on my phone, but I shut it off, strip down, and ease into the water. A week of my own workouts combined with training my athletes has left me tired, sore. And now my father's death, wearing on my emotions, leaves me wrung out. More wine. More deep breathing.

My father makes me think of my hometown, Kansas City. Kansas City makes me think of *him*. Which brings me full circle back to the damn box, and I glare at it through the bathroom door, where it still sits in the front room. Like my father, I want to ignore it. To pretend it doesn't exist, that it can't hurt me.

But it can. It will. My attempts to stay out of the spotlight, both as a coach and as a true crime obsession, blown to bits by a single moment of trust.

I down the rest of the wine, step out of the bath, dripping water and bath bubbles through my apartment. I swipe the box up and use a nail file to slice through the brown paper tape, only stopping when the tape is off and the packing bubbles rest on the floor in a pool of water.

And there's the book, in hardback.

The title says it all: *True Athletes, True Crimes*.

When I agreed to the interview, the author told me it was a book about female athletes and their coaches. Guy Stevenson wasn't a total liar. The book is about athletes—but about athletes who have been victim to, or involved in, crimes. He said he wanted the book to show athletes in their strength. But what he meant was he wanted to expose a nerve—peel back the skin, and show how many of us survived something terrible, only to rise to greatness.

I flip through the pages, each one raising my blood pressure a notch. *How could he?*

A rugby player who beat a murder charge to become a world champion. A long-distance runner who was left for dead by a serial rapist and recently qualified for the Olympics at thirty-five. An entire team of soccer players who escaped and exposed human trafficking by a coach. And then, me—the high school senior who escaped her would-be killer and went on to make sure no one could ever hurt her again.

Guy might as well have stabbed me with a knife and twisted the blade. I can feel the ache even now, knowing I fell for it.

It's then I notice the slip of paper stuck into the middle pages. I yank it out.

Dear Norah,

Sorry this book is getting to you post-publication. I wanted to send you a personally signed copy. Interviewing you for this book was a true pleasure I'd love to repeat. Call me.

Yours,

Guy

I snort. Not likely. He knew what he was doing. If I see him anytime soon, I'm more likely to give him a personal display of my skills rather than *talk* about them.

What kind of name is Guy, anyway?

I turn to the table of contents and flip through until I find my chapter.

> *During my interview with Ms. Silverton, she told a story like something out of a horror movie: The serial killer nicknamed Hansel, responsible for five known deaths, kidnapped both her and August Taylor. Ms. Taylor, her friend, didn't make it out alive, but according to Ms. Silverton, she used her womanly wiles to trick the sexually frustrated serial killer into falling for her. Ms. Silverton told him she would willingly stay with him, but her ailing father needed her as a caregiver. Hansel released her the very next day, reportedly telling her he would, "Wait as long as he needed to." Maybe that's why Ms. Silverton took up mixed martial arts and became one of the toughest and most sought-after coaches MMA has ever seen. Hansel remains at large to this day, thwarting the efforts of the police.*

So much for being a book about women's strength. Womanly wiles? *What the fuck, Guy?* He's right about one thing, though. Becoming tough has been my goal. And it's a goal achieved.

My fingers shake as I fumble to turn the page, but there are only more photos: the first is of August and me, one of the last photos taken of her alive, all dressed up for the school dance, the illusions of teenage hope in our eyes as we hugged one another. I no longer resemble the skinny girl with long dark hair in the photo—I've put on muscle, cut my hair to shoulder length. But August never got to grow up. Never got to change. I linger over it, wondering how Guy got a hold of it, then survey the others. A yearbook photo, a cheesy, innocent smile on my face. Next, a photocopy of the newspaper article recounting the watered-down version of what happened that the public was previously privy to—in this version, I *escaped* Hansel, no details provided.

Hansel, because like in the fairy tale, he left figurative breadcrumbs leading to his victims.

Guy had touched my hand as I shared the horror of that night with him, and now, ten months later, I can't believe I told him what I've only shared with one other person. I hadn't even told Janie the sordid details, because August, my friend who died that night, was her twin. The three of us with our other friend, Esme, joked we were quadruplets, inseparable. Until Hansel came along.

All Guy had to do was buy me a couple drinks, extend his flight home, and spend a few days with me here in L.A. He hadn't been intimidated by a woman who spent her days beating the crap out of people.

It was an intimate experience. One of the few times I've really opened up in my life.

I should have known better.

I snap the book shut and hurl it across the room. It hits the wall, rebounds, and goes right in the trash can, along with the girl I was back then. Weak. Scared. Unable to save August. There are many reasons I haven't been home in a decade. Facing Janie, who looks exactly like the girl I watched die, is undeniably one of them. Because it wasn't just Janie's twin who died that night. A piece of me went along with her into the cold, dark ground.

And now, I'm taking a direct flight right into that world, literally days after this book was published. Which means everyone will know through my firsthand report what happened, instead of the highly filtered version I gave to the police.

My secret is out in the world. I wasn't strong enough then. So, it's not just my father's death I'm flying into tomorrow. It's my past, too, glorified and printed in full color.

THREE

My first stop in Kansas City is to see Janie. The plane lands, I get my rental car, and I head straight for the Country Club Plaza, a swanky little corner of Kansas City full of upscale dining and fancy stores tucked into brick and stone and tile.

Autumn has come to Kansas City—the ruffle of orange leaves, pumpkin-themed decor, people wrapped in scarves and jackets. I shove my hands in the only coat I own, the same one I had a decade ago when I lived here. There aren't many opportunities to need a heavy coat in Los Angeles.

What strikes me most as I walk down the sidewalk to Janie's Cafe, is that almost nothing has changed—the same bookstore I went to with my mother, the restaurant my parents celebrated their anniversary at. Even the people seem the same, in khakis and collared shirts instead of the more laidback style of the West Coast. I've changed—but this place hasn't.

I've seen photos of Janie's Cafe, the culmination of years of waitressing and bartending and then managing restaurants—but to see it in person rocks me. My friend did a thing. She opened her own restaurant. Soon, she'll be married. She's moving forward with her life, and meanwhile, I'm—what?

Arguably, I've become one of the most successful MMA coaches. I'm definitely the most successful female one. That's not nothing. Was it my dream, no, but someone like me doesn't get big dreams. I got to survive. I'm still surviving. That's more than August got.

I shut down the thought. Push my way through the glass front door with the fancy script reading JANIE'S CAFE, and have to stop, pull off my sunglasses, let my eyes adjust. The blustery fall day is replaced by dim lighting, brick walls, a dark bar that looks like it might be a hundred years old and original to the space.

And behind said bar, wiping her hands on a towel, is Janie.

"Norah!"

It hasn't been long since we've seen each other—maybe three months, when she last visited me in L.A.—but she flings herself cross the room, wrapping me in a tight hug. I hug her back, shut my eyes, push away the fleeting moment when, in her excitement, she'd looked more like her twin, my friend who hadn't survived that night.

"I'm so glad you're here," she whispers. "How was your flight? Are you—" She pulls back, meets my eyes. Her brown eyes assess me, focused, all-seeing. "Are you okay?"

I shrug, force a smile, step back. She raises one brow but doesn't comment. Janie knows better than to push. I'll open up if and when I'm ready. That's something I love about her.

"Want anything?"

"Just water, thanks." I find a barstool and she bustles behind the bar, makes up three glasses of water and slides one my way, then excuses herself to deliver brunch to customers. She's back in moments, as though she was never gone. I'm about to comment on her cafe when she leans close.

"Listen." A dark penciled eyebrow quirks. Janie has cut her hair shorter than ever—chin length—and it adds shape to her face, taking her high cheekbones from present to angular. It's a good look on her—very Janie.

"I know you're here for your dad," she says. Her eyes dart away, unsure.

"Janie—"

"No, listen. I wouldn't even bring it up, but I have to have someone cover my shift and make a reservation if you say yes—"

"Janie." I say her name again and grab her hand. It's hot, like she hasn't stood still all morning. "I came back to bury my dad. And help you do whatever wedding crap you can stuff into one weekend." I give her a smile with the last part—it's not my cup of tea, and she knows it. But that's not what matters.

A smile curves at her lips, which makes me notice her lipstick, a crimson red. It reminds me of the girl I went to high school with, so stylish and sure of herself. Did she do this all by herself these last years, or is it her fiancée, bringing her back to who she was before?

"Really?" she asks in a whisper.

"Really," I say.

She whoops. "Great! We'll go tomorrow. I already over-staffed for it."

Of course, she did.

"Speaking of—" Janie looks down at her watch. "Esme should be here any second. She just texted me she was in the parking garage. I'm going to make her a latte. Want one?"

"Just plain coffee."

"Cream, sugar?" It's how I prefer my coffee, and of course she remembers that. But I'm in training mode—less sugar, less dairy.

"Black," I say, trying not to eye the half-and-half on the counter.

"So..." Janie has her back to me at the espresso machine, turning cranks and rinsing a pitcher. Steam hisses from one nozzle, and I watch, impressed by my friend's skills. I knew she'd worked in restaurants. It makes sense she would know these things, and yet—we only see one another on vacation, when other people are waiting on *us*.

I stare at her, trying to remember her fiancée's name—Clarissa? No... Cassandra? No... Chloe. Yes, Chloe. *Jesus.* I bite my lip and know, whatever she has planned for wedding prep, I won't complain. I abandoned her. I fled as far away as I could go, short of leaving the continental United States. And I failed to save her sister—the one who should be doing all this wedding stuff with her. The least I can do is sip champagne and coo over a dress I wouldn't be caught dead in.

"Norah?"

"Sorry, what?" I accept a ceramic mug of steaming black coffee.

"The book," she says, like she's said it a few times. "Did you read the book?"

I blink. Remember wine, bath bubbles, and throwing the damn thing across the bathroom into the trash. I take a long sip, pressing back a surge of anxiety at the thought that my story is out there for anyone to read.

"*Guy* sent me a personalized copy."

Janie's teeth do something that reminds me more of a wolf snarling than a stylish cafe owner showing disapproval.

"The fucking nerve."

"Right?" I take another swallow of coffee.

"Elaine's been snooping around since your dad died."

I'm about to mutter my own curse. Elaine runs the true crime website that put what happened to August and me front and center in the true crime world. Thanks to her, what happened to us has become true crime lore—discussed on podcasts, hashed out on blogs, mentioned in books. But she never got the whole story—no one had. And somehow, she seemed to know it, stalking me all the way to Los Angeles. It got bad enough I had to take out a restraining order. But before I can let obscenities fly, a vaguely familiar man ducks through the front door and waves at Janie. He fills the doorway, literally blocking out the sun.

"Is that—?"

"Yes," Janie says, and she bites her lip. "He stayed in touch with my family after what happened, visits when he's in town, but he—"

I watch as the man makes his way through the room. I haven't seen him in a decade. Since the night August died.

He moves toward me like a phantasm, a speck of the past I'd all but forgotten. I'd lost a best friend that night—he'd lost his girlfriend. August's death had utterly changed the course of both of our lives. I want to run—want to escape—and avoid this homecoming and all the messy emotions all together. But I can't. I don't run anymore.

So I turn and force a smile on my face, ready to greet the other person whose life was devastated that night.

I realize too late, he's not smiling.

FOUR

My dead friend's boyfriend does not look happy to see me.

"Norah Silverton." He sidles up to the bar beside me.

"Owen Andrews." I examine his face, working to figure out the unfriendly vibe. On first sight, the familiarity of him was a comfort, though a bit disturbing—the last time I saw Owen, August was attached to his arm at prom, the same night she and I were nabbed. Back then, he was a wrestler with good enough grades for a partial scholarship to a local university. Like me, he ended up not going.

"Welcome back." He extends a hand, though I'm not sure I should take it. His face is no longer that of a boy's, but has transformed to a man's, a defined jaw, stubble, broad shoulders, the works. His hair is almost jet black, with dark brown eyes.

"Same to you?" I say it as a question, because of his attitude, but also because I hadn't heard Owen was back in town. I left for Los Angeles—he left for San Diego and the Marines and half a dozen deployments to war zones. Our respective boot-camps, so to speak. I take his hand, and it's coarse, like a fellow fighter's.

"Been back about a month," he says.

"Coffee, Owen?" Janie interrupts, distracted as she pours mugs for the table that signaled her.

Owen gives her a nod and slides onto a stool beside me. "Thanks, Janie." She pours a cup, shoots me a look I can't decipher, and disappears to help her table.

I'm about to make small talk, because as good as it is to see a familiar face, the fact of the matter is, I don't know Owen. I haven't seen or talked to him in a decade, and I only knew him back then because he was August's boyfriend. But Owen gets to it first.

"I saw the book." He sips his coffee, and the look on his face is pleasant enough, but there's a stiffness to the set of his shoulders, a flicker in his gaze that tells me where this is going. It also explains the coldness.

"I'm sorry." My voice is strained, because while I *am* sorry, I'm the one who was there. Who's alive now to deal with the shitshow this may become. Who will have to listen to fight announcers say, *And here comes coach Norah Silverton—besides coaching multiple world champions, she tricked a serial killer with her womanly wiles,* like it's a fun factoid, when in reality, it's no one's fucking business. What happened shouldn't be put out into the world for the entertainment of others. My tragedy isn't *fun.*

"The book wasn't supposed to include anything about August. About what happened," I say.

He makes a noise in his throat, the sort that means *yeah, right,* and my hackles rise, my hands tightening around my own coffee mug. I know plenty of guys like him at the gym, guys who think just because they have muscles and a handsome face, they can get their way or share an unwanted opinion.

"So, why are you here?" Owen murmurs. "Why aren't you next door, signing books?"

Ice slides through me, and I take a steadying breath. I search the restaurant for Janie, because it's probably best I go. I need to get on with the day anyway—head to my father's house. I want to see how he was living, but I have another agenda, too. My mother left us the summer before my senior year—and I suspect my dad has had communication with her. I can't imagine two people spending a decade married, having a daughter, and never speaking to one another again. They had loved each other, after all. I asked, more than once, if he'd heard from her. He never said no. Just refused to talk about it. Which made me think the answer was *yes*.

After all these years, I want to know why she left me. How she could defend abandoning her daughter. I understood why she left my dad—it's hard to love an alcoholic—but I never figured out why she'd left me behind. The idea of seeing her—hearing her—makes my heart soar. But also sink, remembering finding that note, the ache of abandonment. She at least could have taken me with her. As it was, she left on a Friday after the last class she taught at the local high school, leaving a mere note stuck to the refrigerator, something about *I deserve to be happy*, and that had been that.

"How much did they pay you?" he continues.

I meet his gaze head on. The skin around Owen's eyes tightens, focuses, like he's not used to others refusing to drop their eyes. That old rage fueled from helplessness burns hot in my veins—about my dad's drinking, my mother taking off, about becoming Hansel's almost-victim.

"Fuck off, Owen."

His shoulders bunch, but I don't so much as twitch. If he's dumb enough to try something, I'm ready. And when he eases back in his stool, I think he must know it. My lip curls with satisfaction.

"What's going on here?" Janie's behind us a beat later, sliding a plate in front of me—whatever their healthy breakfast is, I'm guessing—egg whites, toast with no butter, tomato slices.

She slides something less healthy in front of Owen, apparently his usual.

I don't answer, and Owen turns away, pulls out his phone, stares at it.

It's like someone released me from a chokehold, and I can breathe again. I search for an excuse to leave, nudging aside the breakfast I don't have an appetite for. But Janie looks around, tilts her head, frowns. "No Esme yet?"

Crap. I forgot we were waiting for her.

"Listen, I'm sorry, but I need to get this thing with my dad over with. Can we meet for drinks tonight? Tell Esme I'm sorry?"

Janie gives me a slow nod, mouths, "Text me," with a glance at Owen.

Two minutes later, I'm out in the crisp air, feeling lighter for having left Owen and his bullshit behind me, but the world has grown darker. A gust of wind carrying the scent of rain tells me a storm is coming. Leaves rattle overhead, and I stop, stare at the dark clouds as lightning streaks across the horizon. Lightning is a rare treat in Los Angeles and seeing it here is enough to break the gloom in my head. I watch a moment longer, hoping for a second bolt, but the first raindrops hit, and I move for the parking garage down the block where my rental is.

I get no more than two steps before something catches my eye down the alley behind Janie's restaurant. It's familiar because I've seen a version of it once before.

Ten years ago.

That canyon of dread reopens in my chest. My mouth opens, and if I could find my voice, I'd scream.

Breadcrumbs. Literal breadcrumbs, making a trail from the edge of the alley to beyond where I can see, the brick wall blocking my view. My insides clench up, and my hands tighten into fists.

I can't be afraid. Not anymore.

It's a prank. A sick joke. It has to be. After all, Hansel never used *actual* breadcrumbs.

I force myself to breathe, to take a slow step forward. The alley swallows me up as I follow them, and claustrophobia creeps over my skin in the narrow, dim space. *Not afraid, not afraid, not afraid.*

The rain patters around me, and the bread soaks it up and bloats. One piece disintegrates as a trickle of water streams down the alley, and it hits my running shoes. My heart flutters, adrenaline shoots through me. I kick the speck of bread off as if it's a mouse trying to crawl up my leg.

The rising panic tightens my chest, makes it hard to inhale, and it's enough to bring me back to myself. To the moment.

I'm not *her*, not the scared high school girl with the trembling voice who begged a serial killer for her life. I'm not— *Fuck.* What am I doing then? Walking right into danger? I can train as hard as I want to, but if someone down this alley has a gun, or if it's a reporter—or worse, Elaine—hoping to get a candid photo because she's desperate enough to do something like that for her damn website, I'm walking right into their trap.

I almost turn around.

I almost run.

But then I remember how Hansel killed August. Slicing her arteries, letting her bleed out as he left the breadcrumbs he chose for her—ripped up bits of a love note from Owen he'd found in her purse—giving her the illusion that if someone found the trail fast enough, maybe, just maybe, she could be saved.

Pressure builds in my chest.

What if it's not a joke? What if someone's at the end of this trail of breadcrumbs? What if they're still alive?

I look down. The water is no longer clear with bits of dirt and oil from the alleyway. It's gone red. Blood red.

FIVE

TEN YEARS AGO

"Prom is dumb," I whispered to Janie as we stood in a corner, watching our classmates dance in the gymnasium the junior class had decorated in an attempt to make it look like anything but a basketball court. I tugged at the edge of the strapless bra I had to buy for the occasion, wishing I'd done what she had and gotten a dress with actual straps. Or skipped a bra altogether. I let my eyes wander to the girls nearest us, making sure they didn't notice.

"I told you." Janie moved behind me to pull up the elastic for the fourth time that night. "Strapless bras are basically the devil."

August smiled. "I think your dress is pretty. And I'm happy to leave. We'll have more fun at home, anyway."

"Thanks, August." I gave her a thankful grin—she always had the right words to make me feel better. And she was right— she was referring to the sleepover we planned after every school dance—pajamas, music, and laughter, pedicures and movies and food. It would be more fun.

"Let me say bye to Owen, and we can go." Her gaze flicked

to where he stood with a group of boys from the wrestling team, looking grown up in their suits and ties.

Janie and August were twins, but easy to tell apart, with Janie's usual scowl affixed to her face, whereas August was nearly always smiling. The idea that they shared the same DNA baffled me.

Esme appeared with paper Dixie cups of punch in her hand. She distributed them to Janie and me. August had already flitted off and pulled Owen aside.

"Wait, we're leaving?" Esme's face fell, and she shoved a lock of golden hair back. "We got all done up for this. Makeup and hair and —" She gestured at her face. "This was work. I want to stay. Besides —" Her eyes slid to one of Owen's friends, the tallest of the group, with shaggy blond hair. "I think I finally caught Billy's attention."

Anxiety swirled up inside me—I was excited to leave, not stay here so she could pursue her latest obsession.

"Okay, fine." Janie nodded, decisive. We were all equal in our group, but Janie acted as the social director, and it was her and August's house we always gathered at. "You and August go home. Esme and I will stay a little longer. Maybe you can start the food?"

Relief flooded me. "Sure." I nodded, maybe too eagerly. I came because my friends were here, but they knew I would rather have skipped the dance and all the stares. It was probably my imagination, but I swore everyone knew Mom had left. Taken off, leaving me behind. What they didn't know was the only place I wanted to be less than at prom was home. Dad was no doubt yelling at a baseball game, already halfway through a bottle of whatever was on sale at the liquor store. Plus, I couldn't wait to get out of this ridiculous dress and bra and put on the pajamas mom had gotten me our last Christmas together.

Seconds later, August returned, wide-eyed and breathless, like she and Owen just got done making out, which they probably did. I managed to not roll my eyes. "Okay, you ready to go?" she asked.

She didn't need to ask me twice. I waved goodbye to Janie, locked elbows with August, and walked gratefully out of the school and into the cold, dark night.

SIX

I bolt into action, following the trail beyond the dumpster out back of what must be Janie's restaurant.

At the trail's end, a black high-heeled boot sticks out from behind the dumpster. I step closer, gaze traveling up to see jeans over skinny legs. A silk shirt, destroyed by blood and rain. Pale, lifeless skin.

A dead body.

She's slouched to one side, like someone tossed her to the ground carelessly. I start to reach for her—for my friend—I want to grab her close. Hug her. Bring her back to life.

Esme.

I kneel, my body vibrating with anguish.

I know what death looks like, but I'm not a doctor—I might be wrong.

My hand trembles, but I brush my hand through long, shiny blonde hair to touch her neck, feeling for a pulse. She's still warm to the touch, but no blood thrums beneath my fingers. No heartbeat I can ascertain. I swallow the panic rising from my chest to my throat and take stiff steps backward, my legs unsteady. I feel for the door inset to the brick, the back door of Janie's restaurant. I bang on it until I hear something inside— the click of a lock.

And then I use my foot to stop it from opening all the way.

"Hello?" Janie's voice.

"It's me." I hesitate—because I don't want to leave August out here alone. *No, not August.* Esme. Another friend. A different friend, and I don't want to leave her, either, but I can't stay in the alley. I edge around the door, pushing her out of the way. I slam it shut. Lock it.

I have to keep Janie safe. Keep me safe.

But our safety is an illusion. Not ten feet away, through this brick wall, is our dead friend. And any evidence left behind is being slowly washed away.

"What's wrong? Why were you—" Janie grips my shoulders, gives me a shake. "Norah? What's wrong?"

"Esme's dead." I meet her eyes. The fog of my brain lifts, just a little. "Call 911. Close the restaurant. The alley's going to be a crime scene."

Janie stares at me, mouth agape, but then she nods. Blinks, as though to make sure this is all real. She pulls her phone from her pocket and steps away, dialing and lifting it to her ear. Esme, bloody and lifeless, flickers in my mind, but I squeeze my eyes shut and push the image away. I can't focus on her—can't lose the battle to the grief surging through me, tightening my throat. I have to think.

Hansel was the most notorious serial killer Kansas City has seen in decades. He simply disappeared into thin air after letting me go. Police speculated he'd left the area, gone elsewhere, or given up his game altogether. Elaine and her true crime fanatics liked to guess at when he'd reappear, or wonder about other serial killers in other parts of the U.S., and could they be him? So far as I know, there have been no real leads in a decade.

Is it possible he's back? Yes.

Probable? I hope not. I'd secretly wished he'd died after that night—maybe in the ultimate act of karma. Or maybe, he'd realized he failed—I survived—and decided to call it quits. Thoughts of fantasy. That's not how the world works. I know better.

I lean on the counter to keep myself upright, fighting the panic rising in my chest. If he is back—if he killed Esme—that means this nightmare isn't over. It means more women will die, and I'm not safe. That maybe, I never was.

But it could be a copycat. The book came out a week ago—if someone read it and looked up the newspaper articles, they would have known details about what happened. Not to mention, whoever did it used *actual* breadcrumbs. Every article referenced so-called breadcrumbs, but always as a way of describing what actually *had* been left behind: the torn-up note for August, pages from a favorite book for another victim, smashed bits of a violin for yet another of the women he killed. Trails leading to their bodies, giving the victim the illusion that if someone found that trail fast enough, maybe they'd have a chance of surviving.

No one ever had. Only me, convincing him before he chose my own personal trail of breadcrumbs.

I swallow. It can't be him. It *can't* be.

My phone vibrates in my pocket, and I yank it out.

Rob: *Emailed you your workout for today. Working on tomorrow's. Do you have access to a gym?*

I have to tell him. He'll need to tell Cher. She'll have to get her publicity person on this—someone to control hype. Rumors. Especially on the coattails of that damn book coming out. But not now, not as Esme's body is still going cold outside the cafe's back door.

I realize I'm freezing from the cold rain and shock as Janie returns and wraps her arms around me. We lean on each other until she begins sobbing, collapsing beneath her own weight, and I help her from the cafe's kitchen to the nearest booth. Or maybe she's the one who keeps me upright. I'm not sure.

The police arrive within minutes, officers in dark blue, with stern faces, hands on hips. Crime-scene tape. A woman's sharp voice cuts through the murmur of customers and beat cops, giving directions. And then the woman heads our way, and I go still, another round of shock leaving me breathless and yanking me back a decade.

I know this woman. I dislike this woman. In fact, *hate* might be a better word to describe the emotions I feel for her. My stomach twists itself in a knot—it's not possible. It is not freaking *possible.*

An image of her with longer hair, more makeup, a shade skinnier. The way she wrinkled her nose as I told her what happened when I was seventeen. The way she laughed with another cop not two minutes after walking away from me, as though anything could be humorous at the scene of my friend's murder. How she'd asked if we'd willingly gone with Hansel in the beginning—we *hadn't*—as if even if we had, that would have changed the fact he'd killed August. Lastly, how she asked me without preamble, "Did you kill August?" and when I said no, asked, "Are you sure?" It wasn't the only time she asked me that question, as though she had some reason to find *me* suspicious.

I look up as she kneels in front of us like we're children. "I'm Detective Cron. Which one of you found the victim?"

"Me." I swallow and try to tell myself it was a long time ago. Maybe she's changed. *I still don't trust her, though.* Nausea hits hard, and I clench my fists, dig my nails into my hands to keep myself grounded.

Almost against my will, I release one and extend a hand. She takes it, and her gaze rests on my face too long.

She knows who I am.
She remembers.

SEVEN

TEN YEARS AGO

Prom started at 8 p.m., which meant it was after ten as August and I drove through the deserted streets of Kansas City. I felt lighter than I had all night at prom.

Their house was in a neighborhood that a short decade ago was a wheat field, a beautiful expanse of rolling grass we drove by on the way to swimming lessons as children. But a developer bought it, cleared it, built new homes on it, and as much as I hated knowing someone's family farm had been destroyed for it, I was grateful Janie and August's family had moved there.

I signaled and turned down a quiet road where only the occasional farmhouse stood, horses in fields one second, a Target or a Walmart the next. Kansas was like that. You could go from city to country in about five seconds. I'd grown up wandering the woods around the city, a giant field beyond my backyard. The space, the quiet, was kind of nice.

We climbed another hill, made another turn. Maroon 5 came through the radio, the only noise in the middle of nowhere. I flicked my brights on—no streetlights were out this far, and deer were known to roam across the road. Janie hit one with her car just a couple weeks prior.

We coasted down the opposite side of the hill, but when I hit the gas again, nothing happened—a putter, and then—the car slowed.

"What are you doing?" August looked up from the phone in her hands. She searched the road ahead of us, probably thinking of the same deer I was.

"There's—" I frowned, hit the gas again, but the engine didn't respond. I pulled off to one side. "Something's wrong."

Nervousness crept in—this meant we were stuck. It meant I wouldn't have a car to drive myself to school on Monday. Ugh, that meant the bus.

I braked to a stop, put it in park. The electronics were still working, glowing at us in the darkness of the night. My stomach twisted, but it would be okay—this wasn't the first time my car broke down, and it wouldn't be the last. We had a phone, and Janie and Esme would be headed this way soon. They could just pick us up. Maybe I could convince one of them to give me a ride on Monday, too.

"It just died?" August stared at the steering wheel as though the car would somehow disclose the problem.

"It's an old car." I shrugged and grabbed the key. I tried pulling it out, then putting it back in the ignition, turning the engine over.

Again, nothing.

"That's so weird," she said. "Like, if it were the battery, it just wouldn't start, right? I don't understand how it can just die."

"I don't know." I bit my lip, looked out into the night. It was so dark. My heart beat faster. "I'll call Janie."

"What about your dad?"

"No." I flinched at the edge in my tone but left it at that—he'd be drunk already. He wouldn't be any use.

"Oh." August's voice held surprise, hope. "Oh look." Her voice raised a notch. Relief. My own nerves settled in response

—probably Janie was pulling up behind us right now. But then she said, "Someone stopped to help us."

I looked out the window, and in the shallow red glow of the taillights, saw a figure striding up toward the car. A man. My hands tensed over the steering wheel.

"Where is his car? I don't see his car anywhere."

"That's weird." August twisted in her seat.

Suddenly, the abandoned country road didn't feel so pleasant. In fact, it felt downright dangerous.

My hand inched toward the lock button, but before I could hit it, the man's form filled the window. He yanked the passenger door open.

EIGHT

"Norah Silverton," Detective Cron says. "Hometown hero."

I'm not sure if she's referring to my status as a serial killer survivor, or MMA World Champion coach, and I don't ask, because her tone tells me she's not impressed either way.

"And you are—?" Her eyes slide to Janie.

"Janie Taylor."

Detective Cron gives her a nod, and this time she tries to hide it, but I see her reaction, the same way I see an opponent's tell—the widening of the eyes, the quick blink, that momentary pause before she responds. She knows who Janie Taylor is, too.

She rocks on her heels, looking back and forth between us.

The survivor. The sister.

Great, round two.

"Do you need to see a medic?" she asks Janie, who looks pale. "Or is there anyone I can call?" Janie mumbles something, and my mind wanders. Esme's body. Her eyes, shocked in her last moments of life.

The rivulets of blood streaming down the alley.

Janie and I, alive, but two of my friends now gone. The back of my neck itches, and I swipe at it—take a look around, because it feels as though eyes are on me. And in fact, they are—cops, a medic, a couple customers quarantined off to one side, answering questions. But they're all eyeing me, and the pressure of those gazes builds, leaves me eager to answer the detective's questions and get out of here.

I look back at Detective Cron as she murmurs something to Janie.

It's quite the coincidence Esme was killed and left the same way Hansel's victims were. It's quite the coincidence it happened just as I've arrived home for another death. *Someone* did this, and the big question is—who?

A flash of him in my mind—*Hansel*.

I squeeze my eyes shut, imagining August, imagining Esme —something else is different, too. The cuts. August had her wrists slit. Esme... I hadn't seen *where* the blood came from on Esme, but it hadn't been her wrists. A detail never published. A detail a copycat would have gotten wrong.

"Ms. Silverton?" Detective Cron says. "May I call you Norah?"

I yank myself back to the moment. Reach across and clutch Janie's hand, because she's full-on crying again, and I hope by holding her hand I'll stay in the here and now.

"Yes." I sit straighter, reacquaint myself with my surroundings. Cops. Customers moved to one side, being questioned. Owen is among them, and he catches my eyes before looking away.

"Since you found the victim, it would be helpful if you could come down to the station and give a recorded statement."

"Of course." My own voice feels far away, like someone else is saying the words. I consider asking if a different detective can take said statement—but I'm an adult. I'm not that little girl anymore. I can deal with a detective I don't like.

"Great. We'll need to have you take us through how you found her here at the scene, and then we'll leave shortly."

I take Detective Cron through the scene twice, and then another detective, detail by detail. Janie's mother arrives, and when we finally leave two hours later, it's through a crowd of reporters.

That feeling is back—that someone's watching me—and I look through the reporters, one by one, until I see a familiar face.

Elaine, her blonde hair tied back in a ponytail as she huddles with two others. They nod, eyes wide, like they're taking orders. Then they run off, cell phones at the ready to snap photos, probably for Elaine's website, *True Crime Possessed*. A small army of followers had grown substantially, thanks to her covering the Hansel case, as she was the only person who got firsthand photos of that night—and who figured out where I lived and stalked me.

Elaine looks up, satisfied, like she's happy there's been a Hansel-style murder, and catches my eye. Her mouth curves into a smile before she catches herself—she lifts a hand in a partial wave. Lets her smile droop the slightest, as if to pretend at a grief I know she doesn't feel. This means more followers for her. More money. More content.

I look away from her and move forward. The panic has left me. In its wake, shock, anger. Someone's fucking with us— bringing up the traumatic, morbid past.

And Detective Cron is in charge of finding the killer. She failed the first time, because she was too busy trying to figure out if August and I had somehow *asked* for it, suggesting we'd snuck out of prom to meet with a man when we should have known better. Or maybe I'd offed my friend for some unknown motive.

I swallow the urge to vomit and follow Detective Cron to

the station in my own rental car. It doesn't occur to me I might be a suspect until we arrive, and they ask me to strip—and not because they're concerned about my comfort in cold, wet clothes. Rather, because they want to keep mine as evidence.

NINE

In fresh clothes from my bag, I follow an officer not to Detective Cron's office, but to a plain room. A table. Two chairs. The infamous one-way glass.

An *interrogation* room.

My heart picks up speed as Detective Cron comes in, and every *CSI*-like show I've ever seen tells me I should ask for a lawyer, even though I'm supposedly here to help. It also tells me asking for a lawyer makes me look guilty. I fight the urge to fidget and give the detective a polite smile as she sits across from me. At least, I think it's a polite smile. I feel like I'm walking through a dream, and nothing is quite real. I've done this before —or some version of this.

Statistically improbable. Impossible, even.

Yet here we are.

"So, Norah," Detective Cron begins. I can't help noticing she *looks* the part these days. Short hair, just beneath her chin, dark. Tasteful, minimal makeup. A suit. Staring at me intensely, as though it will intimidate me, but she forgets I'm not the scared girl I was the last time she brought me in for questioning.

Or at least, she won't see that side of me. I keep her tucked safely away, hidden behind the façade I show the world.

Detective Cron clears her throat. "Can you take me through what happened one more time? Now that we're recording?"

I repeat what I said before as I guided Detective Cron through the crime scene. She takes notes. Looks at me. Nods often. I can't help but eye the cameras in the corners of the room. When I finish, she takes more notes, and I sit silently, feeling an awful lot like a suspect. My phone is in my pocket, though, my keys in my bag. Technically, I can leave.

"Can you think of anyone who would want to harm Esme?"

"No."

"No one at all?"

I try to think clearly—try to find a reasonable argument for the truth. "We see each other twice a year when my friends come to visit me in Los Angeles." I shift in my seat, which is cold and metal and uncomfortable. "We're friends, but we don't talk all the time. Janie would be better to ask."

"Yes, we have her coming to help us out, too."

I manage to not snort at her wording—*coming to help us out.* What she means is *to be questioned. Interrogated. Grilled.*

"Didn't you just have a book come out?" She tilts her head.

My head snaps up, the world around me suddenly in sharp focus. "Is that relevant?" I ask, because she's not the sort to make polite conversation.

"It could be."

My heart picks up steam as I process her words, similar to my own thoughts earlier.

"Guy Stevenson had a book come out. Not me."

"But you were interviewed for it, correct? Do you get a percentage of sales?"

"No, I don't. And that interview was supposed to be about my job. Not what happened."

I think it through, and other than thinking I benefit in any way, she's not wrong. If anything will get that damn book attention, it's another murder. But I still want to argue with her. Want to remind her one of my friends just died—that what I went through a decade ago has been called trauma by more than one therapist. That finding Esme didn't do anything *good* for me. That Detective Cron in fact *failed* to solve the case last time, failed to even find a credible suspect, beyond peppering me with rude questions and accusations.

"What's your relationship with Guy Stevenson like?"

"I don't have one. We emailed about the interview. He flew in and we had a conversation." I don't include the three days and two nights we spent holed up in my apartment every second I wasn't training. "We haven't been in touch since. His publisher sent me a signed copy of the book." I leave out the sordid details—they have nothing to do with the case, and quite frankly, it's none of her damn business. The anger is back, and I like it. It helps me focus. Helps me think through what I need to do now. Namely, get the hell out of here and make sure Janie is safe.

Detective Cron spends another half hour questioning me, probing me about my timeline over the past day, then upon learning about my father's death, going back a full week. She requests I provide phone records, which I agree to do—all she'll see are messages between Rob and me, and a couple with Janie. She circles back to what happened a decade ago, and then touches on my MMA career.

"There is a history of violence."

It takes me a second to catch up—to realize what she means.

"My *career*?" I ask.

"You beat people up for a living. *Teach* people to fight. You're quite good at it."

I take a long look around the room. Consider my options. Fight to keep my leg still, which wants to jiggle with nervous energy. All the things I could say stream through my mind, but none of them will help Esme.

So instead, I ask, "Do you think it's him?"

"Him?"

"Hansel."

Her lip quirks. "Do you?"

"He used breadcrumbs," I say. "Real breadcrumbs. Hansel never did that."

"I know."

"The cuts were different on Esme than on August."

Another nod. Another, "I know."

"Do you think it's him? Or a copycat?"

Detective Cron hesitates. "I don't know. There were other inconsistencies, too. My partner believes it's a copycat."

Other inconsistencies.

"You know, speaking of a copycat, I can't help but notice you're back—and the same day you arrive, there's another murder." She raises her eyebrows at me.

There it is. Just like last time.

"Excuse me?"

Detective Cron gives me a tight smile. The same smile she gave me before, right before she suggested I would want to hurt my own friends.

"Another death. Another friend of yours. Plus that book. And you're in town."

I stare at her and take a slow, deep breath.

"You're here, too." I'm not quite sure where I'm going with this—pointing out the obvious. Maybe attempting to prove it's no more a coincidence than *she's* the detective working this case, too—but her face shifts for the briefest moment, that confident exterior betraying something beneath, and I can't help but wonder what it means. What nerve I just struck.

"Are you suggesting I have anything to do with this?" Detective Cron asks.

I don't reply, and neither of us speaks for a long moment. I consider running with it—reminding her of her police department's failure before. Of their refusal to bring in help like the FBI, wanting to solve the case on their own, to keep all the glory. In doing so, they'd failed me. Failed August. And Detective Cron did have something to gain this time—if she could pin it on me, it would make her look good.

"I'd like to go now." My heart quickens in my chest, worried she'll say no. Concerned she'll read me my rights, though I've done nothing wrong. "I've answered your questions. I need to arrange for my father's funeral and see how my friend is doing."

"I will need you to provide your flight information to me, as well as the names and contact information for your alibis. We may need to talk again. How long are you in Kansas City for?"

"Three days. Through Monday."

Detective Cron nods, marks something on her notepad, and lifts her gaze to me. "I recommend you don't leave town until I give you the go-ahead."

And just like that, I'm certain I'm a suspect.

TEN

I shiver in the driver's seat of the rental car, staring through sheets of rain at my father's house.

I don't want to go in there. Don't want to see the remnants of his life—of my old life. It looks exactly as it did a decade ago. Shabby blue, in need of a paint job. The lawn overgrown and weedy. The remnants of the flower garden my mother planted every spring covered in dead leaves and fallen branches.

For someone I haven't spoken to in a decade, I've spent a lot of time thinking about him. Trying to figure out how the man I remembered as a little girl, doting on me and acting the loving father, turned into the alcoholic who disowned me.

I want to force myself into a numb state, where I can enter this house and see it objectively. Look for evidence that he's been in contact with my mother, then leave, and leave him in the past, where he belongs.

If only it were that easy. My throat burns as I swallow down the grief. I have to keep it together. I have a funeral to plan, a house to pack up and sell, a potential serial killer to escape—again. I stare at the front door, wondering if I'd told my dad everything, if it would have changed the slow disintegration of our relationship. Some part of me assumed we'd eventually figure it out—be in one another's lives again. Now that opportunity is gone. Maybe it's for the best. Maybe this is another sign I can move on with life, and leave all this behind me.

Then again, leaving all this behind me won't be possible for a while.

Was it Hansel? Was it a copycat? Are Janie and I next? Do we need to get out of town?

I force myself to exhale. To think rationally. Detective Cron said there were more inconsistencies.

A copycat. It has to be a copycat. Someone who read the book. I swallow down the rage building inside me—at Guy, for writing it. At myself, for sharing that story. At whoever decided to take up where Hansel left off.

And Esme—*Esme*, who smiled enough to make up for Janie's frequent scowl, who always had a new hilarious first date story, who texted me right before my athletes' big fights to wish me luck, even though we rarely talked on the phone. She's *gone*. I can't quite conceptualize it. But I know one thing—I need to keep Janie safe. I'm not going anywhere until we figure out who's behind Esme's murder.

I reach for my phone and text Janie, who still hasn't replied to my last text.

Me: *Are you okay? Let me know when they're done questioning you.*

Then on second thought, I add:

Me: *The detective wouldn't give me a straight answer on what they think. Which makes me think they have no idea what to think. We're not safe. Tell me when you're done. I'll come get you.*

I won't let whoever this is get her the way I let them get August.

The steering wheel is cold in my hands. How long have I been sitting here? I must have shut the car off at least ten minutes ago. It occurs to me I'm doing the opposite of what I should be doing—sitting here like a lame duck, waiting to get picked off. The hair on the back of my neck raises, and I glance around. But the yard is empty. No cars on the street. No cops following me. Not even Elaine, peering around a hedge.

I almost laugh at myself—my paranoia, creeping up on me. In Los Angeles, I'd created a routine that almost let me feel normal. The same places, the same people, a fifth-floor apartment with only one door and windows that locked—here, I'm unbalanced. Unsafe.

But no one's watching me—it's all inside my head. I'm sure of it.

ELEVEN

Inside the house is worse than outside. Worse, because I realize my father hasn't changed a thing. It looks exactly as it did when I lived here—when my mother lived here. When we were a family. The entryway still has the coatrack with her coat hanging off it, a yellow Eddie Bauer number. I know if I pick it up, the interior will be a dark-blue fleece, and inside the pockets, I'll find folded tissues and a Mary Kay lip gloss. Fixtures of my childhood.

The smell is what puts me back in motion—overripe garbage and dishes left in the sink. I blink through the doorway into the kitchen. He hadn't even gotten new plates, new coffee mugs, new dish towels. Every single one is the same, down to the white and blue Corningware and handcrafted pottery mugs.

My hands curl into fists. I wish I could just leave—find a gym with a punching bag to pummel. A sparring partner who doesn't mind taking a little pain, and maybe causing a little, too. Physical pain grounds me. Keeps me in the moment, instead of lost in the past.

I need to get this done and get out of here. Go back to L.A., where there are no reminders of my father, my mother, my life before *him*.

My father's life was in his office—mostly, behind a computer screen where he spent his retirement working on his *memoir*, as though he'd ever done anything worth remembering. A classic narcissist. But the office, as opposed to the rest of the house, is organized.

A tall wood desk holds his computer. A black leather sofa sits opposite, a shelf beside it filled with spy novels and conspiracy theory books; a television on the last bit of wall space. A ham radio sits on the windowsill, and the window lets in the fading light of the cloudy afternoon. Typical stuff for my dad, obsessed with being sure someone was always out to get him—another aspect of his narcissism. As if anyone would give a damn about an old man who rarely left his house and had completely alienated himself from his family.

I begin my search at the desk, finding drawers of bills, photographs from when I was a kid, stacks of CDs I'm not sure he even has a CD player for. The room smells like him, some mix of old-man deodorant, sweat, and the cigars he smoked, and for the briefest moment, one of the few good memories I have comes to mind—right after my mom left. We'd gone to see a movie together, just the two of us, desperate for a dwindling connection. I don't think he knew what to do with himself, much less me.

Mom disappeared on that Friday, and I hadn't heard from or seen her since. The police got involved only briefly—long enough to note the handwriting on the note she left matched her own, and she *had* pulled several thousand dollars out of an ATM—the camera showed her face, clear as day. Apparently, disappearing wasn't a crime. Foul play was never suspected.

A classic case of a woman who wanted out of the trap of marriage. Who took matters into her own hands. Who decided to start a new life elsewhere, free from his obsession with alcohol and himself. I still can't quite believe she would leave us, but I can't believe August and Esme are dead, either, and I know that to be true.

I take a shuddering breath and look around, look for anything to think of besides *that*. Yes, life was hard after she left. But Dad was the parent. He should have gotten his shit together.

I open the closet, stacked with shelves and boxes, and begin sorting. My mother loved postcards, collected them everywhere she went. Maybe she'd have sent a postcard. Or even an email. Some way to contact her in case of an emergency. I just can't believe the mother I knew—who adored me, who came to every school play and every soccer game—would leave and not reach out at some point. She wanted a new, better life, but I couldn't imagine that meant leaving us behind completely. I would, however, believe my father might not tell me if she reached out. Hope rises inside me, the prospect of finding her. Even hearing her voice now, in the midst of all this, would make me feel a little better. I am sorting through a box, when I see the book on the edge of his desk.

That book. *Guy Stevenson* scrolled along the bottom. I fight the urge to chuck this copy in the trash can, too. Was my dad checking up on me? I flip open a page and go still—his copy is signed, just like the one Guy sent me. And like mine, it's personalized: *To Greg Silverton, from one writer to another— Guy Stevenson.*

I go still, blood thrumming through my veins fast and hot. How would he have gotten a signed copy? I flip to my pages, then slam it shut and turn away, deciding I don't want to know. Fuck them both. I've always wondered if he knew how successful I've become. Not because I wanted his approval—I just wanted him to know he'd been wrong. That it hadn't been a pipedream, that I hadn't become a failure. I'd decided I didn't want to go pro, that the limelight was too much, especially given what happened—but I'd become a damn fine coach, helping others work toward their dreams.

I go back to searching. Make it through all the boxes in the study, then move on to his bedroom, searching every dresser drawer and beneath the bed. I even check the closet, but like at the front of the house with her coat, my mother's clothes still hang here, as though no time has passed.

I stand there a long time, then shut it tight.

I turn to survey the room, to pretend I hadn't wanted to touch her clothes, to smell them, to maybe get one last memory of her, when my phone vibrates. Janie. *I'm going back to the restaurant to clean up.*

Of course, she is. I step from the room and spot his laptop on the living room couch. I snap it up to search through when I have time—she could have sent him an email. Crossing the lawn back to my car, I glance around again. I shove the laptop under the passenger seat, start the engine, and drive back toward Janie's Cafe—toward the scene of Esme's death.

TWELVE

I knock on the front door of Janie's restaurant. Her form appears through the frosted glass door, peering to make sure it's me. Mascara still mars the skin beneath her eyes, which are puffy and pink.

The click of a deadbolt, and the door opens.

"Hey." She wipes the back of her hand over her face. She's been crying. "Come on in." I step past her, and she locks the door behind me.

The dim lights are perfect for the speakeasy transformation she gushed about on many phone calls. She gestures for a round booth that could seat eight people, digs behind the bar for glasses and a bottle, and we settle across from one another. She pours—a deep, almost-purple red wine that looks an awful lot like blood. Esme's blood.

I push the thought away and hesitate at the offered glass—I missed my workout, and it's not too late to get a run in.

But fuck, I found my friend dead today. Faced the ghosts of my past at my father's. I need a drink. I accept the glass and take a long draw, waiting for its effects to soothe me.

"They didn't say much," Janie tells me. "Asked about my

timeline for the whole day. Who else saw me, if anyone's been asking around. I mentioned Elaine." Her eyes flick to me. "I confirmed your timeline, of course." She pauses, sips her wine. "They asked about you a lot, Norah. Like last time."

I rub at my face. I'm suddenly exhausted, listening to her own version of the day's events. She relays every question they asked—how long we've been friends, if she's ever seen me act violently, if Esme and I ever fought, if she was sure I'd actually flown in today. The list goes on, variations on the same questions they asked me, but if I ever had any doubt I'm a suspect, it's gone now. They weren't just checking up on me—they were asking others about me, too. Under the table, my knee bounces. This isn't good.

"And," she continues, "they asked me the same things about Owen."

Owen, who was so mad. "Speaking of Owen," I say, "why didn't you tell me he was pissed about the book?"

Janie chews her lip. Her lipstick is long gone, her mascara smeared, and she almost looks like the girl I went to high school with. "I didn't think you'd run into him. I thought he'd left town again, actually."

I take another drink of my wine, then another, finally that murky edge where emotions start to fade setting in. It's what I want right now. What I need.

"He's in the Marines?"

"Was. He got out after his last enlistment, I guess."

We sit in silence. Janie pours more wine. We should be chatting about her wedding dress right now—with Esme.

"Are you okay?" I ask.

Janie takes a minute to respond. "Is that how August looked?"

I want to lie and say no, but guilt breaks through the wine haze at the idea of lying to her. I tell Janie the briefest version of the truth, leaving out that August had different cuts from which she bled out. I hold her hand in mine. Scoot closer and hug her when tears stream down her face.

"Do you think it's him?" she asks.

"I don't know. I don't think so. Cron said there were inconsistencies." I want to wrap up this conversation, make an excuse, get us either to her apartment or the hotel room just a block away. Sleep. Wake up and face tomorrow with a little distance. But someone killed Esme similarly to how Hansel killed his victims. That doesn't bode well for either of us. There's no time to spare. "I'll find out for sure, though."

The words come from my mouth, followed immediately by an internal *And just how are you going to do that?* A responsibility I didn't sign up for. This is a job for the cops. The cops, I remind myself, who never caught him the first time. Who were too busy looking at me, the other victim.

They didn't believe a serial killer would just *let me go.* And they weren't wrong.

I squeeze the wineglass so tight it might break. They didn't need to know the rest, and I hadn't told them.

"Elaine was here today," I say. "With a bunch of her minions. They were taking photos and—" My eyes track to the front door, then the windows along the side of the restaurant. They're tinted, but we're basically on display. A person would only have to get close and look carefully to see in. And Elaine might do that—might snap a few photos for her website. I fight the urge to pull out my phone and navigate to it, to see what photos she's managed to snap of me and Janie. If she got one of Esme's body.

My shoulders tense at that thought. She better not have. No doubt, the true crime world is buzzing with the potential return of *Hansel*, but hopefully they've managed to keep some modicum of respect for the victim.

Janie scrunches her nose. "She's a vulture."

She is. And so is Guy, whose book will no doubt sell twice as many copies thanks to Esme's death. My phone vibrates.

Rob: *Get your run in? Find a gym?*

Shit. I still need to call him. Anxiety seeps into my body at the idea of hashing out everything that's happened today. Reliving it again. Tomorrow. I'll call him tomorrow.

"You know, Esme was dating someone," Janie says. "I know they fought last weekend and haven't spoken since, but I can't imagine he'd—"

She goes silent, something grabbing her attention from behind my shoulder. Like someone's standing there.

I whirl, on my feet with hands up, adrenaline flooding my body. But it's not just readiness—it's fear. Cold, icy dread.

A dark shape is silhouetted just outside the front door. The shadow of a person. Of a man.

My heart seizes up.

I force myself to breathe, to try to settle, to *focus*.

"Are you expecting someone?" Blood pulses through me so fast I can hear it in my ears.

"No." Janie looks down at a silver watch on her slender wrist. "Chloe's out of town until tomorrow, and she already called from her hotel room in Chicago."

"An employee?" I ask.

Whoever it is knocks, and the sound echoes through the empty brick restaurant. My whole body tenses, trembles. Janie clutches my hand.

"Do you have a gun?" I ask.

"No," she whispers. "You know I hate guns."

"This is Kansas City. Everyone has a gun."

"Well, not me."

Another knock. "I know you're in there." A man's voice. A voice I recognize.

THIRTEEN

TEN YEARS AGO

He pulled us from the car. I wanted to fight him, but I couldn't. Couldn't will myself to actually do anything, the fear mounting, incapacitating me. I hesitated, and he produced a gun, put it to the back of August's head.

"Now." His voice was low, gravelly. I hurried. He didn't sound like a human. He sounded like a monster.

Panic left me shaking and unable to think of what we could do, what we should do. It was like I was grasping at straws and coming up empty-handed.

He shoved us before him, down the hill, off an embankment, through tall grass and into a dried-up creek bed.

"Move," he growled, every time we slowed to navigate the dark night, to manage the fact we were shaking.

I tried to catch August's eye, tried to see if there was a flash of something in them that might give me confidence—Was she as scared as I was? Jesus, what were we going to do?—but he caught the look and smacked us both. Pain stung along my cheek, my whole face. It left me stunned, barely able to breathe, on my knees in the mud.

A sob tore from August's throat, and I felt myself lose

control, too, crying quietly as we got back to our feet. She clutched at me, and I hung at her, our dresses caked in mud, prom gowns ruined.

We were going to die.

My breath caught in my chest. At this rate, I'd suffocate before he could kill me. It was impossible to go any faster—it was pitch black, bushes and tree branches slapping at us as we moved over the rocky creek bed. My heels didn't help, and I turned my ankle once, twice. Pain seared up my leg, but I couldn't stop—if I did, god knows what he'd do.

Think. I needed to think.

No one knew where we were. No one was coming to help.

I thought of Janie—she'd see our car on the side of the road. But then what? No one would dream we'd been attacked. Forced off the road and into the woods. And in a creek bed, the rocks underfoot likely reducing any footprints to nothing.

We shouldn't have left prom. Shouldn't have gone out alone.

My mind stalled. My chest squeezed tighter.

We were going to die, and it was all my fault.

FOURTEEN

Owen stands in the doorway, arms crossed, a furrow to his brow that tells me he's not happy I'm the one who opened the door.

"What do you want?" I snap.

His gaze flicks behind me to Janie, who's standing at the edge of the booth, sagging with relief.

"You scared the shit out of us," she calls.

"Sorry," he says. But judging by the look he slides my way as I step back, I doubt it. He shoves his hands in the pockets of a dark brown leather jacket and saunters in, looking around as if seeing the place for the first time. It occurs to me he actually *could* be who killed Esme, and I literally just let him in the door. I barely know Owen—had all but forgotten him until yesterday—and don't they say a killer always returns to the scene of the crime?

Then again, Janie and I are here again, too, and all we want is to keep one another safe and maybe have a good cry. A drink.

"A lot different at night," he murmurs. "With no one here."

"What do you want?" I repeat. Janie, meanwhile, has gone behind the bar and is pouring something into a rocks glass. I suppose he was her sister's boyfriend once upon a time.

Knowing her mother, that means he was like family back then. Might still be. It doesn't mean I have to like him, though.

"I just want to talk. Thanks, Janie." He nods to her, takes the glass, sits across from where she settles at the booth. I pull up a chair because I refuse to be trapped in the booth behind him. I check the windows around us again, wishing we'd found a better spot to gather. We're basically in a fishbowl.

"I think I'm a suspect." Owen sips his drink and seems to consider his words. His gaze shifts to meet mine. "I think you are, too."

It's nothing I don't know already, but hearing the words out loud somehow makes it worse.

"You're called persons of interest," Janie clarifies. "That's different than suspects."

Owen gives her a look, as if he couldn't care less about the specifics. "We should do something. Who would want to hurt Esme? Who would kill her like—" He waves his hand. *Like Hansel*, he means.

I lean forward and grab my wineglass. "We are doing something. You're just not invited."

Owen gives a halting laugh. "The two of you are sitting here getting drunk. You call that doing something?"

"Nope." I ignore the eye-roll Janie sends my way, feel the course rub of irritation at his presence. "For all we know, you did it. You came inside what, five minutes before I found her?"

"Norah—" Janie starts, but Owen cuts her off.

"If anyone looks suspicious, it's you." His voice rises and his words come out fast, harsh. "I mean, fuck, your book just came out. You know how August was killed."

Silence. Janie stares at the table, but not like she's about to cry—more like she's wishing she took me up on a lesson on how to punch someone without breaking her hand.

"Think about it, Norah." His voice changes, drops the sharp anger, becomes *reasonable*. I hate him for it—that he's sitting here mansplaining our friends' murders to me. "You were *there* last time. You survived the unsurvivable—how? And then the guy that took you—*Hansel*—just disappears into thin air. Convenient. And now, you're back in Kansas City *the day* she dies, another friend dead. And that book? It'll be a bestseller now."

My face goes hot and sweat pools beneath my clothes despite the fact I've felt cold all day.

"Who's next? Janie?" he asks.

I lunge, stopping six inches from him. Close. Too close. I stare him down, an old rage boiling just beneath the surface, something I funnel into training, fighting, working out, but I missed my workout today, didn't I?

"Norah, don't!" Janie's on her feet, and she reaches out to put a hand to my chest, stopping me from taking it further.

Owen's eyes go wide. He recoils in his seat, like he didn't think I'd actually do *that*.

"Watch your mouth," I growl. "And no, there's nothing *convenient* about Hansel just disappearing."

"I'm not—" He sits up, straightens his jacket. "I'm not accusing you. I'm just making a point—"

"What about you?" I snap. "You were August's boyfriend. You just got back in town, too. You were *here* when Esme died. And now you're hanging around your dead girlfriend's twin sister?"

"Fuck you both." Janie grabs her wine, spins on her heel, and stalks into the kitchen, calling back, "Figure your shit out. Leave me out of it."

Regret swirls in my stomach as I watch her go. I came here not just to bury my father, but to make up for a decade of missed visits, too. To help her get ready for her wedding. To see Esme.

"Goddammit." Owen drops his face into his hands. "This is not why I came here."

"Me neither." I came here to check on Janie, to keep her safe, and all I've accomplished is driving her away. I look Owen over, consider the fact that he spent the day with the cops, too. It makes a person defensive—ready to point a finger to save themselves.

Owen wipes a hand over his mouth. "Truce? I apologize."

I hesitate, still focused on the guilt over driving Janie out of the room. Finally, I nod. Try to find a neutral topic.

"How's it been being back in Kansas City?" It feels safer than what he did or did not see in the alley this morning.

"Fine, I guess. Nothing's really changed here."

"You get tired of the military or—?"

Owen finishes his drink. Shoots a gaze toward the bar. "I guess I came back to start real life." He looks at me. "That sounds dumb. But I didn't plan to stay in the Marines for ten years. Definitely didn't want to do twenty." He rubs his forehead, distracted. "Look, I'm sorry for what I said earlier about the book. I just thought—"

"I don't get any money from it. I was pissed when I read it, too. That's not what it was supposed to be. It was supposed to be about me as a coach, about my athletes, not—what happened."

I let some of the anger out as I say the words, but my body is still tight, coiled. I want to hit something or run until I can run no longer. Go a dozen rounds with Rob and the focus mitts, until I'm ready to collapse.

Owen scratches at the rough shadow of a beard. "For what it's worth, I don't think you did it. I thought maybe you wanted to promote the book when you came here, but I remember how close the four of you were. I know you wouldn't have killed her."

"I don't think you killed her, either." It's a partial lie. I don't *think* he did, but I barely know him, and I'm not the trusting sort.

"I just can't sit still," Owen says, bouncing his leg. "I've been in my share of trouble, but Jesus, a murder suspect?"

I'm about to agree when my phone lights up where I set it on the table, an incoming call. Rob. Rob, who I still haven't found the time to call.

"I have to take this." I pick up the phone and step away from the booth, weaving through the tables until I have a modicum of privacy. I take a deep breath and answer. "Hello?"

"Norah, it's about time." The slam of a door and then voices—men's voices, echoing. He's at the gym, likely getting ready to teach the evening class. "Are you getting my messages?"

"Yes, but—something happened."

A pause. "Are you okay?"

I give him the run down on finding Esme. My conversation with Detective Cron, and that I may be a suspect, or at least a person of interest. I'm not sure what the difference is.

"Fuck." A beat of silence. I squeeze my eyes shut and hope he doesn't act sympathetic—I don't want to cry right now. Just hearing his voice softens me. "I'm sorry, Norah. I'm sorry your friend died. That you had to find her like that. Are you okay? Do you need me? I can get a flight—"

"I'm okay. Just a little—" A little what? Shaken? Scared? Worried someone picked up where Hansel left off, and Janie and I might be his next targets? But I can't think that way. "I'm okay," I repeat.

More silence. Most people would believe me when I say that, but Rob and I regularly spend every waking moment together—training, coaching other fighters, prepping for the next fight. He knows me better than I'm comfortable with, and maybe that's why he lets the silence linger. Doesn't tell me he knows I'm full of shit. He doesn't have to, because he knows that I know.

"Okay. Okay." He murmurs the words, but he's saying them

more to himself than he is to me. "Keep me updated. Let me know if you need anything. And Norah?"

"Yeah?"

"*Please* be careful."

"Promise."

We disconnect, and I let that conversation settle for a moment. Almost wish I *had* asked Rob to come. But there's nothing he could have done. Maybe I'd feel a little safer, though. Or maybe, I'd be putting one more friend in danger.

An alert comes through, and I swipe to see a new Instagram message.

MMAddict: *Hello, Norah Silverton.*

That's it. Nothing more. Just, *Hello, Norah Silverton.* I get strange messages all the time, but given everything going on, this one sends a shiver through me. I swipe it away. Decide to ignore it. Just another fan, and I'm being paranoid. Same as usual.

I return to the booth, wiping a hand over the back of my neck, trying to expel the feeling I'm being watched. Owen looks at the phone, at me, and I can tell he's curious who called, but he doesn't ask. We stare at our empty glasses, and I contemplate going to find Janie—dragging her back out here so we can all act like fucking adults for a little while, now that Owen and I have sorted ourselves out.

I'm about to do exactly that when my phone lights up again. A local number I programmed in just hours ago—the police station.

FIFTEEN

"Norah? This is Detective Cron." That same no-nonsense voice from this afternoon. Owen pushes out of the booth, heading for the bar, giving me privacy. "Hello?" she demands.

A lash of anger rolls through me, followed by panic. If she's going to arrest me, surely she wouldn't call first. And yet I almost expect her to say as much—to demand I turn myself in or come back to the station. And of course, it's *her* of all people, working this same case after a decade. But maybe it's not a coincidence. My teeth set on edge, considering that.

"This is she." I force the words out through clenched teeth.

"I have some... unfortunate news. I wouldn't usually be the one to break it to you, but given the circumstances, they thought it best—" *She's not arresting me.* I press the phone harder against my ear, eager to know what details she's about to disclose. My inner voice is already guessing at what she will say —it *is* Hansel, or she's *sure* it's a copycat. Or better, they caught him, whoever he is.

A shiver runs through me thinking of that. Of having to face a killer in court. Seeing him, being in the same room as him. And yet, I'd gladly take that news.

"Yes?" I say. "What is it?"

"It's about your father."

I try to piece together the mental puzzle—why is a detective calling me about my father's death?

"Okay." My voice quakes, and Owen eases back into the seat across from me, his brow furrowed, watching me.

"He'd been suffering from liver disease. Cirrhosis from drinking," she says. "He was found with a mostly empty bottle of liquor, and at his age, the coroner assumed—" She pauses to clear her throat. "But he still qualified for an autopsy including toxicology."

I come to the obvious conclusion, unable to summon emotion for him. "So, he drank himself to death." My voice comes out flat, despite the rush of anger I feel—of course he'd effectively kill himself. It would be just like him, more concerned about liquor than his own life or how his death might affect me.

"Not entirely." Papers shuffle through the line, and I go still, her words interrupting my thoughts. "His toxicology report showed a blood alcohol level of .35, which is high, but what likely killed him was the combination of alcohol with a danger-ously high level of trimipramine."

"What?" I ask.

"Trimipramine. It's a type of antidepressant. Was your father taking medication for depression, Ms. Silverton? His levels were high enough to be lethal, and his physician at the VA said it was not a medication he prescribed."

"I don't—" I try to remember that last year living with my father. Could he have been depressed? I wouldn't say *no*, but neither does it stand out to me. But it was a decade ago. I tell her as much, then add, "We weren't close. We hadn't spoken in a while."

But the reality is *He didn't believe in psychology. He wouldn't have taken an antidepressant.* At least, not when I last lived with him. But people change. Maybe someone had convinced him to. Maybe with his wife and daughter both leaving him, he came to the realization he needed help.

"Are you sure?" I ask. Something doesn't feel right about this. "The labs weren't mixed up? That doesn't sound like him. He didn't really believe in mental health."

"I'm sure. They ran it twice." A pause. "I want to be honest with you, Norah. This may be ruled a suicide."

A suicide.

My chest tightens. I can't imagine he would have taken his own life. Beyond not believing in psychology, he looked down on people who claimed to have anxiety, depression, the like. He considered suicide to be weak, and ultimately selfish. When one of my classmates hanged himself, he said as much; same as when I survived Hansel and showed signs of PTSD. I can still hear his words. *"It's all in your damn head, Norah. You're fine."*

I take a long drink of my wine to wash away the memory.

"He probably got some pills and didn't know what he was doing. An accident." Detective Cron's words are meant to be reassuring, and it rankles at me. I don't need her of all people trying to comfort me.

"Of course," she continues, "we'll look into it, just in case. We will be sending someone out to the house tomorrow, just to make sure we didn't miss anything. Let me know if you think of anything else, and I'm sorry for the bad news. Oh, and one last thing, Norah: If you hear from your mother, I need to know."

The line clicks. I exhale, trying to push some of the anger out with it. *If I hear from my mother?* I almost laugh at the idea —Detective Cron clearly didn't bother reading up on the missing persons report my father attempted to make but was refused after it became clear she left of her own accord—but the underlying reason Detective Cron called sits heavy in my chest. I force myself to take slow, deep breaths.

Janie has made her way back into the room, and she comes closer, analyzing my face. "What happened?" she asks.

I try to decide where to begin.

"That was about my father. It wasn't just alcohol in his system. Apparently, he was taking an antidepressant, too."

Her forehead creases. "Your dad? An antidepressant?"

Our gazes meet, that best-friend communication shared without words. She comes and sits next to me, gives me a squeeze.

"What else?" she asks.

I take a breath. Fight back tears. "Cron said it might have been a suicide."

SIXTEEN

TEN YEARS AGO

A cabin stood in a clearing. Well, the shell of one, the roof caving in on one corner. It was cold and sticky with moisture. August huddled against me, and I against her—I couldn't tell if we were shaking from the cold or the fear that replaced everything else in our minds. He took our phones. The keys. Our bags.

We were going to die. I just knew it. There was no escape, no hope. If we tried anything, he'd kill us. And if we stayed here, cowering, he'd kill us. There was no good answer.

He was so much bigger than us, a looming shadow in the slit of moonlight coming through the hole in the roof. He growled to himself, held the gun in his hand, waved it in our direction.

Crazy, I thought. He's crazy.

He dug through August's bag, tossing aside makeup, a wallet. He pulled out a folded-up note, probably one she'd written to Owen, or maybe to me. We were always passing them back and forth. "Fucking kids..." He held it up to the light of a phone, reading the words, ripped in two. "You won't be needing this anymore."

"No, no," August whimpered. "Please don't hurt us. Please don't—"

Hot tears streamed down my cheeks. I wanted to tell her to be quiet, to stop getting his attention. But the words wouldn't form.

His eyes were fierce, and he pinned us with his stare, face hidden behind the ski mask. He wore big, baggy clothes, and try as I might, I couldn't begin to identify him, other than tall. He shredded the note in his hands as we watched. When it was tiny bits, he sprinkled them in our direction, then stepped out of the cabin, creating a trail.

A trail to what?

It didn't matter. Not if we were dead.

He snatched August away from me, and our hands grasped at one another's as though I would somehow keep her safe. A knife flashed, stabbing at me, cutting into my arm. I yelped and yanked my hand back, shoved myself into the nearest corner.

I couldn't do anything. I couldn't save myself, much less her.

"August," I croaked out.

He shoved her against the wall. The cabin shook with the force, and she sobbed. The gleam of that knife, a hand around her throat—

I buried my face in my knees and cried. I wished I could help her, but I couldn't. I couldn't even help myself. God, I was a coward.

"Please, please, please," she whimpered. "Please don't kill me." Her tiny voice squeezed my heart, tore another sob from my throat.

Time slowed as August's shriek cut through my thoughts. I buried my face deeper against my legs. Another shriek, louder this time, filled with pain. I jumped when she hit the floor, unmoving.

Everything went silent, and the silence was somehow worse.

His attention shifted to me, like a weight falling on my shoulders, a weight I wasn't strong enough to bear.

SEVENTEEN

Janie goes behind the bar for more liquor and comes back with a bottle—the same one she poured Owen's drink with. When she sits down, she reaches for a napkin and dabs at her eyes.

We're coldly discussing my father's potential suicide hours after Esme's murder. I try to meet her eyes, to offer her some bit of comfort, but she studiously looks at the bottle as she pours. But I can see the tears already reforming.

"More?" she asks me, and I shake my head—hearing from Detective Cron sobered me. I just want to figure out what the hell is going on, get everyone safe, get home. I regret coming back here.

Janie clears her throat. Forces a smile. "Let's start with Esme. We know she was murdered. We think it's a copycat. Who would have a motive to kill her?"

I stare across the table at her, the question taking me off guard. She sits up a little straighter, with renewed purpose. She can't bring Esme back, but maybe she can do something about it. She consumes true crime podcasts obsessively. Maybe it's not so much that she's fascinated by the worst side of humankind, taking advantage of others' suffering. Maybe she thinks if she pays attention, she'll somehow figure out who Hansel really is, and, therefore, who killed August. That's what happens in the shows, right? The miraculous happens. The killer is found. Usually among people already known.

But is that what we're doing? Playing detective?

The cold memory of leaving Kansas City with no answers comes back to me—Detective Cron and her fellow police department, never finding Hansel. Still casting suspicious looks my way. Will they fuck it up as badly this time around, too?

I wonder, not for the first time, if there's a way the real Hansel could be someone we've met before. But *who*? I try to remember the details of that night—it was dark, a cabin full of shadows. He wore a ski mask from the moment he grabbed us and never took it off. Even his form was obscured—a baggy hoody. Baggy pants. I knew he was tall. Thin, because he'd hugged me, held me. None of that narrowed it down.

"Norah?" Janie says. "You okay?

"What about the boyfriend?" I ask. "You said they were having trouble, didn't you? Could he have done it?"

Janie sets her glass down. "Sure, but why would he kill her like a serial killer did a decade ago?"

"Maybe he knew what happened and thought it would keep the focus off him?" I suggest. "Did you ever meet him?"

Janie hesitates. "No. She was secretive. I think he's maybe married. I think they worked together."

"Like a doctor?" Owen asks.

Janie nods, eyes widening. "She said something about one of his patients once."

"That could be motive," I say. "Especially if he didn't want to ruin his professional reputation. Can you find out who he was?"

"I can try." Janie taps a finely filed nail on the table. "Some of the night nurses come in for breakfast and drinks sometimes, you know, before they go home to sleep during the day. I'll see if I can find a way to ask."

I fidget with a beverage napkin. "Detective Cron asked if I'd heard from my mom."

"Why would she ask that?" Janie says.

I shake my head, but the answer comes to me. "Maybe that would be a reason to suspect foul play with my dad. But she didn't say that. It sounded like it was probably an accident."

My earlier thoughts echo in my head—*didn't believe in psychology. Wouldn't have taken an antidepressant.*

My phone chimes, and I look down to see a text from an unknown number. *Heard about your dad. I have thoughts. Let's talk. —E*

I sigh out and swipe away the message. Yes, let's talk, Elaine, so you can write up the whole conversation about my father. More fodder for your website. Sounds great. Just like Guy's damn book, exactly what I want, more of my private life out into the world.

Speaking of the book. "Do you think—" I hesitate, because even to me, it sounds out there. "Do you think Guy or Elaine could be involved?"

"Guy? As in—" Owen begins.

"As in Guy, the guy who wrote *True Athletes, True Crimes.*"

Janie sips her wine and makes a face. "What would be his motive?

"Another story," Owen answers.

"Same for Elaine. Her career was built on the Hansel story." I spin my glass slowly, thinking it through. "Still. Murder? For a story?"

Owen makes a noise in his throat. "Wouldn't hurt to look into." He meets my eyes across the table.

"I'll reach out to him," I say.

Janie nods in agreement and presses a manicured finger to

her lips, eyes distant in thought. "Elaine stalked you for months, Norah. That's not normal."

"She's not normal," I reply. "She has a whole army of true crime fanatics who practically worship the ground she walks on. And her podcast..." I let my voice trail off as I meet Janie's eyes. It won some sort of award for solving a cold case. It should have been a good deed, but she turned it into a marketing campaign. I can't help but wonder what it would do for her podcast to solve the Hansel case.

"I'll look into Elaine," Owen says out of nowhere. "It'll be less obvious than if Norah does it. If there's something to find, I'll find it." His voice hardens as he says it, expressing certainty instead of wishful thinking.

It occurs to me we're making a plan. It's not the same as having Esme back. Not even close. But it feels like we're *doing* something, and given the police's poor track record, that makes me feel a little less helpless.

EIGHTEEN

I sit up in bed, gasping for air, striking at a monster I cannot see. An arm reaches for me, tries to pull me back down, but I roll away, slide from the bed, put distance between me and my attacker.

But there's no one.

No, there is someone—Janie. Asleep in the bed, her arm flung out, where Chloe usually lies beside her, where I spent the last several hours.

Relief softens my limbs. A dream.

No, a nightmare, about *him*, about the night he took us.

"Norah?" A voice from behind me.

I swing and jerk my hands up, putting myself into an offensive position.

"Whoa." Owen stands in the doorway, hands up in surrender. He blinks at me, squints through the darkness. "Sorry. You yelled out. I came to check."

Of course, he did. Isn't that why he's here, sleeping on Janie's couch? Why we're all here? Safety in numbers.

I feel for my phone on the bedside table, yank it from its cord, and wave Owen back through the door.

My bare feet on soft carpet ground me as I follow him—remind me I'm not in a cabin in the woods in the arms of a killer. I don't have to lie to survive. I don't have to snuggle up to a man who killed my friend, don't have to deceive everyone around me to maintain a sense of self-respect, and I don't have to start at zero to become strong, to be able to take care of myself for the next time.

My therapist said there wouldn't be a next time. The exact chance of being killed by a serial killer is .00039 percent. Almost less than nothing.

All I took from it was that if there is a next time, I won't be so lucky.

"Sorry I woke you." I collapse on one of two couches crowded into Janie's living room. Owen settles on the other, pulls a blanket up over himself—he's in boxers, no shirt, and he looks almost as fit as the men at our training camp in L.A. He catches me staring, and his lip quirks.

I smile. "When you run a gym for a living, you can appreciate fitness. It's not—" *Not sexual*, I was about to say. But to even say that maybe makes it... sexual. My cheeks warm, and I look away, consider brewing coffee. My phone says 4:47 a.m., and maybe I'll just stay up. Get out on a run that includes a stop at my father's house. I want to make sure I didn't miss anything the first time, preferably before the police get there and muck about.

"It's a little harder to keep up with," he says, "now that it's not part of my day job."

"I can imagine." I can't, not really. I've spent a decade pushing my body and others' to the limit—to rest, to do nothing, seems alien. I push the remnants of the nightmare away—a dream that I thought I'd left behind back when I started winning fights. The fights that reassured me that no matter who Hansel is, if I ever encounter him again, I'll have a fighting chance. And if it's a copycat, I have no doubt I'll win. It's what I do.

"What are you doing now that you're out of the military?" I ask to fill the silence and because I'm not quite ready to form cohesive sentences yet.

"Hunting," he says. "Well, trying to, anyway. I just started the business."

"Hunting?" I raise an eyebrow, interest piqued.

"Take people out on hunting trips on my family's land or the national forest. Deer hunting. Elk. Small game, sometimes. Show them the good spots. Help set up camp. Deer blinds. Might do some fishing next summer, too."

It seems odd, but maybe that's because I've never gone hunting. I open my mouth to say as much, but he murmurs, "I hunted people in the Marines. It's—" He hesitates. "Not the same as catching the bad guy, knowing he can't kill anyone else. But I grew up hunting. We killed most of our own meat. Venison, mostly." As if he expects me to object to this, he quickly adds, "I know, I know. But it is more humane than eating an animal bred in a cage only to be killed before they've had a decent life."

Owen watches my face for a reaction, like he cares what I think.

I nod. "Makes sense."

And it kind of does, not that I really want to think about where the mountains of lean chicken and fish I eat come from. Which only means I can better appreciate what he does. It's the *hunting people* part that caught me off guard, and I think in his own twisted way, maybe Owen found the perfect job, too. I wanted to be able to protect myself; Owen wanted to be able to hunt down his girlfriend's killer.

"Coffee?" I ask.

"Please."

We make our way toward the kitchen. He tries to help, but neither of us know our way around the kitchen, and it becomes a game of Twister, reaching for one cabinet, then the other, bare arms brushing, hips bumping. I wave him to the kitchen table, looking away to hide what I suspect is a blush. Once I have the machine perking, I sneak back into Janie's room, use my phone's flashlight to grab running tights and a long-sleeved shirt, take them into the bathroom, change.

When I emerge, Owen has poured us both a cup. He hands me one, and we return to the couch.

"Most people say they're going to get up early and go for a run," he says between sips. "But you're actually doing it."

I smile. "Yeah. I can't afford to take another day off."

"You have some big fights coming up," he says.

"Yes."

"I read about it last night—your career. When I couldn't sleep."

My face warms again, and not from the coffee steam. There are whole days at a time where I can focus on what's right in front of me—the fledgling athlete, the speed bag, the focus mitts, the preplanned meals I hash out with my fighters—I *know* a huge chunk of my life is on the internet for all to see. But to have someone bring it up always shakes me a little—reminds me how exposed I've made myself.

"It's not that big a deal," I say.

"Isn't it?" His brows furrow and he opens his mouth, hesitates a long moment.

He's right—it is a big deal. And I'm not at my training camp with my athletes. I missed yesterday's workouts entirely, theirs and mine. There's an itch at my neck, down my spine, and it's the knowledge I'm not doing what I need to be doing if we're going to be ready. If we're going to win.

But also, I don't have an option. Two deaths. A detective

telling me not to leave. Janie, who needs me. Who I won't abandon again, who I won't leave to potentially fall victim to the same fate her twin did. They're eying me for Esme's murder, just like they did August's. Me, and this man I barely know who I'm sharing these early morning moments with. It feels intimate. Too intimate. Claustrophobia hits, crawling over my skin, and I stand abruptly.

"I should go." The window shows me a dark morning, no sign of a sunrise in sight. Janie's apartment has a decent view of the Plaza, and in a month, it will be lit up with Christmas lights, but for now it's only dark, windy, cold.

"If you need help training, staying in shape while you're here," Owen says, "I'm sure I'm not at your level, but I can hold a bag or spar or—" He shrugs. "Whatever it is you do. There's a gym not too far from here I could get us into."

"That would be good." I drain my coffee mug and look around for my running shoes. "I'll be back in an hour or two."

I slide out the door before he extends our conversation, and jog down the staircase that connects Janie's apartment to her cafe below, raising my heart rate in preparation for the blast of cold that greets me from the back door.

Only one car rolls by as I sprint through the dark streets, illuminated by yellow lamps overhead. My father's house is two miles west of here, and once I'm warmed up, I sprint those miles. Gravel crunches underfoot, slicked in spots with ice, the rain from yesterday freezing overnight. A single light is on in his house as I slow to a walk, climb the patio stairs, and take out the key.

The cops will be here soon, so I need to do this fast. Blood thrums hot through my veins, from the two-mile sprint, from anticipation.

The heat of his house is a welcome relief as I make my way in, but that relief is short-lived, replaced by a pulse of adrenaline. Someone else is already here, her back turned to me as she crouches, shuffling through old videos on a shelf beside the television.

I recognize her, and the same slow-burning rage I felt last night begins to simmer again.

But she doesn't know I'm here yet.

I shut and lock the door behind me.

NINETEEN

"Looking for something?"

Elaine jumps, turns, plasters a bright smile over her face. Her hair is twisted up in a bun, and she wears her signature glasses—thick, round rims, and probably entirely lacking a prescription, to make her look more investigative. You know, playing it up for her fans.

"Norah! It's so good to see you." Her silky-smooth podcaster voice is gone—in its place, a quaking, too-high tone. My body goes hot with satisfaction. Seeing her uncomfortable might be the highlight of my day.

I cross my arms and lean against the nearest wall. "In my father's house? Which you broke into?" I pull out my phone— "At 5:52 a.m. What could you possibly be doing here at this hour?" I decide to bluff. "Tell you what, why don't I just call the police—"

"Don't. Please, don't." Her eyes widen and she glances around, searching, I think, for an explanation. She doesn't seem to find one, and silence stretches between us. Her phone is clutched in her hand—likely, she's taken photos of the house, inside and out. Maybe recorded a TikTok or two, for her fan club.

"Why are you here?" I don't know why I'm asking. I know why she's here—same as why she stalked me out to L.A. and set up camp outside my house after I escaped Hansel. She wants fodder. *Content*, as she might call it.

"I know about the antidepressant. I think your father was murdered." Her eyes widen and she looks at me, waiting for a response. A response I know she would only put in the paper. I keep my face straight, despite a zip of panic running through me.

Murdered. I replay her words, thinking maybe I'm still asleep, maybe I dreamed it up. I have been having nightmares, after all. But I blink, and I'm still in my father's house, and Elaine is still watching me.

"Why do you think that?" I ask.

"The meds—I couldn't find a prescription anywhere in town. Or in the county, for that matter. I thought maybe he'd seen a physician outside the VA, but from what I've gathered that doesn't seem to be the case. So where did he get them?" She poses the question, raises her eyebrows, like it's a great mystifying question for us to ponder. "I think maybe someone *gave them* to him."

I go still. "That doesn't mean he was murdered."

Her theory doesn't make sense. He didn't go anywhere. Didn't see anyone. He didn't have friends. My mother and I were his only family. There was no one who would have murdered him, and given how he died, there's no way it was random. No, she's just trying to create a story—make more of a tragedy, like she always does.

"Did you find anything?" I stroll farther into the hallway until I can press against the entryway to the living room.

"N-no. Not yet." Her eyes flick to my arms, which are

muscular enough to show their shape even through two layers of long-sleeved shirts. She fidgets. Is she afraid of me?

I hope so. God, I hope so. Intimidation isn't a game I play outside of the gym, but I'll make an exception for her. I can't count the number of times I looked in my rearview mirror to see her white van trailing behind me. There were nights I looked out my bedroom window only to see her waiting, ready to pepper me with questions should I step outside. Demanding to know *the truth*, and shouting after me, "How, Norah, *how*? How did you survive Hansel?"

The last time I'd seen her, I turned around and gave her the closest thing to an honest answer I'd ever given anyone: *"None of your fucking business."*

"We can find your father's killer," Elaine says. "I can help. Tell me everything. I know Detective Cron called you last night —what did she say?"

My father's killer. Something rises inside me, a pressure, deep in my chest. I inhale, exhale, fight to maintain the blank face. But then I catch myself wondering how Elaine even knows about the antidepressants if I only found out last night? I stow the question away for later—for Detective Cron.

"You just want a story," I say.

I raise my phone, take a photo of her standing there, pale as the blood drains from her face. And now I've got the ammunition to keep her from pursuing any of those avenues. And hopefully from posting anything she found on her damn website.

"Well, yes, I do want a story." Elaine tries for a smile, but it's not the award-winning gleam of professionally whitened teeth it usually is. It's nervous. Unsure. "But I also want to find Hansel."

I wait a beat, expecting her to explain what finding Hansel has to do with my dad, but the connection forms automatically in my head.

My dad died, and I came home. And then Esme was murdered. Like someone had planned it all out.

A coincidence. It has to be a coincidence.

TWENTY

My watch says I'm running a 7:30-minute mile, but I push harder, let the cold sear through my lungs until they burn. I hit a 6:30-minute mile and hold it, racking my brain for an explanation that makes sense.

There was nothing in the house—no pill bottles, no medications beyond Advil and Tylenol, no business cards from a psychiatrist, no appointments scribbled on his calendar. Nor did I find evidence of my mother. All I found was Elaine and her ridiculous theories.

And they are ridiculous. My father overdosed on alcohol and antidepressants, and yes, it's weird, but it's also been a decade. People change a lot in that time, and Elaine is searching —no grasping—for a story. Something exciting and sickening to make people log on to her website and tune in to her podcast. To get clicks, to get people to sign up for her fee-based fan club, to buy the swag she sells.

Her bottom line is profit—not truth.

I still haven't searched his computer. Maybe he got with the times—maybe any information on what he'd been up to, or my mother, or his theories would be there. I'll find time today to comb through it.

I slow my pace to a walk a block from Janie's restaurant, wiping sweat from my brow with the sleeve of my shirt. I hug myself, as a chill sets in. The bookstore is directly to my left, and I stop, admire a display of holiday-themed novels. Between training, coaching, and fulfilling sponsor obligations, I don't have much of a life outside of MMA. When I do have a moment alone, I'm exhausted from the hours spent training myself and others. In those moments, I read books, escape to another world, another family, another reality. My mother and I used to go to this exact bookstore, where she'd spend whatever money we had to get herself one book, and me half a dozen. Why hadn't one of these realities been enough for her?

I breathe out and change my focus from the book display to my own reflection. I blink, and there's another face there, across the street—

I whip around, searching the nooks and crannies of the storefronts across the way, where I'm sure I saw a face—someone watching me, staring at me. It must have been my imagination, though. The sidewalk is empty.

I turn away sharply, shaking off my paranoia, pushing away thoughts of my mother. In a way, she doesn't matter because I have a new life, now. And I need to get back to it. I stop at the parking garage to grab my dad's laptop from beneath the passenger seat, and take it inside with me.

Janie's already opened the restaurant when I return, counter service only. Two women in scrubs are at one corner of the bar, nursing beers, night shifters just off work, no doubt, and she's busy ringing up scones and coffee for customers who wander in half-asleep.

I take the same booth we huddled in last night, shivering despite my two-mile sprint. Owen wanders over from the bar to sit across from me. Janie delivers coffee and a deliciously carb-loaded muffin, which is still warm.

Owen gives me a nod. "Find anything?"

"Just Elaine." I slide my phone toward him with the photo.

His face hardens. "She was in his house? Why?"

"She was searching it. I guess she wanted to rule out that Hansel had killed him."

Owen widens his eyes. "She thinks he killed your father?"

"It doesn't matter. She was wrong. She found nothing. I found nothing. Other than her." I press my palms to my eyes. "She's just looking for a story. Same as usual."

Sympathy softens his features. "What's with the laptop?"

I slide it onto the table. "It was my dad's. Might be something on it."

My phone beeps.

"You have new messages," he says and slides my phone back.

A text from Cher last night sending condolences. Two emails from sponsors. Messages from fans through Instagram. Which reminds me I haven't posted in two days. This is the part of the job I love and hate—connecting with people who find strength in my strength. But also dealing with the weirdos. It's mostly MMA wannabe fighters, but occasionally, someone figures out my connection with Hansel, and I get that sort of morbid message, too.

I take a selfie with my coffee mug, letting my running clothes show. Add a caption: *Cold-weather running reward!* And post it. Ignore Owen's smirk. I take another photo, this one of the muffin, along with Owen's coffee mug, which has a different design. I set the app to post it automatically tomorrow morning—giving me a day without needing to worry about the gym's damn sponsors. Then, I check the waiting messages.

It's the norm: teenagers, wanting to know if I have any

advice for them to become MMA fighters. A salesperson
promising me free gear in exchange for taking photos and
posting them. The newest message comes from a user whose
name I am familiar with because he messages me at least once a
week, always asking if I like older men. Today, I block him.

It's creepy, yes. But nothing compared to other messages I
receive.

Another one, from that same account as before, makes me
linger.

> MMAddict: *Heard about your father. I'd love to send flowers.
> Is there an address or funeral home?*

I frown; another person who knows about his death. As far
as I know, my father's death hasn't made the news. There was
nothing attention-grabbing—an old man dying alone at home,
his only company his bottle of cognac. Maybe it made the news
somehow. Or perhaps deaths were posted on a website. I had
yet to write an obituary, but maybe the newspaper would do
that.

I swipe away and text Rob.

> Me: *More news. Call me when you're up.*

I need to tell him about my dad. That I may not be back on
Monday after all. I also want to touch base with him on my
workout, because he may change it since I missed yesterday's.

"How was your run?"

Owen watches me across the table, fingers wrapped around
his mug. I set my phone down. Sip my own coffee. Think about
him without a shirt this morning, then immediately flush with
guilt. He was August's boyfriend. Then again, August has been
gone a long time. And we're adults. I glance at him again, letting

myself consider him. He would have been perfect for a one-night stand. A half-night stand, preferably. I'd be gone by Monday if everything had panned out right.

But as it is, I don't want the awkwardness of dealing with him and the aftermath, especially since this may extend well into next week.

I look away and say, "Cold. A nice change from L.A."

"So, you found nothing? Besides Elaine?"

"Nope."

Janie swings by with the coffee pot. "Anything?"

"No. I'll bug Detective Cron later, see if the cops find something. I thought you took today off?"

Janie grimaces. "I did. But I can't bear to go dress shopping. Esme was going to go with us and—" She pauses, her face going blank in an expression I'm familiar with—an attempt to hold in tears. My own eyes burn in response, and I blink, trying to clear them. "I thought I should just do something easy. Like work." She touches the back of one hand to her eyes, dabbing at tears before they smear her makeup. "Anyway, Esme's mom texted. There's going to be a memorial service tonight." She tries to continue, but her voice catches in her throat. She takes a deep breath and adds, "Chloe should be back in town." Her eyes stray to Owen with a brave smile. "You should come, too."

"You good for it?" Owen asks me.

"Of course." I swallow, pushing down the thick grief sitting in my throat. Janie turns to go, the back of one hand pressed over her mouth, holding the tears in. Owen and I watch her go, and I shake my head. Try to come back to the moment. "Are you still good to help me with my workout later?" I ask Owen, because memorial or not, I can't slack another day. And I'm hoping a workout will help me keep my emotions under control. I need to be able to focus.

He nods. "Of course."

I go back to drinking my coffee and thinking about Hansel, the monster who's lived beneath my bed for the last ten years. There's one thing I can't shake—if it is him, if he is back, he's not done.

One of us is next.

TWENTY-ONE

TEN YEARS AGO

August wasn't moving.

My mind screamed it at me over and over. August's still body. His hulking form, standing over her. Blood— Jesus, was that blood pooling beneath her?

I short-circuited, my mind circling, skipping—like one of my dad's old albums. I couldn't quite breathe. Couldn't get myself into motion. Couldn't think.

"Your turn," he growled. My blood roared in my ears, screaming at me to do something, anything.

If I was going to die anyway, I should at least fight. I knew that, and yet—I gulped air, but was suffocating, like a fish left on the shore to die, mouth gaping open. She's dead. August. Was. Dead.

Maybe I was wrong, maybe if I could get to her—but I couldn't even save myself, how the hell could I save her? My mom. I would never see my mom again. I'd never see Janie or Esme again. I'd never go to college or become a psychologist or—

Do something!

Some part of my brain decided to fire.

He stepped closer, dry dead leaves crunching beneath a boot. Two more steps, and he'd be on me. I looked at him. Met the eyes of a monster.

I couldn't think of what to do, what to say, so I settled on, "I-I'm Norah."

The most basic communication. What a two-year-old could manage. Realizing this, I tacked on, "Who are you?"

That's what people in movies did. They got the bad guy talking.

His form went still like he didn't expect that—didn't expect me to introduce myself. To speak to him. To ask him a question.

"Why the fuck do you care?" he bit out. Another step forward.

My hands were clammy, like I was sweating, despite the cold. I swallowed and tried to think of what else people on television did. How did women beat men they had no chance in hell of surviving?

They lied.

Could I lie? Maybe. I risked another glance up and fought the instant desire to recoil. My mind blanked again, but that part of my brain fired in response, and the next thing I knew I was saying, "You don't have to hurt me. It's okay."

I expected him to laugh—expected my life to end in the next moment—but he didn't, and I realized I was still drawing breath. He just stared. Watched. Waited.

TWENTY-TWO

Dear Guy,

Got the book. I thought our long weekend was off the record?
What gives?

I'm game to talk again, but it's my turn to interview you.
Let me know when I can call and a good number.

—Norah

I reread the email, biting my lip, wanting to add a few four-letter words. Then I hit Send and roll off the couch to stretch out my legs on the carpet of Janie's living room. I can hear the murmur of customers downstairs, where Janie is busily working. Minutes later, my phone chirps, and I grab at it, hopeful it's him.

Dear Norah,

Perhaps there was a misunderstanding? I'm happy to discuss
it. I meant no harm.

I'm actually in Kansas City right now for a book signing. I believe I read in the local newspaper you're in town as well. Some might call that kismet. If you're still around, let us meet for drinks tonight. My signing is from 6 to 8 p.m. at Last Chapter Bookstore. You're the local—where will I find you around, say, 8:30? Unless you'll grace me (and your adoring fans) with your presence at the book signing prior?

xo, Guy

I read the email again because I'm sure I misunderstood.

"Motherfucker." I read it right—*he's in town*. One hell of a coincidence, timing-wise. Of course, tonight is reserved for the memorial service. For spending time with my friends as we remember Esme. But this is important, too—what if he's somehow involved? I stand and pace back and forth, trying to work out how to do both. I can't let him get away without talking to him first.

After. I can meet him after. Janie mentioned we should all grab dinner at Esme's favorite restaurant after, but we'll be done with that by eight thirty. I hit reply.

Make it 9 p.m. Janie's Cafe, right next to the bookstore.

I don't give my phone number, nor do I make it a question.

Adrenaline spikes at the ridiculous coincidence he just happens to be here when all of this is going down. I want to run downstairs and tell Janie, but it's just after eleven, and I can hear the lunch rush below me. She's safe with a dozen employees, while Owen went home to grab clean clothes and prep for the memorial tonight.

Instead of bothering her mid-shift, I turn my gaze on my father's laptop, positioned on the coffee table. I set the phone down, stretch over my hamstring, and press the power button, realizing as I do I didn't grab the power cord along with the computer—but miraculously, it whirs to life. I deepen the stretch as it starts up, and I'm thinking about Guy, about how my father must have been in contact with him if he had a personalized copy of *True Athletes, True Crimes* when the home screen appears, and I find myself staring back at an image of myself. A much younger version of myself, caught in my mother's embrace. My father stands a step to the side, with us, but separate, as he always was. Regardless, it's a family photo.

He had a family photo as his computer background.

Which meant he stared at us every time he used this computer, which if he was like most people, was every day. *He looked at me every day. Thought of me every day.* I swallow back a flush of emotion, my face growing hot. I almost reach out and slam the lid down. Almost abandon this task altogether to go for another run, knowing the physical exertion will tire me out, distract me from the ache in my chest.

I leave the computer where it is, pacing the room until my eyes land on the kitchen. A cold glass of water later, I look back at the computer, pretty sure it's worthless and that my dad was likely playing solitaire and reading god-knows-what conspiracy newspapers online. After he served in Desert Storm, after a career where he made no friends, a slow downward spiral into alcoholism, and my mother leaving him—that's what he'd been reduced to. One more man who thought he knew everything and what was best for everyone else.

A text comes through, and it's the distraction I needed—I wanted.

Owen: *Ready whenever you are.*

I exhale. Relish the excuse to put this off a little longer, even if Elaine's bold proclamation—*murder!*—does niggle at my brain. The computer tucked away, I dress once again in workout clothes. This time, I pack an electrolyte drink and a protein shake for afterward. I eat a banana on the way to the car, voice-texting Janie that I'm leaving.

I call Rob on the drive there.

"Sorry," he says, voice hollow, like I'm on speaker phone. "I had private classes to teach this morning. I got your message. I'm so used to you just *being* here, you know?" His words are kind, his voice low, and I can tell he misses having me around. In the background, the sounds of him puttering around his office, a tiny closet with two desks crammed in it, where we've shared many meals and huddled close, watching fights on his computer monitor. The gym is the closest thing I've had to a home and a family since my mother left, and a pang of longing hits me.

"You okay?" I ask.

"Fine," he says with a sigh. "Same shit. You know. Anyway, how are you holding up? How is it being home?"

I almost say *Los Angeles is home.* But I know what he means. I come to a stoplight and put my own phone on speaker. "It's all right." I open my mouth to tell him that Guy is in town but stop before the words come out. He'll only worry. My dead father, my dead friend, they are enough to keep him concerned about me. I decide to keep the bit about the antidepressant in my dad's toxicology to myself for the moment, too—it will likely come out publicly, but the longer I can keep it quiet, the more likely I'll be home by the time it happens.

"I missed a workout," I tell him instead.

"Not a problem." His voice is high, tight with tension. "Which one? We'll work it into today's."

"All of them. I didn't do anything yesterday."

Rob doesn't say anything for a moment, and I glance at the phone to make sure the call hasn't dropped.

"I don't remember the last time you took a whole day off." A smile carries through his voice, and I smile, too, surprised and relieved. *He's not mad.* "About time. Just skip it. Do what we had scheduled for today. One day of training won't matter, but make sure you don't miss anything else."

"I promise," I say. "I ran this morning. Headed to the gym now. A guy I knew in high school is going to go a few rounds with me."

"Ooh, a guy," he teases. "Good-looking guy? Do I need to worry you'll be leaving me anytime soon?" His words joke, but his tone carries a little something extra—concern I'll actually want to move back here, maybe. But then, Rob is protective of all his fighters and coaches. It's his job, his livelihood.

Rob is ten years my senior, past his prime fighting age, though it was a head injury that took him from competitor to coach. We've been friends since he "discovered me" going a few rounds in a shady gym on a Friday night, doing my best to prove I could be tough, take care of myself, in the months after I moved to Los Angeles. Los Angeles was never my goal. It was just the end of the road—literally. I drove until I hit the ocean, getting as far from Kansas City as I could, and then I walked out on the beach, into the water, and debated whether to keep going.

I wasn't suicidal. But I was... something. Something that led me to say yes when he offered to teach me how to be good at beating the shit out of people. And then, when I showed an aptitude for coaching others, taking me on as a full-time employee.

"Ha ha. I'll be back as soon as I can be. Speaking of—" I give him the rundown of Detective Cron telling me to not leave town.

"Not to worry. I'll come to you if they keep you there. Arturo can cover the gym."

I'm about to tell him that doesn't make sense—he needs to be there with our fighters, in L.A.—but I let it go, because I'm determined to wrap this up and get home.

When I reach the gym, we sign off, and just as I'm getting impatient and paranoid—the same car has driven past me twice now, a silver sedan with Missouri plates—Owen pulls up next to me in an aged pickup truck. My heart beats a tick faster, and I tell myself it's because I'm working out after missing a day—but then Owen smiles, my insides tense, and I realize it might be something quite different.

TWENTY-THREE

"You ready?" We climb from our respective vehicles, and I grab my gym bag, all business.

He pulls his own bag from the passenger's seat. "I don't know." He turns to face me, and he's combed his hair, the dark messy waves parted, combed back, an old-fashioned vibe that somehow works for him. "Do I get to just hold a punching bag for you or are we going mano a mano?" He throws his hands up in a few stiff chops.

A smile tugs at my mouth. Okay, so yesterday I hated him, but today, I can appreciate that he's cute. Sweet. A nice distraction from reality. "How about a little of both?"

"Sounds good to me."

We start to move at the same time, bumping into one another. Heat flares through me, but I tamp it down. We're here to train. Besides, the last thing I need is a fling with Owen of all people.

Then I remember the in-person interview I have planned for Guy after that. "Guess what?"

"What?" He beckons for me to step ahead of him, ever the gentleman, and we head inside.

"Guy Stevenson is in town."

Owen goes still, his hand pausing mid-reach to open the door for me. I take the opportunity to open it for myself and leave him slack-jawed just outside what appears to be a traditional martial arts school, the sort I took a year or two of lessons in as a kid. I stop, bow, and remove my shoes, because that's the respectful thing to do, and when Owen recovers, he repeats my actions.

"Tae Kwon Do?" I gaze at a Korean flag in one corner.

"Yeah." Owen sits down and unzips his bag. "The owner is a friend of my dad's. So, what's this about Guy?" His voice drops a notch, threaded with anger.

My own anger builds, too, just thinking about it. "He's here for a book signing. He wants to meet for drinks tonight."

A pause. "And?"

"It's an awfully big coincidence."

"It is." Owen watches me. "What's the plan?"

"I invited him to Janie's after the memorial. I was hoping you'd—" I shrug. "Stay nearby. I'm going to see if I can get anything out of him. Find out how long he's been here. If there's anything suspicious."

Asking for Owen's help makes me feel vulnerable, but he says, "Sure," without hesitation. He looks like he has more to say, but a guy in his fifties strolls in on the balls of his feet, in good shape by his ease of movement. I watch him, wondering if I'll be at all like that when I'm older. MMA is hard on the body in a way traditional martial arts aren't—you can only take so many beatings, spend so many days working out six or eight hours at a time, before your body starts to break down. Rob has already mentioned retirement to me; as an amateur fighter it seems ridiculous, but I know it's not.

"Owen, good to see you, kid." They shake. "And coach Norah Silverton." He extends his hand to me. "An honor to have you working out in my dojang. You're welcome here anytime."

It's kind, and I thank him. He takes his leave, saying something about heading out to grab some lunch.

Guy still weighs heavy on my mind, as does the idea my father would commit suicide, but I need to let it go, even just for a few minutes. I shut my eyes, breathe, and start my warm-up: lunges and squats, arm stretches against the wall, shadowboxing, stretching. Owen's eyes are on me from a folding chair, but after a moment, he gets up and joins in, and I can see the years of training he's had in the way he moves, too.

He's strong. Not just bench-pressing-and-bicep-curls-in-the-gym strong—but that dynamic strength that comes with real work, the sort that activates your core and forces your body to learn to move in a way that is effective in the sort of life we as humans don't tend to lead anymore. When he throws his first punch against an invisible opponent, his body moves with it, opposite hand up, guarding his face.

My pulse speeds, and I grin, because I love a new partner on the mats. The fact he's handsome and game to play doesn't hurt. Add in he's not from my gym, and therefore fair game, and I pull on my own gloves and strap them at the wrist, energy thrumming as we get started.

I go through a couple drills, mostly jabs, crosses, and elbow work. I add in roundhouse kicks eventually, and after thirty minutes, I've worked up a sweat and learned Owen has a brown belt in the Marine Corps' martial arts program.

We both pull on gloves and go to straight sparring next. It's not the intentional focus on one type of fighting at a time I do at my home gym with Rob—boxing, Muay Thai, Jiu Jitsu, wrestling. But it's far better than anything I'd manage on my own, and having a new opponent with techniques I'm not as used to keeps my brain active and my focus sharp.

"What about you?" Owen asks when we take a break.

I pull my mouthguard from around my teeth, tuck it in the strap of my sports bra, and swig water. I glance at him. "What about me?"

"How'd you get started in all this?"

"Mostly by accident." I offer him a smile and find the sports drink in my bag. "After—what happened, I had to leave. Just get out of town. I didn't want to drive by the high school anymore, or—" I hesitate, remembering the first time I saw Janie after it happened. When she gave me a sad smile, and I saw both her and her sister in it, and started sobbing. "You know I'm best friends with Janie, but seeing her every day..."

"I know." Owen sprawls on the blue and red checkered mats, meets my gaze, nods. We look at one another for a long moment of shared understanding, something I've never had with anyone else. Least of all Janie. "Seeing her. Like seeing a ghost."

"Yeah." I offer him the sports drink. "Anyway, my dad and I got in a big fight. I wanted to take a year off before I started college. Travel. Or explore, or... anything. I just needed to get out of Kansas City. He insisted I stay in town. I was supposed to go to Thompson College."

Owen frowns. "That's the liberal arts college near the museum district?"

I nod. "I was signed up for pre-med, the closest thing I could get to psychology that he'd agree on."

"What about your mom?" he asks. "Didn't they get a divorce or something? What did she think?"

It feels almost strange he doesn't know these details, but it makes sense, too. He was August's boyfriend, in our group of friends, but at the periphery. We were a girl gang, first and foremost, the four of us running cross-country and track together since we were freshmen, sleeping over at one another's houses almost every weekend. Boys were part of high school, sure—girls, for Janie. I'd even dated, briefly. But we came first. August would never have mentioned the intimate details of my life to her boyfriend.

"She took off," I say casually. Maybe too casually. "So, she didn't get a say. And anyway," I breeze right past that topic, "It didn't matter. I was eighteen. He said no, so I left. I drove as far as I could, which happened to be Los Angeles, and I met my boss Rob there."

"But how'd you get into fighting?"

I smile, shrug. He's not Guy, ready to sell my private life to the highest bidder. But neither is he a real friend. "I was interested in learning to take care of myself." Not a lie. "He was around. Thought I was good enough to become a competitive fighter. I started winning, but it was too much—too many people's eyes on me. But I was good at coaching, too, so I started doing that, helping others win. I still fight, but just to stay in shape and keep myself on my toes. Amateur stuff. It's enough."

Speaking of.

"You good to go another round?"

"Sure." Owen climbs to his feet, pulls on loaner gloves, and we're back at it.

Twenty minutes later, I'm winning. But then he gets his foot under my shins, sweeps, and I'm on my back, slapping down hard with my hands to break my fall. It was a clean move, fast, and for a moment, I can't breathe, the air knocked from my lungs. It's the moment he needs, and in a flash, my right ankle is under his armpit, his leg over mine. I'm trapped. I slap the ground, signaling he's won the match, and he lets go, collapses back.

"Finally," he says. "At this rate I'll need best out of about fifty."

"That was good." I fall back, too, the mat cool on my back. "I think I'm done."

"I can't believe you do this every day."

"Twice, most days. And I help my fighters do their workouts."

Owen chuckles, pulls himself to a seated position. "I'm gonna be sore for a week. I've always respected fighters—can't imagine doing it for a living. I had no idea."

"Marines couldn't have been easy, either."

His face, lit up with adrenaline and exertion, falters. "It wasn't. But it was fun, too."

The mood in the room shifts, and I regret my words. "Sorry. I just meant—I mean, this is hard, but your life's on the line with that."

"Yeah. Never thought about that much, but yeah." Owen works up another smile, this one sharper on one side of his face than the other, showing off a dimple I haven't noticed before, "Wanna eat? You must be starved."

There's a sandwich in my bag. But Owen is cute, and he's holding his hand out to me to pull me to my feet. I eye the hand, deciding if I want to take it, and he winks. There's a tension between us, and until this moment, it's been funneled into punches, jabs, kicks. With that constant contact gone, it's like a live wire, and I need to ground it. Need to focus.

I put my hand in his. I really should say no, get back to Janie at the restaurant, get ready for the memorial tonight. But the clock on the wall tells me we still have a couple hours, and food would be good. How often do I get to eat out with someone besides Rob?

Owen tugs me up, but he pulls too hard, throwing me off balance, and we're both right back where we started on the mats. But this time, I'm on top of him. A rush of energy fills me, a longing for this. My hand goes to his stomach to catch myself, and his abs squeeze beneath my fingers as he laughs. It takes me off guard—people don't flirt with me. Especially not men at my gym. Rob would kick their ass.

"You did that on purpose!" I say when I've shaken off my surprise.

"No, no, I totally didn't." But he's laughing, and then I am, too. It's a break in the tension—a moment of relief amid the new reality that has consumed me since I got that phone call that my father was dead; since I found Esme.

I start to get up, but Owen catches my gaze with his. That live wire sparks. He grabs my face, pulls me down to meet him, and his lips are on mine.

We're hot and covered in sweat, and it's like kindling to a flame. His arms wrap around me, crush me to his chest. I snag his lip in my teeth, and he rolls, putting himself on top, as though we're still grappling.

This time, I don't throw him off.

TWENTY-FOUR

He kisses me, and I kiss him back, for about two seconds—then guilt crashes in on me, the knowledge of what's happened, that this is the last thing we should be doing. I pull away and press my hand to his chest when he tries to reignite this whole different type of wrestling.

"We have to stop," I say, my breath unsteady. And even though I've agreed to grab food with him, I know I need to put distance between us. Need to get back to Janie. I can't do this here, now.

"What's wrong?" Owen runs a hand through his hair, glances around to see if he missed something or someone walking in on us.

"Just—" I force a smile and my leg up and wrap it around his chest, throw him back, rolling with him, ending up on top. A simple aikido move. I get to my feet. "Nothing's wrong. But I need to get back to Janie. I have to shower. There's the memorial service. Also," I beckon at the room around us, "your friend's gonna be back any second." Not to mention, Esme is dead, and we're acting like teenagers, rolling around like we haven't a care in the world. Maybe that's why we're rolling around, though. Everything feels heavy right now, and this break is exactly what we needed.

Owen hops to his feet and advances on me fast, pushing me against the nearest wall. His hand catches my jaw, holds me still as his teeth tug at my lip and his mouth presses to mine. A growling laugh rumbles through his chest. "I understand," he says, but he doesn't stop, and I kind of don't want him to—my whole body tingling with sensations I usually deny myself—but when he pulls back for air, I duck out around his grip.

I move backward, putting space between us. He takes a slow step toward me, and for a moment, I wish things were normal. I wish we were at my home gym, where I have a key that locks the door, where we could play the hottest game of *catch-me-if-you-can* imaginable. The flicker of excitement in his eyes tells me he'd be excited to play said game.

But we're in Kansas City.

The police are watching us.

We have a friend who needs us.

"Stop." I point a finger at him, raise a brow, and try to keep the smile from curving at my mouth. "I'm going to the bathroom. We have to go."

He clenches his fists, and I think he's about to give chase. But he doesn't, and I walk down the hallway to find the ladies' room.

Five minutes later I emerge. I'm almost hesitant—waiting to see if he's going to jump me again. But he's on a folding chair, utterly still, gazing out the window at the bright autumn day. He's changed into a different T-shirt, a black one, and it hugs his biceps, his chest. I bite back a note of disappointment and appreciate the fact he respected my wishes.

"Ready?"

Owen turns to me. My pulse quickens. His eyes are dark, moody, and they travel up and down my body, still in shorts and a tank top.

"You're gonna be cold." He digs in his bag. Throws a hoodie my way—*his* hoodie. I have my own jacket, but I don't say no when I catch it and his smell floods my senses, bringing back a flash of how it felt to be beneath him, his body heavy over mine. "I'm going to head home and shower, change. Meet you at Janie's at four thirty?"

I grab my bag and locate my keys. Look anywhere but at him for a moment because I need to get my head together. This is not why I'm here. A fun distraction, that's it. That's all this was. A workout and—and a little more. Warmth creeps up my skin, and I'm not sure I'll need anything to keep me comfortable as I step out into the cold.

"Norah?"

"Yeah?"

"You okay?" He reaches out, touches my chin with his thumb and forefinger, a gentle, familiar gesture. Anyone else, and I'd swat their hand away. But something about him, about our shared past grieving for August, about how easy this time with him has been—I let him do it. Our eyes meet. I melt a little, and that's not what I want, but he's being sweet and kind, and Jesus, I'm only here for a few days, and life is hell, so what's the harm? My pulse pounds so heavily I swear I can feel it through my whole body.

"I'm good." My voice comes out too soft, too breathy.

"Okay." He presses a kiss to my lips—quick, careful. Opens the door for me. We go to our separate cars, and I breathe with relief as I close the door, turn on the engine, crank up the heat. I pull away without looking at him, grateful we drove separately.

TWENTY-FIVE

When the same silver sedan with Missouri plates pulls up behind me, I lose my patience. It's not Elaine behind the wheel, nor is it a twenty-something with their phone up, ready to snap photos.

"Hey, Siri, call Detective Cron." I programmed in her number the night prior, and my phone connects to her cell.

"Silverton," she says. "What is it? I said I'd call you when I have news."

I hesitate, then press forward. "Why do you have someone following me?"

A beat passes. It's telling.

"Following you?" Her voice lilts as she says it, and I can tell instantly she's lying.

"They couldn't be more obvious." I open my mouth to say more—but there's nothing to say. They're keeping an eye on me. Again. I can appreciate they're doing their job. I just wish they were looking in the right direction instead of harassing me.

"I don't know what you mean," she says, and by her tone, I suspect she's fully aware I know she's full of shit. "But since I have you on the phone, I do have a question."

"What's that?" I come to a stoplight, hit the turn signal, and check my rearview mirror again. The same sedan is there, two cars back now. When I make the turn, they go straight, as if they've already received a text telling them they've been caught and it's not worth continuing to follow me.

"You previously had a restraining order against an Elaine Gehring."

"Yes." I turn up the volume on the phone, wondering if she found out about Elaine breaking into my father's house; if she found out about me confronting her.

"We questioned Esme's boyfriend—the doctor. He has an alibi. But he mentioned we should look into Ms. Gehring. That she'd recently shown up at the hospital—more than once— trying to talk to Esme while she was at work."

This time, I pull off on the side of the road and put the car in park. I pull my hands from the steering wheel and squeeze them together, repeating her words in my own head.

"She went to Esme's *work*?"

"Yes. We pulled hospital camera footage." Detective Cron clears her throat. "Between you and me, I'd call it an altercation more than a meeting. Obviously, you don't particularly like Ms. Gehring. Nor do I, for that matter. Her website is... obscene. But I was wondering if Esme mentioned this to you?"

"No." I suck in a breath, wondering why she hadn't. The answer comes instantly—she wouldn't have wanted to upset me. She knew as much as Janie did that I hated Elaine. I would have felt the need to do something if I'd known Elaine was harassing her.

"So you don't know what it was about?"

"No, but..." I bite my lip. "I mean, I can guess."

"Guess away."

"Elaine does this every now and then. She knows I won't talk to her, so she tries to get a friend to talk to her. She still checks in with Janie regularly." It occurs to me she might have checked in with my dad, too. She obviously knew where he lived. Hell, she'd broken into the house—it was possible she even knew where the spare key was, the same one I'd used.

"I see." Detective Cron hums to herself. "Well, I'll be in touch."

"Wait."

"Yes, Ms. Silverton?"

I open my mouth to tell her Elaine was at my father's house this morning—that she thought maybe he'd been murdered. But something changes my mind. Makes me shut my mouth and keep this information private a little longer. For one, it might make me look more suspicious—pointing fingers, mentioning the word *murder* when it heretofore has not been mentioned. Second, it's something I have over Elaine. A way to get her to answer my questions and leave me alone. I also can't imagine there's any truth to her theory, so it's pointless, really. But it is interesting she fought with Esme.

"No never mind, it's nothing." I end the call.

I look up just in time to see the silver sedan pass by. I raise my middle finger to the driver and pull back into traffic.

TWENTY-SIX

Janie's wiping down the bar when I find my way inside. I sat out in the car a good ten minutes before coming in, rehashing the day—Elaine this morning, meeting with Guy tonight, and last but not least, making out with Owen. The place has cleared out from the lunch crowd, and a sole elderly man is in one corner, reading an honest-to-god printed newspaper and sipping coffee. I find a barstool, exchange a look with her, and she *knows* what happened, I swear she does. Her lips curl in a coy grin. She winks, and it feels dirty. I cover my face with my hands and groan. *I* feel dirty, even though all we did was kiss. Briefly, at that.

"What did you do?" she asks, her intonation making it clear I did *something*. I raise my brows at her. She claps her hands. Guilt follows in the wake of excitement, but Janie is smiling for the first time since I found Esme, and I give her a smile and let the mood continue.

"Please tell me it was Owen," she whispers.

I hesitate, watching her. "You don't think it's... weird?"

Janie rolls her eyes. "Why would it be weird?"

"He and August—and..."

Janie leans across the bar, presses a hand to my forearm. The playfulness is gone from her gaze. "Owen is like family. It's been ten years. It's not like he was a shitty ex-boyfriend. She died, Norah. So, no, it's not weird. Besides, when was the last time you so much as flirted with a man I didn't think was complete trash?"

I breathe out, take a barstool, nod. I figured she wouldn't mind, but I had to say something. Had to... acknowledge it. Whatever it is. We made out. That's hardly something worth talking about.

"So, how was he?" She leans in, stares at me with her wide eyes, and this is as much a distraction for her as it is for me. I have things I need to talk to her about, and I need to ask if she knows about Elaine bothering Esme, but so many bad things have happened, and in this moment I decide to go with it.

"We didn't really do anything. We just kissed. Once—no, twice."

Janie sighs. "Norah, when are you going to let yourself just have some fun?"

My phone vibrates where I set it on the bar.

Rob: *How was your workout? How was the new sparring partner?*

Janie snorts. "*That's* what you were doing? *Sparring?*" Her eyes are still lit up, but then something passes over her face— guilt—remembering, I think, that our friend is dead.

"Something like that. You okay?"

She nods. Turns away and grabs a menu. I watch her, wishing I could bring back that Janie energy, distract her to keep her from hurting.

"Tell me more." She pours herself a tall glass of wine. A

forced smile. Trying to look happy again. "What happened with Owen? *Exactly?*"

I almost suggest we go upstairs and have a good cry. Janie needs it. I hate crying, but of all the people in my life, I'd cry with her. But she's downed half the wine already and is wiping at her eyes, pretending to be okay. And if that's what she wants, I'll help out with fun tidbits from my afternoon.

I summon my inner gossip—which is not me at all, but for Janie, I'll do it—and launch into the story. "We were sparring and then—" I try to remember the details. It all blurs together. The heat of jabs, kicks, blocks, tossing one another to the ground, then pulling one another close. I give her the shorthand, and she croons with delight.

But then reality hits, and I break the mood, adding, "*Guy* is in town. The Guy who wrote the book."

Her smile vanishes. "What?"

"Book tour." I point. "He'll be right next door."

"Shit. What do we do? Maybe we could have Owen kick his ass—" Her eyes widen. "Or you could. That would be the ultimate payback."

"Rob will be pissed if I get arrested." Janie pouts. "Besides, I want to talk to him. He just *happens* to be in town when Esme dies? And I told him..." I pause. "A lot. He knows details about what happened back then." He *did* know details, but there was a lot I left out, too—like where arteries were cut. He could be the copycat. I also want to know why my father had a signed copy of his book.

She sighs and sets down her wineglass. "Yeah. Yeah, you're right. And like you said, he's probably benefiting from it all. Did you see the newspaper? There was an article this morning about Esme dying and you being back in town. They rehashed everything about you and August, too." She makes a face, picks at a smudge on the bar top.

"Did it mention my dad?" I force myself to let it go for the moment, to move on, remembering the Instagram message.

Janie makes a face. "I don't think so."

"I'm bringing Guy here for drinks after the memorial."

Janie nods, eyes unfocused, thinking. "Owen and I can hang out. In case you need backup."

Behind her, the cook slides a plate of food out, and Janie sets it down in front of me.

I pick up a fork. "Did Esme ever mention anything about Elaine bothering her?"

Janie props her elbows on the bar, her brows furrowing. "No. Why?"

I share what Detective Cron told me, but leave out the part about Elaine's theory on my father being murdered. It's not worth making Janie worry even more.

"Huh. I didn't know. I guess I should have—Elaine comes here a couple times a year to have a glass of wine and see if she can get me to talk. But going to the hospital Esme worked at?" She shakes her head, but then her eyes go wide. "Norah, do you think Elaine would..." Her voice goes ghostly soft.

We exchange a look.

"I don't think so," I say.

"Me neither."

We exchange a look again.

"What about her fans?" Janie asks. "Some of them are..." She cringes. She hates using the word *crazy*, but I can tell it's the word she wants to use. She whispers it, instead.

"I don't know." I chew a bite of salad and stare down at the woodgrain of the bar. I wouldn't say it's impossible. A true crime fanatic becoming a copycat killer?

Possible. Very possible. I need to ask Elaine about it. She might even be aware of fans of hers who aren't quite... normal.

I eat, and Janie signs off to an oncoming bartender who will manage the restaurant tonight. We head upstairs in short order, where I shower, and we both dress for the evening—a black and violet velvet number for her, a simple black cotton dress for me. Chloe's meeting us there since her flight was delayed.

We're headed for the door when my phone lights up.

"Who's that?" Janie stops us. "Another boy toy?"

"No. It's—It's Owen." My heart quivers for a half a second before I shut it down. *Not the time.* "What's up?" I press the phone to my ear.

"You two okay?" He's breathless.

"Um." I glance at Janie. We're in the back stairwell from her apartment to the rear exit of the restaurant, where she comes and goes when she doesn't want to attend to business. "Yes? We're leaving for the memorial."

"Good." His voice slides into a more neutral tone, but I heard the note of panic it.

"What's wrong?" I grip the phone tighter. Janie's fingers touch my elbow. She leans close, brows furrowed.

"Nothing, probably nothing, it's just—could you give me a ride? I can text you my address. It's out of the way, but someone slashed my tires. My first thought was it was—" He pauses. "Related. But it's probably not, probably random. I just saw it and worried about you and—" He stops. He's talking a mile a minute, nearly out of breath.

"Owen, it's okay. We'll come get you. We're fine." I hang up.

"What in the world?" Janie asks. "In this part of town?"

I shrug. "The Plaza is fine, but a couple blocks east..."

We get into my rental, and Janie looks his address up in her phone. But when we arrive, he's not waiting inside his house, out of the cold—he's scrubbing at the windshield of the old truck, and though the light of day has started to fade, I can see the faint tracing of what was red paint.

"Owen?" I step out of the car. "What did it say?"

He turns to me with a frown, eyes filled with anxiousness, waiting for my reaction.

The car. The red paint. I can see the faint outline of the words he was scrubbing desperately at. Trying to erase before I saw them.

YOU'RE NEXT.

TWENTY-SEVEN

TEN YEARS AGO

"Some people like to call me Hansel." He took that final step, closing the gap between us, and crouched, putting us face to face. I felt like I was in a zoo, facing down a snarling tiger, but no cage separated us. I was not supposed to be here. Humans did not survive creatures like this.

My whole body trembled. He reached out and touched my face, examining me for a reaction. Fear. He wanted fear. I could see it in his eyes.

It's what he got from August.

And then I replayed what he'd said. *Hansel.* The media had named a serial killer that for the breadcrumbs he left leading to his victims. He'd killed at least four women, they suspected, and there were no leads.

And he was here in front of me.

What little control I'd gained slipped away. A tear escaped my eyes, and he pressed a fingertip to it.

"I'm waiting," he said.

Waiting for what, was the appropriate response, but my mouth couldn't form words. I couldn't convince any part of my brain to work right, this time.

"You're very pretty." His words rasped in my ear, so close, too close. My gaze skittered around the room. August. A liquid around her, reflecting light. Blood. She had to be dead.

I focused closer, on his shoulder, on his arm. "You look strong," I stammered, shocked to hear my own voice working. He didn't look strong. But he complimented me. I had to compliment him back. Had to say... something. Anything.

Or I'd die. I'd lie in a pool of my own blood, just like her. I shuddered, and he mistook it for me being cold, moving closer, wrapping an arm around my shoulder. I squeezed my eyes shut.

"I've been watching you."

My stomach twisted, gnarled, threatened to eject the punch I'd had. I wanted to close my eyes and wake up from this nightmare. *Wake up, wake up, wake up!*

"We can be different. You're different." He beckoned at August's still form.

"What do you mean?" I asked, when I convinced my lips to form the proper movements, my lungs to expel the air necessary for speech.

"She screamed and begged. You're..." He tilted his head, got close again, the fabric of the black mask skimming over my jaw. "Different."

My whole body tensed. I'd learned about fight or flight response in biology, but I couldn't do either—couldn't run, couldn't defend myself. All I could do was sit there, helpless.

"You're not scared," he said after silence that seemed to stretch for hours.

I was. How could he not see that? I was terrified. I was seconds from death. Seconds from my eyes fluttering closed never to open again. Another glance at him—almost too close for me to be able to focus on him. I said the response I thought he wanted to hear.

"No. I'm not." A lie. I summoned the semester I took of drama and lived it, became it. I crossed my arms, pretending to be cold, but really, I was hiding the shaking that could nearly rattle my teeth from my mouth. He was insane. Absolutely, truly living in another world.

"Here." He pulled me into his lap. I forced myself still, forced the scream to stay in my throat.

"You're special." His voice up to that moment had been curt, robotic, one order after another. But now it was soft, tentative. Vaguely familiar, though I couldn't place who or what he reminded me of. Maybe of the first time I met my one and only boyfriend at age fifteen. Too nice, too available. And now, knowing I'd never see said boyfriend again, I wished I'd been nicer in return. A warm hand smoothed from my shoulder to my elbow. My prom dress was ragged, muddy, still damp where the fabric gathered. I couldn't stop shaking. I could barely think straight.

"So are you." I just had to keep agreeing with him, saying yes, letting him believe whatever tale he was weaving.

His eyes were trained on me, and for the first time, a glimmer of hope stirred inside me. My brain rebooted. This might work. I just had to keep it up long enough to be rescued or find a way to escape.

"Not like the others," he continued. "You're... unique. Strong. Do you think you could like someone like me? Maybe love someone like me?" he asked.

"Yes," I said automatically.

"You don't have to be scared." He hugged me against his body.

After a while, he started talking—about how everyone was afraid of him. How no one understood him. How the world focused on the unimportant bullshit, but how he thought I was different.

When he asked questions, I answered them. Everything he said, I agreed or praised him. He liked that. After a while, I thought he fell asleep, but the moment I moved, his hands clenched around me tighter. Somewhere in the horizon, a hint of light emerged. We'd both fallen asleep in the darkness. Exhaustion tugged at me, in a tug-of-war with the flagging bursts of adrenaline.

"I want you to stay with me," he said as the sky turned a soft blue. "Forever."

TWENTY-EIGHT

We call the police, even though Owen is nervous to.

"I started wiping it off," he says. "What if—"

But Janie interrupts, "What if there's evidence? That could lead us to Esme's killer?"

Owen goes quiet then, looking over the half-washed red paint with regret. "I didn't want it to upset the two of you."

Janie dials. I ease back into the driver's seat, unable to take my eyes off the vehicle. The message someone left for Owen. For us. Owen is pale, and he runs a hand through his hair, watches Janie and I as though we might freak out.

But I'm not freaking out. I'm mad, squeezing my fists, glancing around, like I'll catch someone with a bottle of spray paint.

Detective Cron appears twenty minutes later, dressed all in black, headed for the same destination we are—the memorial.

Someone from a lab comes and takes samples. Detective Cron scolds Owen for trying to wipe it away, but her face softens when he says he didn't want Janie and me to see it. To *worry*.

"It's probably nothing," she says. "Local kids who know who

you are, that August was your girlfriend. Someone being an idiot." She stares at the vehicle, and I almost call her out on this statement—she has no idea who did it. Minimizing the possibility it was Hansel or a copycat does nothing to help any of us.

"Do you have any news?" I ask.

Janie looks over at me, then at Cron. Owen moves closer, making himself part of our group, and this time, I don't mind.

"Are you planning on bringing in the FBI this time?" Janie asks, her voice sharp. A question her parents asked more than once last time.

Detective Cron stiffens. She gives Janie a long look and adjusts the set of her shoulders. "You can all go to the memorial. We'll finish up here." She's effectively dismissed us, and in doing so, ignored Janie's question. But she pauses as she turns away. "Nothing on your dad yet. Hopefully you'll be able to plan a funeral soon, but they're holding his body in case..." Her voice trails off. *In case what?*

She stalks away before I can ask.

Ten minutes later, we're bundled into my car, heat blasting. It's dark out. Night has settled in, the temperature has dropped, and all I can think of is that there's something Detective Cron isn't telling me about my father. That Elaine thinks he was murdered. That I'm the only thing Esme and my father had in common, and that I'm also what Owen has in common with them.

But Owen and I barely know one another. We went to high school together, but that was a decade ago. And yet...

And yet, if someone had walked by the martial arts studio, if they'd held their hands to the glass, peered in, they might have caught a glimpse of us rolling around. They might have assumed he meant something to me and targeted him.

Shit. It was entirely possible I'd just put Owen in the worst position possible—*next. You're next.*

I realize I'm grinding my teeth. We should have been more

careful. Damn it. Even that silver sedan with a rookie had been able to follow me—has someone else been?

I look behind us, but it's too dark to make out the cars nearby. I steal a look at Owen in the rearview mirror. He's deep in thought, and so is Janie, and I wish we could just be normal. Just be friends, just laugh and remember Esme and have drinks and *live*.

"You okay?" I ask Owen. He meets my eyes, tries for a smile, but something stirs in their depths. I thought it was worry in that distant look, but it's not—it's rage. I understand rage. "We'll get them," I say. He doesn't reply.

"I'm sorry this isn't the visit you wanted," I tell Janie, reaching over to squeeze her arm.

"You're here," she says. "I'm glad you're here."

More silence. Detective Cron is also a common thread in all of this. And Detective Cron would know how to not leave behind DNA evidence. She's, yet again, not asking the FBI for help. I swallow, stare out the window into the darkness, watch the night flashing by. But that's crazy. It doesn't even make sense. She's a detective. It's been a decade.

But there's someone out there doing this. I only wish I knew who.

TWENTY-NINE

We reach the university where Janie and Esme graduated, where I was supposed to be their third roommate before I ducked out, and I find a parking spot. People in heavy coats mill around. Candles are lit in front of a chapel, flickering in the darkness, almost *cheerful*, and I know this is supposed to be a celebration of life, but god, I just wish Esme were still here. "Where's Chloe?" I ask.

Janie looks around. "She should be here soon."

I don't see the soon-to-be-wife anywhere, but I do see Elaine, and when she spots me, I can see the battle in her mind —to approach me or not, after we faced off this morning. To try to get a quote for the next podcast or to get a photo of the infamous Norah Silverton. Or to slink away, like the snake she is. I consider going after her right now, but Owen's hand encloses around mine. The shock of it—god, have I ever held someone's hand?—makes me look down, makes me take it all in.

"Just for now." He winks.

I relax. Good. He didn't read too much into earlier. Janie eyes us but says nothing, and moments later, a dark-skinned woman joins us. Her eyes are the lightest shade of amber, and she smiles, and Janie smiles, and I've never seen her so happy. For a moment I do nothing but watch them—incredibly grateful that despite everything, Janie has found her soulmate.

"Chloe," the woman says, and we exchange handshakes. "I'm sorry about your friend. But it's so good to meet you. Janie talks about you all the time."

"Norah," I reply. "And likewise. I can tell Janie adores you."

We go inside and find a bench. Esme's family is several rows in front of us. I should say hello. I should offer condolences. But I'm the one who found her, and that might be worse than simply fading into the background. I focus on what I can control —myself. Owen's warm beside me, his leg against mine. The service doesn't start for a few minutes more, so when I see three messages from Rob, I check them.

Rob: *How was the new sparring partner?*

Rob: *Call me when you have a second—want to catch up on a few things. Cher called.*

Rob: *Norah, why aren't you answering?*

Owen shifts beside me. "Everything okay?"
"Yeah." I type a quick response.

Me: *Everything is fine. Sorry. Busy. I'll call you tomorrow, memorial tonight.*

"He's my boss," I say. "He's worried about me being out of town with the big fight coming up."

"I can work out with you again tomorrow," Owen says. "If I can walk after today, that is. I know you have a lot to do, though, so... just let me know." He's casual. Forced casual. His eyes linger on my phone, his cheek twitches. Hopeful? Jealous? I tuck my phone away and ignore that I'm secretly pleased he seems interested. This isn't the time, place, or situation.

The service starts. A man in robes talks up front for ten or twenty minutes. Esme's mother approaches the podium, and then a sister. Jesus, her sister, who looks so much like her. It's not like Janie and August, but it's spooky all the same. I shift in my seat and Owen takes my hand again. Janie exchanges a tearful smile with me. I wish I could take her pain away. So much pain. But at least she has Chloe now, and Chloe wraps her arms around her.

I sneak a look toward Elaine, who sat too close to the front, but she's gone. Good. Maybe someone said something to her. Another woman sings a song, and people share stories, and Janie gets up and shares one, too.

And then it's over, and we wander around with plastic cups of white wine from a box and Ritz crackers with slivers of grocery store-cut cheese.

You're next, the paint said. And if it's Hansel, or someone continuing what Hansel started, he'll kill again.

I check the ground, like I'll find the breadcrumbs here somewhere, but of course, there's only a splash of the wine, a bit of cracker turned to dust under someone's shoe. When I look up, I catch sight of Elaine near the closed casket, murmuring to Esme's mother.

My patience snaps.

"Excuse me." I step away from the circle of friends I'd been half-listening to. I stride across the room without hesitating, clutch Elaine's elbow, and press down on a pressure point, forcing a squeak from her throat.

I yank her away down a private hallway. "We need to talk."

THIRTY

"What do you think you're doing?" Elaine's face creases in anger, but her eyes go wide again when I advance half a step.

"What do *you* think *you're* doing?" I demand. "This is Esme's memorial, and you're grilling her mother?"

"I wasn't grilling her."

"Yes, you were. That's what you do. You sneak around and get the *inside scoop* and expose people's private lives for public entertainment."

A beat of silence. Elaine presses her lips together as though she'll deny this accusation, but she can't. We both know it's the truth.

I'm about to tell her to leave—about to threaten to send Detective Cron the photo of her tampering with a potential crime scene—but then I remember she'd known things she shouldn't have. And that she was bothering Esme. *And* our theory that maybe one of her fans had decided to take matters into their own hands.

"How did you know about my father? And the antidepressant in his system?"

Elaine rolls her eyes. "I have contacts everywhere, Norah.

Everywhere. When you're me, everyone wants to help you solve the crime. If you would just let me help you—if you would stop holding back on what happened—we'd probably have him by now. I know you're hiding something." She lifts her brows at me, as if she's proved some great point, and that I should take great significance in her words.

"So you have people committing crimes to help you? Tampering with evidence, obstructing justice—"

"Oh please, stop being so dramatic."

"What did you want with Esme? Why did you follow her to work? What did you argue about?"

This makes her shut up. She presses her lips together, staring at me, thinking hard. "How did you find out about that?"

"I have *contacts*," I say, imitating her own words. "Getting in an argument with someone before they are murdered looks suspicious. Did that occur to you?"

Elaine crosses her arms. "I didn't do anything to Esme. I just asked her about you. Your friends are annoyingly protective of your privacy, you know. I even offered—" Her nostrils flare. "I even offered her money. She wouldn't say a word."

Emotions rush through me—my heart aching for Esme's loyalty, for the loss of my sweet friend—anger that Elaine would dare do that.

"Why can't you just drop this? Leave my friends alone. Leave *me* alone. I'm not going to tell you anything. Besides, there's nothing left to tell. Didn't you read Guy's book?"

"Is that really everything, though?" Elaine's brows shoot up, and she's got that look on her face again—the one that tells me she's memorizing everything I say.

"What are you suggesting?" I ask.

"You escaped a serial killer, Norah. People want to know *how*. What if you could save someone's life by sharing your methods? I mean—"

"My *methods*?"

Her smile grows. "Yes. We've had *True Crime Possessed* fans get themselves out of bad situations because of what they learned from the podcast. Tell me what you did. It might save someone's life someday."

I realize I'm sweating—hot, fevered, the anger coming out of my pores in liquid form. I can't let her get to me like this. But she's suggesting I tell her every gruesome detail from that night because it might *save* someone? It's bullshit. Utter bullshit. And besides, there was no method—there was just pure terror. Doing my best to survive one moment to the next.

"Listen, you went through something traumatic." Elaine's face smooths into a façade of concern. She reaches out and touches fingertips to my arm. "If you can't remember—it's common, with PTSD, to block out memories."

"What?" I snap.

"I have someone who can help you remember what *really* happened that night. Not what you think happened, not what the cops convinced you to say—"

I start to pull away—to force myself away from her, from this situation that is going to get me in trouble if I don't leave now. I don't need help remembering. If anything, I'd prefer help *forgetting*. But I can't leave until I ask my last question.

"You have a dedicated following."

A pleased smile. "Yes, I do. Thank you for noticing."

"It wasn't a compliment. Would one of them kill for you?"

"Excuse me?" She goes still, goes pale. Blinks at me, unbelieving. "Kill?"

I inspect her face, her posture. I almost wish I knew her better, so I could understand what it means. But I do notice one thing.

She doesn't say no.

THIRTY-ONE

Elaine frowns at me. "I have tens of thousands of fans. Hundreds of thousands, maybe, if you count the people not in the fan club. I have no idea. I can't be responsible for their actions."

I want to argue with her. Want to tell her if she's running a true crime website, she damn well *is* responsible for the content, for what she encourages her followers to do or say or investigate. But that is a far cry from committing murder.

"Anyone obsessed with the Hansel case?"

Down the hall, a song starts to play—a piano melody, one Esme learned in high school and swore she wanted to play at her wedding. It's like a knife to my gut, painful, momentarily distracting, but Elaine is talking, and I force my attention back to her.

"Everyone loves the Hansel case," Elaine whispers. "It's... Hansel." She tosses her hands up, as if explaining the obvious— everyone's favorite serial killer.

It's sick, is what it is.

"Have you found out anything else?" I lower my voice a notch, try to relax my posture into something less threatening.

Elaine crosses her arms over her chest, rubs her elbow where I pressed into the pressure point. As usual, her makeup is on point, her blonde hair perfection over one shoulder, atop a black blazer.

"No." She forces out a breath. "I haven't. Although—" Something flashes in her eyes. Something that means she's either lying, or at least holding back the truth.

"What is it?"

"Don't be mad." She gives me another look that makes me think she's scared of me. I wave a hand for her to get on with it.

"Your father's library card. I found it. He never setup an online account, so it was easy to make one with the card number. I looked at his borrowing history."

My mind whirls, trying to understand what she's telling me. My initial reaction is annoyance she stole his library card, but more, I want to know why she's sharing this with me. What it could possibly mean.

"And?"

"He was researching true crime. Specifically, unsolved cases." Elaine's voice is just above a whisper. She casts a glance down the hall, back toward the memorial service, as though someone might overhear us. "Maybe he got too close to figuring out who Hansel was."

Detective Cron's words thunder through my brain—the overdose. And then the word Elaine proclaimed.

Murder.

I clear my throat, try to sound uninterested. "Yes?"

"Well." Her hands come up in a gesture I take to mean *isn't it obvious?*

"Lots of people read about true crime." Inside, my heart beats faster, and I have to fight to keep my breathing regular. I start to wonder what exactly I'll find on his computer when I work up the guts to actually go through it. Which I need to do. *Tonight.*

"Norah?" Owen calls from behind me, pulling my attention away from Elaine. I hold up a finger to him to indicate *one minute*.

"Anything else?" I ask.

She shakes her head, then hesitates, words on the tip of her tongue.

"What?"

"Are you—are you *sure* you don't want to tell me the rest of what happened that night?"

My face turns to stone. "Excuse me?"

"I know you didn't tell the police everything. The fact you told Guy so much more is proof of that. I can't help but think you didn't tell Guy everything, either."

My ears ring. The world shifts around me, as her words sink in, as what she's suggesting penetrates, as I flash back to those terrifying hours in Hansel's clutches, and—

I shut the memory down. I keep my face as blank as I can, but the way her eyes are boring into me, like she's memorizing my every feature, I suspect I'm failing miserably. I want to push her away. Run for the nearest exit. Leave Kansas City again and never turn back.

My fingers tremble with the desire to ball into fists and cause her the physical trauma equal to what I went through emotionally then—to what I deal with every day now, even though I try to force it back, try to keep it from engulfing me. Usually, I can manage. Being here, though, makes it harder. I swallow it back, force myself to inhale, exhale.

"I want to know if you dig up anything worthwhile," I say. "If I find out you know something and you didn't tell me, I'll tell Cron you were at my father's house that morning. Otherwise? You should go." I nod toward the exit, opposite of where Owen stands, looking as though he's trying to figure out if I need help or not.

Elaine's face twists—she smells a story, one she wants badly.
One I'll never give her.

THIRTY-TWO

Dinner is lovely. A glimpse of what this trip could have been. Chloe is beautiful and charming and intelligent. She's a security specialist, the sort who works for powerful people, keeping their lives safe by organizing personal protection in the form of bodyguards. Janie is head over heels for her. Chloe's halfway through a rant about one of her employers when I notice the time.

"I have to go. I'm meeting Guy." I push back from the table. Janie glances at her watch, eyes wide.

"Wait," she says. "You can't go alone. It's *Guy*, and he—" She stops, but she doesn't have to say it. I know.

"I'll be fine," I say. "It's not like we're meeting in his hotel room."

"I got it." Owen presses the white cloth napkin to his mouth, wiping away the remnants of dessert and wine. He stands and buttons his jacket.

"We'll pay and be there soon." Janie cranes her neck to look for the waiter.

Janie's Cafe is packed, twenty- and thirty-somethings in twos and fours, seated in booths, around tables. The bar is standing room only. An older man with a long white beard sits on a makeshift stage in one corner, strumming a tune.

So much for a quiet conversation.

I slide into a booth tucked into a private corner as a couple vacates it, and Owen walks in a second later—all part of the plan. Make it appear I'm alone.

When Guy walks in, he looks exactly like he did the first time I met him. A twinge of pain leads to anger as I take in his slicked-back hair tied in a short ponytail, very '90s-era, very *I'm a fucking writer, and don't you forget it.* He even wears a hat, or maybe a cap would be a better term for it, the sort men obsessed with their Irish heritage wear. He sports a brown leather vest over a long-sleeved shirt, jeans, and I suspect there's a godawful suit jacket to go with it. If I didn't hate him, I might appreciate he has his own style, that it fits nicely over his tall, lithe form. As it is, I do hate him, and it's only through pure willpower I don't stand up and take a swing when he approaches the table.

"Norah." Guy grins with too much teeth. "So good to see you. I was really hoping you'd make the signing, though. A photo-op would be great for business at the bookstore."

More like your Instagram—look, a photo with the woman who survived a serial killer!

"I was at the memorial for my friend who was murdered."

"I'm so sorry." I wait for a change in his expression, a moment of hesitation, a glance to the left, the universal *I'm lying* signal. But he doesn't do any of these things. He frowns, the expression even reaching his dark brown eyes, and he reaches out, touches my shoulder, tries to pull me in for a hug.

"Don't." I yank away and point. "Sit down."

A slow smile forms at his lips, an eyebrow hitches, and my god, is he getting off on this? My hands burn with the desire to wrap around his throat.

"You're still upset with me," he says.

"Yes."

"I told you before we got started—" Guy rolls up a sleeve, pulls out the largest cell phone I've ever seen, and swipes through screens. "Look, this is the form you signed. If you look at line twelve here—" He's pointing to words, and my digital initial is there, but I don't care.

"You know what you did. You know that I thought what was said about that night was between us." I pin him with a glare. "You used me. Led me to think—" *Think what? We were starting something? Yes.*

Which is one of many reasons why things will stay casual with Owen. This is what happens when I don't look before I fall.

So, I won't bother falling again.

A waiter steps up to the table then, pulls a pen from behind his ear, poises it over a tiny notepad. "What can I get for you two?"

"Ladies first." Guy gestures to me. "And I've got the check, so feel free—"

"I can buy my own damn drink." I ignore the startled cough from the waiter and pick up the special drinks menu Janie spends hours on each month, designing cocktails specific to the season. I know it will please her if I order something from it. "I'll have the Autumn Old-Fashioned," I say, hoping to god it's not the pumpkin spice latte version of my favorite cocktail.

"Same," Guy says, and I almost tell the waiter to wait so I can pick out something else. My hands clench around the menu, but I lower it to the table, glance around the restaurant— Owen is two tables away, sipping a beer—Janie is behind the bar, and Chloe has found herself a stool nearby.

Guy reaches across the table to take my hands. I yank them away.

"Why did you agree to talk to me if—"

"It's my turn."

"Your turn?" He adjusts his *cap*, checks his *ponytail*, and *he's* the one I'd like to take into the cage with me. I wouldn't knock him out in the first round, though. No, I'd toy with him, like a cat with a mouse.

"To ask you questions."

"By all means." He smiles indulgently, like I'm a child.

"When did you get in town?"

"Two days ago. Thursday morning."

"Let me see your flight information."

A quirked brow. "You think I carry my boarding pass around?"

"Your phone. Pull it up on your phone."

He's *still* smiling, but it's the smile of *I'll play along*. My neck itches. My arms tingle.

"How are sales?" I ask. He slides his phone across, an email pulled up with his flight information.

"Steady. Good first week. Not quite a bestseller—but solid."

"Yeah?" I ask. "They didn't boom after Esme's death yesterday?"

Guy sighs. "Is that what this is about? I was very sorry to hear about her death, and admittedly the timing is—odd."

"Really?" I give him his phone back. Meet his eyes. "You lied to me. Exposed something that was private. I was known as the female MMA coach. Now? I'll be known as that chick who tricked a serial killer with my *womanly wiles*." I'm off on a tangent now, and I take a breath, pull myself back to center. "So, if you'd lie to me, expose my private life to sell a few books" —I focus on him—"you wouldn't take it a step further? Bring a serial killer back to life, so to say?" There, I've said it. My stomach flutters, and I wait for his reaction.

Guy's eyes widen, but then he laughs. "Are you kidding me? Murder?"

"Did you interview my father for your book?" I switch tact.

Guy's smile fades, and his lips press together.

"Did you speak to him?" I ask. "Is that why he had a signed copy of your book?"

"Yes. I did. And yes, it is."

I half expected him to say no to this question. I go still, curiosity and annoyance racing through me in equal parts. "When?"

"Which time?" Guy's good-guy routine is gone, his voice dry, his expression flat. He looks at me across the table, and he's a whole different person. Like a fucking sociopath with more than one side to his personality. A chill runs down my spine. A lot like how Hansel moved from one personality to the next that night.

"When did you last speak to him?"

"Here's the thing, Norah Silverton. I'm working on another book." His gaze flicks back to me, and he waits, like I should have something to say about this. "So, I've spoken to your father quite a lot. Turns out he had a lot to say about you. What led you to be a fighter. Why he thinks you were able to survive a *serial killer.*"

"He wouldn't do that." I keep my face blank. Try to think through everything I know—*knew*—about my father. I can't see him talking to a reporter. Then again, he was apparently writing a memoir. What if Guy took that angle? The *I'm writing a book, and we're writing buddies* angle?

And worse—another book? On me, apparently.

"Excuse me." The waiter is back. He sets down our drinks. Neither of us touches them. Behind Guy, two men stand, pull on jackets, and Owen takes their spot. His presence bolsters me a little.

But then Guy slides his hand across the table, runs his fingertips down my arm, smiles all charming again, just like he did that fucking weekend, and I don't think—I just act.

I grab his hand, yank him toward me, twist. He's face down on the table in half a second, and I bend his hand back and press on the back of his elbow, and he *laughs*, and I smack my forearm down, and there's a *crack*. And then he's not laughing anymore.

THIRTY-THREE

TEN YEARS AGO

"I want you to stay with me. Forever."

Panic burned through me, and I tried to say something, but my vocal cords were paralyzed. I was paralyzed. To stay with him meant death. I knew that much. Either because by forever, he meant he wanted to kill me and keep my body in a freezer, like I'd seen a serial killer do in a movie, or because he literally meant he wanted to keep me with him. Where he could touch me. Talk to me. Where I'd be his prisoner. Where god knows what might happen, what he might expect me to do.

No, no, no—

You can't panic. You can't. If you do, he'll kill you. Think. THINK.

"I would like that," I said. "But my father, he's really sick."

"Oh?" He sounded interested. His hand closed over mine, pressed it to his chest. I fought the desire to pull away, to strike out.

"Yes." My brain engaged, and I dragged a list of symptoms from my memory, but they weren't my father's. They had been my grandfather's, who'd been dead for five years. These were the symptoms I remembered seeing with him. "He coughs a lot.

He can't walk very far before he has to sit down. It's something with his heart. He has this medication, and if he doesn't take it—"

I went on and on. I let this stranger pull me tighter into his embrace. He rested his chin on my head, as though we were girlfriend and boyfriend, watching the sunrise together. He was delusional, but I needed that delusion.

I had hope.

I had lies.

This was all I had.

THIRTY-FOUR

Guy yelps. Across the room, Janie curses and shoots me a glare, the sort that says *don't get the police called*.

I let him go short of breaking his arm and shove him back across the booth. We're hidden from the majority of the room in our corner, but a few sets of eyes have turned our way, the murmur of the crowd quieting for a beat, but the musician wails something about Kansas City and jazz and barbecue, and Guy is back in his seat, holding his arm like I *did* break it, which maybe I should have.

"When did you *last* talk to my dad?" I ask. I stare him down, hoping he sees how serious I am. That I'm not the same woman he met and spent a weekend with.

Guy grabs his drink and downs it like it's medicine. "Fuck, Norah. Maybe a week ago? I don't know."

"When are you talking to him next?"

Guy shrugs, miserable with himself, and I hope he's one of those men who's got a complex about women being tougher than him, because if he is, he'll beat himself up over this for days.

"When?" I demand.

"We don't have anything set up. I finished my research on you weeks ago."

Finished his research. That meant he was ready to write the second book. I sit back, thinking about him and my dad talking, my dad researching true crime. The computer.

I take a sip of my own drink. Guy doesn't know my father's dead. Or he's doing a damn good job lying about it.

"So what exactly was my dad helping you with?"

"I asked him about you, of course."

"That's it?"

Guy nods, fidgets, looks generally uncomfortable. *Good.*

"What's the second book about?" I give him a look, hoping he takes it for a subtle threat—but there's only defiance in his eyes.

"It's a true crime, centering around Hansel. And you, obviously. The other victims. What happened. Digging up who it could have been. I interviewed the families of the other victims, too. Profiled Hansel. Interviewed law enforcement on the case." A swift shake of his head. "I'm sorry, Norah, but I'm writing it. It's giving people closure, the chance to share what happened. And nobody ever looked at the cases at the level of detail I'm taking it to. I can't back out now."

I let his words settle, carefully keeping my emotions in check. "What do you mean, level of detail?"

"I hired a profiler to help me." Excitement flashes through his eyes, and his good hand spasms around his drink as he clenches it and sits forward. "We know so much about serial killers now. So much more than a decade ago." He looks at me like this is significant, but his lips curl up, like the cat with the fucking canary, like he has a secret. "If you'll help me with the chapters on you, then I'll help you figure out what happened with Esme. I've read a *ton* on serial killers, and I've learned—"

I almost hit him.

If I help him, he'll help me.

Esme is dead. Owen had red paint splashed across his car in a clear threat. And the man across from me is a liar who could help if he wanted to, but won't unless I give him something first. My stomach turns. Guy is sneaky and slimy and being around him sets my teeth on edge. My skin all but vibrates with disgust, and I get to my feet, holding back my anger enough to grit, "Get the fuck out," through my teeth.

Guy's mouth drops, his words falling short. He blinks. Starts to say more, but I shake my head—give him a look—the look that says *I'll break your arm for real this time*—and he steps away from the table awkwardly. Wanders to the bar, pulling his wallet from his pocket, glancing back at me warily.

Guy Stevenson had lied for a story. Maybe he would kill for one, too.

THIRTY-FIVE

I'm dissatisfied, like I got just enough out of him to worry, to find him suspicious, but not enough to do anything with. I pull out my phone to send a message to Detective Cron.

Me: *Just talked to Guy Stevenson. He's in town. Coincidence?*

I'm waiting for a response when Janie, Chloe, and Owen crowd into the booth. Janie has four glasses and a bottle of something expensive looking. She pours us each one.

"Jesus, Norah." Janie takes a sip of hers. "I thought you were going to get the cops called."

Owen gives me a little bump with his elbow as he hands me my glass. "That was badass."

Chloe just looks at me, uncertain.

"He's writing another book. He talked to my dad. And it seems like he doesn't know he's dead." I glance up and around the room, making sure Guy actually left. I'd swear I can feel eyes on me, but I did nearly break someone's arm—probably other patrons *are* looking at me.

Janie furrows her brows. "Another book? On what?"

I tear my gaze away from inspecting the room and hold up my hands. "Me, apparently. Hansel. The whole—" I wave my hand. "Everything."

Owen leans forward in his seat. "I'm going to follow him."

"Owen." Janie reaches over, puts her hand to his. "Are you sure?"

"Yes." He looks dead serious. "He'll never know I'm there. I want to see if he talks to anyone. Make sure he's not waiting for Norah outside. Can I borrow your car?" Janie hands him her keys, and with that, he's gone.

I look in the direction Owen went. "I'm worried."

"He's a big boy." Janie sighs and refills her drink.

"I really don't think he knew about my dad, though."

I pull out my phone and double-check Guy's publication history—magazine articles, a couple books. *True Athletes, True Crimes.* I have an email from Cher reminding me that if I want to keep the sponsorships I need to post more on social media. I snap a photo of our fancy drinks, including in the photo where my hand ripped open over one knuckle while training this afternoon with Owen. I put it on Instagram with a filter and write something like *Train hard, play hard.* Already there are a dozen likes, and someone sends me a DM in response.

MMAddict: *So glad you're enjoying a little downtime in your hometown. It's got to be hard, losing two people close to you. I recommend having a drink. Or two.*

I pause, unsure of what to make of it. My skin crawls that this person is suggesting I have a drink when—my gaze moves to the beverage I ordered—that's exactly what I'm doing. I look up sharply, that feeling of being watched back full force. Furthermore, I haven't posted that I'm in my hometown, though I know an article about Esme—and that I found her—was in the national news. I forgot to double-check on my father's death being published before, but it's possible whoever this is is local and somehow heard about it. I shiver, glancing around, as though I'll catch someone's eyes on me.

Stop being paranoid.

"Have you seen anything in the news about my dad?" I ask Janie again.

She purses her lips. "Nope. But I haven't checked since earlier."

"I read the Kansas City news every day. I haven't seen anything," Chloe adds.

We wrap up our evening, and I text Owen.

Me: *Where are you? There's not enough space at Janie's for all four of us, but I don't want anyone to be alone tonight. Want to share a hotel room? Two beds, of course.*

Or a suite, maybe. I do like him. I wouldn't mind kissing him again. But Guy was a stark reminder of the luck I have with men. Even if Owen does seem to be different, even if he's a little like family to Janie, I have enough on my plate.

I grab my bag and my dad's computer, and Janie and Chloe walk me to the hotel a block down and escort me to a room I book on the twelfth floor. I can't help looking over my shoulder as we walk, aware there might be more than one person with an interest in keeping an eye on me: Guy, Elaine, Hansel.

"Norah, honestly, we could make it work."

I summon a smile and wink at her. "You guys haven't seen each other in a week, and I don't think Owen, nor I, want to sleep on the floor. I'm sure he'll be here soon. It's fine. Just lock your doors. I'll come by in the morning, and we'll go dress shopping. Besides, you look exhausted. Go home. Pretend everything's normal for a night."

"I am tired," Janie says. She nods, we hug, and I'm alone for the first time since my run this morning. Silence settles in the room, and without thinking, I give in to a sudden urge to do what I do at home—to check every nook and cranny, behind every door, under each sink, behind the shower curtain. To make sure I truly am alone.

THIRTY-SIX

The time alone relaxes me, though it's a little creepy. Okay, a *lot* creepy.

After I check the room and conclude I really am alone, I change into workout pants and a tank top. The room is larger than hotel rooms I stay in for fights—big enough for the two queen beds, with plenty of space left over. Sleek, stylish furniture, and willowy off-white curtains at the French doors that open to a balcony.

Stepping out through the balcony doors, I shiver as I make my way into the cool night air. I'm a dozen floors up, and far below is a pool, a smaller hot tub to one side. Both are lit up and glow blue, and a handful of people splash around in them. Heated, even in the winter.

It occurs to me someone could be down there, staring up at me—watching me. Just as I'm staring down, watching them. But I can't live every moment paranoid, so I breathe in the cold winter air and stare out at the Plaza, the sea of twinkling lights makes me feel calmer somehow. After a while, I wrap my arms around myself and step back in, glancing at the laptop from where it taunts me from one of the beds.

Murder.

I open it, press buttons until the monitor glows to life. I'm not sure where to start, but his internet history seems as good a place as any. Mostly, it's news sites of the conspiracy theory sort, and I scroll through them, disinterested in going down any rabbit holes that remind me of my teenage years. I go back weeks, randomly spot-checking days and times. He spent a lot of time on the internet, from the thousands of sites I'm scrolling through. It's the Google searches for "Hansel serial killer" and "Norah Silverton" that eventually give me pause.

So he had been looking into it, into me, too. If briefly. I check the date—only three weeks ago. I scroll more, and the history ends soon after. As though from time to time, he simply deleted his history. Which I'd expect from him. It would have never occurred to me to clear my internet history, but then, I was checking email and watching news on other fighters. I didn't think anyone was out to get me. Well, that's not entirely true—more, I *knew* who might be out to get me, and I was fairly certain Hansel—or his copycat—wasn't interested in my browser history.

So he was doing web searches. No big deal.

My phone chirps, and I pull my attention away from the computer to pick it up.

Owen: *Guy met with Elaine.*

Hmm. They could be working together on this. And I'd just spoken to them both. I try to think back, remember if I gave Elaine anything she could hand off to Guy, or vice versa—

Owen: *They argued. Then he went straight to his hotel room and hasn't left. You still at Janie's?*

I text back details for the hotel and go back to my father's computer. The websites he wandered to on Hansel are the official true crime sort—not a random Wikipedia page with the highlights; no, the sort that people obsessed with true crime like to build, sprinkling in facts with theory, things they swore they overheard, or citing a source that can't be verified.

I bite my lip, because I, too, spent some time on these websites, once upon a time. I thought maybe, just maybe, I'd find answers to the question of who Hansel was, and where he'd disappeared to, could be crowdsourced.

But the reality was these people didn't see me as a human—they saw me as a *thing*. A source of entertainment. It was sick. Twisted. It dehumanized me, and every single one of the women Hansel had successfully killed. The worst part were the theories—how *I'd* survived when no one else had. How I'd walked out of the woods with a mere gash on my arm and my dress destroyed, but otherwise intact. At least, physically.

Mentally was a whole different matter. And furthermore, it didn't matter how I'd survived. I had. Wasn't that enough?

It's only when I switch from poring over the websites he frequented—the ones that wove tales of what happened between Hansel and me, the ones speculating where he might be now—and switch to his word processor, that I find something that might actually be useful.

There are multiple files, true crime words like *murder, suspects,* and *leads* scattered among them. But the first file name says it all: HANSEL—WHO IS HE?

THIRTY-SEVEN

TEN YEARS AGO

He let me go.

He kissed me and whispered, "I'll wait for you, and someday, you'll come back, right?"

"Yes, of course." I didn't hesitate to agree with him one more time.

He pointed me down a trail not far from the cabin. "Walk that way. Stay on the path. You'll find the road."

I was sure it was a ruse. This was just a game he wanted to play with me, dragging it out instead of finishing me off quickly like he had August. I let my gaze slip to her one last time—still, unmoving.

I was almost afraid to accept his offer to leave. Terrified to step away from him. To turn my back.

My legs threatened to stop working, but I force them to move forward.

Darkness closed in around me as I stepped onto the wooded trail, like stepping back into the night. I stopped once and looked back over my shoulder. He stood there, watching. A shadow against the shadows. I raised my hand in a little wave, pretending that's why I'd turned, not to see if he was following me.

I tried not to hurry. Tried not to make it clear I was all but about to break into a run, to run for my life. I turned a bend, and when I glanced back and could no longer see him, I let myself break into an adrenaline-, fear-fueled sprint. I ran like I never had before, tears streaming down my cheeks, sobs racking my whole body.

I thought only of escape.

THIRTY-EIGHT

For a moment, I considered that my dad might have been onto something—that in all his conspiracy theories and narcissistic memoir bullshit, maybe he'd actually done some good. But as I skim through names of potential Hansels alongside explanations of why he thinks that person would make a good Hansel, all I can think is that he was grasping at straws.

The list is long and vague.

It includes kids who lived down the street from us in my childhood. It includes Rob, my coach, with the line "awfully convenient how he and Norah met, isn't it?" Janie is on there —"jealous of her twin?"—completely ignoring the fact I had no doubt in my mind it was a man who took us that night. "Janie's dad, Carl." Then he gets into the people he used to work with, with explanations like "wanted revenge for the way I left."

He hadn't left. He was fired. And nobody became a serial killer because of something like that.

I breathe out annoyance and keep scrolling. More names, including Esme, boys I went to high school with, Owen, but then "no, he was at prom that night." He lists out all of Owen's friends, but all of them have similar explanations—at prom or "stomach flu," meaning he did a fair amount of research.

My heart swells as one page turns to three turns to eight, with theories randomly interspersed with potential Hansels—I have to admit he tried. Something happened to me, his daughter, and though he hadn't so much as reached out to me to make sure I was happy or healthy or okay, he had been on the hunt for the serial killer who'd taken me.

At the end of the document there is a line, and beneath that, he's written, "Conclusions: Male. Probably in his twenties. Not local. Likely went home after he failed to kill Norah, wherever home is. Potentially someone who doesn't like me—Norah and Amy connected?"

I go still. Amy was my mother.

What's more, this implies he truly didn't know what happened to my mom—that he hadn't had contact, that she'd disappeared as much for him as she had for me. I'd hoped perhaps she'd reached out to my father to try to contact me— that I'd find an email on his computer that he'd never bothered to show me, an address or phone number she'd sent so I could get in touch with her, but this destroys that idea. This means she truly *was* gone. He was implying Hansel had something to do with her disappearance. And that maybe he blamed himself.

I push the laptop aside and lay back on the bed. The past decade reconfigures itself in my head. My father, who I was completely estranged from, had been on the hunt for Hansel. Not just because of me. But my mother, too.

For the first time I consider something I've never let myself think.

She might be dead.

No. No, that's not possible. She left a note. They had video of her pulling money at the ATM.

I roll off the bed, close the file, ignore the list of other files, snatch up the laptop, close it, shove it back in my bag. My dad's conspiracy theories were just that—and as usual, he was full of shit. Making me doubt myself and everything I knew to be true, just as he had growing up. The last thing I need is his crazy ideas casting doubts, making me wonder about something that never happened. She *left*. She wasn't killed by Hansel. Besides, she left before Hansel ever struck. She didn't fit his pattern. She wasn't a teenager or in her early twenties. She'd been a grown woman, a tired wife done with my dad's alcoholism and refusal to get help.

I crawl onto the nearest bed, press my hands to my eyes, and shove thoughts of him and the laptop away. I don't have the energy to rehash his theories. Like everything else, it was never about me. It was about *him*. And though I would have never wished him dead, he is dead, and I intend to leave him where he belongs, firmly in the past.

THIRTY-NINE

A ping on my phone startles me awake. A strange ceiling. A beige wall that is not mine.

Adrenaline spikes, my muscles tensing, but then I remember—I'm in Kansas City. In a hotel. No one's nabbed me and carried me away like Hansel did that night. My mind goes immediately to the files I just read, but I shut the thoughts down. That isn't going to help me, and I don't want to think about my father anymore.

I fell asleep.

I groan as I roll over to grab at the phone. I get myself comfortable on a stack of pillows and open my email to find the workout Rob sent me. I skim through it—a detailed warm-up and workout—and stop at the bottom when he goes from fellow coach to friend.

Everything okay? I said it before, but it sure is strange not having you here. Didn't realize how much a part of this gym you've become. We should talk about that when you get back. Long-term plans for—

I let the phone drop from my hand. The fabric of the pillow is soft on my face, and I sigh into it. I'm not ready for this conversation. Not now. Not here. Not with everything else going on.

Rob is going to ask me to buy into the business with him, to become a full partner in it. And I should say yes because it's the only type of work I'm qualified for.

Laughter carries through the French doors, which I left open. I go to stare out into the night again and wish I'd brought a bathing suit—a dip in the hot tub would feel incredible on my sore muscles, not to mention the tension in my shoulders. Then again, a sports bra isn't so different than a bikini top. Hell, it covers more. I turn and eye my bag, indecisive. I'm halfway through wrangling it on when a knock comes at the door.

"Who is it?" I call.

"It's me." Owen.

"One sec." I throw a sweatshirt over the sports bra, pull on the closest thing I have to swimsuit bottoms—my skintight lifting shorts—and open the door. Owen is still in his suit, and this time, I'm not shy about looking. I am, however, a little shy as I let him in the door and his hand brushes over my back.

"You okay?" he asks. "Sorry I took so long."

"I'm fine. I was just getting ready to go down to the hot tub." I sit on the bed I've claimed as my own. "You find anything?"

"Guy met with Elaine. They argued." Owen frowns, and our eyes meet. "Seem weird to you?"

I chew my lip. "Yes. That seems very weird." I try to think of why they would meet up, but nothing comes to me.

Owen tosses his duffel on the bed opposite and shrugs out of his suit jacket. He looks even better in the white collared shirt beneath it, buttons almost bulging around his chest. The fabric is tight over his biceps and shoulders, and he unbuttons it from the top down.

"The hot tub sounds amazing." He pulls the shirt off, runs a hand through his hair, which leaves it a bit disheveled. He blinks at his bag. "Shoot. Guess I didn't think about swim trunks. All I've got is gym clothes."

I smile, welcoming the distraction of him, shirtless. "Me, too. We can be the odd ones out."

Owen gives me a half smile and finds gym shorts. "Be right back." He heads for the bathroom, then stops short. "Oh, I brought you something." He digs again in his bag, but this time he pulls out a shiny brown and gold canister and announces proudly, "Hot cocoa. After I left Guy, I thought I'd pick up wine or"—his cheeks go pink—"you know, something nice. But I was thinking you probably don't drink much with how much you train, so I thought..." His voice trails off, and I can feel his eyes on me. Waiting for approval.

This is a *gesture,* the sort Janie might tell me to pay attention to, because this is indicative of his love language, or something like that. I tense, because he thought of me, thought of getting me *something nice,* and I'm not sure I want him doing that. Then again, we had fun today. We're spending the night in this hotel room together. We're trying to solve Esme's murder together, with any luck. And... god, even if Guy's company did repel me from ever spending time in a man's company again, this is Owen, and I like him.

"I love hot cocoa." I take the canister and peer at it. "Looks fancy."

"It's *cinnamon* hot cocoa," he specifies.

"I'll make some for us. There is a minibar if you want to spike yours."

Owen raises a brow. "From what I understand, I have another harsh workout coming tomorrow, too."

I busy myself with the tiny coffee maker in the kitchenette, heating water for cocoa, finding the paper coffee cups, and minutes later, we're walking side-by-side down several sets of stairs. There's a tension between us, the sudden knowledge we'll be spending the night together in the same hotel room. Half of me wants to jump him and get it over with, lose myself in the distraction he would bring. The other half likes him in the way that makes me want to not lose his company and sleeping with a guy often goes that direction. Sometimes, staying friends and nothing more is the better move, a lesson I've learned the hard way.

"So, do you think Guy had something to do with it?" Owen breaks the silence.

"Maybe? It seems a little crazy, but he doesn't seem quite right to me. He knew what he was doing when he interviewed me. Like he purposely created a"—I search for the word— "rapport. But more than that. We emailed for weeks before that interview. It started off very professional, but it got pretty..."

"Intimate?"

"Yeah."

"I get that. Kind of like online dating. You start to feel like you know someone you've never met."

I nod. "It's dumb. I mean, I should have known better. But I'm around these jocks all the time. I *am* a jock, so I can say that. And they're all good guys, but at the end of the day, they just want to talk about the fight they watched, or they want to go drinking, which you can do if you're not serious about it, but Guy... We talked about going for a run to explore a city on foot for fun, not because it's *cardio*. We'd read the same book, and we discussed what we liked about it. He told me the best restaurants to visit in New York, because his brother lives there, and he visits sometimes. And then we finally met when he flew in for the interview, and it was the same." I pause, realize words are spilling out of my mouth faster than I can keep up with. "With online dating—which, yes, I've tried—most of the time, you meet the person face to face and it's awful. No one's as good as they seem online."

"But," Owen prompts, and pushes the door to the pool open for me.

"But he was. He was exactly in person like he was in his emails." I scoot through, cocoa in my hands, and the humidity and stench of chlorine hits me. The pool is divided, half of it inside, half outside. Fake palm trees decorate corners, and a built-in waterfall trickles near the window with a small opening to let swimmers go outdoors. It's after ten at night, and mostly empty.

We take another door to the outdoor hot tub. It's set into the ground, surrounded by lush grass covered with a tumble of fall leaves. A wrought iron fence stands tall around the hotel property, and the whole area is lit with floodlights that cast a harsh glare and blind us to what's beyond the fence. I scan it anyway, but only see empty cars in the night. No one peers from one, watching us, and no other hotel guests are out here. We're alone.

The freezing air hits me, and I kick off my sandals and toss away my towel to hop right in the warm water, paper cup of cocoa and all. Owen laughs from a nearby table, where he lays out his towel and kicks off his shoes. He pulls his phone from his pocket and sets it down, then slides in beside me, our thighs brushing.

"So, he interviewed you and...?"

I almost switch topics—the hot water loosens every muscle in my body, and I'm considering telling Rob we need a hot tub in the women's locker room back home. "We had a few drinks. He stayed the weekend." A bitter twist comes to my lips, and Owen reaches out, touches it lightly with the tip of one finger.

"Don't be ashamed. You believed in someone who'd shown you a piece of himself. It's normal to want to offer a piece of yourself in return. It's brave, really."

I make a face, and Owen laughs at my expression, which feels somewhere between a wince and cynicism. "Too much?"

"You sound like you're in a Hallmark movie." I soften my words with a smile.

"Ouch." He laughs and settles back, his arms going over the edge of hot tub, one around my shoulders. His fingertips brush my back, and I close my eyes, trying hard to ignore the flutter in my belly.

"Anyway." I shift to put a jet directly on my back, and our legs brush again. "He did the interview. Then he shut his notebook. He put it away. We moved from the cafe to a nice restaurant, from coffee to dinner with wine, and it was different. It changed from 'What's your inspiration as an influencer to young women?' to 'Tell me your life story. Tell me who you really are.'" A tremor of anger runs down my spine. I sip my cocoa and shift away from Owen, blood hot at the memory.

"I'm sorry." Owen pulls back his arm and shuts his eyes. He sinks deeper, letting the bubbles from the jets cover his chest, his neck, until only his head bobs above the water. "We can talk about something else. You don't have to think about him."

His words are kind, caring. But the fact of the matter is, I *do* have to think about Guy. And Elaine and her fan club, too. Because right now, they're the best suspects I've got, even if it might be a stretch. It occurs to me both of them knew my father, too—at least, in some context. Guy visiting him. Sending him a book. And Elaine... well, being Elaine. And then they met tonight. That doesn't make sense. If Elaine is right, if my father *was* murdered, if it wasn't accidental or a suicide... and if she was in some way responsible, she wouldn't suggest it. She wouldn't *suggest* he was murdered. Except... she would. Because she wants the story.

Unless... *unless,* she wants it to look like Guy did it. They were fighting tonight. He's the one who got my story. The story she'd been begging and stalking me for the past decade. Maybe this was her own version of revenge.

Or... maybe it was neither of them.

I exhale a shuddering breath. "Tell me more about Guy and Elaine."

Owen adjusts to a more comfortable position. "They met down the block. Well, more like she'd been waiting for him. I couldn't hear what they said, but she looked mad."

Maybe I should call Elaine and grill her. "Weird. Maybe she helped him research Hansel. She's an expert on him. But that doesn't explain why she would have been mad." I decide to say it out loud. "Maybe because he got the story she always wanted."

Owen makes an affirmative noise, and I glance over—his eyes are shut, and his face, so tense today, has relaxed.

"Owen, have you thought about leaving town?" I ask after a beat.

"What?" His eyes snap open and he sits up, splashing water with the suddenness of his movement.

"Your car." I give him a pointed look. "It said, 'You're next.'"

Owen frowns. "Yes, but—"

"What if he gets to you? What if you really are next?"

"We don't even know it's Hansel who left that. It could have been anyone. Hell, we don't even know that's who killed Esme."

I go quiet, lost in thought. We don't *know*. But I suspect. I feel it in my bones. An echo of the terror of the past.

I think through the people I find suspicious so far. Could Hansel be Guy? Guy, Hansel? In my memory, Hansel was tall and skinny, like Guy. And Guy seems to know a lot and be incredibly interested in all of this. But then, so is Elaine. So are Elaine's fans. And anyone could have read Guy's book and gotten details. Become a copycat.

I breathe out, frustration building.

"Besides. I'm not leaving you and Janie to handle this yourselves. If I'm next, and I skip town, then what? You're next?"

Our eyes meet. His hand finds mine in the water, and I hold on for dear life. It takes me by surprise—this rush of panic and gratefulness that he won't leave Janie and me hanging.

I make a decision. I have to trust Owen. I have to tell him everything. Because if it *is* Hansel, we're in for the fight of our lives. Literally.

"I've been getting messages on Instagram." I stare into my cocoa. "Someone who knows about my father's death. It's not a secret, but it hasn't been published anywhere, either."

Owen shifts closer and pulls the cup from my hands. He sets it on the pool deck then takes my hands in his. "Have you told Detective Cron?"

"No. I mean, it's only happened a few times. But it's weird. And I get *a lot* of weird messages from fans."

"Can I see?" His voice is soft, thick with concern. I look up into his dark eyes and melt for just a moment.

"Sure." I step from the hot tub, snatch my phone off the nearby table, and get right back in, already shivering from the cold. I navigate to Instagram. And in that exact moment, as Owen watches, a new message comes through. I tense and click on it.

> MMAddict: *Finding comfort in friends is all well and good. But I wouldn't recommend giving mixed signals to the men in your life.*

"Fuck." The word escapes me, like a final breath.

Owen frowns. "What—" His voice stops short.

I scan our surroundings. The fence around the hotel. The empty cars. The door that leads back inside. The rows of windows and balconies above us. Not a single soul in sight, and yet... my gaze flicks back to the message.

"Norah," Owen says. "Someone's watching you."

FORTY

The hotel room no longer feels spacious and tasteful. It feels like a place to hide. I close the sheer curtains and pull the thicker blackout curtains, too. I lock the door and add the bolt. I'm a lion, and this room is my cage, and I pace one way, then the other, and when I turn again, I nearly smack into Owen's chest.

"Hey, come here." He enfolds me in his arms. I inhale, exhale, catch the scent of chlorine and *him*, and I bury my face in the fabric of his shirt, hot tears streaming down my cheeks. We came up from the pool. We climbed the stairs. We dressed. And I held back tears through each activity, forcing myself to keep it together.

"It's okay. Whoever it is can't see you here. It's just us."

"How, though?" I pull away, look at him, then step out of his embrace. "How could whoever this is know where I am? What I'm doing?"

Although, it wouldn't be that hard, come to think of it. I've felt like eyes were on me since I arrived in town. Janie's glassed-in restaurant. The dojang with windows lining the front. Then again, I always feel that way. I'm always looking over my shoulder.

"Well..." Owen's forehead wrinkles in thought. He sits on the edge of a bed. "It could be someone you know. Someone who knows you're back here. Or someone you work with at home? Or Rob?" He looks at me, eyebrows raised. "Is he—jealous? Were you ever a thing?"

"Rob?" I blink, perch on my bed. "No, we never dated. Besides—"

I'm about to say Rob is in Los Angeles. He doesn't know I'm spending time with Owen. But he kind of does. How many times did he ask about my new sparring partner? Once? Twice? Rob usually *is* my sparring partner. And he keeps telling me he misses me.

"We're not like that," I say, but didn't Rob just invite me to buy in to the business with him? That the gym isn't the same without me there? My head buzzes with the possibility. "I don't think he'd do that. Why would he pretend to be someone else? No." I shake my head, clearing it. "He's not like that. We're friends—*more* than friends. He's my coach. He's like family." But I can't help but analyze when we met—how we met—how easily I fit into his life and he into mine.

Owen watches me, nods slowly, no judgment in his gaze. "Okay, well if not Rob, then... who?"

"It could be a fan," I say. "I have—" I blanch. "*Superfans*, as Rob calls them. People who are obsessed. Mostly MMA people, but a few true crime weirdos, too. Elaine's type of people, who know about my past. If there's a superfan here in Kansas City, if they happened to see me or overheard a conversation. That could be it." My mind wanders back to my father's list—the long, haphazard, seemingly random list of suspects that included nearly everyone I'd known when I lived here. For a moment, the world shrinks in on me—do I really need to worry about every single one of those people? A rush of panic, anxiety clawing through my chest.

But then Owen catches my eye. He eases from his bed to mine but doesn't touch me. "Norah, I think we need to consider the possibility that it's him."

Him.

"Hansel."

Owen nods. "And he's trying to communicate with you." My heart jumps into my throat. My hands go numb, and I have to take slow, deep breaths to keep from hyperventilating.

"Let's look at the messages again." I scroll up and read the first out slowly. "This one just says, 'Hello, Norah Silverton.' But then... 'Heard about your father. I'd love to send flowers. Is there an address or funeral home?'" I pause, chew my lip. "I read that one this morning. And then earlier this evening: 'So glad you're enjoying a little downtime in your hometown. It's got to be hard, losing two people close to you.'"

Owen leans close, his shoulder pressed against mine, and he reads the last one out loud. "'Finding comfort in friends is all well and good. But I wouldn't recommend giving mixed signals to the men in your life.'" He scratches his chin, runs a hand over his mouth, shakes his head. He presses a finger to the screen and scrolls up to read them one more time. "It has to be someone here. Or someone who can tell where you are."

"How'd they know about my father, though?" But Elaine knew, allegedly through one of her many connections. And if she and Guy are talking, then despite what he said at Janie's, he would know, too...

Owen's gaze goes to me, then back to the phone. "Someone close to the case? Someone who knows Elaine? Who overheard you talking to Janie at the restaurant? It could be anyone." He examines the phone. "Or... I don't know how to check for spyware. Or how easy it is to tap into someone's phone. But I know it was something we took precautions for overseas."

The phone feels heavy in my hand at his words. I'm not sure which is worse—the idea someone may be tracking me, or able to read my texts, listen to my calls—or the idea someone's actually following me.

"I have to tell Detective Cron."

"I agree." He glances at the clock on the nightstand. "Maybe tomorrow, though? It's after eleven."

He's right. I nod. Hesitate, then pull the battery out of my phone and put the pieces in my bag with a shudder. When I come back to the bed, Owen lays back and takes my hand, leading me to lie down beside him in the crook of his arm. The room is dark, a single bedside lamp casting yellow light through the room, the thick walls and blackout curtains blocking noise, and I lie there in silence against Owen's warmth.

I'm glad he's here.

I'm glad I'm not by myself.

I'm glad he's strong enough to protect himself, and I'm not so worried about him like I am Janie. She's one of the toughest women I know, but she's August's sister. Somehow, that makes her seem more vulnerable. Not to mention, she's never learned to throw a decent punch. God, what if they're watching Janie, too?

Owen curls his arm, drawing me near, and presses a kiss to my temple. "Get some rest. We'll deal with this in the morning."

I close my eyes and snuggle against him, wrapping my arm over his chest beneath his shirt. His muscles tense at my cool touch, but then he relaxes, and I realize just how exhausted I am. The day, the night, the worry fades away.

I sleep like I haven't slept in a very long time.

FORTY-ONE

I wake to heat, to soft breathing, to darkness.

Last night comes back to me in bits and pieces. The memorial. Elaine. Guy. Owen. The hot tub. The message on Instagram. *Three* messages.

Owen's arm is heavy over my torso, his chest to my back, one leg over my ankle. Cocooned, and half of me wants to stay here, to fall back asleep surrounded by his scent, his breath on my neck, his hair tickling my cheek. The other half of me needs to move, needs to be free of anyone's grasp. The claustrophobia wins.

I disentangle myself and shiver as I climb out from beneath his limbs, the comforter, from the hot bed to the cool plush carpet and early morning air. The curtains are still closed tight, and I push them aside to peer out at the city. Still dark. Still a sprinkling of traffic lights and streetlamps and one lone runner out there with a headlamp.

My phone is in my bag, and I shove the battery back in, then sweep into the bathroom, shutting the door so as to not disturb Owen. It comes to life slowly, and I brush my hair and tie it in a ponytail as I wait.

I shoot a text off to Janie as I perch on the side of the tub, scrubbing at my face, wishing for a cup of coffee.

"Norah?"

I jolt, nearly drop the phone.

"You okay?" Owen's voice carries through the door. "I don't mean to pry, just wanted to make sure you're in there. I woke up and you were gone."

Of course, he's checking on me. A killer is on my trail.

"I'm okay." I open the door, and he's turned on a light. The coffee machine perks in the corner. He's watching me with mussed hair and dark eyes, and he looks cautious. Like maybe I'll run after a night wrapped in his arms. "I was texting Janie. I didn't want to wake you."

"Oh. Did you get"—he pauses, and his eyes flick to my phone—"any more messages?"

I breathe out. Open the app. Owen steps closer, but the coffee beeps, and he moves off to pour cups for us, and somewhere in there, we meet on the edge of the bed. I have three new Instagram messages. But none of them are from MMAddict.

"Good." Owen sips from his cup, makes a face. "God, this is awful."

"There's a coffee shop downstairs." I eye the clock. "It might be open. Or we could go for a run and stop at Janie's on the way back."

"Do you—" He hesitates. "Is that safe?"

"I don't think any of us are *safe*," I say. "But what else are we going to do? Sit here and wait for the cops to figure it out?"

He's quiet a moment, then nods. "Okay. If you want to run, I'll go with you."

We dress for the cold, and twenty minutes later, we're racing through the Plaza, the world moments away from morning dusk, the two of us mere shadows. Today's run is short and fast. Three miles at a 7:30-minute mile, and already Owen is struggling to keep up. I temper my pace—something I usually wouldn't do, because this is my work, but we need to stay together. He catches up, breath fogging before him.

"How much more?" he asks.

"We're halfway there."

We turn down an alley, and a shadow catches my eye. I pull him to a stop, stretch, and a moment later, a car eases down the road. A car we've seen twice already.

"What is it?" he asks.

"Hold on." I grab my phone, dial Detective Cron despite the hour, wait while it rings.

"Cron," a tired voice says.

"Stop having me followed," I growl.

A beat passes.

"Huh?" she says. "Who— Is this Norah?"

Real surprise in her voice.

And then, "We don't have anyone following you right now, Silverton. Stop being so damn paranoid, and don't call me this early again." She hangs up.

Owen's eyes widen, and he glances back the way we came, where I saw the shadow, the car. I look down at my phone, almost embarrassed, but after last night—likely someone is following me. It's just not a cop.

I nod Owen forward, and we keep running, albeit more carefully.

Through the dim, growing light, a vast expanse of lawn opens up, giant white statues of shuttlecocks and a silver tree, a sculpture, signaling we've found the largest museum in Kansas City, the Nelson-Atkins Museum. I take us up the path that meanders through a sculpture garden, then to huge stone steps, and behind me Owen laughs.

"It's like Rocky," he calls as I reach the top. "And later, you'll beat me on the mats, too."

I stop at the top and take a long look around. From up here, the entrance to this giant stone museum that was once the location of the home of William Rockhill Nelson, its benefactor, I can see fairly well. A hint of sunrise plays over the green lawn, frozen dew creating a sparkle. It also means I can see the figure at the edge of that lawn, and the flicker of what looks like a camera flash, and now that I think of it, I can hear it—the *click* a digital camera makes, mimicking the sound a film camera once made.

I smile. Motion at Owen to join me. Let him engulf me in his arms in a hug that is both hot at our cores, and chilled over our arms and fingertips and noses.

"Someone's watching us," I say, and he doesn't miss a beat. He holds me tighter, sways with me gently, as though we're lovers goofing around, and turns me so he's blocking my face.

"Who?"

"Don't know. They're mostly behind a tree, but they have a camera."

"Elaine?"

"It looked like a guy."

I bite my lip, heart racing at the possibilities: Guy? A superfan? Hansel? I don't feel fear, though. Only adrenaline-fueled readiness, that feeling of potential action that consumes me right before a fight. "Pretend we're hugging goodbye. You go to your right and come around on the trail." It's wooded. Unless our watcher pays specific attention solely to Owen, there's no way he'll be able to keep an eye on him. "I'll go the other way. Whoever he doesn't follow—"

"Got it." Owen says a little louder. "See you soon," and like that, his warmth is gone.

I pretend to take another lingering look at the view, then lope off in the opposite direction, tucking myself behind a stone wall that borders the museum's property. Our watcher was another couple hundred feet forward, on the other side of the fence. Owen is skirting around the opposite side, so will theoretically be coming up behind him.

My phone buzzes. A new Instagram message.

I freeze. My heart pounds.

Is this him? Is this it?

I open the message.

MMAddict: *The hunted? Or the hunter. We shall see.*

FORTY-TWO

TEN YEARS AGO

Sometimes, I'm not sure if I remember that night quite right.

It blurs. The edges go fuzzy.

A common side effect of PTSD, more than one therapist informed me. It didn't help I had to tell the story no fewer than a dozen times. That every time I repeated the story, someone tried to poke holes in it.

Detective Cron had once said, "And then he just let you go?" with such a look of disbelief, I found myself racking my brain, trying to recall what I had missed. She was right—a serial killer just letting a victim go? That didn't happen. It *never* had happened, in fact. Hansel had killed five women already, it didn't make sense he would just let me go.

"Maybe he was someone else," I suggested.

"You said he was Hansel," she said.

"He told me that. Maybe he was lying. Maybe he's a copy-cat, maybe—"

"How did you get him to let you go?" she interrupted.

I went quiet, remembering the revolting tingle of his touch over my skin.

"Norah, you need to tell me the truth."

"I am telling the truth!"

Around me, the square room seemed to close in. White walls. A mirror. A mirror where I looked up and caught only my expression, but someone was watching me from back there, *someone* had their eyes on me, and I knew it wasn't *him*, it wasn't Hansel, but what if it was? Or what if I stepped out of this building to go home to my father, who'd shake his head and tell me *life goes on*, but Hansel would lie in wait, ready to snatch me up and take me away?

Forever, he'd said.

Suddenly, I couldn't breathe. My lungs stopped accepting air, my throat closed up, my chest stopped working.

I would never be safe. Not with a serial killer thinking I was coming back for him.

FORTY-THREE

I can discern his outline, silhouetted against a tree, hunched over his glowing phone. I press my form against the cold concrete wall and size him up. He's tall, but thin. Wiry. And as he lifts his head and glances around, furtively, I wonder if this can really be the person who sent the texts. Then again, I've fought fighters with similar builds. They weren't strong, but they were fast, with a good reach, and could land a hit before you realized they moved. And not everyone plays fair. He could have a weapon. Hansel had a weapon when he took August and me. His face is long, narrow, with dark hair. I don't recognize him.

He types at his phone and mine buzzes.

I step back behind the wall and look down, ready for another taunting Instagram alert, but this time, it's from Owen.

Owen: *I've got a clear view. What's the plan?*

Me: *No plan. I want to see what he does.*

The phone goes back in my pocket. I take a deep breath,

check my surroundings, make sure we're alone. And I go back the way I came. I stop and stretch, peer at the pink sky once more, then take off at a brisk pace through the grass.

In moments, I'll be within feet of him.

I keep my eyes forward. Pretend I'm unaware of him.

My heart seizes with electricity, and it crackles down my limbs. Adrenaline thrums through me. Now that I'm so close... I'm scared. I am, and I'm not afraid to admit it. But I'm also ready for this. And if I'm not, well... Owen is here. Owen, who's a part of this, too.

The trees of the trail block the pink light here, but I hear a crunch to my right. Fast steps.

And then a rough hand on my arm. It grabs tight, yanks me back. I swivel on one foot and go with the motion. It's him. *It's him.* I barrel into him, and we both go down. He's easily six-foot-five, even taller than I thought, and his eyes are wide and luminous with excitement.

"I got you," he whispers, and he rolls, putting me beneath him. But it's not that easy, even if he is twice my size. I grab his shirt, crossing my arms, and pull him close, which shoves my forearms against his airway. It effectively cuts off his oxygen supply, and as he struggles to recover, I snap my hips up, throwing him off and over one shoulder.

"Don't fucking move." Owen, barking an order. He's beside me then, a gun I hadn't known he had in a two-handed grip, and he's no longer the sweet-natured guy who brought me cocoa. He's the Marine who's faced death more times than anyone else I know.

"Owen," I start. But then I stop. Because I was going to say, *Not yet. I'm not finished with him.*

The man starts to get up, but Owen makes a sound in his throat like I've heard people do with dogs. A clear *No.* The man lays back, hands raised, eyes still wide, but the excitement replaced with fear. Something stirs deep in my gut—satisfaction? I only wish I'd caused that reaction on my own.

"What's your name?" I ask. I peer through the dim light, taking in a narrow face, thick eyebrows, but little more. The sun is slowly rising, but we're in the shadows, sheltered by trees. The man just stares, a grin spreading over his face. My insides clench. Now that I've got a better look at him, I can see he's not old enough to be Hansel.

"He's got a camera on," Owen says.

"What?"

"GoPro. Strapped to his chest." He points with his chin, eyes and hands never wavering from the man on the ground.

"I'm going to post this online," he says with a little laugh. He glances at me, but his attention is all on the gun. "I mean, you're Norah Silverton."

A hundred things go through my head: *He's a crazy fan. God, he looks young. He attacked* me, *a woman trained to fight— of course he's crazy. Yes, he seems psychotic enough to follow me, to listen in on conversations, to send me strange messages.*

And lastly, *Thank god, Owen stopped me—this is being filmed.*

"Call the police." Owen's voice breaks through my thoughts. I consider taking the camera. Beating the shit out of him. My hands are still clenched, my body still ready for a fight. How does Owen hold it in so well? How does he stay so still, so ready, yet not *do* anything with that energy? I'm almost jealous.

I count to ten in my head, then say, "Okay." I feel for my phone. Dial Detective Cron.

A voice thick with frustration. "Norah, I know I gave you my number, but this is getting ridiculous. I have certain hours—"

"I think you'll be glad I called."

Silence. And then an exasperated, "What is it?"

"I was attacked."

"What? When? Where are you? Are you okay?"

"I'm fine." I give her the details. Within seconds, sirens wail in the distance.

"I'll be there as soon as I can be," she says, and we disconnect.

Owen glances my way for the briefest moment. He winks. And it feels like we've won.

Like maybe, just maybe, things will get easier now.

FORTY-FOUR

Janie serves us victory cocktails.

Okay, so they're actually fancy coffee drinks, and I refuse the Baileys she holds up, eyebrows raised, but the idea is there.

"You did it." She reaches over the bar and grabs me for an awkward half hug. Chloe sits down beside me and offers a more subdued, "I'm glad you're okay." Owen, on my other side, just grins, but is more than willing to take the offered Baileys in his coffee.

"You should have seen her," Owen says. "Actually—maybe you can. Think Cron will give us the camera footage?"

"Camera footage?" Chloe asks, cupping a mug of hot tea between her hands.

"He was filming the whole thing," I say.

"A GoPro," Owen clarifies.

"He wouldn't admit to anything. Maybe because the camera was on." I set my mug down, but it lands hard, sloshing over the side. "Shit. Sorry." I reach for a napkin, which is when I realize my hand is trembling. The adrenaline of catching him followed by the pure shock it was so easy, so fast, has left me hollow, unbelieving.

Owen's hand smooths up and down my back, comforting, like he understands, and likely, he does. Is that what it's like to be in a war? To prepare, and then you win, or you lose, but there's the aftermath regardless? I exhale, realizing this also means I can stop going through my dad's laptop—stop rehashing theories of his not-quite-right mind, reading his thoughts as he came up with his own excuses as to why my mother would leave him.

"Breakfast is on me." Janie passes out menus, and once I've ordered, I slip away for a moment to myself. Outside, the air has warmed a few degrees, and in the sunshine, it's almost comfortable without a coat. Red and orange leaves flutter in the breeze, and I close my eyes, breathe it all in. Relax, for just a moment. And then I call Rob, awash in guilt I'd even considered thinking of him as a suspect for the briefest moment the night before. He's Rob. He's dedicated the better part of a decade to teaching me to be a coach and a fighter. Of course, he's going to offer me a partnership. Of course, he's going to check in on me. It's in his job description, both as my coach and as my friend.

"Hey," a warm, sleepy voice murmurs.

"Shit. I forgot about the time change." I pull the phone away to see the clock, 8:47 a.m. Which means it's not even seven there, on a Sunday morning, no less.

"It's okay." He clears his throat. Blankets rustle. "How's it going?"

"We think we caught him. Maybe. Hopefully."

"Caught... caught *him*?"

"I was out running with Owen, the guy who worked out with me yesterday. And we saw him following us." I relay the rest of the story, and this time, include the details I'd left out— my father's questionable death, the Instagram messages, the paint on Owen's car. "I'm sorry," I say. "I should have told you." And though that's not the whole of it—because I'm sure as hell not telling him I'd considered he might be the one sending me messages—I feel lighter for having come clean with him.

"Shit, Norah. Just tell me next time." A harsh laugh. "Wait. I take that back. No next time, got it? Bury your dad. Get your ass back here. The fights are in seven weeks. Oh, and there are some guys coming over from one of the Las Vegas gyms next week."

"Okay." I lean against the cafe wall, and my eyes stray to the bookstore window.

The book is there. My face one of a dozen on the cover. I catch myself staring into my own eyes, wondering if I can move on from this now. If I can go home. I let hope fill me up.

The cafe door jingles, and Owen peeks out, sharing a smile with me. A rush of heat as I notice a dimple, take in how his arms fill out the sleeves of his long-sleeved shirt, a deep autumn red color that somehow makes his eyes darker, deeper. If this is really over, maybe I have time for that half-night stand, after all.

"Your food's ready," he murmurs. "Everything okay?"

"Just talking to Rob. I'll be in in a second. Thanks." Owen hesitates, words on the tip of his tongue, but he shuts his mouth, nods, and goes back inside.

"I have to go," I say. "I'll probably stay a day extra to take care of everything. I'll look for a flight on Tuesday night, or Wednesday at the latest."

We sign off. I go inside. I eat breakfast with my friends, and I finally feel like I'm home.

* * *

Late that afternoon, Detective Cron calls with news.

"He's been following you since you got here. He fessed up to that much. Demanded a lawyer. But we're working on it. It looks good. We've found communication between him and Esme on a dating site from several months ago."

I'm in my hotel room, alone since Owen went home, and I listen carefully, tallying his offenses in my head. Wishing I'd had more time with him before Owen stopped me, regardless of the video. I inhale. Exhale. Thank her.

I've already worked out twice since this morning—the run with Owen, followed by a couple hours of flirtatious sparring, minus the make-out session afterward. No, we kept it together because tonight, we have a date. A real date. But that's not for another two hours, and I can practically feel the anger radiating from my skin, so I lace up my shoes for another run, this one solo.

Without Owen to temper my pace, I sprint, letting that energy spill from my pores as I race down the hill to Brush Creek and hop on the trail that runs alongside the concrete-rimmed body of water. It's Sunday, and bright with sunshine, so there's a small crowd of Kansas Citians wandering, laughing, lining up for the dragon boats along the shore. I skip by them and up the hill opposite, racing past apartments and the Plaza library and homes that might as well be castles, until I reach Loose Park, where my mother used to bring me as a child. My mother, who I've decided is still alive out there somewhere. A flicker of anger makes my jaw go stiff. My dad's *theories*.

Even in death, he cast a shadow over my life.

I halt and watch a mother show her toddler how to feed pieces of stale bread to the ducks near the pond. When I begin again, it's at a slower jog, and soon, the world around me settles into dusk. My watch tells me I've run eight miles, and I need to head back to the hotel to shower and find something suitable for my date with Owen.

Your *date!* Janie would exclaim, except I didn't tell her. There would be too much pressure. But tomorrow, if all goes well, when we wander the bridal boutiques, I will. I circle one last neighborhood and head back toward Loose Park, where the families have gone home because it's a school night, and only an occasional lone jogger such as myself roams the trails.

I'm halfway down the hill back to the Plaza when I hear the footsteps. I stop, and so do they. I don't turn. Rather, I bend, pretend to tie my shoe, and drop my phone in a place that requires I turn just enough to catch a glimpse behind me.

Empty sidewalk.

Dusk has arrived, and there are no dark shapes. No movement. Likely, I heard the echo of my own footsteps.

Yet the hair on the back of my neck tingles. My breath comes a little faster. My hands curl into fists. When I start running again, I listen, and I don't hear the echo. Which makes me think someone might have been there.

FORTY-FIVE

TEN YEARS AGO

I escaped, but that didn't mean I was free.

I found the road, a barren section, my car nowhere in sight. The sun was up, but the world seemed black and white—dead, burned grass on the side of the road, gray asphalt, a gray, cloudy sky. Like the sun would never truly rise again, like my world would never again be in color.

When a car crested the hill, headed my way, I almost dove for the trees—but I needed help. Needed it badly. I waved, and the car slowed, a guy my age, eyes bugging out of his face from the look of me—ruined prom dress, mud streaked, dripping blood, shivering.

"Are you okay?"

"Call the police, please. It's not safe. I was attacked. My friend—" But he had already yanked his phone out and dialed. He talked into the phone, and I watched the woods, trembling at the inner vision of that dark form coming out of them and after me.

I wasn't safe, not yet.

Maybe I'd never be.

"They're coming. You wanna get in? It's cold."

Yesterday, I'd have said yes.

But today, I shook my head. Took steps to put space between us, realizing I was close enough he could grab me. No way in hell was I getting in a stranger's car.

Ten minutes later, two cruisers emerged from the same hill he'd come from. Their lights were off, as were their sirens—no one in enough of a hurry, realizing a serial killer might come for me. No one realizing maybe there was some chance August still breathed, though I knew it was nothing more than a fantasy.

She was undoubtedly dead. If she hadn't been when I left, he'd have finished her off by now.

The first cop took one look at my torn dress and called, "Female officer." When I told him the briefest version of what happened, he called, "Female detective, too. Call homicide." He offered me a wool blanket while we waited. I shook, hoping he was better with a gun than Hansel was, in case he came for me.

I kept waiting to feel relief—help was here—but it never came. I didn't trust he wasn't watching from the woods. Wasn't circling us at this very moment, ready to snatch me away back into the forest to kill me.

More vehicles arrived: an unmarked car, an ambulance.

Someone knelt before me. "I'm Detective Cron. What's your name?"

I started. Time had passed. I took her in, whispering, "Norah. Norah Silverton."

"Norah, are you hurt?"

"No." It was a lie, but I didn't want the medics, all men, to get near me. I didn't even want her near me. "My friend—" I didn't want to think about it, relive it, but I had to tell her. His eyes seared through my brain every time I blinked. I could smell him on me, sweat and men's deodorant. God, I could feel him, still touching me. I didn't realize I was brushing off his memory until the detective reached out, placed a gentle hand on my shoulder.

"Tell me what happened to your friend. Is she in danger?"

I explained the best I could—in the woods. The trail. The cabin. A man. How he pulled us from the car.

"A gun," I added quickly. "Be careful, he has a gun." And then I remembered the news the last few months. "I think it was the serial killer on TV."

Her eyes widened. "Hansel?"

I nodded.

Another car pulled up right then. Another woman appeared, a handheld camera at the ready. Her face flickered like the trees, crimson, blue, white, but I didn't know then who she was.

"Goddammit," Detective Cron muttered.

An understatement. She already had footage of me, huddled in a wool blanket, looking pathetic and helpless. The way I'd look for years to come when Hansel's name came up— the lone survivor of the notorious serial killer.

I knew I'd see him in my nightmares.

And for years after that, I saw Elaine in them, too. If it wasn't Hansel coming after me with his knife, it was her, and her camera, ready to immortalize me in the worst way. Demanding to know just how I'd escaped the unescapable.

An hour later, at the hospital, when Detective Cron showed back up and asked, "Listen, is there any way you gave this man the impression you wanted to go with him? Had you met him before? Are you sure August hadn't planned this meetup?" I knew she'd join them as one more character in the nightmare that became my life.

FORTY-SIX

I'd showered and dressed, and Owen was supposed to knock on my door any moment when Elaine calls. Had I known it was her, I wouldn't have picked up, but I've been playing phone tag with Detective Cron's partner for half the day, so I answer.

"Norah, I want to talk to you about what happened this morning."

I pause, shoving my hand into a Ziploc bag in which I've dumped all the bathroom supplies I might need—everything from deodorant to tampons—but I finally find a tube of mascara and withdraw it.

"No." I put her on speakerphone, which is dumb, because I should just hang up. But with the threat of Hansel's copycat gone, I'm feeling generous.

"Listen, Norah, the true crime community *knows* someone was caught in connection to Esme's murder. Detective Cron won't tell me a thing. My sources haven't been able to—" She comes up short, clears her throat.

"Not my problem."

"Listen, the story *will* be told. Wouldn't you rather it be the real story? *Your* story? I'll let go about what happened in the past. Just tell me about—"

"Stop. Just stop. My life is not entertainment. Being kidnapped and nearly killed is not—" I heave a breath, squeeze my eyes shut, shake my head. No. I will not let her ruin this day. I will not get mad all over again about this. It's hung over my head for a decade. I change tack. "Are you currently in search of a boyfriend?" I swipe mascara at my eyelashes, makeup never my forte, and when I've decided it's decent, screw it back into its plastic sleeve.

"Excuse me?"

"A boyfriend. Because I know someone who you'd get along with *fabulously*. You've met him, actually."

A growl over the line. "I don't need your sloppy seconds, Norah." Another noise follows—something feral.

I was about to hang up on her, but her words give me pause. Not just her words, but the tone, which has gone from professional to angry.

"Who are you talking about?" I ask.

A huff over the line. "How do you think Guy found out about you in the first place?" she asks. And she hangs up on me.

I'm left staring at my phone—Elaine *had* told Guy about me. But the anger didn't make sense. Unless... she'd said *sloppy seconds* referring to Guy. She was *jealous*. Jealous of Guy and me. Hah! If only she knew the truth. She *wanted* him. Or hell, maybe he'd seduced her for information the same way he'd seduced me.

A knock at the door interrupts my thoughts. A muted "It's me."

I take one last look in the mirror, push away thoughts of Guy, because I have better things to do than worry about him, and I should feel nervous, right? A pitter-patter of my heart? A clenching of my insides? I can't remember the last time I went on a real date. But it's Owen. And we've already been through bad shit together. Tonight will simply be fun, and I'm not worried what he thinks, because I know he likes me, and besides, I'll be home soon.

This is just one night, the sort of night I can think back on fondly, but never have to worry about or regret.

FORTY-SEVEN

I'm not nervous, but Owen is.

We talk down the hall to the elevator, which I don't hesitate to get into, because Owen is not a stranger, and it's like he doesn't know what to do with his hands. He touches my shoulder, gives me a sideways smile, avoids my eyes when we step in and press the button for the lobby, and then the air is thick with energy, like the moment before a fight.

Or, before a first kiss.

Mom would have liked him. The thought occurs to me before I can stop it. Mom actually *had* liked him—she'd taught his junior year English class, and suggested I go to junior prom with him, not realizing he and August were together. I take a breath, and as I exhale, let thoughts of her float away.

"Don't be nervous. It's just me." I reach for his hand and peck him on the cheek. He's in the same brown leather jacket he wore the day I met him—or, met him again. Hair styled back in a way that seems so old-fashioned it's fashionable. And his dimple shows as he smiles, meets my gaze, looks away.

"Sorry. It's different. Before, we all *had* to be together for safety. Tonight..." His shoulders lift in a long, slow shrug. "Tonight, you're *choosing* to be with me."

Now my heart does pitter-patter, but I'm not sure if it's because something in me yearns for someone to feel this way for me—or because I'm afraid for *him* to feel this way. I've always thought if a serious relationship were to happen, it would be with someone who understands the lifestyle. Another fighter, another coach.

"Just relax. Have fun."

Owen nods. The elevator chimes and the door opens. In moments, we're in the yellow lamplight of the Plaza, headed hand in hand past Janie's Cafe, to another restaurant several blocks away. I stop us in front of the bookstore, my face still on display.

"I was looking forward to going to this bookstore, too," I murmur.

"We could still go." Owen beckons at the door. "Want to? We'll avoid... whatever section your book's in."

I shake my head. "Maybe later. Maybe after a drink."

We walk through the Plaza, like any other couple out on a Sunday evening, and my phone buzzes repeatedly. When I check it, it's Janie.

Janie: *I saw you and Owen walk by! Are you on a date?!*

I stifle a laugh but can't help the groan that escapes my lips.

"Rob?" Owen asks.

I look up to see Owen peering down, respectfully at me instead of my phone.

"Huh? Oh, no, it's Janie."

His gaze softens. "Everything okay?"

I hesitate, because what I saw flash in his eyes and disappear was none other than jealousy. Another swirl of emotion through me, and I'm not sure what it means, so I shove it aside and read the text out loud.

"Caught, red-handed," he says with a grin. "Tell her we'll come by after for drinks. If you're okay with that, that is."

I am, because I've been feeling guilty I'm out with Owen instead of Janie, and this way it doesn't look like we're actually in hiding.

The Plaza is known for a series of statuesque fountains, and the restaurant takes a corner slot facing them. The water is shut off this late in the season, but their lights are on, and I gaze at them as we wait for our table. Then we're seated, and Owen orders a bottle of wine after consulting me. It's clear he put effort into tonight. A quiet table in a corner near the fireplace. Candlelight in a dimmed dining room. A bottle of wine that costs three times what I buy myself.

"This is really nice," I say.

"I hope you like it." He meets my gaze across the table, and quiet swallows us as the moment stretches out between us.

He leans forward. Our hands meet between us, and they're warm, and I wonder, for the briefest nanosecond, if this could work. When was the last time I *wanted* something to work?

"I know you probably hear this from fans all the time," he touches my face tentatively, "but you're truly beautiful."

I tilt my head at him and deflect. "I have more scars than you do."

"Tell me about them. I want to know. This one?" A finger traces over my bottom lip where a slender line runs a quarter inch down my chin.

"Busted lip. Street fighting. Before Rob found me."

"And this one?"

His finger caresses down my neck to my collarbone. I fight a shiver.

"Broken collarbone. Surgery. They put a screw in."

"Ouch." He's about to touch the scar on my forearm, the

one Hansel left, the only one I'd rather not talk about, but the server comes up just in time in a long black apron and begins to pour wine. The moment breaks. I'm hot, practically trembling from a mere fingertip. My armpits are damp, and I wish I'd worn the men's deodorant I put on before I work out, because it's stronger than women's, but undeniably leaves me smelling like a man.

Owen's cheeks are pink, and our eyes meet, and we both laugh, dispelling the heat, the tension of the moment.

I bite my lip and wonder if it's too soon to invite him back to my hotel room. He *had* spent the night there last night, even if we slept in our clothes.

An appetizer arrives, and we talk about our lives in the past decade. For me, what living in Los Angeles is like (more urban than I prefer, but convenient), how I feel about spending most of my time around men (they're smelly, but so am I after a day of training), and what I think about posting photos for sponsors all the time (shit, do you mind if I take one now?). For him, the Marines (his father was one), the places he's traveled (everywhere), the time he nearly died (okay, the two times), why he decided to get out and come home (he wants to settle down), and his general business plan for the hunting business. It's then he pauses. Looks indecisive between bites of a steak and lifts his napkin to pat at his mouth.

"What's wrong?" I ask.

"Nothing, I just—" A glance at me. A glance anywhere *but* me. "This is a fun night out. Two old friends. Two new friends, sort of. But... I could do this hunting business almost anywhere. Just so you know. If we ever... Not saying we would, but if we did. You know, in the future." A forced smile.

The implication behind his words hits home. *If we ever*. If we ever get together. Make this into something beyond a casual date. Butterflies. Or maybe a snake, coiled in my stomach, writhing.

Owen's face has gone white, and his fork is limp in his hands, like he's regretting his words already, but I find his foot beneath the table with my own, and he looks up.

"I'm glad you told me that."

Another stare-off. The glimmer of an embarrassed grin. And we change the topic, both maxed out on admitting that maybe, someday, something. It leaves me warm, happy.

After dinner we stroll arm in arm back toward Janie's. We're each half a bottle of wine in, and I'm relaxed, knowing my stalker is in jail. I'm warm, pressed up against Owen, and pleasantly fuzzy from the alcohol. It's a feeling I'm most familiar with after we've won a fight, when Rob and Cher and fighters from my gym and I all go out for a nice meal and drinks and to let loose.

We round a corner, nearly at Janie's, when I spot Elaine—her head down, stabbing fingers over her phone screen, then looking up, watching—waiting, I think, for me. After our phone call, and what I'm pretty sure was jealousy from my weekend with Guy, I'm anything but interested in talking to her. I check our surroundings, making sure we're not about to be ambushed by any of her fan club.

I sigh, nod at Owen, and we duck down the nearest alley. It allows us to skirt around the building, avoiding her, and when we arrive at Janie's, she's let the same bartender take over and has commandeered the giant booth we shared just yesterday morning. God, has it been such a short time? She beckons us in and hugs me and winks at Owen, and Chloe has her best friend there, and soon, we're all laughing so hard I can't even remember why, like we're high on friendship, high on life in the shadow of so much death.

Owen goes to the bar and gets another round for everyone, setting a tray on the table and handing them out one by one. When he comes back his arm goes around me, and an hour later we're back in my hotel room.

Owen stopped being shy sometime during dinner, and his hand brushes over my abdomen as we pass one another, me toward my closet to pull out shorts and a tank top, him to the minibar, where he crouches and calls, "Want anything?"

I turn my back and pull off my shirt, replacing it with a favorite T-shirt, then shimmy out of my jeans and pull on sweats while he's still sorting through the tiny fridge.

"No more alcohol for me."

"Cocoa, then?" He gets up, his lips twitching when he sees I've changed clothes before he could notice.

"Not exactly a nightie..." I shrug and look down, but he's right in front of me a beat later, his fingers skimming under the hem of the shirt, warm against my skin.

"Nah. You're not a nightie kind of girl."

"Girl?"

"*Woman*," he corrects himself, and he bites his lip, but he's staring at my lip, like it's mine he wants to bite.

Our eyes lock.

"What kind of woman am I, then?" I lean close, let my breath tickle his jaw, feel a rush of triumph when a tremor runs through his body and his hands spasm over my skin, gripping my hips.

He lowers his mouth to mine and hovers, brushing his lip to mine, murmurs, "My kind of woman," and we're kissing, and then we're on the bed, and eventually we get to hot cocoa, but not before we're naked, laughing, then not laughing, the excitement and chase of the day before at the martial arts school coming back full force.

We fuck. And then we fuck again. He makes cocoa, and we drink it on the balcony staring out at the city. When we lie down, I pass out once again in his arms, thinking *maybe, someday, something*, forgetting entirely to mention what happened earlier, when I could have sworn I heard the echo of someone following me.

FORTY-EIGHT

TEN YEARS AGO

"Can't you just be normal?"

My father's words resonated through me, over and over. He'd yelled them when I broke down in tears after the mail carrier rang the doorbell. After I'd refused to go out to dinner with him. When I'd declined movie night.

Instead, I lay asleep in the same bed I'd slumbered in for a decade, but I wasn't the same child. The same teenager. My hands gripped the blanket for dear life. I felt cold, so cold, like I might never be warm again. My chest squeezed, and every time the air conditioner clicked on or a branch swayed, brushing against the house, I was sure it was him.

Hansel.

He said he'd wait for me.

He said he wanted me forever.

I took finals but skipped graduation. I avoided the stares of my fellow students, and shut my phone off rather than see Janie's calls. When she came knocking at the door, I pretended I wasn't home. She looked just like August, and worse, I should have been the one checking on her. I gazed at photos of my mother, wondering if she came back, if maybe then I'd feel safe again.

Every time I shut my eyes, I'd see him. The darkness was like him—all encompassing, like death. And August, poor August.

I should have kept us safe. I should have locked the doors. We should have never left prom early. If only I were normal—a normal teenage girl who *liked* prom. If only we'd stayed with Janie and Esme.

If only, if only...

"Norah?" My father's light knock on the door all but sends me into another panic attack.

"Yeah?" I sit up, pray he won't notice how tight and fearful my voice sounds even to me.

He opens the door, comes in in the darkness. "Honey, you can't change the past." His weight dips on the bed. His hand lands on my ankle over the covers. I have to inhale to keep from yanking away from his touch. We've never been close, never ones to hug spontaneously or tell one another we love each other—but casual touch was never a problem before. Now? Now, it's different.

"I know," I say, but not because he's right. He's not. He doesn't understand. He doesn't know what it's like to nearly die at a serial killer's hands. He doesn't know what it's like, thinking said serial killer might be lying in wait, ready to grab me the moment I'm vulnerable.

"So you have to look to the future."

I swallowed back the reality—that he was still out there. Waiting for me. That Hansel *was* my future, even if it was me figuring out how to keep myself safe from him always. The police had no new leads. I had no hope they'd catch him, not now.

I'd come to accept a new reality—that I have to make myself invulnerable. And until then, I was in danger.

FORTY-NINE

I'm in his arms. His arms. Not Owen's.

Hansel's.

Hot breath spills down my neck, and it boils over my skin like acid, and somewhere in the distance I can hear a ringer I've heard a thousand times. August's phone. It's probably Janie, sick out of her mind because August's not answering, I'm not answering, no one is picking up their damn phone. But Hansel tossed our phones away. How am I hearing August's ringer if—

I startle awake, sitting straight up, yanking away from the man in my bed, yanking away from—

I gaze down at him, and I can breathe again, because it's Owen, and he's safe, and I'm safe, but my phone is ringing. Where is my phone?

The covers are heavy, and sweat has pooled beneath my back, my shoulder blades, my knees, but I pull myself out from beneath them and rub at my eyes and blink into the dark, last night coming back in a tumble of groggy memories.

The phone goes silent.

Cool air greets my naked body as I grope through the early morning murkiness of the room, of my mind, a dull ache at the base of my skull, radiating to my temples. How much did I drink? Too much. Way too much. Wine with Owen and then Janie made her favorite cocktail and then Owen went back for another round, passing them out as we laughed over Chloe's latest debacle at work—

My phone rings again.

I find the bathroom light. It casts an off-white glow on the hotel room, and my coat is there, slung over a chair, and that seems right. I feel for it, the hard rectangle vibrating, and when I pull it up, it's a local number I don't recognize.

I've missed three calls. Which means I slept through the first one.

"Hello?" My tongue is thick as I say the word, and I say it again, because I barely recognize it as it slides from my mouth.

"Norah?" A woman's voice, one I recognize, but it takes me a second to place it.

"Chloe?"

"Norah, is Janie with you?"

"What?" I frown and pull the phone away long enough to check the time, 4:47 a.m. "No, of course not. What—" I take a breath, try to remember last night. "Owen and I left, and you guys—"

"We went home. We went to bed." Her voice drops and it sounds as though someone's strangling her, and it's a gasp, a sob. "But I woke up to go to the bathroom, and Janie's not here. She's not answering her phone. She's not in the restaurant. She's just... *gone*."

I swallow and search for the right words. But I can't speak, because my chest is heavy, and I can't quite get air into my lungs, and I have to sit down, or rather, *melt* down, find the floor beneath me before I collapse.

"She's gone?" I whisper, and Chloe says yes. I blink into the darkness as I try to assimilate her words, what this means. Janie's *gone*?

My phone vibrates—an alert, a message on Instagram.

"Hold on," I tell Chloe. Pressure builds in my chest as I swipe, click, open the app. My heart picks up speed as I see who it is, as I tap on his name, as I murmur the message to myself.

MMAddict: *You know what they say about making assumptions.*

"Fuck." I'm wide-eyed as the little bubble pops up indicating someone's there, someone's typing more.

MMAddict: *It's just like last time. The only thing missing is you.*

My heart spasms in my chest, my hand flies to my mouth, and I can't stop the gasp that comes out. Last night was an illusion. The promise of which we haven't actually earned, because whoever we caught yesterday was just what he seemed to be. A superfan.

Not *him*. Not Hansel. Not even Hansel's copycat?

"What is it?" I startle, Owen's voice coming from behind me, and he's rubbing his eyes, squinting at me through the light from the bathroom. He peers at his phone on the bedside. "It's not even five. Are you okay? Why are you—" Then he stops, taking in the expression on my face, the fact I'm collapsed on the ground.

"I'll be right there," I say to Chloe. Adrenaline spikes my blood, and I pull myself up to tear through my suitcase.

"What is it?" Owen's out of bed, too, and he comes up behind me. "Norah, what—"

"Janie's gone. Chloe can't find her anywhere." I pull on underwear, running tights, search for a shirt.

"Janie's—" He comes up short, watches me furiously dressing. And then he's dressing. "What did she say? What exactly?"

I answer him as I grab my wallet, a room key, and Owen yanks open the door and hands me a coat. We take the elevator. I watch the numbers over the door illuminate—seven, six, five—and Owen reaches for my hand and squeezes.

"It's going to be okay," he says. "We'll figure this out."

I try to smile. I manage to nod. We rush out into the cold dark morning. If ever I thought Hansel had returned, it's now.

And he's repeating history. He's got Janie, August's twin. And like he said, the only thing missing is me.

FIFTY

Chloe lets us in through the alleyway door, her eyes red-rimmed, lip trembling, streaks of dried tears leaving their path down her cheeks.

"What happened?" I pull her in for a hug, and her body is hot, feverish, and it looks as though she hasn't slept. Chloe hugs me back, slender fingers grasping my shoulders. Her body heaves with another sob.

"It's him, isn't it?" she asks. "He took her, just like he took her sister. I knew I should have had a security system installed."

"Take some deep breaths." I hug her close and walk her past the cafe's kitchen. The restaurant is dark, only yellow sconces illuminating our way to what I now think of as *our* booth. It still smells faintly of whiskey—god, how much did we drink?—and I sit beside her and hold her hands. I try to be strong, because though Janie is my best friend, the closest thing to a sister I've ever had, and Jesus, we just lost Esme, but she is *Chloe's* fiancée. Chloe's whole world. And I just *left* them here. The two of them. We had no proof that whoever attacked me was the guy, or at all related other than being a fucking psychopathic fan, and honestly, those aren't unheard of.

What was I thinking?

I go still, remembering the footsteps during my run yesterday. It could have been him. I could have turned around, and maybe I'd have seen him. Maybe I'd have realized we didn't catch the right guy, and Janie might still be here.

Owen makes coffee behind the bar, and after a few minutes Chloe nods, sniffles, wipes her nose with a spare napkin, and gives me the details.

"We went to bed around midnight. I woke up at—well, before I called you. Maybe five minutes before I called you?"

So, right around 4:45, given how many times she'd tried my cell phone.

"And?"

"And she wasn't in bed. Which isn't that uncommon. I thought maybe she'd come down here to start preparing for the breakfast crowd, but then I realized it's Monday, and the restaurant isn't open today. But still, sometimes she can't sleep and she..." Chloe's voice trails off. I follow her gaze to the kitchen, where a little cubbyhole of a closet is Janie's office. "She wasn't here, though. She wasn't outside sneaking a cigarette, either."

"Janie smokes?"

Chloe's cheeks pink, and this was a secret, something Janie held back from me because she knows I hate it.

"Not often. But occasionally. But she wasn't there, and all the doors were locked and..." Another stop as a thought occurs to her. "I didn't check the windows."

"We'll check them," I say.

Owen arrives with coffee.

"Go on," he says, sliding in across from us, eyes wide and focused and determined as he watches Chloe. "Tell us everything."

"There's nothing to tell, not really." More tears make a path to her jaw where they drop onto the table. "I looked everywhere. She's not answering her phone, either. It goes straight to voicemail."

I pull out my phone and dial, just in case, and Janie's voice comes over the line: "This is Janie. Leave me a message—" I end the call, abruptly cutting her words off. They hurt to hear, and again, I shouldn't have left them alone.

"You didn't hear anything?" I ask.

"No. It must have been..." Chloe beckons at imaginary beverages between us, where last night a dozen glasses in varying degrees of fullness contained whiskey and wine and whatever else we ordered. She puts a hand to her forehead. "I fell asleep, and I woke up, and... and she was gone. I didn't even wake up to go to the bathroom."

"We'll find her." Owen swings out of the booth. He gives me a look, and I follow, and that's when I remember he's a hunter. He's hunted *people*. There's resolve in the way he looks around the room and begins checking anywhere one might make their way inside, and I take the opposite end and do the same, and I think maybe, just maybe, we'll be able to find her before Hansel or his copycat starts ripping something up to make breadcrumbs.

Chloe watches us, and somewhere in there we remember the police. Chloe calls while Owen and I climb the stairs and search the apartment, and we find nothing, and with every room explored, every window still shut and door never unlocked, something inside me grows and grows, and it's all I can do to keep from hitting something.

Owen takes me in his arms. Squeezes me tight.

Downstairs, voices murmur, maybe the police, and all I can think of is *I can't lose Janie, too*, and somewhere in there I say it out loud.

Owen hugs me tighter. "We won't lose her," he says. "I promise, we'll find her."

FIFTY-ONE

TEN YEARS AGO

Summer was once a haven, when my friends and I would go to the local lakes and swim and sunbathe, and occasionally someone would steal a wine cooler, and we'd pass it around, pretending one of them was enough to make three of us *so tipsy*.

But this summer, there were no friends. No lakes. No warmth, period.

I didn't leave the house until the weekend before July Fourth. Everyone in the neighborhood was in celebration mode already, so no one was on our quiet street—they were gathered at parties or inside getting ready for the big day.

I stepped out on the front patio and let my eyes adjust to the brightness. My clothes hung off my slender-turned-skeletal frame. I inhaled, hoping fresh air would somehow bring me back to life, but it didn't. The smell of the trees only reminded me of being in the forest, of being forced through the woods to our deaths.

My hand reached for the doorframe, like it would somehow hold me upright.

In the last week, something had become clear to me—I was going to die. It was that simple. And at the rate I was going, that might not be such a bad thing. Except... I didn't *want* to die. But I didn't want to feel this way, either. And in the moments I wasn't filled with crushing anxiety, it was, quite honestly, boring.

My mother wouldn't have let me lie about like this. She would have been far more understanding than my father, but she would have booted me out of bed after the first week. Got me a therapist. Probably dragged me to the park for long walks along the lake. Anger lashed through me, thinking about her off wherever she was—ignoring me. Ignoring what happened. It made national news. Why hadn't she come home? Why hadn't she *called*?

I liked anger. It was easier than pain. I could be angry at her, and at my father for failing so miserably. I could be angry with Janie for looking like August. Angry with Esme for not understanding how I could shut them out.

Angry at the world.

Angry at—

"Norah!" A woman's voice, bright and clear.

My hand on the doorway squeezed, and I was ready to bolt inside, but I forced my feet to stay planted where they were. It took twenty minutes to get myself out on this doorstep—I wouldn't go inside now.

The woman looked familiar. She paced up the street in front of my house, in slacks and a teal blue shirt, hair in a ponytail.

I didn't panic. I didn't run away, lock the door, hide under the covers. I ignored the trembling as she grew closer. It was a woman—not him, not Hansel—and she smiled at me, and she was *so* familiar, maybe a friend of my mom's—

"Listen, I know the police have been giving you the side-eye, but I believe you. I saw you that morning. You were terrified and covered in mud and blood and god knows what else. Listen, Norah—" She knelt down in front of me, enunciating slowly, like I was a girl raised by wolves, or somehow otherwise lacking the mental capacity to understand her.

And that's when I realized where I recognized her from. *Elaine.* The woman with the website. The one responsible for my photo being online, covered in blood, in that damn prom dress.

"I will tell your *true* story. I will make sure everyone knows what really happened. We'll get the public on your side, and then the police will have to back down. You were the victim here." A patient smile widened over her face. "We both know you did what you had to do to survive."

My body wasn't listening to me anymore. Shock took over. My mind raced into overdrive—her expression, her words, they meant something. My brain couldn't quite sort out what it was, what she was suggesting, but at that exact moment, a car pulled up.

Janie burst from the driver's side.

"Get away from her. Leave her alone! Don't you think she's been through enough?"

Time blurred. I couldn't recall what happened next, only that Elaine was gone and Janie had gotten me back inside and was fussing over me, but inside, I was still stuck on Elaine's words.

We both know you did what you had to do to survive.

FIFTY-TWO

Detective Cron stands utterly still as she stares at the scene before her. Or rather, as she puts it, the lack of a scene. My frustration mounts with every word pouring from her mouth.

"There's no evidence she didn't leave of her own will. The Instagram messages you received don't prove anything." The detective takes another glance down the dim hallway, into the bedroom, shakes her head, taps a pen on the little pad of paper she's got in her opposite hand. "No struggle. No locks broken. Her purse is even gone. She left and locked up behind herself."

"Or someone else did." My jaw tenses. "This is *Janie*. August's *twin* sister."

Detective Cron's eyes soften at the mention of August. "Your attacker from yesterday—his name is Brandon Sands—he checks out. We even found footage of him talking to Esme the day before she was killed. He hasn't admitted to anything, but..." Her voice fades off. "Wait, isn't Janie engaged?"

Chloe looks up from a gray loveseat a dozen feet away, tissues clutched in one hand. Her whole body goes rigid, her sorrowful expression, the slumped posture dissipating.

"Yes," she answers, though the detective was talking to me. "*We* are engaged."

Detective Cron stiffens, realizing the fiancée is mere feet away. "It's common for—"

"No." Chloe's word comes in a quick snap, and the room falls silent. Behind us, techs check for fingerprints, and I catch one of them giving her the side-eye.

"Janie's the happiest I've ever seen her." I cross my arms and examine the room as though maybe this time I'll notice something about of place. But the detective is right—everything is as it should be. Of course, Detective Cron would want this case solved more than anything else. She has her man. It makes sense she would want to play this off as prewedding jitters. "She wouldn't just leave," I press.

"Given the situation and who she is, we'll look into it." Detective Cron nods decisively. "But Mr. Sands looks good for it." She pauses then. "We haven't been able to tie him to the messages you received on social media. But otherwise, everything checks out. We believe he's Esme's killer."

"Can you trace the messages back to who it actually is?"

Detective Cron hesitates. "No. Not unless you've received threats. Have you?"

I shake my head. I haven't. I have no proof of anything. Even if I do suspect the messages were—are—from Hansel.

An officer strides in. "One of the techs found this," he says, and at first, I think it's Janie's phone, but he swipes up and points and Detective Cron frowns down at the screen. Then, she laughs, but it's humorless, and the sharp angles of her face become fierce, angry.

"Right. Great." A glance at Chloe. "I'm sorry, Ms. Dearborn, but it appears your fiancée is fine."

"What?" Chloe's on her feet, and I move closer, eager to see what she means.

"See for yourself. This is her profile, right?" Detective Cron grabs the phone and turns it our way.

Janie. Smiling. Arms up to the sky like she's about to twirl. Trees behind her, a lake somewhere beyond that, stars. The photo is backlit somehow. "A moment of freedom after a chaotic few days," reads the caption.

"But—" Chloe begins, and Detective Cron is muttering to herself, returning the phone to its rightful owner. Orders are barked at the techs, and Owen texts me at that exact moment.

Owen: *I can't find her car anywhere. Not on the street, not in the garage.* And a moment later, *Did the police find anything? Did you ask if they can trace her phone? I'm trying to get in touch with a friend who might be able to, but he's not answering.*

I tuck it away for later.

"Wait." I make it an order, and Detective Cron freezes in the doorway. "You have no proof she's actually okay."

"She looks pretty okay in that photo. No sign of break-in or a struggle. Her car isn't in its usual spot, keys are gone. Looks like she just... left."

"Where is the photo taken?" I ask. "Do you recognize it?" I'm desperate to keep her here, to make her understand Janie would never just wander off after everything that's happened without saying anything.

"How the hell should I know?" Detective Cron sighs. "Listen, Norah, I get it. But she seems fine."

"How do you know that photo was even taken today?"

"I'll follow up with you later on. If she's not back by this evening, we can..." Detective Cron shrugs. "But I'll bet you'll hear from her." At the look I give her, she adds, "I'll see if I can figure out where the photo was taken. If we can get a uniform out to locate her. Happy?"

And then she's gone, and once again, the police are failing us.

All I can think is *But who took the photo?* Because Janie couldn't have.

Across the room Chloe gasps, and I look up, and her hand is in a drawer but she's looking at me.

"What?"

"Our spare key. We keep it in here, under the cookbooks. I was going to give it to you. It's missing."

"Who's had access to the apartment?" I cross the room to her and search the same drawer.

Chloe presses her lips together, shakes her head. "Anyone who's been in the restaurant. We rarely lock the door up to the stairwell. I always tell Janie we should, but she forgets—"

I go to stop Detective Cron, but her car is already pulling away, and Chloe and I are left alone in the apartment, and I know he has her.

Hansel is back.

FIFTY-THREE

Chloe calls in her friends at the security company, checking for contacts who might be able to access local security cameras. She's busy at a desk in the corner, where she occasionally works from home, her hair tied back from her face, and that initial shock has passed. Her eyes narrow, she's drinking espresso, and she's on the warpath to find Janie.

Owen returns, shivering from searching the nearby streets without a proper coat, and he drinks coffee and mutters about the police not doing their job. He tries again, unsuccessfully, to call his friend to trace her phone.

I'm on my third coffee and struggling against an aching head and lingering exhaustion, thinking of all the nights to have more than one drink, this was possibly the worst.

"That's illegal, right? Tracing a phone like that?" I perch on the couch beside him as he tosses his phone down on the couch.

"Probably." He runs a hand over his face, through his hair, and looks around bleary-eyed. "Fuck."

"That's my line." My lip quirks up, but it's not a smile. My phone buzzes. "I'll be right back." I take the call into the bedroom.

"Hey!" Rob's voice is quick, excited. "Are you coming back tomorrow or Wednesday? I'll try to pick you up, so you don't have to get a cab."

"Shit." The vision of what we were supposed to do today— wedding dress shopping. Champagne. A workout somewhere in there. Spending one last night with my best friend and her fiancée, figuring out if *maybe, someday, something* might be a thing with Owen. Petty, everyday pleasures and concerns, and now they are a world away, in another reality that may or may not ever occur.

"Norah? What is it?" Rob asks.

I try to put together the words. "Janie's gone. We woke up today, and she's—just gone. The cops think it's no big deal because she posted a photo on Instagram, but—" *But who took the damn photo?*

"I thought they had the guy."

Air hangs between us on the line, an unspoken truth dawning.

"They got the wrong guy," Rob murmurs after a moment. My chest clenches, and all I can think is Janie is scared to death right now. Or she's not, which is worse, because that means he's already killed her. *Breadcrumbs.* Fuck, I should be out looking for breadcrumbs. But where do I even start?

"Yeah." I say the word and take a deep breath, pressing down the rise of panic, of tears.

"What now?"

I fill him in on the details. He stays mostly silent, not at all like him. "Should I assign another coach to your fighters?" he asks. "I mean that seriously. I'm not mad. You have a lot going on."

"No, Rob, don't do that."

Another pause.

"You're in danger, Norah. You can't deny that."

I don't argue because he's right. And I'm not the only one.

The red lettering over Owen's truck comes back in a flash, *You're next*, dripping like blood down the windshield. We should have left town. All of us. Detective Cron would have shit a brick, but Janie would still be here. We would still all be together.

"Can you leave?" he asks, following my train of thought.

"No. I can't leave until we find her. We're going to find her." The words come from my mouth, but inside, other words echo: *Finding her means finding Hansel.* Dread pools in my stomach. I thought we had found him. Or at least his copycat. This was supposed to all be over. Probably, while Hansel looked on, amused we thought we were safe.

I think through all the possibilities—all the things we could have missed. My dad's laptop is still in my hotel room. There are more files I chose not to go through. It's possible there's something worth looking at there. Doubtful, but—but if he *was* trying to figure out who Hansel was, that meant he at least had a head start on us. And we need to know who he was—*is* —desperately.

Rob mutters a curse in Spanish, then switches to English and says, "I'll call you back." It's abrupt, and I wonder if he's mad at me, despite saying he wasn't, but he finishes with, "Be careful," in a voice that softens something inside me.

He disconnects, and I look up to find Owen in the doorway.

"I want to go look for her," I say. "Look for breadcrumbs. He always leaves breadcrumbs. He didn't just—" I stop and start again, forcing the words out. "He didn't just kill her like he did Esme. So, maybe..." Maybe there's a chance. Maybe for once, we'll follow the breadcrumbs and find her in time.

"I'll tell Chloe," he says.

"Did you see the photo?" I ask. "On Instagram?"

"Yeah, but I didn't recognize where it was taken. I know most of the lakes around here. But the photo was dark..."

"It might not be close."

Owen steps inside and kneels in front of me, putting us eye-to-eye, fingers brushing my calves. He takes my left hand and kisses my palm. The tenderness is too raw, too real, painful, and yet, I can't look away. "Can you think of anywhere he would take her? Anywhere of significance?" I gaze at him and hope to god between the two of us we can find her. Especially considering the cops don't seem concerned.

"I don't know." I look at my hand in his, thinking. "Maybe..." I freeze, a thought occurring to me that's so obvious I have to think it's the early wake-up and shock that kept me from thinking of it sooner. "Maybe where he took August and me."

"Where?" He peers at me like this is important, so important, and though it's been ten years, I can remember the path exactly.

"I'll show you."

FIFTY-FOUR

TEN YEARS AGO

It was late July when Detective Cron came to my house for the last time.

She strolled up the sidewalk in her boots, to the front door, hands resting on her hips as if she didn't assume that position, people wouldn't think she was in charge. She raised her hand to knock at the door, but my dad had seen her coming—he could see out the front from his office—and he let her right in.

"Detective Cron. Have you found the man who kidnapped my daughter?"

"Still working on it, Mr. Silverton. I'm here to talk to Norah. A few questions."

I'd been listening from the hallway. I always listened now—to phone calls, to my father's footsteps as he rambled through the house, to every conversation that happened within these walls, to the noises coming from outside. I realized I could tell quite a lot just by doing that much—could tell when someone was approaching my door, most importantly, or entering the house by the way the front door creaked. Another line of defense.

Detective Cron and I settled in the living room, and when

my father lingered, she gave him a look. "I'd like to speak to her alone this time, if you don't mind."

I hadn't felt normal in months—but having the detective here, in my home, brought back the tremble to my hands, the tightness in my chest, that had loosened at least some of the time. At first, during our many conversations, she'd asked me to come to the station. She had come here once or twice before, but my father had always sat with us, so this was... different.

Something about her demeanor left me uneasy. Her eyes, searching mine. Her body language forward, leaning toward me, as though she might spring at any moment. While it was her job to find out what happened to August, it had become clear we were not allies—if anything, her goal was to find someone to pin the murder on. And it was obvious I was as good a suspect as anyone else.

"Norah, I'm going to record this, if that's okay?" She didn't wait for a response, just turned on a small handheld recorder and set it on the table before us. "Hansel has... abruptly ceased his activity. I wanted to ask if you might know why that is?"

I rubbed my hands over my knees, searching for an explanation. There was no way I could know the answer to that, and yet she was asking. I shrugged. "Maybe because he's afraid of being caught? Everyone's looking for him."

I add silently *and now there's a witness. Me.*

"It's just strange, you know, that he let you go and then..." Her hands splayed out, palms up. "He disappears."

"I don't know."

She'd asked me a version of this question already. A couple times, actually. My palms sweat, hands slick against one another, and I wanted nothing more than to go crawl back into bed for another day or two. To hide beneath my covers and pretend none of this ever happened.

"How about this, Norah. I can't help but wonder, how was it that you just happened to have car issues at that exact spot where he was lying in wait? How did he know where to wait for you to pull over so he could—" A small smile touched her lips then. "Grab you?"

I shut my eyes, but it doesn't block out the memory—if anything, it makes it that much stronger. I open them again and stare at her.

"I don't know. I—" I forced myself to take a breath. "I wondered that, too. I wondered if maybe he was following us, or if—" My words fell short. It was a good question. A question I didn't have an answer to.

"Are you sure you don't know who Hansel is, Norah?"

The question comes fast, catching me off guard as I try to catch my breath, try to think through her question and the further questions it raises.

My eyes fly to her.

"How could I possibly know? He *kidnapped* us, he—"

"I just have to be honest, Norah. How else could he have known unless someone tipped him off? Unless he knew where to wait for you? And August is dead. Which leaves only you. So either..." An energy builds in her words, in the way she positions her body. "Either you know him and helped him. Or you are him."

FIFTY-FIVE

I'm standing in the sunshine, but the trail entrance before me promises thick, dark woods. A PRIVATE PROPERTY—NO TRES-PASSING sign hangs on one tree.

We shuffle from the gravel apron of the road where we left the truck and step onto those leaves, and a shiver runs through me. I haven't been here since before. Since *then*.

It looks different in the bright midday sunlight. Innocent. Just another trail in the woods to wander, no hint of what happened here a decade ago. I want to leave. Want to get back in the car and get the hell back to civilization. I can't, because I have to find Janie, but I *want* to, a pull so strong I have to steel myself from turning my back and walking away.

Owen examines my face. He reaches for my hand, gives it a squeeze, then says, "Wait here a sec." It's dead silent, save a whisper of wind in the trees, which have only half-dropped their leaves. The scent of burning wood is thick in the air, one of those smells that brings me right back to my childhood, the sort of thing you don't smell in Los Angeles, where you're more likely to catch the scent of diesel or piss than anything else.

"What?" I ask.

Owen crouches and studies the ground.

"Is this a Marine thing or a hunting thing?" My tone is light, trying to add a dash of humor to the situation, or maybe because my heart's pounding wildly in my chest, returning to the scene of the crime after so long. But Owen doesn't respond, and I switch to watching the trees around us.

"There's mud." Owen motions to a few spots. "Footprints. Too many leaves to make out much, though."

I squat and examine where he points, but I don't see what he does. I switch to what I am good at—being ready. For whatever awaits us down this trail. My ears ring with the stillness, the quiet, after the chaos of waking to the phone and the cops tramping through Janie's apartment. I peer around the street, the brush across the road, the woods we're about to enter—other than an occasional bird fluttering by, we're the only sign of life.

Owen shifts his weight, and his jeans grow dark where the wet leaves brush them. A sudden urge to hug him comes over me, but I stay where I am and watch him work. I'm grateful to not be alone here. Not only here, on this trail where nearby I nearly died, but in the sense of trying to find Janie. We shouldn't have been so quick to assume we had it figured out.

Owen moves another ten feet down the trail, still searching the ground, and my phone beeps. I pull my phone from my pocket to check for messages. One email—from Guy, requesting an interview, an exchange, he writes, since he technically could press charges for assault. I stare at it, wondering where *he* was last night, then delete it. And a missed call from Cher, a voicemail I don't bother listening to. I don't have time for her, for the business side of things. If Rob can't handle it, it can wait.

Owen's fingers brush along the vegetation on the side of the trail, then he stops to look up at the branches overhead. One hangs low enough that I could reach up and grab it, and he examines that next.

I peer into the woods again, making sure no monsters are

emerging to grab us, then go to Instagram. The last message MMAddict sent is there, baiting me. I slide another look toward Owen, but he's turning in a slow circle, taking a long look around like maybe he'll find a clue. And maybe he will. But I'm not like him. I'm a fighter, and the best thing I can do right now is a different sort of hunting.

My fingers poise over the keypad, and then, slowly, I respond.

You said you miss me. Why not tell me where you are so I can join you?

I hit Send. I wait.

A tremor runs through me that has nothing to do with the cold. It has entirely to do with shifting the game. It's like in a fight when I figure my opponent out, when I see an opening, when I know I'm going to win.

Except winning this time doesn't mean I come out on top. It means I keep Janie alive, one way or another.

Soon, Owen is back on his feet, and he holds his hand out for mine. I hesitate because I want my hands free in case something—*someone*—attacks us. But the desire for comfort, from about the only person I'd accept it from right this moment, wins out. I press my palm against his, fingers intertwining, and we walk down the trail. I catch him watching me, likely afraid I'm going to lose it. It's the sort of thing that, at any other time, would piss me off. I'm not that woman. I don't *lose it*. But coming here is different. It's like stepping back in time, knowing I'm going to see where August's body lay, where mine nearly joined hers, where I instead swore I could love a monster.

"You okay?" he asks after a mile or so. I shrug, and he leaves it at that. I spare a moment to mourn what this morning should have been. Wake-up sex. Coffee. Laughter. Eventually, we'd have gotten breakfast with Janie and Chloe, and then we'd have trained for hours before I went about taking care of my father's business in preparation for leaving. Somewhere in there, I'd have helped Janie find a wedding dress.

Now, I'm hoping she's still alive.

The cabin is off the trail, and I can't recall exactly where, but when I see a craggy boulder with dead, yellowed moss over one side, I know it's close.

"Do you remember much about that night?" Owen stands on a rock and scans the woods, looking for any sign that might indicate a cabin. I'm strolling the edge of the path, which has narrowed here, almost requiring us to walk single file, looking for the trace of a trail forking off. Once upon a time, someone lived out in these woods. Did they die in that cabin, too?

I almost say *No* to Owen's question. But that would be a lie, and *maybe, someday, something* comes to mind, and I tell him the truth. "I remember most of it like it was yesterday."

He doesn't say anything, and I turn to see his reaction, and indeed his eyes are on me, but his face is blank. He studies me a long moment, then asks, "Most of it?"

I shrug. "Sometimes it's blurry around the edges. The police questioned me so much, and I was so..." I bite my lip. "Hopped up on adrenaline. Not quite right in my head. You nearly die, you kind of shift into this other..." I search for the word. "Other mindset. Where things are a bit foggy. So I remember it, but sometimes I have a hard time telling if it's all my memories or..." I let my voice fade off. *Or suggestion. What the police wanted me to say. What they* suggested *happened, rather than what* actually *happened.* Or maybe, *things I wanted to forget.*

"Do you want to talk about it?"

I shake myself. "Do you really want to hear about it?" The unspoken: *Your girlfriend was there. I watched her be murdered.*

"I want to listen to whatever you want to share with me."

The light shifts as a cloud covers the sun, and without its blinking light, the temperature drops a few degrees. I cross my arms and look past Owen, mostly because I'm not sure I want to tell him the sordid details he was spared when he found out his girlfriend had been killed. But something catches my eye—a glint, as the light changes.

"What?" He turns to follow my gaze.

"I saw something."

Owen suddenly has his gun in his hand, and it's aimed in the general direction I'm staring. I start forward, but he stops me with a swift shake of his head. "I have the gun," he murmurs. "I go first."

"But I—"

"I can't shoot him if you're in the way." Our eyes lock, and he's right. If Hansel is here—if there's a chance to rescue Janie— this isn't about me being tough or proving myself. This is about us doing what makes sense.

I let Owen go first, and we move slowly. The brush thickens off the path, scrubby trees and rockier terrain. We step through a dried-up creek I don't remember, and we duck around a tree, ivy climbing up the branches and draping down over our path.

We're twenty feet from the cabin now. With each step, my muscles tighten, my alertness grows. I keep waiting for Hansel to jump out. For a trap to be sprung, to have to fight for my life. Every step that leads to nothing is a surprise and a relief. I can see what glinted in the light—a tall, slim cylinder, rising from the roof, part of what was once a chimney. The rock around it has crumbled, and I can see the inside off the chute. The cabin itself looks mostly in one piece, though a shutter hangs side-ways, and when we skirt around to the front, half the roof is missing.

There are no signs of life.

Owen lowers his gun but doesn't put it away.

I stare at the cabin, rock and mortar crumbling into history. One day it will be just another pile of rocks. Someone will walk by it and think, *Huh,* and that will be that, but awful things happened here.

I approach it, no longer cold, no longer feeling much of anything outside my body. The doorway is open, a maw more than happy to take in anyone who enters. To hold them captive. But it's just a cabin. A structure a human built eighty or a hundred years ago, and a murderer took it over for a night. The police hadn't found DNA of anyone else. It wasn't his *usual spot,* as the other detective informed me back then. When I'd asked what that meant, he'd clarified—this wasn't where he took his other victims. It certainly wasn't where the photos on Janie's Instagram were taken.

The last time I entered this cabin, I didn't step in so much as I was tossed in. I remember hitting the dirt ground hard, rocks under my hands, my arms, gashes and scrapes left as a consequence. And then, after I'd told him I *could* love a monster, I *would* stick around, except my father... Hansel had washed my wounds with water and said he *hadn't meant it,* and held me close, and all I wanted to do was throw up.

My body is tense, rigid, as I run through the motions in my head. *Elbow to the gut. Turn, knee to the groin. Arm around his throat and* tighten *until he can't breathe anymore, until he turns blue, until he feels like his head will burst from lack of oxygen, and then, squeeze tighter...*

A chipmunk scurries from the cabin across my feet, and I jolt back, hands into fists, ready to swing.

"Norah." Owen's voice is soft behind me, and I turn to find him watching me. He steps closer and smooths an arm around me, and I let him pull me against his body into a tight hug. "I've got you," he says.

"I would know what to do now," I say, gazing into that cabin.

"And what is that?" he asks. He turns me to face him.

But I don't answer because I'm running through a different

version of it now. A version that would have meant August lived, starting before we came to this cabin, back where he grabbed us off the road when the car died. *Lock the doors. Call the police. Why hadn't we called someone,* anyone *for help? Why hadn't we paid attention?*

"Maybe we should go. Janie's not here." Owen's voice interrupts the memory, and I swallow, nod, think maybe all this reminiscing is better saved for after we find Janie, anyway.

I push away the final word echoing in my thoughts.

If. If we find Janie.

FIFTY-SIX

It's the only time in my life I've wished to find breadcrumbs.

We go back to Janie's apartment, but Chloe is gone, leaving a note saying she'll be back in the evening and that she's working on getting the security videos. I wish she hadn't gone out on her own, but she's a grown woman. I search the apartment again, in case we somehow missed something before, but turn up nothing. My heart hurts, imagining where Janie might be, what might be happening to her right now.

Instagram offers no answers, only Likes on the last photo I posted and a handful of inappropriate comments. No response yet to my message, either.

Owen and I force down a silent lunch. Rob calls and leaves a message. Somewhere in there we go back to the hotel, and Owen pulls me into his arms, murmuring, "We'll find her. As soon as she doesn't show, the police will get on it." And I don't believe him, but having someone nearby who wants to comfort me helps, and I pass out in his arms.

When I wake, two hours have gone by, the grogginess has finally faded, and I make myself a cup of cheap hotel coffee. Owen doesn't budge, as exhausted as I am from the late night and drinking, and I pull on clothes and let myself out on the patio with my dad's laptop. I sit at a small wrought iron table, the breeze over the city bracing, and wish I'd grabbed a blanket. I stare at the computer a long moment.

Part of me wants to assume there is nothing of use to be found in this damn thing. I want to chuck it out and put it in the past along with him. But we were wrong. Janie is missing. And I don't know where to start. My dad might have something more in all those other files—something that either helps us or keeps us from exploring an avenue he may have already discovered was a dead end. I at least have to look.

The next file after HANSEL—WHO IS HE? is labeled JOURNAL. I click, and my jaw drops open when I see what the file contains—my father kept an actual *journal,* but it's not day-to-day observations—it's about his own investigation into what happened to me.

The websites have been unhelpful. All those people do is decide some other serial killer is responsible. Then they show evidence they are sure *proves it. It's coming to a conclusion before gathering evidence. Then finding evidence that supports whatever you've already decided is the right answer. It makes no sense!*

One man's idea did catch my eye, though. There was a serial killer by the name of Arnold Tilly rampant in the early 2000s. He killed primarily in St. Louis—not too far from Kansas City. He disappeared the same way Hansel did. Same guy, new city? Maybe. He didn't leave trails of items to his victims, but it was believed he kept a piece of their jewelry. It's a possibility, something to look into.

The other theory I saw that was notable involved families. Similar to Ryan Alberts in Florida. It doesn't quite fit, but if he first took Amy, and then attempted to take Norah... it just might. The only missing piece is that I'm still here writing this.

I freeze.

I'm still here writing this. Except, he's not. Not anymore.

I frown and scroll down, skimming more journaling about true crime websites he monitored, but there's nothing else about this theory. It takes a web search for me to learn Ryan Alberts would toy with whole families—killing first one, then two of them, in a manner that looked like an accident. A tragedy followed by a *real* tragedy—two people lost from a family, so close to one another. After three entire families were killed in a single year, it caught the attention of a criminal justice college student who read the papers obsessively.

My father discounted the theory—after all, he was still alive.

But... now he's not.

Which means maybe Ryan Alberts should be a suspect. But that would mean he killed my mother, too. I frown and keep reading only to find the following:

> *Guy Stevenson called again. I'll give him this—he's determined. He has some good ideas, though. Might let him come by. Tell him about Alberts and Tilly, see what he thinks.*

There's no date on the journal, but dozens of pages follow this one—so it's likely they were in communication for some time. I pick up my phone and dial Guy.

"Norah, this is unexpected."

I pause, deciding where to start. "Is it? You didn't hear about Janie? I would have guessed you'd be first on the scene."

Guy clears his throat. "I heard she left."

"She didn't leave."

"How do you know?" he asks.

"He took her."

"He who?"

He wants me to say it. I can picture him now, scribbling notes as I talk, planning his book around them.

My gaze flicks over my father's journal, coming to rest over the serial killer names. Are one of them born again as Hansel? Maybe. Perhaps my mother is dead, and Alberts meant to kill me next, and after a decade of waiting for me to return, went for my father.

I clear my throat. "Hansel. Who else?" It doesn't matter. Not anymore. Hell, I'll give him whatever he wants if he can help me find Janie.

"Do you have proof?"

"Help me. Please."

"How would I do that?" Guy's voice is silky smooth, like that first night together. I want to punch him. It's too bad I need his help.

"I have my dad's files."

The line goes quiet.

"Your father was trying to find your would-be killer, Norah. The monster who destroyed your life, as he put it. Unfortunately, he wasn't very good at it. I wouldn't bother wasting your time going through all that. You'll find he has hundreds of pages of... utter crap."

My heart palpitates, hearing that confirmation. "He showed it to you?"

"Sent me half a dozen files. I wasted a whole week on them. The only thing helpful he did was tell me about you."

I bite back a scathing remark. "He wrote down Ryan Alberts and Arnold Tilly as suspects."

"We discussed them at length. Alberts was arrested just last month. Tilly doesn't fit the profile."

Frustration squeezes my chest. "Are you sure?"

"Yes." The finality in his voice makes me think he really is sure, though a part of me wants to explore it as a possibility anyway. But we don't have time for that. Janie's life is on the line.

"You said you read everything there was on serial killers. What now?"

A chuckle. "I have no idea, Norah."

"You said you studied Hansel. Profiled him. My dad has all these people he thinks could be suspicious—"

"Your father was grasping at straws. Hansel—or whoever this is—is breaking all the rules. Serial killers have patterns. It's not unheard of for them to break their patterns, but this isn't normal. My professional opinion? This feels more like someone who you pissed off. Look at who's died. Your father. Esme. And now your best friend is missing. One of those happened to have *literal* instead of figurative breadcrumbs. I don't think it's him." Guy clears his throat. "And if it is? You're the expert. You're the one who flirted your way to freedom."

Someone I pissed off. That list wasn't exactly short. It would also mean this is my fault. Hell, it's my fault either way—I either helped create a copycat by telling Guy every last detail, or Hansel is back. For me. I scrub a hand over my face and blow out a breath, repeating Guy's words in my head, forcing myself to stay calm.

He mentioned my father's death in that list.

"Detective Cron says my father overdosed, accidentally or maybe—maybe suicide."

Guy goes quiet for a beat.

"It's possible, Norah. But likely?"

My heart is suddenly audible in ears—a whomping *thump-thump-thump.*

"What are you saying?"

"I'm saying I think he was murdered."

FIFTY-SEVEN

Guy thought my father was murdered, too.

Questions fill my head: *Who would have killed him? And why?*

But maybe I need to think of it in reverse. Why would someone kill him? Either to get to me, if this was Hansel—or because he'd gotten too close to figuring out who Hansel is. Which both led back to Hansel killing him.

I look over my shoulder at Owen, still passed out on the bed, his chest rising and falling in a slow pattern.

Something else Guy said sticks with me, too.

"You there, Norah?" His voice comes over the phone. I blink down at it and hit the end button. I *had* flirted my way to freedom, as he'd suggested. I pull up Instagram. My last message is there unanswered:

Norah Silverton: *You said you miss me. Why not tell me where you are so I can join you?*

I type, backspace, type again.

Norah Silverton: *Maybe I miss you, too.*

I hit Send. I wonder if this is even him. If this is worth my time. I navigate to Janie's Instagram, and there's a new photo: her hand, clutching a mug of coffee. The little tattoo of a purple heart she put on her ring finger in favor of an engagement ring is in the photo, so I know it's her, but I also know she's left-handed and always takes photos with that hand. Which tells me either someone else took this photo, or she's signaling me all is not well.

Or I'm completely nuts.

But I'm not. Something isn't right, and my skin crawls with that knowledge. Even if this does break the pattern, even if Guy thinks I should consider others, it has to be Hansel. I can *feel* it in some untouchable place inside me.

I go to the window and inspect the road below, cars driving by, kids in costumes out for some sort of trick-or-treating festival, and an idea forms in my head. Before I can change my mind, I duck inside and dress for a run. I bring my phone, my wallet. I don't leave Owen a note.

I take a settling breath and don't let myself think about what I'm about to do. I step outside alone, and I head down the first deserted street I find.

Inviting Hansel to nab me.

FIFTY-EIGHT

For six miles, I pound the pavement, weaving through the Plaza, taking every quiet, dark alley I come across. I glance over my shoulder for someone shadowing me. I check my reflection in glass shopfronts, hoping to see someone peering at me from across the street. I even wait for that tingle on the back of my neck, the one I've gotten since I arrived in Kansas City.

But there's nothing.

I stop to walk along Brush Creek, pretending for a moment to be a normal person. I crave that same feeling I've had the last several days—I *hope* someone is watching me. But it doesn't come. Almost like Hansel knows I'm baiting him and is refusing to play the game.

But someone recognizes me—a teenage boy, whose mother looks embarrassed and annoyed—which of course leads to others pretending to recognize me, too.

I take my time and sign a hat, a shirt, even a random piece of paper from someone's purse. And I let myself attract attention, casually looking up and down the creek for anyone acting suspicious or watching me. My pulse is fast, thready. Inside, I'm quaking—this is a risky idea. But I'm out of options. I have to get her back. I can't lose her like I lost August.

My mind flicks to my father—to the idea someone drugged him purposefully. To Guy's words, that *everyone besides Detective Cron and I* think it was a murder. By everyone, he must mean himself and Elaine. I get stuck on that for a moment—the idea of them colluding. It makes sense—it could be mutually beneficial—but it also feels so odd.

Only one person, a man in his early twenties, gives me a look and raises his phone to snap a photo—I assume he's one of Elaine's goons and turn away, ignoring him.

But so far, no Hansel. No attacker.

No echo of footsteps.

Not even a catcall, which is remarkable in and of itself.

I check my phone—still, nothing.

I'm nearly back to the hotel when my phone lights up. A message on Instagram.

MMAddict: *Do you miss me, Norah? Do you really?*

I tremble, the sensation of spiders crawling down my spine leaving me sure whoever this is, he's creepy as fuck.

It's impossible to tell his tone over a message on my phone. But I decide to assume it's sincere, because I don't have much I can do with sarcasm.

Norah Silverton: *Sometimes.*

I hesitate, then add more.

Is it really you? Hansel?

I press my back to the brick of the building and stare at the screen. I debate typing more. But I can't. I shouldn't. He has to believe it. And if he's been watching me, there's no doubt he's seen that I'm angry. Scared. A scared and angry woman doesn't profess her love for someone she hasn't seen in a decade. Especially if she's not entirely sure she loves him. Or if maybe she once did. Uncertainty is my friend.

Three dots. He's typing.

I suck in a breath and wait. My phone lights up, but not with his message; with Rob, calling again. I hit end and wait for Hansel. The dots go away. I curse under my breath, sure I've screwed it up. But just as I'm about to shove the phone back in my pocket, they reappear. Is he hesitant? Scared? Distrustful?

My hands go numb from holding the phone in the cold, and I press them into the sleeve of my jacket. It occurs to me I'm in front of a perfectly good bookstore—save the book in their display window—and I duck inside, avoiding yet another display where my face stares back at me.

The message comes through, the haptics jolting the phone in my hand. I maneuver past a line waiting to check out and stacks of bestsellers waiting to be picked up. I find a corner next to a row of journals and sit on a stool and give my phone my full attention. I very likely have a serial killer on the other end of this message.

MMAddict: *When?*

When what? I review our messages. He's avoided answering my question about who he is, which maybe could have allowed me to get the police involved. To trace the messages to whoever's on the other end, wherever he is. I blink, try to focus on what he's asking.

When do I miss him?

Damn it. A headache begins at the base of my skull, and I rub my eyes. For the first and likely only time in my life, I wish Guy were here beside me with his months of serial killer research. Or even Elaine. Not that their knowledge has done me a hell of a lot of good up to this point. I breathe in. Think through what I know.

Hansel takes young women. He kills them and makes sure people find them.

What does that mean?

I have no fucking clue. I do know he asked if I could ever care for someone like him. I know that I said yes, and that he believed me, and that he went so far as to let me go instead of killing me, believing the only reason I wasn't staying with him was because of my father. My dead father.

An idea comes to me so fast it's as though I'm watching it fly off before I can fully understand what it is—what it means. With my father gone, did he think I'd come back to him? I stop, ruminating on this, turning it over in my head, trying to see it from the perspective of a psychopath.

I don't answer his question. Instead, I think of a truth he might believe. A way I can get my foot in the door. With trembling hands, I type the message.

Norah Silverton: *Have you ever seen something you wanted that also scared you a little?*

No. Not quite right. I backspace.

Have you ever touched a lion?

I cringe at the words. But it's the best I can manage. I hit Send.

Three dots. My heart surges, adrenaline tingles through my veins. I wait.

"Aren't you—" I look up to see a girl who can't be more than thirteen. She has a copy of Guy's book in her arm, and she's pointing at my photo on the front. I bite my lip and fight off a flush of annoyance. Five minutes ago, I wanted to be recognized, but now I just want to focus. But I can't brush her off.

My phone vibrates, and the girl's eyes are wide, terrified at asking this question, and yet she did.

I press a finger to my lips. Wink. Mime signing and lift my eyebrows in question. She scavenges in her little pink purse for a pink pen, and I sign the book and whisper, "Our secret, okay? I'm trying to keep a low profile." I take a selfie with her, ignoring yet another buzz of the phone in my lap. I tell her to stay strong, because that's what I needed to hear at that age.

And she walks away, peeking at me one last time around a bookshelf, and I finally can look at the phone in my hands.

MMAddict: *A lion?*

MMAddict: *Don't fuck with me.*

Nausea rolls through me. My fingers jam at the keypad, picturing Hansel angry, picturing him angry and taking it out on Janie.

Norah Silverton: *I'm not. Lions are beautiful. Strong. But also frightening. Capable of devastation.*

Do I need to spell it out for him? A little *you're like a lion, beautiful but frightening*? Unless he's completely oblivious, he should get it.

A longer pause this time. I pace from my corner to the cafe, half my attention on my phone. I order a coffee. The man behind the counter gives me a disgusted look, like I'm one of those twenty-somethings obsessed with their phone. If only he knew.

My phone finally buzzes, but it's Owen.

Owen: *Where are you?*

Owen: *Are you okay?*

I wince. He's clearly worried, and I caused that. I type back a reassuring message.

Me: *I'm fine, I'll be back in a few minutes.*

But I'll need an explanation. It's past 3 p.m., which means I've been gone for more than an hour by myself when a killer might be on the lookout for me. I need to hold on to Owen, who's been one of the few people I can depend on through all of this. Despite myself, I want more nights where we drink hot cocoa together, have sex, fall asleep in one another's arms. I just want to know Janie is safe at home with Chloe when we're doing it.

The minutes tick by with no word from Hansel. Owen texts *Where are you? I'm worried.* And then Rob calls again. It's like the whole world wants to talk to me except the serial killer I need to answer me.

Finally, he says

MMAddict: *I've been waiting for you for a very long time. You don't need to be afraid. I know you didn't mean what you said.*

And all I can manage is to stare at the words and wonder what the hell that means. But then Guy texts, and his message pops up as a banner at the top, and the pieces fall into place.

Guy: *Help me with my next book on you and Hansel, and I'll help you find Janie. I have something that might help.*

The book. Hansel read the book.

I grab a copy from the closest display and flip through the pages until I find the chapter on me again. The words blur together as I fight to breathe normally, but I find the part I only vaguely remember reading.

During my interview with Ms. Silverton, she told a story like something out of a horror movie, the serial killer nicknamed Hansel, responsible for five known deaths, kidnapped both her and August Taylor. Ms. Taylor, her friend, didn't make it out alive, but according to Ms. Silverton, she used her womanly wiles to trick the sexually frustrated serial killer into falling for her. Ms. Silverton explained she would willingly stay with him, but her ailing father needed her as a caregiver. Hansel released her the very next day, reportedly telling her he would "wait as long as he needed to."

He read this, that I used my "womanly wiles to trick" him. I'd called him *sexually frustrated*. I'd *convinced* him. And this whole time, he's been *waiting for me*.

My hands shake as I slap shut the book and set it back on the table. The world tilts, and I find the nearest chair. The last decade of my life reconfigures in my head. I thought I'd left Hansel behind. I thought he'd left town or disappeared, or at least, stopped killing people. After a year, then two, then five... I thought he'd forgotten about me.

Jesus. Has he been keeping tabs on me this whole time?

My phone vibrates.

Rob: *Where are you? Some guy answered the door to your hotel room.*

And a second later, another message comes in from Owen.

Owen: *Why didn't you tell me your coach was coming in town?*

Fuck, fuck, fuck.

And last but of course not least, another message from Hansel.

MMAddict: *Are you there?*

FIFTY-NINE

TEN YEARS AGO

Detective Cron's theories went nowhere. They had no proof I'd done anything wrong, and how could they accuse a victim publicly? They couldn't. They didn't. They stuck to quiet bullying. Beyond the police, Elaine was not deterred. Her true crime website had flourished with her firsthand account at the scene of a serial killer's only surviving victim, and she was like a starved animal, viciously stalking me for another meal.

Worse, my father grew less understanding with time. My world grew smaller and smaller, until even on days I felt I *could* leave my bedroom, I didn't, because I'd have to be around him.

By late summer, I knew I had to leave.

I tried to discuss it with my dad, but he wouldn't so much as listen.

"You're not going anywhere. You can't take care of yourself. You're only eighteen, you're falling apart, how could you possibly—" This was always followed by, "It's all in your damn head, Norah. You're fine. A thing happened. It's over. The police will stop bothering you. You'll go to college and be a normal college kid—you'll be *fine*."

And when I looked out the front window to see Elaine

waiting in her car, as she did many days, waiting for any opportunity to launch herself at me for a story—*The real story, Norah, tell me the real story. Girls don't just survive serial killers. So what really happened that night?*—I knew leaving was the only way to escape it all. I didn't think leaving would fix all my problems. But it would let me get out from under them—Elaine, Detective Cron, my father, even Janie. It would let me breathe.

I'd given up hope that my mother was going to run to my rescue. She was gone. That much had become clear.

The most difficult part about leaving wasn't leaving these people behind. It was going out on my own, into a world I'd become terrified of. But I wanted to live. And I couldn't live like this, surrounded by these people who all wanted something from me. I couldn't live in a place where Hansel would expect to find me.

And so, one night I packed a bag and took my car, and headed west on I-70. The first mile was the hardest, then crossing the state line from Kansas into Colorado.

But dawn emerged as I crossed the flatlands leading up to the Rocky Mountains. I rolled down the windows. I inhaled mountain air—not Kansas air, not the woods where we'd been taken—and for the first time since that night, I felt like I could breathe.

SIXTY

I want to tell Hansel, *Let's meet.* Or, *Can I come to you?*

But it's too soon. He'll know my game. He has to be the one to suggest it. Tension tingles through me, and I write back with slow, cautious words:

> Norah Silverton: *I'm here. Sorry. People ask so much of me. Like, because I'm on TV, my time isn't my own.*

And I close the app, hoping he'll reply, then wait for *my* response, the way I waited for his. It's not ideal. Janie is intertwined in this, and if I fuck up, she gets hurt. Or worse. If she hasn't already.

I turn to go, only to nearly run into Elaine. Her eyes are locked on me, and I realize she's been watching me for some time now—me, too distracted to realize I was being observed. Heat licks through me, the sort that burns hot with rage, but not at her—at myself. I don't let people sneak up on me. Especially not *now,* with everything going on.

"You looked pretty intent on your phone." Her eyes flick to the phone in my hand, then back to me. "Find something new?"

"If I did, do you think I'd tell you?"

A one-shouldered shrug. That coy confidence I usually associated with her, the attitude she'd dropped with our more recent run-ins. Like she knows something.

I want to brush by her and escape out the door. Instead, I shift my weight and watch for other tells.

"What do you want?" I finally ask.

"Just a story. Some new tidbit for my readers. They're your biggest fans, you know."

I think of the MMA superfans and consider arguing that fact, but the true crime crowd is committed. She might be right.

"Did you take a photo?" I nod at her phone.

Her smile is slow, overly sweet. "Would I do that?"

"Yes."

Her smile dissipates. "I'm sorry your friend has gone missing. Have you thought anymore about what I said about your father?"

I want to give her the middle finger and walk out. But she's as much an expert source as Guy is. Maybe even more so. At first, I couldn't give credence to her idea about my father because I couldn't imagine who could dislike him enough to kill him—he had no friends, no family he was in communication with. But if it was Hansel... If Hansel was killing my whole family, slowly, or if the whole point had been to get me back here, well—that was motive, I suppose.

Though if I went with the former theory, that meant my mom... I bite my lip hard.

"I've thought about it."

"And?" She takes a half step closer.

I shrug. "It's a theory. There's no way to know for sure what happened." I look away. I don't want her to see the tears in my eyes. "Listen, you and your contacts—have you found anything else?"

Elaine opens her mouth, closes it, and I sigh. She doesn't

have anything—she's just here for a photo, a quote, anything to keep people refreshing her website and making her money.

"Bye, Elaine." I brush by her and out the door, only to run into another familiar face.

SIXTY-ONE

Rob's back is to me when I first catch sight of him, but I'd know him anywhere.

When he first invited me to train at his gym, I'd been in awe of his physique. The way his arm could snap out and back faster than my eyes were capable of seeing, how his body could go from one spot to on top of an opponent in a flurry of movement that was both brutal and graceful. Since then, I've become capable of doing these same things, my body the feminine match to his.

And I know much more than that—he's too dependent on his mother, dates the wrong kinds of women, has a heart of gold. I know that catching sight of him, my whole body warms, like I've come home after a long time away.

When he turns and smiles at me, that's all I can think of. My annoyance fades, and he comes close, and we hug.

"Glad to see you're in one piece."

"You weren't supposed to come," I mumble into his shoulder.

"My best coach? In trouble? I had to come." I pull back and

he catches my eyes. "So, who is this man in your hotel room? Do I need to be worried?"

"His name is Owen. I..." My hesitation is all Rob needs. The grin reappears, teasing. He presses a playful fist to my shoulder in a mock punch. "I like him. No, you don't need to be worried. I'm not getting married and buying a house in Kansas City anytime soon."

"Does he know that? The jealous type doesn't suit you, you know. Too many men in your life."

"You are not a *man in my life*," I remind him. Rob chuckles.

I feel eyes on me, that tingle over my shoulders. I flick a gaze up at the balcony, but Owen isn't there watching. But someone else might be. Or I'm paranoid. I wave Rob toward the hotel door, using the motion as an excuse to look up and down the road, but only shoppers, the occasional car, a group of women out speed-walking.

Rob shakes his head because he notices stuff like that, knows exactly what I'm doing. "Jesus, Norah. You were supposed to bury your dad, now all this. What are the cops saying?"

"Nothing. They think Janie took off, for some space." I show him the photos on her Instagram as we make our way upstairs, and when I get to the door, Owen opens it like he's been waiting, his dark eyes looking between us before he steps back and lets us in.

Tension fills the air, a thick haze through which I walk, suddenly self-conscious about the man I slept with, the coach who showed up uninvited.

"Rob, Owen. Owen, Rob." They shake, a smile comes to Owen's lips, and maybe the tension was all in my head.

"Nice to meet you, man," Owen says. "Sorry about before. I didn't realize who you were." And his tone is kind, but once they break apart, Owen strolls to me. He touches my hip with one hand, a casual gesture, a gesture I suspect that is meant to send a message to Rob. "I was worried," he murmurs in a low voice. "Everything okay?"

"I was looking." I pull off the long-sleeved top and toss it in a dirty laundry pile.

"Looking?"

"For Janie. For Hansel." I almost whip my phone out to show him the messages, but something stops me. I didn't show Rob, either. I suspect at some point I'll have to go to Hansel. Agree to a trade, me for Janie, or at least see him in person. At which point I can go past my ability to use my womanly wiles to get what I want and into my ability to beat the shit out of him. *Hopefully,* anyway. Neither of the men in the room will like that, but I'll have to do it, for Janie. So, I don't tell them. Try not to think about it too much, for that matter, because if I do, I might run away screaming.

"You shouldn't be out on your own," he says. And when I raise a brow at him, he adds, "Neither of us should. Nor Chloe, for that matter."

Chloe. We should be over there, checking on her.

Beyond Owen, Rob has made himself comfortable on the edge of the bed. He's watching us quietly, drawing some conclusion. He calls, "You realize Norah can take care of herself?"

Owen spins. His tone is controlled, but to the point. "Yet you flew in from halfway across the country because you're worried."

"Guys—"

Rob only smiles. Before his traumatic brain injury—literally one too many hits to the head—he was known for his cool in the ring. His utter inability to be rattled by any opponent. It's the sort of thing I tease him about, a calm that can border on creepy at times. He's doing it now.

"Her father is also dead. Her friend has been murdered. Her other friend is missing. Moral support seemed like something she could use," Rob answers.

"Cut it out," I snap. "Owen, Rob is one of my best friends. Rob, you shouldn't have shown up uninvited." I look back and forth between them. "We good?"

I go to the bathroom instead of waiting for an answer. I shut the door on the premise of changing, but what I really want is to check my phone without either of them looking over my shoulder.

The message came in ten minutes ago.

MMAddict: *I know what it's like to have to hide from others.*

Norah Silverton: *You've been hiding for a long time.*

MMAddict: *I have. I was waiting.*

My lip curls. Waiting for me. Words escape me as I stare down at the screen. I'm not good at this. For all Guy used the term *womanly wiles*, I had no idea what I was doing then, I was just surviving, going along with what Hansel said. I sure as hell don't know what I'm doing now.

I change into clean clothes and exit the bathroom to find the guys at opposite ends of the room. Owen's on the phone with someone, muttering about setting up a hunting trip for the week before Thanksgiving, and Rob's at the French doors, staring outside.

"You really like him?" he asks when I walk over. I sort through my duffel, tossing most of it out, piling dirty clothes in to take to Janie's apartment and wash.

"Owen?"

"Who else?"

I shrug, glance behind me, but Owen is still busy on his phone. "Yeah. I like him."

"How long have you known him?"

"We went to high school together." I explain his relationship with August, that he joined the Marines, that he's only recently back. "He's the one I've been training with."

"And now more?" A twist of his lips into a wry grin.

"He's helping me figure this out. Find Janie. But yes. Now more."

Rob nods and runs a hand through his hair. "That's good. You could use someone like that in your life." He lets a moment pass. "Did you get around to reading that email I sent?"

I grimace.

"Yikes. That looks like a no."

"Let's talk about it after I get back to L.A." *If I make it that long.*

Rob nods. "Fair enough. So, catch me up. You've got your Owen to help you out, but you've got me now, too. Let's find your friend. Get you home. Back to your fighters."

My phone vibrates, and it's probably another message from Hansel, but I'm making him wait, making him sweat.

Rob makes it sound like it will be so easy. I know it will be anything but.

SIXTY-TWO

Rob heads to the lobby to reserve his own room, and Owen practically flips a switch.

"I apologize." He approaches me in the bathroom, where I'm tying my hair up in a bun to get it out of my way. He crosses his arms and leans in the doorway, meeting my eyes in the mirror. His shadow of facial hair has become a full-on beard, and with his arms crossed and in a white T-shirt, he's almost passable as one of those men on the fronts of underwear packages. I let myself admire him a moment, think *he could be mine*, wrap myself in the warm cloak of the moments before Chloe's phone call this morning.

And now I have to lie to him.

Or, at best, keep the full truth from him. But there's no other option—if I share my plan to trick Hansel into believing me yet again, there's no way he'll let me leave. Not by myself. And I can't risk Janie's life.

"Apologize for what?" I ask.

"I was worried. You were gone and not answering my messages. Then someone knocked on the door, and I thought it was you, but it was *him*, and he acted—" Owen chews his lip and sucks in a breath. "Like he had the right to be here. Like you were... *his*."

"I'm not anyone's." I secure the bun with a hairband, twisting it an extra time to keep it firmly in place.

A slow nod, processing my words. "You're right. You're absolutely right." But he's taking it to mean something different than what I mean. I can tell by the way he drops his arms and turns to leave.

I grab his arm and pull him back in the bathroom, a different sort of panic flickering in my chest. I don't want him to walk away. Don't want him to leave me.

"Owen."

"It's okay, Norah. I knew it was—you know, just fun."

"Owen, that's not—" I sigh. Of all the times to do this. "I like you, Owen. I want whatever this is. But you have to understand, Rob's in my life. He's my coach. He's the reason I more or less have my life together. And that's not going to change."

"I wouldn't ask you to change that."

I widen my eyes at him. "Then there's no problem. But I'm not something to be fought over. I can be friends with Rob *and* be your—" Shit. I almost said *girlfriend*. It's been three damn days. Too soon.

Owen's lips twitch. The set of his shoulders relaxes, and he pulls me up against him. Lowers his mouth to mine. Kisses me softly, and when he stops, he stays right there, his breath tickling my lips. I shut my eyes and settle for a moment in his embrace. It's intimate in a way I haven't been with a man. Ever. Breathing one another's air, able to feel the warmth radiating off him.

"Okay, then," he says.

"Okay," I say back. Heat flares through me. I swallow and open my eyes, and he's watching me again, eyes glowing with warmth in the pale light. It's not that I don't want to do more right now—and possibly right here, in the bathroom, on the counter. But *Janie*. Not to mention, I hear the hotel room door open, Rob muttering under his breath as he returns.

"I'm going to call Detective Cron," I say. "I want to go by the station."

"I'll come with." Owen backs me up against the vanity. His arms circle my back and crush me tight against him. His lips press to mine again, and we kiss, then kiss some more.

A gentle *rap-rap-rap* at the door a minute later.

Rob calls out, "You've got a visitor."

My insides jolt. A *visitor*? There's a blip in time when everything is surreal enough I think it just might be Hansel. But then Owen says, "Expecting someone?" and I shake myself. Hansel is too smart for that.

My phone rings from the other room as I untwine myself from Owen.

"Want me to grab it?" he asks.

I hesitate. Nod. He can answer the phone without getting access to Instagram and Hansel's messages.

I wipe my suddenly damp palms on my jeans and go to the door while Owen answers my phone.

"Chloe?" I hear Owen say from behind me.

I crack the door open, heart pounding with anticipation.

Rob fixes me with a look that says, *Do I need to kick his ass?* while simultaneously asking, "You know this guy?"

Guy's cheesy grin turns my stomach the second I see it. He's wearing the damn hat, and the black leather vest over a button-up shirt, the sleeves rolled up to his elbows. I have no clue how the hell he knew which hotel I was staying at, much less which room, but it irritates me I was so easy to find.

Rob says something in the background, and I realize I don't know how he knew where I was staying, either. And Elaine had no trouble finding and following me. It's as though I have a GPS tracker attached to me, and anyone who wants to know where I am can find me just like that. Anyone but Hansel, apparently.

"Thought you might want my help," Guy says.

I shift my attention back to him. "You didn't seem terribly interested in helping me on the phone."

"You caught me off guard." Guy glances at Rob, who's stepped back and crossed his arms, well aware of how his arms and shoulders bulge with muscle when he does it. "This your bodyguard?"

"I don't have time for this, Guy."

His lips curl up in a smile that reminds me of a Disney villain, and he leans close. Rob shifts behind him, ready to do something about it. "Trust me," he murmurs. He looks into my eyes and something's there, like he *knows* something I want to know. And he's probably full of shit. But what if he's not? "It's now or never, Norah. I've got a plane to catch tonight. You want my help? It's all right here." He holds up a briefcase, a leather satchel-thing as pretentious as he is. And I want to give Rob the okay to get rid of him, but what he knows might make a difference. It might help us find Janie and keep me from endangering myself in the process.

Owen taps my shoulder and whispers, "Chloe thinks she found something. Can you talk to her?"

"Sure." I step back and leave the door open. Not welcoming Guy in. Not refusing him entrance, either. Owen and Rob do a manly nodding-at-one-another thing, and from the way they're looking at Guy, I'd say they're united now that they have someone to mutually dislike.

"I'll just set up right here," Guy says. He pulls out the chair to the tiny desk that houses a Bible and a notepad with the hotel's logo.

"You okay, Chloe?" I step out on the balcony with the phone, much in need of fresh, cool air, a moment of privacy.

"I have it." Her voice is quiet, forceful.

"Have what?"

"Video footage. Of him. Of whoever did it. It's grainy, and

from the side, but can you come? Maybe you'll recognize him. If you can confirm it's Hansel, the police will do something."

Energy revitalizes me. A lead. We have a lead.

"Okay. I'll be there. It might be a few minutes, Guy just showed up, and he thinks—"

"Norah, please. I wasn't exactly quiet about getting this. I don't feel safe here on my own. I tried to call Detective Cron, but she said something about Janie posting on Instagram again and how—"

Panic zings through me at her words. But there are three of us, and we're all skilled enough to fight off anyone without a gun. Shoot, Owen *has* a gun.

"Can you go down to the restaurant?" I ask her.

"It's closed on Mondays. No one's there."

Fuck. Of course, it is.

"I'm sending Owen," I say. "I'll be right behind him. Is that okay?"

"That's fine. Just ask him to hurry."

I hang up, and there's Hansel's message still waiting for me on Instagram, but there's no time. I spin and go back inside. Rob's making coffee, and he tries to hand me a mug, his brows knitting when I wave it off.

"Everything okay?"

"No," I say. "Owen, can you go to Chloe? She found video of... of *him*."

Owen's brows shoot up. "Really? Should we call Detective Cron and have her come—"

"She tried that already. I need to talk to Guy, and she doesn't feel safe. I'll come in just a few minutes, if you wouldn't mind—"

"What about you?" Owen takes a half step forward, then seems to remember Rob. "Okay." He nods to himself. "Okay, that works. Just be careful." His gaze touches on Guy. "Call if you need help with anything. I'll keep Chloe safe." He's pressing a kiss to my forehead and out the door in the next moment, leaving me with Rob and Guy.

Guy turns his smug *I'm-a-fucking-writer* smile on me and beckons me over. "Pull up a chair, Norah. We're about to figure out who Hansel is."

SIXTY-THREE

"There are four known serial killers who have passed through Kansas City in the last decade." Guy pushes his glasses up on his nose and points to a list of four names. "All men. None of them fit."

"Okay." I'm on my feet, bending over the desk, close enough Guy's cologne is about to choke me.

"Norah." Rob pulls over the other chair and beckons for me to sit in it.

"Thanks." I flash a smile at him and turn back to Guy. "So, that tells me nothing."

"Just wait." Guy shuffles through pieces of thick paper that are off-white, and no doubt have a fancy name like *candlelight* or *mother-of-pearl* or something else ridiculous. Leave it to him to avoid a regular notebook. "Here are common serial killer attributes. I've circled the ones that fit Hansel. Which, might I add, none of your father's suspects fit."

I pull the chair closer and peer at the list. I'm dubious, but I have to give Guy the benefit of the doubt. I have to explore every avenue that might help us find Janie and stop Hansel.

"He shows characteristics of what the criminal justice

system calls organized and nonsocial when talking about serial killers. Which is different than *asocial*."

I frown. "How so?"

"Asocial is someone who lives in a basement and has no friends. No normal life. Usually, nocturnal. *Nonsocial* is somewhat of a misnomer. They may have a normal life, have an education. Decent job. Might even be married, though I'm guessing not for Hansel. In other words, think of nonsocial as blending in. Not attracting attention."

I bite my lip. "Like Dexter."

A single nod. "Yes. Exactly. Follows the rules. Is good at pretending. They are also harder to catch than the other variety because they tend to be smarter. But—" Guy holds up a finger and points farther down the list. I see words like *Likes to play games—with police. Uses seduction to his or her advantage. Returns to crime scene. Fancy car. Good hygiene.* "Think *American Psycho*. Have you read it?"

"No. But I've seen the movie."

"Like that."

I blow out a slow breath and nod. This wasn't a mistake— Guy does know his stuff. Maybe this will help. Between this and Chloe's lead, maybe we'll be a step closer.

"These aren't strict lines. Not every serial killer fits perfectly into a category. But it's somewhere to start. The most noticeable thing about Hansel is that he's broken his pattern. *If it's him.*"

"I noticed," I murmur.

"It's become personal," Guy goes on, and he looks at me, and I know what he means. "He wants something."

Me. He wants *me*. But I knew that already.

"You said figure out who he is. How do we do that?"

Guy flicks his gaze behind me at Rob, who's typing away on his phone, then looks back at me. "The evidence we have would suggest," he lowers his voice to a whisper, "it's someone who's integrated themselves into your life."

I have to catch my breath, because I feel as though I've stopped breathing.

"What?" I know what he said. I know what he meant. But I still can't wrap my head around it.

"Think about it. How else would they know so much? Know you were coming back, know where your friends would be, who your friends are in the first place? Hell, I'd be as good a suspect as anyone. I don't blame you for confronting me."

"Are you being serious? You're saying you think it's someone I know?"

"Yes." One short, exact nod. "Likely a male, but possibly a female given we believe it could also be a copycat. Do you think Janie could be behind this?"

"Of course not." I fix him with a glare. Since we realized it wasn't Brandon Sands, I've moved on to being nearly certain it's Hansel. But Guy thinks it might not be. I'm not sure if I should feel relief there's still a possibility it's not him—or frustration, because I just want to know who the enemy is.

Guy shrugs. "Doesn't mean he was working alone. Doesn't mean it's not someone else this time." His lips twitch. He pulls the stupid hat off his head and spins it in his hand. "Janie was never jealous of her sister? Never got in a fight with Esme? She didn't want you, her best friend, back in town so badly she'd help your father overdose to force you to come back? And those photos that are showing up on her Instagram now that she's supposedly disappeared. She's in the center of it all, Norah, and now she's bending over backward to get you to come looking for her. Or not. Maybe, she's really the victim." A pause. Another glimmer of a smile that's darker than anything. "Did you know she used to take the same antidepressant that showed up on your father's toxicology reports?"

It takes me a moment to respond, and then I ask, "Are you

serious?" Janie and I shared everything—I would have thought she'd tell me if she were taking an antidepressant.

"Yes." He raises a brow and grins, far too pleased with himself. "It's probably a coincidence. It's a commonly used drug. But something to keep in mind." Again, he lets his gaze wander to Rob. "Or Rob, also known as *Roberto Cordeiro*. How much do you actually know about him?"

"A lot. I've worked with him for a decade. We're close."

"Right." Guy gives me a smile that tells me he thinks that's bullshit but doesn't comment further. I can't help but remember my own father's comments about Rob's timing, how he *just happened* to find me in Los Angeles. And now, here he is, in Kansas City. I watch Rob a long moment, hating that I'm even considering it.

Guy slides another paper my way. Two names are written on the top. "Speaking of women." *Detective L. Cron.* And below that, *Elaine Gehring.* "Detective Cron is up for a promotion next year. She was passed over last time. Don't you think it would look awfully good if she found someone to pin these murders on?"

I look at him—remember Detective Cron's newest accusations in my direction. Her refusal to bring in the FBI. Her certainty we caught the guy and Janie is fine.

But Guy isn't done. "And Elaine," he says. "Oh, Elaine."

"You slept with her, didn't you?"

Guy's lips slide into a slimy smile. "She went after me, not the other way around. I can't help it that women find me attractive."

"You think she's a killer?"

A shrug. "Maybe? Maybe not. Maybe her or one of her minions. She's mad she lost out on this story last time because you wouldn't give it to her. Then I published the book. Would she bring a serial killer back to life to get more attention for her website? She did stalk you, Norah. That's not... *normal* behavior." I stare at him a beat. He's not wrong.

"So," he continues, "take a look around you. Anyone look like a serial killer?" He pushes the list of serial killer attributes closer to me. "Rob, Chloe, Janie, Elaine, Detective Cron..." Another smile. "Me."

My patience snaps. "What's your point, Guy? Everyone fits some of these characteristics. *Everyone*. Even me. Look..." I trail my finger down the first list. "I had an alcoholic emotionally abusive father. I'm prone to violence." I point out others, then add, "That doesn't make me a murderer."

Guy shrugs. "True. But think about it. How many of these characteristics does your new boyfriend fit? Or Janie's fiancée, for that matter?"

I stare at him, patience gone. "I appreciate you coming here to help but accusing the people I care about is not helping. You should go."

Guy's face stiffens. "I'm not trying to cause trouble. I've spent years analyzing the previous murders. I've spoken to Detective Cron, and I've spent the last two days learning as much as I can. The only way this makes sense is if it's someone you know." He slides the list of characteristics to me. "You keep that. And good luck. I'd hate to see him—or her—win at this particular game." Guy shoves the other papers back in the briefcase and gets up. He's about to turn, to leave, to get the hell out of my life, thank god, but then he stops and looks at me one last time. "I mean that. I enjoyed the time we shared. Even if it was..." A shrug. "Business."

And with that, he's gone.

I stare at the door. In a way, he's helped. In a way, I feel worse than I did before, and no closer to finding Janie. Figuring out who Hansel is. And I can't shake his words from my mind.

The only way this makes sense is if it's someone you know.

SIXTY-FOUR

Guy takes his leave. I rush around the hotel room, grabbing my father's laptop and pulling on a jacket. Five minutes later, Rob and I take the stairs, moving at a fast clip. Guy's words echo in my head the whole way down, and I can't help but slide a quick look at Rob. He can't be Hansel. He was too established in L.A. when we met. And besides, I can't believe anyone could carry on a charade like that.

My heart aches. I don't *want* to believe it. But if it is someone close to me, that means someone is doing exactly that. Someone is deceiving me.

The BTK Killer lived right here in Kansas for decades, working at a supermarket, married to the same woman for most of his adult life. Hell, I remember hearing on the news he was on the church council and even helped out with a local Boy Scouts chapter. He maintained a totally normal life, and not even his wife or children suspected him.

It's possible someone close to me has a second life, just like the BTK Killer had. I just can't imagine *who*.

My phone is in my hand as Rob and I burst from the hotel doors and stride toward Janie's Cafe. I check her Instagram—

and sure enough, there's a third photo. This one of her feet, nails freshly painted, and she's on a deck overlooking a lake. The image of relaxation. But even if she has taken off for some R&R... Janie doesn't post to Instagram like this. She just doesn't. Unless there's a side to her I don't know, but we've been best friends for most of our lives. That said, I see her only a few times a year, and it's been that way for a decade. People do change.

I check messages next.

MMAddict: *Did I lose you?*

I hesitate, wondering who's really on the other end of this message. A response comes to me, something along the lines of *You'll never lose me again*, but footsteps smack the pavement, coming closer, and Rob's hand comes to my forearm, tightening. I look up.

It's Owen, his face flushed. "Is Chloe with you?" he calls, stumbling to a halt, his chest heaving.

I freeze. "Don't tell me she's gone."

He presses his hands to his thighs, shakes his head, huffs out a breath. "She's not there. I looked all over the apartment and the cafe. I just circled the block in case she got scared and started walking toward us." He nods at the bookstore. "Think she'd go in there?"

I grab at my phone. "I'll call her."

"What's she look like?" Rob asks, his hand already on the bookstore's front door.

"Five foot ten. Slim. Dark skin. Light brown eyes." Owen shakes his head, curses, takes another look around. My chest is tight, and I raise my phone to my ear, but it just rings and eventually rolls over to voicemail. I try her one more time.

"Fuck." My hand comes to my forehead, and I rub it over my face. "She found something, and now she's gone."

Or she's Hansel.

The idea comes to me too fast, too conveniently. And yet, she *had* conveniently been out of town when Esme died. She was *with* Janie when Janie disappeared. And it's entirely possible she made herself disappear—calling pretending to be in a panic as she took off, a gleam in her eye.

No. That can't be right. I remember the arms that tucked me close as August lay still on the ground. The voice that whispered in my ear. Hansel was undoubtedly a male. It would only make sense if Chloe were working *with* him, or if she's... if she's a copycat. There were mistakes. The breadcrumbs. The cuts.

And she is the new girl in town.

I pull out my phone and reply to Hansel.

Norah Silverton: *I'm only lost without you.*

It's cheesy. The sort of thing that would make my stomach roil if a man sent it to me. But it implies what I want next. An invitation to go to him. Or her. To find Janie. And maybe Chloe, too.

Rob's back a second later, and the three of us go to the apartment over the cafe, where once again, we find nothing. No one. And no sign of a struggle. But there is one thing missing.

"Her computer's gone," I say. A bare desk. No cell phone. "She was scared. Someone took her in—" I shake my head. "In minutes. Literal minutes." I don't say the rest of it. *What if she's a part of all this? What if she took Janie? She was here, with her, when she disappeared. She was supposedly in Chicago when Esme was murdered.*

"We should call the police." Owen shifts closer, takes my hand, grounding me. "Detective Cron will at least think this is suspicious. Did she say who found the security footage? If it's on a network, they may still be able to access it."

"She didn't say."

Owen squeezes my hand. "I'll call the detective."

I can't look away from the empty desk. She was here. *Right here.*

"We'll find her, Norah. And we'll keep you safe." Owen's words are meant to be reassuring. I wish I could collapse into his arms, and wish everything would be back to normal. I wish I could flick a magic wand, and it would make me disappear back to L.A., when Esme was alive and we were safe. As it is, I'm at the center of all of this, and I don't totally understand why, but I need to find out. My friends and family are disappearing, dying.

It's my fault. And Rob and Owen are going to get hurt next if I don't do something.

"Excuse me a second," I say. "I'm going to use the down-stairs bathroom. I need to pee, and we need to call the police. I don't want to worry about messing up evidence by using the apartment one."

I brush by them both and hurry down the stairs. I open one of the two unisex bathroom doors, hit the lock, then shut it, never stepping inside. Then I scribble a note on a napkin and leave it where they'll find it, because to keep them safe, I have to do this alone.

I'm going to find Hansel.

SIXTY-FIVE

The first thing I do is run.

I run as fast as I can to the parking garage and my rental car because I have no doubt one of them will come after me.

The highway out of the city is clear, and I hop on it, ignoring the texts and phone calls that light up my phone for the fifteen minutes it takes me to reach my destination. The private lake community of Swan Estates was once home to my maternal grandmother, a tidy white house in a corner lot down a twisty road. The community is mostly retired people with a handful of younger families tossed in. It's small, private, and rarely patrolled by police, in case the guys convince Detective Cron I'm in danger and to start looking for me. Here, I should be just out of reach, so I can do what I need to do to find Janie and Chloe. I park behind a detached garage where my car can't be seen from the road.

Nine text messages. Five calls.

I ignore them all and go to Instagram. Janie has no new photos, but I have two messages waiting, both from Hansel. One came in half an hour ago. The other, mere minutes.

MMAddict: *So, you've been lost these past nine years.*

I frown. Nine? It must be a typo. Or... I clench my hand around the phone. Or, it's a copycat, and they have their numbers wrong. It's been a decade. A decade and five months and two weeks and—I force myself to stop counting.

MMAddict: *Is that why you do what you do?*

I settle in, wish I really had peed before I'd made a run for it, and reply: *Fight, you mean?*

MMAddict: *Yes.*

His answer comes almost instantaneously.

Norah Silverton: *Something like that.*

I fight the urge to roll my eyes. *Sure, I learned to fight because I've felt lost without you, dear serial killer who murdered my friend right before my eyes. It has nothing at all to do with the desire to kill you with my bare hands.*

MMAddict: *I've felt lost, too.*

Norah Silverton: *I'd like to hear more if you want to share.*

I send the message, then add, as if it's an afterthought, *I understand if you don't want to, though. Not pushing, not prying. Just available.*

If it's him, I can fix this. I can do what I couldn't do ten years ago—strangle the life from his body, save my friend, make sure he never hurts another soul. End this.

And if it's not him, well—I can still do those things, even if it's not quite the same resolution. Even if it means the real Hansel is still out there somewhere. But the most important thing is rescuing Janie and Chloe.

Three minutes pass. Messages appear in the notification banner from Rob, mostly *Where are you?* And then *Goddammit, Norah. Not cool.* Owen calls back to back, then finally leaves a voicemail.

My chest feels heavy as I hit the Play button. Rob is like family—unconditional love. Owen is new. Untested.

"Norah, it's Owen. Listen, I know you think you have to go after him on your own. But, you don't. I'm here for you. So is Rob. We're not mad." In the background, Rob yells something that sounds an awful lot like "The hell I'm not!" and I can't help but smile as a tear trails down my cheek. I'm scared. Really scared. Utterly alone, in a way I haven't felt since my mother took off. If there was a way to do this with them, I would. But there's not.

"Well, *I'm* not mad," he goes on. "So, call me. Even if it's just to talk. I won't try to force you to do anything you don't want to." My heart about bursts, and time is running out on the message, and I wish it wouldn't. "I was serious about what I said. I'll follow you, if you'll have me. Just stay safe, okay?"

The voicemail ends.

For a moment, I'm tempted. My heart swells with emotion. But I can't call Owen. Not only would Hansel no doubt sniff out my lie if I brought him along with me, but I'd endanger him. Maybe, away from me, they'll be safe.

A buzz. Instagram, again.

MMAddict: *I tried to change for you.*

His words take a moment to comprehend. What does he mean, change for me? I type out the question and hit Send.

Norah Silverton: *Change?*

MMAddict: *I didn't fail. I didn't succeed, either. I just got... carried away.*

I frown. Try to figure out what to say to that, but he's still typing.

MMAddict: *You know what I am?*

I swallow. Dare I say it? Yes. If I push for honesty, maybe he'll open up. Maybe he'll invite me over.

Norah Silverton: *It scares me a little to say it. Because I shouldn't feel this way considering... who you are. Do you mean a serial killer?*

I hesitate. Hit Send. My heart thumps wildly in my chest, and heat builds under my arms. I pull off my jacket and crack a window, wishing my nerves would go away. I don't get nervous like this even for a big fight.

MMAddict: *So, like I said, I tried to change for you. Become normal. I'll try to show you. Try to prove it to you.*

My stomach flutters. Try to *prove* it to me? I type a few words, dread pooling in my stomach at what his words might mean.

Norah Silverton: *I don't want you to be anything other than who you are.*

Lie, lie, lie. I grit my teeth. A surge of rage leaves me hotter than before, and I open the car door to let a gust of cool air in. He tried so hard he apparently couldn't help but kill Esme.

> MMAddict: *Do you think you could ever love me?*

The words aren't meant as a taunt. They aren't meant to steel my spine and send some mixture of animosity and rage through me. But they do because it's the same thing he asked me *then*. I swallow my pride. Allow myself a moment to remember this isn't about me, or the things I've been running from and fighting off for ten years. It's about saving Janie. Making the world safe for myself, for Owen, for anyone else he would target.

> Norah Silverton: *I answered this once before. Have you heard the quote, "Absence makes the heart grow fonder"?*

I send the message, then close my eyes and wait, anticipation burning through me. His reply is instantaneous.

> MMAddict: *You're almost too good to be true.*

My breath catches in my throat as I murmur the message to myself. I'm not sure how to take it—a statement, or maybe a question. He might be overwhelmed with emotion, or he might be suspicious. I type something out, then backspace. Type again. Delete again. Finally, I come up with:

> Norah Silverton: *Almost.*

And I follow up with:

> Norah Silverton: *We deserve to be happy, though. We deserve one another.*

I wait, and overhead, clouds gather. A few stray raindrops hit the windshield, and I shut the door, raise the window, close myself in the car. More messages come through.

Rob: *This is fucked up, Norah. Please, don't do this. Let me help with whatever—*

Detective Cron calls, and I let it go to voicemail. It pops up a minute later, and I switch over to see visual voicemail, the service that transcribes voicemails to the best of AI's ability. The message is a mixture of *Your friends are concerned about your whereabouts* and *I would discourage you from going after—* I hit Delete. I don't need her help or whatever she thinks she's doing.

And then, Hansel messages back.

MMAddict: *I'll show you how much I care.*

My breath catches in my throat. Those three little dots shimmer over the screen. Another message comes through.

MMAddict: *Tonight. At sunset. The last place we saw one another.*

I take a shuddering breath. *Finally.*

SIXTY-SIX

Sunset is at 7:18 p.m. according to the weather app on my phone.

Four hours away.

Where we last saw one another.

I've been there already today, with Owen. The forest path. The glint of metal between the trees. The abandoned cabin, the roof caving in on one side. Would Hansel send us there if he knew how I really felt? That merely seeing the structure sends waves of anguish through me?

I shut my phone off to silence the incoming buzz of texts and another call from Owen, a call I want to answer. Not only because hearing his voice would soothe me, but because this is where I really could use his help—a decade of experience in the Marines. Staking out a killer. A gun, so I wouldn't have to get close enough to have to touch him. Regret flits through me. Maybe I played this wrong.

No. Keeping safe the people who matter is the goal. It's why I've dedicated the past ten years to training myself to be danger-ous. So if this moment ever came, I could do something about it instead of wilt like a flower before it dies. Taking it a step beyond my *womanly wiles* and beating him for real. Not just a trick. Not just agreeing with everything he says to survive the night.

My emotions swirl—some combination of dread and resignation. But also hope.

Tonight is going to be the fight of my life, and I intend to win.

* * *

Hansel is a planner. I have no doubt he'll show up at least an hour early, which is why I'll get there two hours early.

I stop at a sporting goods store and buy a warmer jacket in a woodsy camo pattern. I walk the aisles, grabbing a bag of trail mix, a pair of binoculars, a small backpack, and find myself at the gun counter. Handguns rest beneath bright lights and glass, and behind the counter is a row of rifles. Some are longer, with woodgrain stocks, and others are black and look more like something Owen might have used in the Marines. But I haven't touched a gun in over a decade; I wouldn't remember how to even load it.

So, I turn away, check out, and drive toward the same spot where Owen and I parked earlier. The patter of rain is a continuous background as I drive past the trailhead and park half a mile beyond it. The next hour is spent picking through the forest, finding a different path to reach that trail, to get a view of the cabin. One that doesn't involve the most obvious trailhead, the most obvious trail, the way Hansel would expect me to go.

I arrive with an hour and a half to sunset, and I climb into a massive oak with enough leaves to still provide protection from being spotted. I wait. A trickle of rain gets past the camo and slides down my neck. I shiver and wish the rain was the only thing leaving me chilled.

Hansel is somewhere out here. Or will be soon.

I can't freeze up—can't let him have the advantage, or let him have a chance to hurt me, to capture me. Years of training, of mental preparation to face my fears will keep me from that. But what will he expect? A hug? A kiss?

The thought of his hands on me turns my stomach. I have to act the part, at least until I can save Janie and Chloe. Which means that unless he's brought them with him—and I can't imagine he has—I'll have to go *with* him. Willingly. Pretending to be the woman who messaged him things like *we deserve one another*.

A knob in the tree sticks in my back, and I adjust, clutching the damp branch for dear life. I'm about twenty feet up—not so high a fall would kill me. Nor would it feel good. I shift and find another branch I can stand on, leaning against the bark, wondering what Owen is doing. If he and Rob have gone separate ways, looking for me, or if they've stuck together. If I'll ever see either of them again.

Because when two people fight, there's always a loser.

I lift my binoculars and check the cabin yet again, the sky slowly fading from the dark gray of the rainstorm to the dusk of sunset.

I go still. Stop breathing.

There's movement.

I blink, wipe rain from my eyes, and look again, because I can't tell, it's almost too dark—

There's someone just in the cabin door, slouched against the wall. Someone I recognize.

SIXTY-SEVEN

I climb down far enough I won't injure myself dropping to the forest floor. A carpet of cold, wet leaves cushions me as I leap to the ground and take off at a sprint.

I dodge a boulder. Hop a fallen tree. Stumble as rocks slide beneath my feet.

But I don't stop, my attention focused squarely on the cabin. The person there, unmoving.

"Janie!" I shout her name as soon as I think she may be able to hear me, but she doesn't turn or so much as react. It might be the rain, covering my voice, but adrenaline dumps through my veins, floods my body, and in its wake, fear.

The rain blurs my vision, and I swipe it away as I navigate over the dried creek bed that now flows with a trickle of water. My foot slides and is doused, and it's cold enough for numbness to creep up my ankle.

"Janie!" I scream her name at the top of my lungs. My chest constricts as she again doesn't respond. She might be dead. And if she is, I'm running straight into his trap.

I stutter to a stop. Take a long look around me, squinting

through the dark canopy of trees, the patter of rain. But there's no one else here, not that I can see.

Of course, there are a hundred if not a thousand hiding places.

Behind a tree.

Within the cabin.

But it's *Janie*. And she might be alive.

I continue, albeit at a slower pace. I watch the woods around me, check the trees in case he's climbed one like I did. He said he would *show me how much he cares*. I force myself forward, that flush of fear I can usually keep away settling inside. It makes my moves jerky, steals my confidence, leaves my hands trembling.

No. *No*. This is not who I am. Not anymore.

I'm twenty feet from the cabin. It's Janie, alright. On a folding chair, not standing. She's slumped to one side, her dark hair mishappen and over her face. Her hands are behind her, tied, I presume. Her eyes are shut.

She's dead. Or maybe, unconscious.

I pray for unconscious.

I forget the rest, and I sprint for her. Press my fingers to her throat, like I did Esme, and she's *warm*, and I whisper her name. Her eyelids flutter. The heaviness in my chest dissipates, and my insides positively vibrate with excitement and relief. I hug her, and she murmurs, "Who are you? Where...?" Her voice fades off as she drops into unconsciousness again.

The happiness drains out of me as I take her in.

Spit pools at the corner of her lips. She's still not opening her eyes, looking at me. Or responding, even. Something is wrong. Drugged? Forced to drink alcohol?

And we're at this cabin more than a mile from where I parked. I'm strong, but Janie is taller than me. She weighs at least as much as I do. Could I carry her out of a bar and into the car? Sure. But through these woods, where I myself can barely walk without falling?

No. Not likely. And it's nearly dark, now. Janie's features are suggestions of shadows. We're soaked, and I'm shivering. She probably should be shivering, but she's not, which makes me wonder what Hansel gave her, and how much of it.

I need help.

But I didn't want to drag anyone else anymore into this. What if Hansel is out here, lying in wait? And I bring them within his grasp?

But *Janie*. I find the driest spot on the cabin floor, where a wood plank rests, where the wall is still mostly in one piece. I hug Janie close and pull her to it, and I sit beside her limp form. I shrug the backpack off and pull her into my lap like she's a child. And when we're as warm as we can be, I reach into the bag and feel for my phone. Turn it on.

It lights up with over a dozen various messages, but only one catches my attention.

Instagram. Hansel.

MMAddict: *Do you like my gift? I know she is important to you. Now you know how important you are to me.*

I swipe it away and go to the phone app. Dial the one person who can help me right now.

"Norah?" Owen's voice comes over the phone instantly, like his phone was in his hand. Like he was waiting for me. Warmth spreads through me. A trembling smile comes to my lips.

"It's me," I say. "I need help."

"Are you okay? What is it? Tell me where you are." And in the background, Rob, cursing, again. I'd laugh if I had any humor left.

"I'm in the cabin."

"The cabin...? Shit, *that* cabin?" He's incredulous, like, *How could you go there by yourself?*

"That one."

"I'm coming."

"Wait, listen to me."

"What is it?" I can hear a door slam. Keys rattling. Rob asking a question.

"I have Janie. But she's not well. Bring blankets. Water. I think he drugged her, and we're out in the cold and it's raining—"

"Got it. Here, I have to drive. Stay on the phone with us."

And then Rob's voice comes on the line, warm, husky, soothing. I shut my eyes and listen to him, and answer his questions, and think maybe, just maybe, everything's going to be all right. But then he asks, "Do you have Chloe, too?" and, somehow, I'd forgotten her.

The woman Janie loves.

"No," I say. "Did you find anything? Detective Cron left me a message—"

"Chloe's background checks out," he says. "Cron finally started an investigation when you disappeared, too. And Chloe was definitely in Chicago. She contacted two of her co-workers and verified it. They even sent photos over."

"Fuck. I mean, that's good, I just—"

Hansel wants me to trust him. He *gave* me Janie back. But he still has Chloe.

Which means this is far from over.

SIXTY-EIGHT

Rob and Owen finally arrive, and the three of us manage to get Janie back to Rob's car.

Janie huddles against me, the seatbelt sideways over her. The car starts to move, and Janie wakes enough to murmur, "I'm fine, just take me home," but I only smooth a hand over her pale, cool face, and say, "I got it. Go back to sleep. Don't worry."

Rob has a rental SUV with plenty of space and a heater that's cranked up. He meets my eyes in the rearview mirror. I mouth, "Hospital," and he nods and asks Owen for directions.

I can breathe again. Janie's here with me, alive. Owen and Rob came fast, though huddled in that cabin, it felt like a lifetime. But only thirty minutes passed from my call to their arrival, meaning they must have sped the whole way, then sprinted from the car down the trail. By the time they arrived, Janie and I were both soaked through, shaking, hypothermic. I could no longer feel my fingers, my toes.

Somehow, we all got back to the car. It was chaotic and messy: tears and mud and Rob giving me a look that made me feel like a child—that *what the fuck, Norah?* look—a look I haven't seen in a very long time.

We arrive at the hospital with minimal words exchanged. The nurse at the front desk takes one look at Janie and gets her in a bed immediately. Our information is taken, and Detective Cron shows up—someone called the cops, I guess—and the four of us are in a private waiting room, and she's gone through her series of questions twice now.

I can't be certain she knows I'm lying. But I suspect she does. I can't tell her the truth, though, or my only means to communicate with him—to try to find him again—will be cut off. I can't trust her to do it right after she's failed so many times. And I can't bring Rob or Owen into this any more than I already have.

"Tell me again how you knew where to find her?" Detective Cron sits on the edge of a plastic chair. I have a blanket thrown over my own shoulders, a cup of coffee from a vending machine clutched in my hands. Rob sits to one side, fingers pressed to his jaw, like he's about to tell her to shut the hell up. Owen is motionless beside me. He hasn't said a word.

"That's where Hansel took us before. I just thought—" I shrug. Wipe a stray tear away. "I thought maybe he was trying to repeat what happened." Not a total lie.

"You didn't find a letter or pay a ransom?"

"No."

"You didn't see anyone out there?"

I press my hands to my face. "Are we done, yet? I'm exhausted. I'm freezing. If I don't get a hot shower and clothes, I'll be the next to be admitted to the hospital."

Detective Cron shakes her head. Stands up in a swift movement. "We're not done, Ms. Silverton. But that's enough for now. I've got people looking for Chloe. I'll update you if I hear anything. In the meantime, you shouldn't go back to your hotel room. Or Ms. Taylor's apartment. Go somewhere new. Hotel or"—she shrugs—"somewhere safe." She turns to go, then stops.

"What is it?" I give her a weary look.

"News on your dad." Her eyes flick to the guys, then back to me, taking the measure of us all. "Not good news, I'm afraid."

I sit up straighter.

"We ran further tests. Trace amounts of the antidepressant were found on his hand."

I frown, searching for the meaning. "So?"

"It suggests he voluntarily took the pills. That he held them in his hand before he swallowed them. Which would further suggest either accidental overdose or suicide. It doesn't really change anything, but..."

"This seemed like the right time to tell her that?" Owen's voice is low. I open my mouth to reply to Detective Cron, but nothing comes out.

Accidental overdose.

Suicide.

Neither feels right to me. I think of the computer he left behind. His theories. Maybe he had stumbled on something. Or maybe, someone knew he was looking. Guy had known. Elaine, too.

"Have you considered someone forced him to take those pills?" I ask.

Detective Cron's eyes widen. "Excuse me?"

Owen and Rob look at me.

"I told you that wasn't like him. He wouldn't have taken an antidepressant. Even if he was depressed, he wouldn't have."

"If he was suicidal—"

"He wasn't. But his death did get me back here. Back to Kansas City. For the first time in ten years."

A silence fills the room.

"We haven't looked at it like that," Cron finally says.

Owen reaches out and takes my hand. Something like relief floods me—that he's here, with me. I'm not facing her alone this time. And like he's forgiven me for taking off, with this one movement. I hang on to him like I'm holding on for dear life.

"I'll look into it," she says, then takes her leave. No one moves. No one speaks. For a solid minute, there's silence, and it's the sort of quiet that is louder than if someone would just say something.

Finally, I say, "I'm sorry."

Rob curses in Spanish. "No, you're not, Norah. You knew what you were doing. You knew what could happen, and you did it anyway."

"I found her, though. We *have* Janie." She's safe. She's alive.

"Don't do that again. I mean it." Rob crouches in front of me and our eyes meet. He raises his brows. "Understand? Not again."

Owen's hand smooths down my back. "Come on. Let's get you somewhere safe."

"I don't want to leave Janie."

"Nothing you can do," he replies. "Nurse said she's being admitted."

Rob sighs. "He's right. Come on. I'll get us a room somewhere with better security."

I say goodbye to Janie, and though she's only semiconscious, I think she knows I'm here with her, holding her hand. A cop is posted outside her door. Hopefully that means she's safe, at least for tonight.

Rob and Owen and I exit the hospital and find Rob's car, and all I can think is *she's safe, but we're not. None of us.*

I pull out my phone in the backseat.

There's a new message.

MMAddict: *You're welcome.*

SIXTY-NINE

"You're welcome." I whisper Hansel's words under my breath.

I hold my phone in my hands and try to type out a response. What is there to say? *Thank you?*

Thank you for not killing my best friend? For leaving her in the same place her twin sister was killed, unconscious and hypothermic, assuming I'd get to her in time?

I can't quite focus. I can't hold still. I'm twitchy, on edge, and even Rob seems to notice, glancing back not once, but twice.

"You all right?" he asks.

I nod. Fight to not fidget. I'm still cold, in soaked jeans, a T-shirt, my jacket long ago given up to Janie. The heater blasts warm air, but maybe that's it. Maybe I'm just too cold to focus.

What does he *want* to hear? What would make Hansel happy at this point? He's given me what he considers to be a gift. A simple thank you might be all it takes. A simple thank you *and*... hadn't I thought he would be there?

Norah Silverton: *Thank you.*

I breathe out, push Send before I delete it.

Norah Silverton: *That's not who I thought I'd see there. But I am so relieved she is safe. So, thank you.*

"Norah, are you hungry?" Owen twists in his seat, and I jump, drop my phone. Nearly caught, communicating with the enemy. An enemy no one knows I'm talking to. His luminous eyes meet mine and glint in the passing of a streetlamp. He holds out a hand and touches my knee. Gives me a reassuring smile. "We can stop."

"I'm okay. I'll get something at the hotel."

Owen nods, leans his head on the seat, watches me. "I was worried I wouldn't get you back."

I was worried I wouldn't come *back.*

Minutes later, we pull into an underground parking lot.

We make our way to the lobby, where Rob checks us into a room on what he calls the locked floor, and when we get in the elevator he murmurs, "It's where celebrities stay. Professional athletes. I didn't give them your name, but I mentioned fans who stalk you, which apparently isn't far from the truth."

The room is bigger than my apartment. It's actually *rooms*, to include a foyer, a living room, two bedrooms, two bathrooms, and a balcony. There's plush white carpet and white leather couches, lots of dark wood and the smell reminds me of going to the massage therapist, all lavender and eucalyptus, but I can't bring myself to care.

I call the hospital and check on Janie. Once I'm reassured she's okay, that no one's come and taken her, Rob goes back into coach mode.

"Shower. Food. I'm going to go grab your bag from the other hotel."

And then I'm alone with Owen, and he's softer, more careful, hugging me, stroking my hair. If it were anyone else, I'd tell them to go to hell, but after today, I want someone to hold me. I want *him* to.

The problem, of course, is that we're filthy, and I'm still shivering.

Owen pulls his shirts off in layers, peeling them over his head, the chiseled planes of his abs exposed a little at a time until he's shirtless. He's pale, not the sort to take up tanning in autumn, I guess, and he smiles ruefully when he catches me watching.

"I'll get the shower going."

He steps from the bedroom to the bathroom, but I call out, "Owen, wait." He pauses and sticks his head back out, eyebrows lifted in question. "Are we okay?"

"One sec." He holds a finger up. Disappears into the bathroom, and the spray of water hisses. He comes back with a white fluffy robe, and he sets it beside me on the bed. "You should get out of your wet clothes."

"You didn't answer my question."

"We can talk in the shower." His lips quirk. "When we've stopped shivering and no longer smell like a swamp."

I strip, and I let him help, because I'm not sure I can do it on my own, I'm shaking so hard. We step from the thick carpet to the cool tile of the bathroom, and then we're in a shower that rivals any I've ever seen.

It's big enough half a dozen people could be in here at once. There's an overhead rain shower, a regular angled nozzle, two that come from the wall at about chest level. Owen fiddles with them until just two are spraying, soaking us both in steaming water without blinding us.

"That okay?" he asks. I nod, and he pulls me close, our bare chests against one another. "Are you okay?"

"I thought he'd be there. I thought that's what I was walking into."

Owen stills. "That was very brave of you."

Regret leaves the moment empty of the emotion I want to feel. That I'm not being entirely honest with Owen. That I'm baring my soul, but not really. Because I know what happens next. I go to Hansel again. For Chloe. And because this won't stop until he's in prison. Or dead.

"I'm glad to be here with you now." There, honesty.

"You asked if we're okay," Owen murmurs into my hair.

I wait. This is when he tells me we're not okay. That he likes me, *but...*

But all he says is, "If you and I are enough of a *we* you're asking if we're okay, then you should know I'll always support you. I have no doubt you felt you had to do it your way. So, yes. *We're* okay."

We take turns washing one another, the heat between us growing under the drizzle of hot water. His hands smooth over my bare skin, touching every scar. His mouth finds mine, and he kisses down my jaw and throat until he's lower, much lower, and I gasp, and only his hands clenched on my thighs keep me upright.

Neither of us has any business trying acrobatics in the shower after the day we've had. We roll into bed naked. The numbness from the hospital has worn off. The knowledge it's not over pushed aside.

I kiss Owen like I may never get to again, because there was a moment today when it seemed like that might be the case. And I know this isn't over. So, for this moment, I'll be here, with him. The first person I've thought I might want *maybe, something, someday* with in a long time. Except it's *yes, us, right now.*

SEVENTY

The smell of coffee wakes me.

I'm rolled in the thick quilt of the hotel bed, Owen's form half draped over me. I now understand the term *spooning*, and though part of me doesn't want to disentangle myself from him —the coffee, and my bladder, call to me. Not to mention I'm so hot I can't imagine how just last night I was borderline hypothermic.

The robe I never bothered with is strewn on the ground, and I shrug it on. I use the toilet, lingering to admire the white tile, the large mirror, the granite countertop—such a stark difference from my cheap Los Angeles apartment. I've brought my phone in with me, which Owen was kind enough to plug into a charger at some point between sex and sleep.

One new message.

MMAddict: *I would do anything for you. Anything.*

I settle back to perch on the bathroom counter and mull over an answer. The goal is to get Chloe back and end this for good. I've never killed anyone. It happens, on rare occasion, in

MMA. A punch just right—or rather, wrong. An attack on the street, some asshole wanting to prove how tough they are. I'm thankful for that. But for Hansel, if there was no other option, I would do it.

> Norah Silverton: *Don't take this the wrong way. But talk is cheap. I meant it when I said I thought it would be you I'd find yesterday.*

> MMAddict: *Don't take this the wrong way. But yesterday was both of us proving ourselves to one another.*

His response comes over immediately, and I stare at it. Turn it over in my head. He was testing *me*. Maybe to see if I'd still talk to him after we got Janie back. Maybe to see if I'd come alone, or if I was bringing the whole police force with me.

> Norah Silverton: *I understand your concern. I can wait as long as I need to.*

I can't. Not really. But I'll say I can.

I hop down and splash water on my face. No doubt, Rob won't let me out of his sight today. So, I'll go along with it. We'll go to the gym. We'll spar.

I'll wait.

And then I'll go after him again.

Owen's rolled on his other side and sprawled out, but his breathing is still slow, steady, and I tiptoe through the room. On the other side of the door, Rob's sipping coffee from a hotel mug and shoving scrambled eggs in his mouth.

"Food," he grunts and points at a rolling cart. I pull a tray out to reveal the same meal Rob has—eggs, toast, sausage, a side of sliced tomatoes and fruit.

"I'm after coffee," I say, but he's already pouring me a cup from a carafe.

"Your stuff's over there." He uses his fork to indicate my duffel in one corner. "You were asleep by the time I got back."

No, I wasn't. And I'll bet he knows it. But he's busy sipping coffee and staring at a newspaper and ignoring me, and that's fine by me.

I take my coffee and plate and find a spot to curl up on the couch and eat as I call the hospital to check on Janie again—vitals stable, temperature normalized, definitely drugged, but the nurse isn't sure with what yet. She's sleeping. She'll be discharged this afternoon if all is well. The nurse adds, "A woman named Elaine tried to visit her, said she was a relative. Janie was asleep, so I turned her away."

I tell the nurse who exactly Elaine is, and the nurse promises not to let her in. I have half a mind to call Elaine and tell her off, but no doubt she'd only use it as an opportunity to ask more questions.

I drink my coffee, pondering Elaine's motives, staring at Instagram, waiting for another message to pop through, but it doesn't.

Hansel has gone silent. Dealing with Chloe. Planning the next murder. Or... something. My heart trips over itself, imagining what he has planned next. Maybe I should message him again. Keep his mind occupied. Keep him from whatever the next thing is. If that's even possible.

"Got a gym we can go to?" Rob calls.

I look up, startled. "Yes. Owen knows the guy who owns it."

"Good." Rob downs the rest of his coffee. He's still mad, but he's talking to me, so that's progress. "Finish up. We leave in thirty minutes." Then he disappears into his room, and I'm alone.

If I'm going to take off, the time is now. But I don't know where to begin. Hansel is silent. My rental car is still parked in the middle of nowhere. And I'm not ready to disappear again, just yet. Maybe once I talk to Janie. Maybe after another hug and kiss from Owen. Maybe once Rob has had the chance to go a few rounds with me and work it out of his system, and I feel forgiven at least for the moment.

Owen's still asleep when I enter the room with my duffel bag. I pull out gym clothes in need of a wash, get dressed, and scrounge for a sweatshirt. My hand closes over one, but it's not one of mine—it's Owen's. The one he loaned me just a few days ago, though it feels like weeks now. Months, even. I pull it on, bask in his scent, remember last night.

It started out sweet. Kissing. Touching. Heat building between us. And then it became something else. Something more intense. A game of catch-me-if-you-can around the room, ending with an intensity and a relief and a moment of forgetting everything except one another I've only ever found during a fight.

Now, I lean over him. Press a kiss to his mouth, but his eyes fly open, and he pulls me down on top of him.

"Mmm, you kept this," he mumbles, fingertips reaching beneath the sweatshirt to my stomach. "My favorite hoodie, too."

"Want it back?"

"Maybe." He growls. His hands cup my face, pull me in for a kiss. One hand wanders south, tracing a line down my cheek, to my neck, over my arm, reaching for my hand. He does this. Holds my hand as he kisses me. It's odd, and yet, it's intimate. I like it.

"You'll have to take it then," I whisper.

"I think I can manage that."

"Can you?"

Owen releases my hand and fingers bury themselves in my hair, tight enough I wince, but it's not the bad pain. It's the good pain. I hiss. His whole body tenses, his giveaway when we spar, too, and he rolls me beneath him. That's when I realize he's still naked. Which only makes it easier.

What stops us dead is Rob rapping on the door.

"Norah? Let's go."

"No," I groan.

Owen chuckles. Pulls away. Presses a kiss to my mouth. "Better go. Coach is calling you. I'll be here when you get back. We'll go see Janie."

I find my clothes and let him wrap me up in a hug.

"See you soon," he whispers.

SEVENTY-ONE

Rob gets right to it. We start with a dynamic warm-up consisting of squats, frog-walking, pull-ups, and more. After twenty minutes he has me shadowboxing, then we move to working on strikes against a bag. We move onto focus mitts, then finally, full-on sparring.

I'm only an amateur fighter, with no intention to go pro, but I fight like one, regardless. And in exchange, Rob trains me like one. Like the next fight might be the most important one in my life. Almost no words are exchanged throughout. A quiet intensity fills the room, and we go one round, then two. Rob sweeps my legs and takes me down for the third time using the same combination of moves to maneuver around me, wrap his legs around my lower body, his arms around my upper body, and choke until I tap out.

"Fuck." I sigh, roll away when he releases me, and get to my knees. I stare at the mat, right where he had me, and try to visualize it. But it's not happening. I can't see it from the outside, can't quite wrap my head around a counter.

"Let me show you again," Rob says, but I shake my head.

"Gimme five." I find a bench and swig water. Rob goes to

chat with the gym owner, to thank him, I imagine. And I sit and stew, but it's not the moves, the takedown I'm thinking about. It's Janie. Chloe. Hansel. I look up, let my eyes linger on the windows where maybe Hansel himself watched Owen and me rolling around mere days ago—just before he left that threat across his windshield. Has he looked in on us now? If I could just watch behind me at all moments, maybe I'd have caught him.

Or maybe he's someone who people don't notice. I swig more water, trying to think of who that could be. When I check my phone, I have only a message from Owen.

Owen: *Thinking about you.*

I type out a quick message. *Same. Wish I were sparring with you right now ;-)* And I can't help but grin because *sparring* is one word for it.

I switch to Instagram.

Still nothing from Hansel since I sent the message saying I would wait as long as he wanted. I type out a quick Norah Silverton: *Feel like I'm losing you here.*

Minutes pass. Rob reappears.

"Done texting with your boyfriend?" he asks. And I open my mouth to defend myself, but he smiles, just a little, and I breathe. He's joking. We're okay.

Rob takes me through the moves in slow motion. The moment he shifts his weight, and I go sideways. The moment I land, but he's already moving to the next hold, which leaves me helpless.

"Shove your arm down," he says, "then pop your hip and you'll—yes, like that." I break free of the hold. "Now reverse it." And I do, and finally, I get it. We repeat the chain of movement over and over, and then we go back to sparring. He throws it in randomly, and eventually, I make it happen on the fly.

"Good," he says. Another half hour of sparring. Students trickle in, bowing at the entrance, dressed in white pants and white tops, an array of colored belts at their waist. One of them recognizes me as the woman who trains world champions, and then they recognize Rob, too, from his fighting days. Word spreads through the crowd, and we're signing various things—a book, a brochure for the studio, a baseball—before Rob finally pulls me from the crowd, and we go for coffee. I watch the side mirror as we chat, for Hansel, for Elaine... for anyone who might tail us.

"I hope that cleared your head. Biggest thing is finishing all this—" He waves a hand, indicating Kansas City at large, I guess. The serial killer at large. "Getting you home safe." A long pause. "Assuming you plan on coming back to Los Angeles, that is."

I've been quiet, watching, considering my next move—Message Hansel again? Make him an offer? Wait for an invitation?—but Rob's tone, tight with emotion, yanks me back to the moment.

"What?" I blink and look over. He spins the steering wheel, pulling us into a coffee drive-through. There's no line, and he orders for us both without hesitation—this is every day for us. He can order for me at most restaurants, too.

"You met someone," he says. He pulls forward. Puts the car in park. Looks straight ahead. "Been a long time since you met someone."

"Yes..." I think through my words. My reality. "But I'm still a fighter. Still *your* fighter. A coach. I can't just leave my athletes. Owen is great, but I'm not moving back to Kansas City for him." Would I, though? I shove the thought aside. It's too early to know. And it doesn't matter, anyway. He's said he'll move to L.A. if we get to that point. Which makes me wonder where exactly that point is. What happens after I go home? Months of long distance?

Rob takes the coffees from the barista and hands me one. We head back to the hotel. He talks about the gym, a new student, who his brother Art is dating, and his thoughts for adding a couple yoga hours to the gym's class schedule. "It helped you, right?" he asks.

I nod. Ask questions as appropriate. Pull out my phone and check Instagram again, but still nothing from Hansel. My chest tightens. I hope I haven't screwed this up or put Chloe in greater danger than she already was.

"You okay?" Rob pulls the car into the underground lot and finds a spot. He cuts the engine. We sit in silence for a moment.

"Distracted," I say. "Thinking about Hansel." My gaze darts to the mirror one more time, but no one pulled into the garage behind us.

"I know. I was trying to—give you something else to think about. Get you a workout in. That usually helps."

I nod. I knew that already. And I'm glad for it. But now, I'm ready to get back to figuring this all out. And I need to call Detective Cron. I hadn't thought of the question at the time, but maybe the news on my dad means I can finally bury him. Finally get his house taken care of.

"Want to head on up?" Rob and I step onto the elevator a moment later, but I'm too exhausted to even consider feeling claustrophobic in it. And I can't imagine climbing the fifteen floors of stairs to our room. "I'll swing by one of the hotel restaurants and grab food?"

"Sure." I lean on the elevator wall and shut my eyes, grateful that I'll have a few minutes alone with Owen. Rob steps off the elevator on the ground floor, and I take it up alone. The only moment I've had alone since yesterday.

The elevator door dings.

I step onto the patterned carpet and wind through the floor, turning the corner to our room.

I stop dead in my tracks.

The door is cracked open. A gaping hole into a dark room. The curtains were open when we left, letting sunlight in, but they must be shut tight now, because it's dark as night through the doorway. And between me and the door are pieces of paper littered in a rough line.

Pieces of... I suck in a breath. Kneel for a closer look. Reach for the wall to keep myself upright as my head spins.

Owen's face in one. My shoe in another. It's a photo of us, ripped into a dozen pieces.

I recognize the background—red brick. Another snippet of paper is my face. It was taken when we were in the booth, at Janie's. I can't tell when, but one of the times we sat across from one another, first annoyed and snapping, then at ease, enjoying one another's company.

A paper trail. A figurative trail of breadcrumbs.

My heart drops into my stomach.

Hansel wasn't following us, because he was here.

SEVENTY-TWO

The bits and pieces of us—a torn-up photo, our faces, our smiles, our hands, our bodies—come to an end in the doorway to our half of the suite. My phone is in my hand, the flashlight on, trailing them faster than I should be because *Hansel might still be here*, but either way, Owen *is* here, and if how Hansel killed August and Esme is any indication, if he's not dead, he will be soon.

The white glow of the phone's flashlight shines through the doorway to the room, illuminating the pale edge of the bed. The hotel room is otherwise black and still. It's only darkness. Only silence. But the weight of something more sinister sits heavy all around me. I've heard serial killers referred to as the evil here on earth. The devil personified.

Is the devil waiting for me in this very room? My fists clench. I hope so.

If Hansel is here waiting for me, if I can save Owen, I'm no worse off than I was before. I flick the light on. Step forward. Wait for my heart to lurch the moment I see blood and empty, staring eyes.

But the bed is made and empty. I step in and turn in a slow

circle. The room is perfection, as it was when we arrived last night. The only difference is my duffel bag in the corner, tidily zipped and waiting for me.

The bathroom. He's in the bathroom. I stride across to the entrance, flick that light on, but—but nothing, again. White walls, white tiles. No marring of perfection with spilled blood. Even the air still smells sweetly of lavender and eucalyptus.

Time moves slowly. I turn yet again, leave the bedroom, pull back curtains, turn on every light I can find. And the hotel room is put together, pristine. Plates are left on the rolling cart, but otherwise, nothing's out of place. The only difference is the trail of breadcrumbs littered across the floor.

The only thing missing is Owen.

SEVENTY-THREE

"It's exactly the same." Rob meets my gaze from across the room. He's repeating my search—checking every nook and cranny.

"No, it's not." I crouch low, taking photos of the cut-up photograph, because Detective Cron will be here soon, and then my chance will be lost. "Janie and Chloe were just gone."

"That's what I'm saying—no evidence of break-in. No evidence of a fight."

"But there are breadcrumbs, and that means a trail to some-one's body." I look up to find him leaning on the counter, fingers pressed to jaw in thought.

"But not this time."

"Not this time."

"So, maybe he's not dead." Owen's cold, still body, flickers in my mind. A wave of nausea, panic. I grasp at the nearest thing to balance myself, the edge of a couch.

Rob means it to be comforting, I'm sure. But *he* is Owen and using him in the same sentence as *dead* crushes me with grief.

My stomach clenches at the thought of someone coming in here. Attacking Owen as he still lay in bed. Jumping him in the shower. Dragging him away. But how? Like Janie and Chloe, it doesn't make sense. The only difference this time... "We were warned," I say. "The message on the car."

"That was days ago. Janie and Chloe were taken in between." Rob shakes his head. Comes close to inspect the photos with me. "No way you could have known."

"What gets me is that Hansel was *able* to take him. He's big. He's strong. And he can fight."

"Maybe he drugged him."

That's true. Janie was drugged. My thoughts go to my father. If he were going to commit suicide, I know for a fact there's at least one pistol in that house.

A knock at the door. Rob answers it, then eases over to me. We step outside the room, and it becomes a crime scene, because finally, Detective Cron is taking all of this seriously. We answer her questions for the better part of an hour, accounting for our whereabouts down to the minute.

When she leaves us, and Rob excuses himself to use the bathroom, I slide my phone from my pocket. I check for messages, and there he is.

MMAddict: *Missing something?*

My first reaction is uncontrolled—stabbing the keys until I've typed out *Where is he?* And *Don't hurt him* and *If you hurt him, I'll hurt you.*

But none of that will help Owen. I swallow my anger, my fear, my pride. Force myself to take slow, deep breaths, and shut my eyes, center myself.

It doesn't work very well, but when I type out a message and hit Send, I've stripped it down to something that shouldn't endanger Owen.

Norah Silverton: *There are better ways to get my attention ;-)*

MMAddict: *I've been watching. You like him.*

He's been watching.

The hotel has brought up a cart of basic catering items—coffee, tea, a water pitcher. Cookies, a fruit tray. I pour myself water and wander the hallway. The officer posted at the door eyes me, but I ignore him. Detective Cron said not to go anywhere. She didn't say I had to sit still.

Norah Silverton: *I like you, too... But a girl can only wait so long.*

MMAddict: *Has it been too long?*

Norah Silverton: *I'm just saying there's no need for dramatics. We can skip to the chase.*

Rob comes into view down the hallway. He stops, has a word with the officer. Detective Cron comes to the doorway and looks in my direction, then says something to Rob.

"We can go," Rob says when he gets to me. "I gave them my number." He breathes out, looks around as though answers will appear. "I don't know how he found us here."

My shoulders are tense as Rob beckons toward the elevator. "We'll find him. Detective Cron said it's a good sign there was no—" His voice fades.

"No body," I fill in and walk stiffly beside him. My stomach is hard as a rock, my breathing shallow. All I can think of is the way he smelled. How safe I felt in his arms. How he said he would be here when I got back, how we'd go see Janie, how he'd *see me soon.*

We exit the elevator and head for Rob's rental car. Owen is gone. *Gone.* Maybe, dead... the breadcrumbs. Only Rob's grip on my arm keeps me moving, keeps me steady.

Out of the garage, and onto the street, and I'm almost too distracted to notice Elaine—standing there, just outside of the garage, a camera held up, snapping photos of me. I school my features to something more normal—less shocked, less devastated—but it's too late, and I know those images will be online within the hour.

How long has she been waiting here for me? Not long—we just entered the garage, but somehow... somehow, she knew.

I bury my face in my hands.

At this rate, Rob will be next. And then, I'll really be alone.

SEVENTY-FOUR

I wait for dark to escape.

We're in a house on a corner lot in suburbia arranged by the police and under guard, the thought being Hansel has no trouble accessing apartments, hotels. Perhaps a single-family house will present a challenge. A plain-clothes police officer is posted across the street, watching.

The hotel cameras caught nothing, and due to its status as the hotel of celebrities, the locked floor our room was on had no security cameras.

"Too easy for a security guard to find and sell the footage," the hotel manager had said. So, Hansel got in and out unseen.

Rob's in the living room going through my father's files for anything I've missed, and I'm upstairs under the pretense of a hot bath. I run the water, I pull on my warmest clothes, and I pocket my phone. He'll be mad. He might even drop me as an athlete and fire me as a coach, assuming I make it back in one piece. But he'll be alive, and that's the goal here. To keep him from harm's way.

I lock the bathroom door as I exit the room, because when I don't respond to him coming to check on me, that will buy me another minute or two. My bedroom is the closest to the staircase, and the floorboards creak as I step over them. I go in my room, and lock it, too. The window squeaks as I press it open, and I pause. Wait. Listen. No footsteps.

My phone picks that moment to buzz. I pull it out.

MMAddict: *Interesting choice of words. I think you know what I want.*

Yes, I know what he wants. And just like he's baiting me, I plan to bait him. I force back fear, anger, every emotion. I don't have the time, nor the headspace for them. There's a ticking clock, and when it ends, Owen and Chloe die. I have to hurry.

Norah Silverton: *It's what I want. Like I said, the dramatics aren't needed. They've got people watching me. But I'm leaving. I have nowhere to go. But I'm leaving, all the same. Just in case.*

A pause. I duck through the window and grip the ledge with my hands, lowering myself until my arms are fully extended. It's still a drop, and leaves crunch underfoot as I let myself fall and roll. The phone buzzes, but my goal now is to put distance between me and the house. Between me and Rob, and the danger I'm putting him in every second I'm near him.

But before I can take a step, my feet are swept from beneath me. My wrist is snatched up, twisted, and a foot plants itself firmly in my armpit, pinning me.

"Going somewhere?" I blink into the black night and find dark eyes.

Rob.

* * *

Rob escorts me back inside.

The plain-clothes officer is asleep at the wheel and doesn't even notice as he pushes me through the front door. I swing on him when he releases me, fury lashing through me as he locks it behind him.

"What the fuck, Norah?" Rob's hands whip into motion, as they do when he feels intensely about something. He gestures at me, at the street outside, at the world at large. "Are you *trying* to get killed?" The lecture goes on.

I stand there, stoic, but my mind has drifted elsewhere. How to lock Rob in a room long enough to leave. How to choke him out and make a run for it. How to move forward with my plan, though it's not much of one, so I can rescue Owen, and how I wonder if Owen is even still alive.

I don't realize tears are streaming down my face until Rob goes silent. Sighs with his whole body. Steps forward, wipes the tears away, and pulls me into a hug.

"You don't have to do this alone," he says. "I came here for *you*. To help you. And yes, I thought that would consist mostly of helping you deal with the death of a friend and packing up a house, but I'm here for this, too." A pause. Then, "You'd do the same for me."

I would. I definitely would.

Something gives way inside me, and I hesitate, then say, "Okay, then. But you have to let me do this. I can't wait for the police to get their shit together. Because it'll be too late."

He presses me back and searches my face. "Let you do what?"

I pull out my phone and motion to the couch. We huddle on it, legs pressed together like we're back in his office in Los Angeles, studying footage of fights, figuring out how to best coach our fighter to take out their next opponent. In fact, it's exactly like that.

I open Instagram and hand him my phone. I let him scroll

through the messages, which by now go pretty far back. When he's read them, I say, "Don't be mad. I'm trying to keep everyone alive."

"And what about you?" he asks. "You're going to go to him, aren't you?"

I look down. Try to think of something to say. Decide to go with honesty.

"I didn't get into MMA because I thought the money would be good."

Rob winces. "You told me what happened to you, I just didn't realize—" He stops. Shakes his head. "Fine. We'll do it your way. But Norah?" Our gazes meet. He lifts one brow. "You better win."

SEVENTY-FIVE

We need a game plan. Rob and I huddle together on a couch, poring over my father's computer and my phone.

"Did you find anything in my father's files?" I ask.

Rob's brewed a pot of coffee, and we drink it black. It's acrid on my tongue, but I sip it anyway, for the caffeine, the alertness.

"No, but he really liked Elaine's website. He has notes from there about other serial killers, about Hansel theories." Rob points to a list of suspects, a different list of suspects than the one I saw before.

"He doesn't have any proof, though. Look, he even listed you."

Rob's lips press into a thin line. "Yeah. And Janie, and..." The rest is self-explanatory. Literally anyone I came into contact with in the past decade.

My head pounds with the knowledge he, too, seemed to think it had to be someone I was close to.

I pull up the photos I took of the hotel room, of the "trail of breadcrumbs," and show them to Rob. I can't help but think of Elaine, so often tailing me, then taking photos of us just after Owen disappeared. And now this.

He asks the most obvious question: "Who took the photo?"

I shake my head. "I don't remember it happening. Elaine is handy with a camera, though... as are all of her followers."

"A still from a security camera? What night is this?"

I peer at the photo again. We're dressed up. "Saturday. After Esme's memorial. Guy was there that night. That's when I talked to him. I wonder if he—"

I close the photo and text Guy. *Did you take a photo of Owen and me the night we met at Janie's Cafe?*

Three dots appear almost immediately. Then disappear. I copy the message and send it to Elaine, too, then navigate to her website. She captured me, pale with wide eyes, like I'd seen a ghost—not far off, considering it was a very real possibility Owen is dead.

Tears fill my eyes at the thought. I swipe them away and tap my foot against the coffee table, debate more coffee, debate asking Rob to go for something stronger.

Elaine responds immediately: *Nope. Why, what'd I miss?* and then *Detective Cron is looking into it now. Thought you should know. What can you tell me about your boyfriend? Maybe I can get my fans to help out looking for him.*

She's full of shit, but I'm desperate enough to take her up on that offer—I send her a selfie of us from our date, his full name, in case anyone has seen a man fitting his description being dragged off.

Then a slew of pictures come through from Guy. My eyes widen, and I open my mouth to call for Rob, but the words die on my lips.

Photos of Owen and me. At Janie's. Walking outside. Sparring in the dojang we'd borrowed. A photo of Owen and Rob and me carrying Janie's limp body from the woods. I stop breathing. Dread pools inside me. Rob sits beside me on the couch to look, and when he sees them, goes still.

They aren't cell phone photos—they look professional, crisp

colors, taken with a lens that has the ability to zoom in, because otherwise, we would have seen him. Seen him stalking us. Taking photos for what—his next book?

I type back *What the fuck, Guy?*

And he replies a smiley face. A fucking smiley face.

Coldness seeps through me and rage spirals through my veins. I don't like Guy, but until this moment, I hadn't seriously suspected him of anything other than being a pain in the ass. Other than making a profit off of others' misery and grief. But photos? Of Owen and me?

I enlarge the photos he sent. Go back and forth between one of us at Janie's and the photo of the fragmented bits left at the scene of Owen's disappearance.

Rob says it before I can. "It's the same photo."

I swallow. Hear Guy's voice all over again. *Someone who's good at pretending. Someone who has a normal life. Someone who blends in.* And the timeline fits for everyone except my dad, but Detective Cron said he likely fed himself those pills.

"It's him." My heart pounds, throbbing in my chest. Realization dawns through me, hot, tingling.

What else had he said? One of the types of serial killers returns to the crime scene. Writing a book on it is the ultimate version of that. He gets to pick it apart. Expose every truth. Look like a genius while doing it, and of course, no one suspects the mild-mannered writer.

I switch to Instagram, the message running through my mind. Something along the lines of *I know who you are*, but Rob's hands come down over mine.

I look up and meet his gaze.

"Wait," he says. "Are you sure?"

"It's the same photo, Rob. He sent me photos that prove he was *spying* on me. With Owen of all people, not anyone else. And Owen happens to be who just went missing. And then—" I go back to messages. Point at the smiley face emoji. "Tell me this is normal."

But Rob can't, because it's not normal. If anything, it reeks of sociopathy.

I start to type out an Instagram message, though it feels almost ridiculous at this point—if it's Guy, why not text him directly? But this is our game. This is how we play it.

Norah Silverton: *Isn't it time already?*

A pause. Rob pours more coffee. I can't bring myself to drink it or do anything besides stare at the screen, waiting for a response.

MMAddict: *You're right. We've waited long enough.*

A long pause, and then an address comes through.

MMAddict: *Don't bother knocking. Just come right in. I'll be waiting.*

Rob's already putting it in his phone.

"It's two miles away," he says. He presses the phone into my hands, but I don't look at it, because I know that address by heart.

It's my father's house.

SEVENTY-SIX

We avoid the cop by sneaking out the back door and crossing through the neighbor's yard. We hop the fence and jog down an alleyway. Rob wouldn't let me go alone, and I'm okay with that. His presence at my side as we speed through the cold night air reassures me.

I'm about to face him. *Hansel*, who is Guy. Guy, who this whole time has seemed to have two personalities. One the warm, friendly writer. The other a cold, calculated professional willing to do whatever it takes to get what he wants.

Who has been in town since the killings began.

Who straight up told me to my face I probably knew the killer. Anger rolls through me at the thought of him supposedly coming to help me at the hotel—knowing full well he'd be back later to nab Owen. And not only that, he befriended my father. *Used* him to gain access to me, to my past. And then... then Guy, *Hansel*, killed him, to draw me home.

I hesitate, the memory of my father's notes running through my mind—that he thought maybe Hansel killed my mother, too. Was slowly taking out my whole family? If he'd gotten to me, that's exactly what would have happened. Tears burn my eyes, thinking of my mother's body cold, decayed, wherever he'd left her. God, I hope I'm wrong about that—I hope my father was wrong.

He'd tricked me into being with him all those months ago. Sleeping with him. I try to puzzle that out, understand why he didn't kill me then—he certainly could have. Nausea rolls through me at the thought. I'd slept with the man who'd killed August. Whose memory haunted me this past decade. Whose actions changed my entire life.

We clear the neighborhood, and hop onto a road without sidewalks, but it's a country road, the sort that were plentiful in my childhood and seem to decrease every year. The raw edge gives way to a ditch, and we hop it to run in the grass when a car rolls by.

"We're almost there," I say. "Up the hill and a couple blocks south."

"What do you think he's doing at your father's house?" Rob asks.

I shrug. Don't answer. But I think I know. I think Guy is ready to brag about it all—about fooling me. About reeling me in over drinks that night, and when he found out how I really felt about Hansel, about *him*, he decided to get revenge.

Fuck. I blink. Try to focus on where my feet are landing, on not falling on the cold ground. But I can barely see straight I'm so mad. It's so obvious now that I think about it. I have no idea who Guy was before he became a writer, but it was a good ploy to get close to me. To understand my side of things. And now that the book is out, to continue the tale. Probably with me dead. I was wrong. He doesn't *want me for himself.* He wants revenge, period.

"Norah." Rob's voice breaks through my ruminating. He grabs my arm, yanks me back. "Pay attention," he snaps.

I look up. A car is halfway through a four-way at a dead stop, lights blinding me.

I'm not paying attention, not thinking clearly.

"Sorry. I just—I'm so mad. I can't believe I didn't realize—"

"I'm sure I can't understand what's going through your head right now. But Norah?" He does that thing he does during matches—where he grabs my chin and makes me meet his eyes, except I can barely see him now, on this freezing, moonless night. "Snap out of it. You said it yourself. You didn't become a fighter because you thought the money would be good. You've trained for tonight. This moment. So, focus. Guy is just one more opponent."

"Except he has Owen."

Rob breathes out. Nods. "Except he has Owen. But you're not alone in this fight. I'm here to help."

We run until we reach the edge of the property. At least one light on inside, a gentle glow beyond a blue curtain that blocks our view of what's beyond the window.

"He said to come right in," I say.

Rob nods. "I'll go around the back. See if I can find a way inside."

We separate without another word, and I step over the paving stones that create a pathway to the front door. The smell of dead leaves reminds me of my early morning visit here just days before. I touch my hand to the brass knob. It gives way, spinning under my grip.

I ease the door open, almost expecting Guy's smug face to be waiting for me just beyond it. But the foyer is empty.

I step inside. Glance sideways into the kitchen, still full of now foul-smelling dishes that a week ago held my father's last meals.

A floorboard creaks just ahead in the living room. I move into the doorway and freeze.

Guy stands there. A camera in one hand. His ridiculous hat on his head. He glares across the room at—*Owen*. Owen, who's backed up against the wall. Whose eyes are wide, spooked, who has a slash over one arm, across one cheek, who's lips are swollen and bloody and bruised.

He's been beaten. Badly.

My teeth clench, and I have to hold myself back to not fly at Guy.

Owen's gaze moves to me. "Norah?" he asks, like he can't quite believe I've walked into the room. Like he might be hallucinating. He sways on his feet—drugged, maybe?

"What the fuck?" Guy snaps.

I swallow. Move forward and put myself between them

"He has a knife," Owen says. "Norah, be careful."

And indeed, he does. I couldn't see it before from the angle at which I stood, but in his left hand, Guy holds a blade no shorter than ten inches. A butcher's knife. The exact brand—likely the exact knife—I grew up with. Stolen from the kitchen.

"Are you okay?" I call to Owen.

But Guy steps forward, closer to me, his hands coming up. His face is red, jaw tense, and sweat beads down his brow. I raise my hands, cupping them inward, the best way to defend against a knife attack—keeping that blade from my arteries the best I can.

"What the—" Guy looks between us. "No, I'm not trying to fight you."

"But you are trying to hurt him," I growl.

Guy falters, or trips, or lunges—I can't quite tell which it is. The knife gets too close to me, and I smack it sideways, grab his wrist, shove up with the palm of my hand. His elbow cracks, and he shrieks.

Rob appears behind Guy, coming from the dining room. I keep my eyes trained on Guy, who has dropped the camera—the camera he's been spying on me with—who clutches the knife in his good hand now.

He takes a step back, like he's going to make a run for it, but then Rob is there, snapping his knee from behind. Guy buckles.

Hits the ground. The knife goes flying. I'm on top of him in the next moment, smashing my fists over and over into his torso, and when he loses all fight, I wrap my body around his, the V of my elbow up against his throat. He's unconscious in seconds, but I don't let go.

The fear, the anger, the frustration of every death, every kidnapping, every moment since he held me prisoner and I narrowly avoided death, fills me.

It's only Rob's gentle voice, his fingers prying me off Guy, that keeps me from killing him. From killing Hansel.

SEVENTY-SEVEN

Detective Cron escorts the paramedic pushing an unconscious Guy on a gurney, giving us the side-eye, which later turns into, "Why didn't you call me?" and "I could arrest you for this." Cops swarm the house, taking photos, collecting evidence.

Elaine's face pops through a back window before an officer shoos her away, and Detective Cron threatens to arrest her for interfering with an investigation.

Rob gives a statement, then hovers in the background as I do the same. We're eventually pulled aside by Detective Cron, and I stare longingly at Owen, who mumbles responses to two cops who question him. He's slid down the wall, clutching a dirty kitchen towel to his bloody arm, looking pathetic, but the EMT is busy with unconscious Guy. When Detective Cron has the details, including enough information to hopefully gain access to Guy's—Hansel's—Instagram account, she dismisses me with a wave of her hand and follows an officer who's indicating to the camera bag Guy left behind. I go right to Owen, whose gaze finds mine and doesn't let go. His eyes search mine, takes me in, as though to make sure I'm still in one piece, when he's the one who's all cut up.

"You came for me," he whispers. I kneel beside him. Step back a little when the EMT finally comes over to check his wounds, but I don't leave him.

"Of course, I did." I lean in. Wrap my arms around his neck, pull him into me, hug him carefully, while the EMT tapes his arm up. I can barely believe he's here in front of me—*alive* in front of me.

"You'll have to go to the emergency room for this," the EMT says. "We can give you a ride in a few minutes. What's your pain from zero to ten? I can give you meds."

"No meds." Owen tries for a smile, but it pulls at the cut on his face, and he falters. He's dazed. Eyes too wide. Taking in the scene around us—cops, Detective Cron, Rob.

And then Detective Cron shoos the EMT away and crouches before us.

"You okay?" she asks, and at his nod, continues. "Good. What happened?"

"I don't remember most of it." Owen looks at me. "I was in the hotel room. Then everything was black. And I woke up, and I was here. Where is—" He sits up a little. Winces. The wound on his arm saturates the gauze and tape the EMT wrapped his arm in, and I press my hands to it, holding pressure. Owen stares down at my hands, then up at me, and this time he only tries for a quarter smile. He presses one palm over my own hands. "Where is here?" he asks.

"My father's house. We're at my father's house."

Detective Cron makes a noise in her throat. "Guy's being rushed to the hospital. Paramedic said his blood pressure is crashing." She pins me with a look. "Likely internal bleeding." But she doesn't sound too mad about it. "Off the record, Norah. There were pills found in Guy's camera bag. It looks like he's been sleeping in one of the rooms upstairs. The fact he was camped out here suggests there was some—attachment—to your father. I'll let you know if the pills are a match for what killed him. If I had to hazard a guess—" She lowers her voice another notch. "Killing your father was a sure way to get you back here."

I nod. Hold my face expressionless. Regret not choking the life out of Guy when I had the chance.

"My father knew him," I tell her. "Guy interviewed him for a book."

Detective Cron starts to ask a question, but a rise in volume behind us snares my attention and Detective Cron's, too. She stands, yells, "EMT!" and there's a gasp, a shrill cry, then sobbing.

"What happened?" Owen tries to turn to look.

And then Rob is there. "Chloe. They found Chloe. She looks okay."

I motion for Rob to take up my position with Owen. I wind through the small crowd and into the doorway that leads to what was my father's office. An EMT, a paramedic, two cops, and behind them, Detective Cron. And on the ground, Chloe. Bound. Blindfolded. A gag on the floor beside her, as one of the officers works at the blindfold.

Another cop sees me, nods for me to leave. And I don't want to, but I can't do anything to help her. Owen needs me, and Janie needs to know she's alive. I return to Owen's side. Ask for Rob's phone to call the hospital.

And through the chaos, I know everything is done now. Everything is going to be okay. I'm sure of it.

SEVENTY-EIGHT

The hospital has a soft buzz of fluorescent lighting and medical equipment. Hazy light. No antiseptic smell, but other smells, none of them pleasant. Owen is in the emergency room getting stitched up, and I'm at Janie's bedside, and she's wide awake, and we're sharing a cup of pudding.

"Wait, so he killed your father to get you to come into town?" Janie gives me an incredulous look, scooping more pudding into her mouth.

"We think so. They're working on identifying the pills. She said she would call the second she found out."

Janie shakes her head. Waves the little plastic spoon. "That's fucked up, right there. I can't believe it was him this whole time." She pauses, a faraway look in her eyes. "Does everything line up? From before?"

I frown and rub my fingers over the scratchy blanket covering her bed. "Detective Cron said he was living here in Kansas City then. So, the timelines match up. And come to think of it, isn't it weird he never mentioned he was from Kansas City? Knowing I was from here, too?" I sigh. "Chloe said she never saw him because she was blindfolded or unconscious the whole time. Just like you and Owen. They haven't found whatever video footage she came across. But we caught him in the act." I pause. "And he got into town the day before Esme was killed. Plus, he wanted to write the new book, and this gave him plenty to work with. Did you know he's been spying on Owen and me? Taking photos of us together? It makes sense in a fucked-up way."

"Sociopath. I wish you had killed him." Janie looks down at her now-empty pudding cup. "Think the nurse will give me another one of these?"

I smile. "I'll go ask." I stand and press a kiss to her head. "I'm so glad you're okay. That Chloe's okay." I step outside the room to find Rob at the doorway like a sentry. "What's up?" I ask.

Rob nods. "Detective Cron is wandering around looking for you. They found the same drug in both Chloe's and Janie's systems."

"The antidepressant my father took?"

"No. Some sort of..." He searches for the word. Shrugs. "Something that makes you sleep hard? That's how she described it. She wants to take a blood sample from you, in case you were drugged somehow. They got a sample from Owen when they stitched him up. Something to present in court. She thinks that's how Guy was able to take everyone so easily. He slipped something in their drinks."

"But how—" I try to remember. Guy was at Janie's the night of the memorial, not the night after the supposed copycat was captured. Or was he? I can't remember—we drank so much, so fast, it's a haze. And somewhere in there, we were drugged. Guy could have easily been there that night, and we'd never have noticed.

If we hadn't been so sure we'd caught the guy—if I had abstained, as I so often do—this all could have been avoided.

Rob studies me. "This isn't your fault, Norah." I don't

answer, lost in thought. "I'll call Cron. She had a lab tech with her."

Janie calls something out the door, and I snap back to the moment. I ask for more pudding while we wait, and five minutes later, a woman in dress-casual appears. "I'm from the police department lab," she says. "Sorry to make you wait. The hospital can't do your labs since you're not a patient. This'll just take a moment, and we'll have results sometime tomorrow."

An alcohol swab to my arm. A needle. I look away. Rob smirks.

"You can get punched in the face but don't like needles?"

I roll my eyes at him.

Even if Guy drugged us, he's going to prison now. Hope-fully, forever.

The lab tech leaves, and Rob and I join Janie for another pudding. Eventually, my phone lights up, and I answer to find Owen on the other end, and he, too, joins us in Janie's room, our own little reunion. Lightness and laughter and long looks of relief. It's only when a nurse comes in to announce that Janie—but only Janie—can visit Chloe that we take our leave.

"Wait," Janie says. The guys have already left the room, but I turn, brows raised. "You won't be able to stay at your hotel if it's still a crime scene. Stay at my place."

We take our leave, and Rob calls a cab to get us back to Janie's. Rob takes the couch, Owen and I share the bed, and sweet, peaceful sleep starts to descend over me, Owen safe at my side.

As I feel myself drift off, I reach for his hand beneath the sheets, careful of the bandage just above it.

"Owen?" I whisper.

"Mm?" He's already on the verge of sleep, too, probably thanks to pain medicine the emergency room finally convinced him to take.

I hesitate, blood rushing through me, warming my cheeks.

The words on the tip of my tongue are words I wouldn't have thought I'd say ever again, much less so soon. But there's no way to know what life might throw at us. The soft edge of everything being over, of everyone being okay, dissipates, giving way to a nervous flutter in my chest. We get a second chance. We're alive. Owen is safe. I need to say it now, or I might not, and who knows what happens tomorrow, or the day after. The present being a *present* and all.

I almost laugh out loud at the thought, then take a deep breath and force the words out. "Is it too soon for me to tell you I think I love you?"

Silence. Then a soft chuckle. "It's soon. But not too soon. I think I love you, too."

I fall asleep, no longer thinking *maybe, someday, something*, but *yes, now, us*.

I fall asleep feeling safe.

SEVENTY-NINE

Rob books a return flight for the following afternoon, and I book one for the day after—I still have to see Janie and Chloe home safely and arrange for my father's house to be taken care of. I spend the next day doing this, and snuggling with Owen, who has no serious injuries, but whose cuts and abrasions leave him sore and worn out. I go for a run, not once looking over my shoulder.

When Elaine calls, I hit ignore, tuck my phone in my pocket. Think about how, without the need to check my Instagram for Hansel's messages, maybe I'll leave my phone at home more often.

I climb the stairs to Janie's apartment and find Owen in the kitchen, half braced against the corner of the counter, because he took a knife slash to his lower leg, too. He turns, lets that charming smile light up his face.

"It's a little early, but I thought I'd make dinner for you. Since we missed a lot of the uh—" Another smile, this one with a flush. "You know, normal dating stuff."

I hold up a bottle, the one Janie's bartender shoved in my

hand when I went in after my run to grab a glass of water. "I have wine."

"A perfect night in." Owen and I kiss, and I go about opening the wine bottle, helping him chop garlic since he's only got one good arm. Half an hour later, lasagna is baking, a salad sits ready in a fancy bowl, and we're sipping a Merlot on the living room couch. Outside, the wintry night, complete with fluttering snowflakes outside the window, gives us the perfect background.

"How are you feeling?" I ask.

"When you're not sure if you'll survive the night, a little pain doesn't seem like such a big deal."

He leans toward me, and I tilt my head, resting it on the couch as we sit sideways, staring at one another. One kiss. Then two. Then his mouth curves into a smile against mine. "I was worried I wouldn't see you again. That—" His voice breaks. He pulls back and takes a deep breath. Sips the wine, carefully sets it back on the table. "I tried to get free. To warn you. That's when—" He gestures at his arm.

A beat of silence. I crawl closer, until our foreheads rest against one another. It's intimate in a nonsexual way, in a way I haven't had with a man in—well, ever. It's somehow better than sex.

My phone vibrating in my pocket breaks the moment.

Owen pulls back, murmurs he'll check on the lasagna. I pull the phone out, and it's Elaine again, likely calling for an *update to the Hansel case!* for her website. Or to interview Owen, or heck, maybe both of us. Wouldn't that make her website buzz? *COUPLE SURVIVES HANSEL—TWICE!*

I tuck it away before he comes back—better to not bother him with her. With her stalking tendencies, and with a new story, I have half a mind to file for another restraining order. But that would require I stay in town longer. And as much as part of me wants to, I can't. It's time to go home. Get back to training my fighters. Fulfilling obligations to the gym's sponsors. I'll fly back another weekend to go shopping with Janie, when she and Chloe are both up to it. Hell, maybe they'll want to elope after this. I wouldn't mind joining them on a tropical island if that's their thing.

Speaking of getting home...

Owen settles back on the couch. Winces. Replaces it with a painted-on smile. I'm all too familiar with pain, having had plenty of cuts, bruises, and stitches myself.

"You said you would move to L.A. if we... you know, became a thing," I say.

"I did."

"I'm not saying you should look for a place. But you could come visit. I need to come back and see Janie soon for wedding dress shopping and to help her plan the wedding. We could go back and forth a few times. See if—" I shrug.

Owen's hair falls forward over his forehead. His dimple appears. "I'm down for that."

We eat dinner on the couch, our bare feet and knees tucked up against one another. It's almost embarrassing, the way I feel like a teenager, my heart thumping away in my chest, how my body is warm, even when I strip down to one of my training tanks. I was attracted to Owen before, but now, knowing we can relax together, knowing we're *safe* together, and that we've already gone through hell and back—well, it feels right. As corny as that sounds.

When the kitchen is clean, Owen suggests we get out and do something. "Something easy," he adds. "I've been cooped up all day, but I don't want to overdo it."

"Ice cream?"

"Too cold."

"Hmm." I hesitate. Then, "The bookstore? I think they pulled all the books after it hit the news today. The local NPR station mentioned it."

"Wandering the bookstore for entertainment. Feels like high school." He flashes a grin, but the mention of high school brings back other memories—August-like memories. A moment of sober reflection. I grab our coats and help him into his.

"Let's do it," I say. "We can't live in the past forever."

EIGHTY

A sunny day, white-yellow light shining through orange and red leaves. The wind blows, and they flutter to the ground and cart-wheel along the pavement. It's beautiful. Autumn in Kansas City.

All I think is they're dead. The leaves are dead.

I'm walking now. Hand in hand with someone. *But I can't see who. I spin, and I yank my hand away, and yet, I can't detach myself from him. From* Hansel. *Even if I can't see him, I know it's him. Know he won't let me go.*

My eyes open, but I don't move. The ceiling is old-school popcorn style, and I study the misshapen bumps as my breathing slows, a trickle of sweat runs from my neck to my back to the soft sheet beneath my body. Owen is fast asleep, his eyes shut, mouth slightly open. One leg is slung over mine, trapping me. I reach for my phone. Prop myself up on one elbow. Scroll through photos that make me happy, hoping maybe that will shake the nightmare from my consciousness—Janie and me, the last time she visited me in California, and we went to the beach. Owen and me, taking a selfie at the bookstore last night, mugs of hot cocoa from the cafe in our hands. I send Janie a quick text—*Awake?*—because she's an early riser, but she doesn't answer back.

It's 4:32 a.m. Too early to get up. And yet... I slide out from beneath Owen. Pace into the living room, the kitchen. Start coffee. Shuffle through the dark to the big window that looks out over the Plaza, and just stand there, the dream running through me again.

I had nightmares for years after August died. They mostly stopped when I started fighting. Started winning the fights, started putting the past behind me, one punch-jab-hook at a time. I thought this would end in a true fight between Hansel and myself. Do I wish it had? Maybe. But it's over now, and that has to be enough. It's more than I could have asked for, really.

I settle on the couch with a cup of coffee, extra cream, extra sugar, pull a soft blanket over my knees, and go to work. I post a photo taken during a photoshoot last month, but one that hasn't been on social media yet—tag a sponsor. Add a quote by someone inspirational. I type up a quick post for Twitter, saying I can't wait for the upcoming fights. I answer two fan emails with semi-personalized responses. And somewhere in there, my phone buzzes, a text.

Not Janie.

Detective Cron: *Call me when you're up. I have news.*

I roll off the couch and hit Call. Pace the floor as the phone rings.

When she answers she says, "That was fast," but jumps right into it. "The antidepressant in your father's system was the same one Guy had in his bag. We will be investigating his death as a murder." She pauses, as if to let me digest this information, and I can't deny a ripple of pain rolls through my chest.

My father didn't drink himself to death. He didn't commit suicide. He was murdered.

She goes on, "It's possible Guy does actually have a prescription for it, but I can't find one anywhere in his hometown. And Guy's currently in a medically induced coma, so I can't ask him about it." She says that last bit with a dry tone, and satisfaction zings through me. *Good.* I'd gladly put him in the hospital again.

Detective Cron rattles off more facts, ones I'm not sure the meaning of, but they seem important to her. Then she adds, "Janie and Chloe both had a pain medicine known for its sedative properties in their systems. I should have results back on your and Owen's toxicology later this morning. I'll call with an update. But everyone reported sleeping hard the night Janie was taken. Waking up woozy." More details, and then, "Plus, there's plenty of evidence to tie him to it. Photos of Owen tied up and Chloe unconscious on his camera. Damning evidence. I'll call when I have an update."

We disconnect.

I change clothes. Scribble a note for Owen—*Gone running. Be back soon*—and step out onto the icy sidewalk.

I take off at a sprint, hoping the run will siphon off the tide of rising anger in me, thinking about everything Guy has done. I'm two miles from Janie's when she texts back, and I step behind a building to block the wind. *I'm awake. Hopefully discharged later today. Chloe's okay. How are you? How's Owen? Why are you up so early?*

I answer her questions one by one, then run a few more miles, contemplating the day, the week. I'll fly home. Rob will pick me up, and maybe things will feel almost normal.

Except *normal* means alone, and that doesn't feel quite right after nearly a week in the company of friends.

But Owen is flying out to spend a long weekend with me. My heart warms thinking of that. He's one good thing that has come out of this.

That afternoon I tick more items off my to-do list: I meet

with a woman who will clean out my father's house in exchange for part of the profits of selling everything he owned. I book a flight to come back to Kansas City in a month to see Owen and help Janie pick out that damn dress we never managed to go shopping for. I visit Esme's grave, the dirt still raw and turned, and I tell her we found him. We got justice for her.

At 3 p.m., my bag is packed. My stomach churns. Owen's truck is still in the shop, having the paint touched up where the red spray went beyond the windshield, and he took a cab to retrieve the rental I left near the woods *days* ago. He insisted on it, even with his injured leg. "It's an automatic," he'd said. "I'll be fine." And I'm expecting him back any minute to drive me to the airport.

I look around the apartment, wishing Janie and Chloe were here. They were supposed to be—for me to see with my own eyes they are okay, to say goodbye—but the discharging physician got drawn away to a sicker patient, and so their discharge was delayed.

"We'll *just* miss you," Janie said over the phone. "But go catch your flight. Go home. You'll be back soon."

And so, I packed my bags. I texted Rob.

Me: *Yes, I'm coming.*

I smiled when he replied with *Good, we have fights to train for.*

I grab my jacket and shove it in my bag, and look around Janie and Chloe's apartment, making sure I haven't forgotten anything. My running shoes still sit near the door. I grab them, tie their laces together, unzip my bag—and my phone buzzes. Repeatedly.

Elaine. Again. When I don't answer, she sends a text.

Elaine: *You told me to update you if I found something. I have*
a source in the hospital. Here's what all the lab tests showed.
Attached a screenshot of that. I'll have police lab results soon,
too, and send those along.

I sigh out. She's grasping at straws—hoping I'll decide to
talk to her. Hoping in the aftermath of all this, I still won't send
her the photo I took of her break-in to the scene of my dad's—
murder, I suppose. But the case is over. We got the guy. We got
Hansel.

I don't want to think about it—about what he had planned
for me. Owen. Chloe.

I open the file, taking a quick glance over it. Janie's and
Chloe's names. Screen grabs of their labs coming up positive,
some complicated drug name. Other screenshots from their stay
at the hospital. My lip curls in disgust. This is a huge violation
of their privacy. Elaine's website is popular, but it's ridiculous
that someone is willing to break the law to send her this, especially considering it's over.

Owen pulls up in front of the building in the rental car. He
climbs out slowly, pauses, shuts his eyes and breathes in the cold
winter air. I smile. Savor this moment because I'll miss him until
I see him again. He starts around the car, and my stomach flips
—it's our last few minutes together. He'll come in to collect me.
We'll go to the airport. We'll say goodbye.

I hesitate, because maybe I should stay a little longer. For
him, for Janie, for Chloe. But... I shake my head. No. I've been
here long enough. I'll be back soon. I need to get back to real
life, back to my gym. And what's more, after this week, I *want* to
feel like life is normal. That requires L.A., not Kansas City.

When Detective Cron calls, literally as Owen's footsteps
are audible up the staircase, irritation prickles along my skin. I
want a few more uninterrupted minutes with him, that's all.
The news won't change between now and then.

The door creaks open, and Owen comes in. "Hey." He smiles and unzips his coat. "What have you been up to?"

"Just getting ready." I beckon to the bag. My smile wavers, and he sees it, and his forehead furrows.

"It's okay. I'll see you in a week. I'm—" Owen holds up the bandaged arm. "Almost good as new."

I tighten my mouth. Refuse to cry because I am not that kind of woman. I'm going to carry my own damn bag down the stairs, put it in the car, and get on a plane home. I breathe deep. Nod. Say, "I'm okay," and almost mean it.

"We've got a bit before we have to leave. Let's sit down." We go to the couch, and he pulls me into his lap with only the slightest wince.

"You're cold," I say.

"It's freezing outside again. You're getting out just in time, big snowstorm blowing in tonight." He hugs me tight. I shut my eyes, let my head rest on his shoulder. Wish I could fall asleep like this, then remember, in just a week—less than that, actually —I can do this again.

"Want some tea?" He presses a kiss to my forehead.

"Sure, but I'll—"

"No, you stay here." He meets my eyes, all warmth and coziness. "I'll make the tea. I can do that one-handed."

I stay on the couch and watch as he strides over to the kitchen. His shoulders flex beneath his thermal as he reaches for the kettle, and I long to smooth my hands over them. To feel his strength, to feel secure with him in a way I haven't felt with anyone, ever.

Owen turns, flashes me a dimpled smile, then goes back to finding mugs and tea bags. In my lap, my phone buzzes again—another email from Elaine. This one is titled POLICE LAB.

I sigh and open it, because I want to get it over with—I want to leave Kansas City with nothing left to wonder about, no stone left unturned, with no excuse to ever communicate with Elaine again.

It's a series of screenshots again, but the formatting is different, because it's the police lab. My name, followed by *positive*, the drug name, more details. Below my name is Owen's, and next to his name is...

I blink down at the phone.

Negative.

His drug test is negative.

The world around me goes still. For a moment, every sound is filtered out, and I exist in a vacuum of silence, all by myself. Then the heavy *thump-thump-thump* of my heart takes over.

It's not possible for his drug test to be negative. If anything, he should have higher levels than the rest of us. He was drugged that night at Janie's bar. He was drugged again when Guy—when *Hansel*—nabbed him. It's a mistake. It must be a mistake.

I hit reply and type out *Are you sure these are right? It says Owen is negative. That's not possible.* I hit Send. A second later, the reply comes through.

> *My source says this was double-tested for accuracy and that strict protocols were followed. Why?*

I blink at her words. She hasn't put it together yet. She doesn't realize what it means.

But I do.

I look up to find Owen leaning against the counter, watching me with a small smile. His eyes are that same warm brown, but I blink, and it's like the mirage fades away. I know those eyes. I've seen them before. A thousand times, even.

In my nightmares.

EIGHTY-ONE

When my phone buzzes again, it's a phone call from Elaine.

"Everything okay?" Owen turns back to the kettle. The hiss of the water boiling, like the rain falling that night—

I blink, snap back to the moment. I silence her call, and a second later, another notification pops up. A voicemail.

My body doesn't feel like my own. I have to move. Have to do something. My gaze flicks to the door. Maybe I can escape. Maybe I can—

"Here you go." A mug is pressed gently into my hand. Owen lowers his body next to mine, the couch shifting beneath his weight, the creak of the frame, and still, I can't quite get myself to move. To react.

Shock. This is shock.

I glance down, and the visual voicemail read out pops. *I just realized what the labs mean. I pulled some background info— Marines—Owen was a medic, with knowledge of drugs. He was kicked out when too many went missing. He had access to the same antidepressant that killed your father, the sedative that—*

I swipe away before he can see my phone screen. None of

this is what he told me. He said his enlistment was up, that he—he'd been gone this whole time, a soldier in the Marines.

The whole time the murders had stopped, he'd been gone.

He'd *hunted* people—he told me himself.

And he was August's *boyfriend*.

That stops me. Why would he have killed her? But then, why had he killed any of the half dozen women who were found at the end of a trail of figurative breadcrumbs during our time in high school?

Because he's a serial killer, that's why. Serial killers don't need motive.

But then, why is he killing now after all this time?

Guy had said someone I knew. I couldn't have imagined it would be Owen. We have a connection, the sort I've never felt with another man. Though when it gets right down to it, I suppose I barely know him.

"Are you okay?" Owen sets his mug carefully on the coffee table and reaches out, taking my hand with his one good one. "I'll miss you, but I'll see you this weekend—" He's still talking, but I'm stuck inside my own head. I need to react. I need to *do something*, but my body and mind just won't work together.

I nearly killed Guy. He's in a medically induced coma. Meaning he can't defend himself. If Owen had kidnapped Guy he could have planted all the evidence. Given himself the cuts. Taken those photos. Or had Guy taken some, and then Owen took some of himself when—

"Norah?"

My heart goes wild in my chest.

Maybe I can get out. Maybe I can tell him I need to grab something from the car or the restaurant downstairs. Maybe I can—

Wait, wait, wait. This is *Owen*. Owen, who I think I love. Who I cooked dinner with last night. Who helped me carry Janie back to the car after Hansel left her at the cabin. And

Chloe—*shit*. He'd been the one to go keep Chloe company when she was scared, while I stayed behind with Guy. And then she'd disappeared.

I look up at him again, at those deep, dark eyes I've slowly fallen for over the past week. The planes of his face, the dimple as he smiles, the concerned look he gives me now.

I thought there was familiarity there because we went to high school together. Because he was August's boyfriend. But that's not it. There's familiarity there because... I inhale, exhale.

It *wasn't* Guy who did these things.

It was Owen.

And Owen is Hansel.

"Just... just a second. Janie texted. She said—I'll be right back."

I set the tea down and get to my feet. My body is stiff, but I move toward the front door as naturally as I can. Like Janie mentioned something was being dropped off, or like I just need to grab something.

"Norah?" His voice climbs a pitch, a thread of concern woven through it now. But he's far enough away, still sitting on the couch, that maybe I can do this. Maybe I can get out before he catches me.

I'm nearly there, holding my breath, clutching my phone in my hand like it's a lifeline.

"Norah?" Again, and louder, like he's right behind me.

Time slows down. I sprint those last few feet to the door.

The phone vibrates, but my hand is on the knob, and I'm close, so close.

The door opens an inch, giving me entry to the hall, but then he's here. Beside me.

"Norah."

Owen grabs my arm. Turns me to him.

"What's wrong?" He frowns, those dark eyes peering into mine, full of concern. "Are you okay?"

For a moment, I think I must be in a dream. An awful, horrible dream, my mind playing tricks on me. This is *Owen*. Who's been part of this battle since day one, since he walked in the door of Janie's—*shit, shit, shit*. And not ten minutes later, I found Esme in the alley. Dead.

It's so fucking obvious. How didn't I see it?

But I smile. Force myself to take a breath. Grab his hand, yank him into a hug.

Not because I want to ever fucking touch him again. But because he has to believe it. Believe me. Believe I can love him.

It's the only way I'll survive.

Again.

EIGHTY-TWO

I notice two things in quick succession.

One: he knows something is wrong. He takes me in his arms, but he's stiff, and he breaks the hug before I do.

Two: when he presses me back, my arm catches on something hard on his hip. His gun.

I consider going for him—a knee to the groin, circling and sweeping his legs, taking him to the ground. But he's bigger than me. Stronger. And he knows how to fight. Add in his gun, and I'm on dangerous territory. In a fair fight, I think I'd beat him— hell, I did beat him on the mats, plenty of times. But this isn't fair. And there's that extra element—he's a *serial killer*.

"What's wrong? Norah?" Owen ducks, putting us eye-to-eye. It takes everything in me to meet his gaze. To hold it. To force a smile to my mouth.

"Sorry. I just—" *Think.* "I thought I saw Janie outside. I got distracted and—" *Good. This is good. Keep going.* "One sec. I think they're home. I want to say goodbye."

I turn to open the door—to get the *hell* out. But my phone buzzes, and I jump, drop it and it smacks to the ground, the screen lit up with *Elaine*. It buzzes once more and goes still.

"Shit. Clumsy." I lean to pick it up, and it lights up again. This time, *Rob*.

"You should answer it. He's your ride from the airport, right?" Owen kneels, snatches up the phone before I can. Movement surprisingly quick, considering his injuries. He hits the green button to accept the call, then the speaker phone. He holds it out to me.

Our eyes meet over the phone screen.

And I know, right then, he suspects something.

"Hey, Rob—"

"Norah, I just heard from Detective Cron. Elaine said— well, never mind that. Are you safe? Did you get away from him? Where are—"

Owen ends the call. Sighs. Drops the phone into his pocket.

"This isn't how I'd hoped this would go."

A memory flashes—Hansel, so close, too close. My whole body trembling. A frightened little girl. I steel myself, try to press back the fear and wait—wait for him to come at me. To reach for me. To pull the gun and—and I don't know what. *Do something.* But he doesn't. The silence stretches, and I mentally measure the distance to the front door. Close. A foot, maybe two.

Close enough? He's just as close.

But Owen—*Hansel*—he's got that other look to his eyes, fierce, determined, and another memory hits me. A memory of seeing those eyes the night August died. The light dim, and he wore a mask, but I saw that same look slanted my way, and if I were still doubting this is *him*, that doubt is dispelled from my mind.

This isn't Owen. Not really.

This is Hansel.

Hansel smiles, and his dimple appears, and I flinch. I stare into the eyes of the man I've been falling for, and the pain in my gut is sharp, like a knife twisting deep. It rises through my chest, into my throat. Anger flares in its wake—anger at him for everything he's done. Anger at myself, for falling for it.

"How exactly *did* you think this would go?" My teeth are clenched, but I keep my tone neutral. Not letting the anger come through. Not yet.

Hansel tilts his head. "My goal is for us to be together, of course."

Of course.

But I knew that already. I wait for him to go on.

"This has all gotten pretty complicated, Norah. We should sit down. I'd like to explain. I think once you see all I've done to make this happen—"

He turns, gestures at the couch, like it's yesterday, like we're going to curl up and sip wine and have a nice chat. And all I can think is I *might* be able to get out the door, but if he pulls that gun out, which I've seen him do with blinding speed, then I'm dead. Or at least shot. And neither of those lead me to living to see tomorrow, nor keeping Janie and Chloe safe. Janie and Chloe, who will be home soon. And Jesus, Owen is a *family* friend.

Fear clutches at me as I imagine August, cold and dead. And then I see Janie there beside her. And Chloe, too. I can't fuck up. *I can't.*

"Okay." I summon a smile, but it falls flat. His features crease in sympathy, and he takes my arm, like he *understands what I'm going through*, and he leads me to the couch. I sit. He presses my tea mug back into my hands, and again, if only he didn't have a gun, this would be so easy.

"Here. This will help." He sits beside me and turns toward me. He waits for me to take a sip, and he nods. "Good."

And he's still searching my face, my eyes, like I'm a lover who wants to break up with him, and he's here to plead his case. I take another sip. Take a slow, settling breath. And I play my part. I mirror his body, turning toward him slightly. Meet his eyes. Try to look attentive, interested.

Round two.

"I'm going to tell you everything. Because I want honesty between us, always."

I smile. Nod.

And then something shifts. His eyes, nervous just a second ago, now gleam with slow-simmer excitement. His hands fold in his lap, a posture I've never seen him take. Even his face is different. His features seem to relax. And he's calm. *Too calm.* Whatever anxiety he's shed, I've gained, because this is not the man I know. It's like I've turned a corner and come face to face with a giant tiger, contemplating its next move with quiet focus.

"I haven't always killed," he says. His voice is different. Unemotional. Apathetic. Distanced from the here and now. Like he's caught in a different world inside his mind, and he's channeling it to me through his words.

It's the same voice I heard the night August died. Automated. Devoid of humanity.

"You've probably heard what"—and now, the hint of a lip curl—"*people like me* are like. That we kill small animals. Enjoy torture from a young age." A shrug. A beat of silence. And then, "That wasn't me. I was normal. Normal as could be. I just liked —" And his eyes slide to one side, like something or someone is standing there. "Knowing I could, if I had to. Life wasn't always great at home, and knowing I could, you know—" His eyes flash to me. And I force myself to not move a fucking muscle. "Stop it all. If I decided to. Thankfully, it never came to that. My parents are both still living. Siblings, too."

"I remember your brother from high school. He was a couple years behind us, right?" *Keep him talking. Act supportive.*

Hansel tilts his head, and he's definitely somewhere else. Somewhere I can't see. And I'm glad for that. He continues as though he can't hear me. "But I got to high school, and high school was stressful, you know? So many people. Thousands. Crammed into one building. Attitudes, too. Everyone thinks they're fucking great. Well, you know how that went."

And now he looks at me. *Really* looks at me. "No one really cares about you in high school. Not the teachers. Not the other kids. Your parents think you're finally old enough you should have your shit together, so they go back to basically being teenagers themselves." The quarter smile again, but it doesn't reach his eyes. His eyes are dark, dark brown, almost black, orbits of... *Insanity* is the word that comes to mind.

"You were the first person to really care, Norah. That night, in the woods. You *saw* me. The real me. And to think, I was about to—to kill you, too." He stops himself. The smile fades. "You saw what I did to August. My own girlfriend. And I even liked her. I thought she liked me, too." He reaches out, takes a sip of his tea. "I was wrong."

"What do you mean?"

"She didn't tell you?" For a moment he's back—*Owen* is back. But it's just a mask. I see that now. A mask he wears for me.

"Tell me what?"

"We broke up at prom that night. Well, *she* broke up with me. Right before you left."

I think back, remember August had come away breathless after saying goodbye to Owen, but I assumed it was because they'd been making out. I hadn't imagined she'd ended things with him.

"She said it was because we were going to college. Had our whole lives in front of us. That bullshit. But then you—" He shifts closer, suddenly. His hand brushes my knee. I force myself to stillness. Let his fingers trail a line across my cheek. "You told me you could care for somebody like me. The *real* me."

EIGHTY-THREE

I remember the moment I looked at him and asked him his name. Was that the moment he meant? The moment I treated him like a human being. *Him*, Hansel, not Owen. No one had ever acknowledged that other side of him. That must have been the moment that saved my life.

Owen pulls away, and I try not to look relieved.

"When you asked for time, I gladly gave it. Your father was sick. I could understand that. I needed to get away, myself. And you—you made me want to be better. I watched you go home that night. Watched you go to your little house. I saw as the police and press descended on you, and I wished I could be there. To help. I realized who I am, no matter how you felt, might not mesh with who you are. With the future you wanted. So, I decided to change. I had time. Why not, right?"

Hansel stands. Goes to the window. Stares out of it. His voice drops again, that monotone that sends spiders up my spine. "So, the Marines. I'd talked to the recruiter a few times already. Anything to get out of my house. And that's what I did. Until..." His shoulders raise and lower in a sigh. "Until they noticed meds missing. I wasn't abusing medications. Wasn't selling them. I was just stockpiling. Just in case. And then... a decade had passed, and I figured—if you weren't going to come back to me..." His voice trails off.

When he turns back, that glint in his gaze has become a hardened focus.

"The decision was made for me, though. They kicked me out. I came back a month ago. And you're the only thing I could think of. I watched your career, of course. I knew where you were, what you were doing."

My stomach churns. This is what it is to be in the public eye. To know anyone and everyone has some level of access to you.

"But I wanted to see you in person. I had to know if—if you were still right for me. And then—" His chin lifts. "Then Guy's book came out, and I knew the truth." He takes the spot beside me, motions smooth, mechanical. And like he's read that damn book a thousand times, he recalls, *"According to Ms. Silverton, she used her womanly wiles to trick the sexually frustrated serial killer into falling for her. Ms. Silverton told him she would willingly stay with him, but her ailing father needed her as a caregiver."*

A grim smile. "You clearly weren't caring for your father. But I thought maybe your career was a way of caregiving. Providing money. And I knew if I killed him, you'd have to come home. Either way, it was better your father was dead. I'd been patient long enough. And honestly, my dear Norah, I was pissed. Telling another man you tricked me?"

He did kill my father. I think of my mother—her absence. My father's theory was that the serial killer meant to kill us all, but that hadn't been Hansel's goal, it sounds like. He let me live because I saw him for who he was. My father came after that, to pull me home. Which means surely... surely, my mom is still out there in the world somewhere. I tuck that idea around myself like a warm cloak. *Come to think of it, I am feeling warm... and tired. So tired.*

Hansel's head swivels back and forth slowly. *He* moves like he's in slow motion, sitting back, turning to face me. "But then I met you again, after all this time." Hansel reaches out, presses his thumb to my chin, meets my gaze. He's fuzzy this close up. He leans in, and he's fuzzier still, and I realize something is wrong. With me.

"I know Guy lied. Or maybe you *had* to say those things, to protect yourself. To protect me. After all, it's not *normal* to love someone like me." A chuckle, distant now. My body sinks into the couch, and all I can think is he said *this will help* when he gave me the tea, and I've almost drained the mug, and *of course* he would drug me. He drugged everybody. "I tried to become someone normal, Norah. For you. For *us*. For ten years, I didn't hurt a soul outside of what the military required of me. But then your father had to die. There was no away around it. And then I had to show you I'm still here, I'm waiting for you, and Esme was just *there*, and it was easy, and before I knew what happened, she was dead."

He goes quiet.

Or rather, I go unconscious.

EIGHTY-FOUR

Owen's voice hits me before anything else. Murmuring to himself—"Wine or maybe something warm. Coffee? No. Let's see—"

My eyes open. Trails of yellow light from a single lamp over wood paneling. It's dark out. A window shows me deep purple-blue sky, a single star, twinkling between the slowly swaying branch of a tree. The sharp smell of cedar.

These observations come to me in fragmented bits, my reality building around myself slowly, combining until I realize I'm awake. Alive.

And it hits me. Not Owen.

Hansel.

My chest feels like a giant claw has reached in, snatched up my heart, squeezed. I fight for a breath, try to push back the rising panic. I raise my hands, and I'm not tied down. I take a longer look around myself, already weighing my options.

Hansel faces away, busy at what appears to be a makeshift kitchen counter. We're in a cabin. New-ish, the paneling still rough, raw. One relatively small room. A fire crackles in a wood-burning stove, with one of those giant thick iron chimneys that goes straight up the inside. A door, but it's past where he stands now, his back to me, sorting through items in a cabinet above the counter.

I slam my eyes shut, force my breath to slow. Pretend to still be asleep. Which isn't hard—the edges of my consciousness are soft. Like they were a few mornings back, the morning Janie went missing.

How did I miss it? It seems almost... obvious now. But that doesn't matter. What matters is surviving. Just like last time.

I slit my eyes open enough to watch him. Open and close my fists, squeeze my toes, tense my legs. Everything seems to be working. I might be okay to run. Might be okay to take a swing at him. Then I spot my phone. It rests on a table made of the same wood as the cabin but sanded down and smooth on top. His phone is there, too. But where is his gun?

It must be on him.

Which means I need to be careful. If there were no gun in play, I'd go for it—go for him. Fight the fight of my life.

Instead, I take in the room one more time—noting objects I could use as weapons (a broom, a chair), escape routes (that door, the window), and trying to estimate how long I've been out (four or five hours, at least—it's dark through the window).

Then, I say, "Hey," in a soft voice, and when he looks over his shoulder, force a shy smile.

"You're awake." A grin—Owen's grin, dimple and all—but I see it now in his eyes. Hansel's eyes.

I don't know how I missed it this whole time.

"Coffee? Wine? Hot chocolate? I have some tea, too."

I want to say yes, because my throat is dry, my head is foggy, and yet accepting beverages from him has been anything but a good idea.

"Let me." An excuse to get up. To move around, to see how much the drugs have affected me. He hesitates—turning halfway to intercept my attempt to come to the countertop, but then he lowers his arms. Steps back. The gun is indeed at his hip. I purposefully don't look at it and instead reach for a box of tea. Tea is sealed in individual packets—not something he can add drugs to without me knowing. "Kettle?" I ask.

He turns his back on me and steps in the direction of the wood-burning stove. In the half-second I have, I ease a drawer open to find it empty. The next, however, has four knives in it. I memorize which drawer it is, shut it silently, because I have nowhere to hide a knife. And he's back with an old-fashioned kettle, holding it with a fuzzy hot pad holder.

"Thank you." I watch as he pours into the mugs I've prepared. His free hand skims my back, the way he did before, and it takes effort to not react. "I'll bring them over," I say, and he turns his back, and I swap them, just in case, giving him the one that I would have been most likely to take.

Hansel pulls the table close to the daybed, and motions for me to sit there. He pulls up the only chair catty-corner to it.

"I'm sorry I had to drug you," he says. "But we couldn't stay at Janie's. She and Chloe were going to be back soon, and we have more talking to do."

I nod. Press the hot mug between my hands, realizing it's chilly in here. "Understandable."

"Is it?" he asks, and when I look at him, he seems curious.

"I'd prefer you don't do it again. But I understand why you did."

Hansel studies me. "You're very good at being understanding. What's the last thing you remember me telling you?"

"My father. Esme."

Again, that change—someone personable becoming someone focused, lost in his own world. Cold. "I began messaging you, hoping you'd realize it was me. I wanted to have *honest* conversations with you. I took Janie, but we had been spending time together. I could tell you... *liked* me. That version of me. And I wanted to understand you better. I also no longer wanted to hurt you or the people you cared about. I wanted to prove to you I could—" A shake of his head. "—*not* kill someone. So, I decided not to kill Janie."

"Why did you take her, then?" I ask.

"Originally, she was going to be the lead-in for taking you. For fixing what I should have done a decade ago. I took her, posted photos on her Instagram, set the whole thing up to draw you out." His eyes meet mine, and I'm not sure which side of him I'm seeing—cold-blooded killer, or the warmer version of him, Owen, which might be even creepier considering it's an act. "The best revenge for tricking me. Kill your best friend. Make you watch. And perfect symmetry, what with them being twins. But since I'd realized you either didn't mean what you told Guy in the interview for the book—or that Guy was lying —" Hansel pauses. Sips his tea. His motions are almost... robot-like. Like he has no control over this side of himself, as though someone has a remote control and is puppeteering him from afar. The skin at the back of my neck crawls, watching it. "I decided to use it to prove to you I didn't have to kill. That I could be—" And he pauses. His lips and tongue adjust, as though tasting the word. "*Normal.*"

"You drugged us then, too?"

A glazed smile. A nod. "Yes."

Neither of us speaks. Part of me wants details—part of me doesn't give a fuck.

But then he says, "I wrote on my own truck, of course. It made you feel *concerned* for me. Shifted suspicion away. Win-win. I used a third-party app to time messages to send on Instagram at the same time we were together, so you wouldn't suspect me." He stops, smiles vaguely, savoring it, it seems like. "But my favorite part of all of this has been seeing how much you hate Guy. It meant I could do something about him for you. It meant I'd been wrong all along, and maybe you were still for me. And I decided to be the normal version of me. To be Owen.

But there were already murders, disappearances, and—someone had to take the fall."

"Guy."

"Yes. If Guy did it, everything could end. I could be Owen. Hansel would be Guy, and in jail. We could have a life together. But someone figured something out." Hansel's eyes land on me. "What was it? What did I forget?"

I open my mouth and find I'm reluctant to tell him. But what does it matter at this point?

"Labs. They took blood from all of us at the hospital. Including you. You were the only one who didn't test positive for the drug you used to sedate us the night of Esme's memorial."

"I should have known better. I *do* know better." A grim smile. "I don't make a very good pretend victim. I tried to just go along with everything."

"I believed you," I say. "The cuts on your arm and leg? The way you looked like he'd hurt you—" I pause. Swallow. Relive that momentary anguish of seeing the man I thought I loved hurt, how much it hurt *me*. In the end, Hansel is the one who tricked me, *again*.

Hansel had been living his life this whole time, just waiting for me to come home. I'd been living in the public eye, which meant he could watch me from afar—from literally across the world. He'd tried to *change* for me. A gag works its way from my stomach to my throat, and I squeeze my eyes shut, force it back down. My father's and Esme's deaths were because of this. Because of me. Because of the words I'd spoken to him *a decade ago* promising him I could love someone like him, and the psychopath had *waited with bated breath*. Meanwhile, I'd trained, in case I ever met him or someone like him again.

What was that statistic of being attacked by a serial killer? .00039 percent. And the odds of it happening a second time? They'd assured me it wouldn't.

They called me the lucky one.

I almost laugh, thinking I *proved* them *wrong*. But tears are in my eyes, and Hansel makes a sound in his throat. I open my eyes to see his gaze boring into mine, and his hands come up, carefully lift the mug from my hands. He sets it on the rough wood table. He adjusts, and he telegraphs his next move, and I let him come in for a hug, and I let him hold me tight, and I fake-sob into his shoulder.

I have no idea what he thinks I'm crying about. And I don't care.

Because from this angle, I can grab his gun.

EIGHTY-FIVE

It's been years since I've shot a gun. But it was one of my father's hobbies, and after my mother left, when I was spending a lot of time alone, he briefly made it his mission to teach me to use one. I've forgotten a lot—but I remember guns are more difficult to yank out of a holster than they make it look in movies. Which means I can't just grab it. I need to distract him.

Hansel strokes my back. Whispers, "It's all going to be okay. We can disappear together. Forever."

Forever. There's that word again. It steels my spine.

"You promised you'd come back to me. Told me you could love someone like me."

His words worm their way into my head, alongside Elaine's and Detective Cron's questions—*how did you survive? What really happened that night?*

This time, I'm not a terrified kid. This time, I'm a woman who's not afraid.

So when Hansel wraps his arms and pulls me close, I let him take my weight. Let him pull me into his lap, like *Owen* did, just a few hours ago. I can't just say *look over there!* but I can hit him. Which might throw him off. Mess with his equilibrium. So, when he finally pulls me back, his intent to inspect my face, a hand already rising to wipe tears away—

I strike hard. I strike fast. The outer ridge of my palm below his jaw, and it knocks his head back, and I draw the gun at the same moment. But his hand is already on it, and there's a moment where we both yank in different directions. The gun comes out, goes flying, clanks against a wall.

Hansel grunts in pain as I heave my bodyweight into another strike, this one with the hand that went for the gun. My fist hits the side of his jaw, and I feel something *crunch*, but it doesn't stop him like it would the average person, too stunned by a face blow to react. He shoves me off him, puts distance between us. I land on my back hard, but roll to my feet, trained to ignore the pain and react.

And suddenly we're facing one another. My heart beats wildly in my chest, and Hansel's eyes are wide, angry. I take a step backward. Feel the table, pocket my phone. My eyes never leaving his. I size him up, measure the distance to the door. Wonder if I should stay and fight or run and get help.

"Why would you do that?" Hansel snaps. "I love you. You said you love me. You said you'd *come back*. I did this for us. I brought us back together after all this time."

I scoff, raising my fists, ready for this fight—the fight I've trained this past decade for. "Are you kidding me? I lied. I was a *child*. You kidnapped me. Killed August. Would have killed me, too. I *lied* to survive. To get away from you."

His eyes widen, and he stares at me, like he can't comprehend what I'm saying.

He had believed it a decade ago, all of it. Believed I loved him. That I wouldn't mind he'd killed my friend, that it didn't piss me off he'd drugged me and taken Janie, that it was okay he'd knocked me out to drag me here. Wherever here is. Another fucking cabin in the middle of nowhere, like last time. But he thought this one would have a fairy-tale ending. The only ending it will have includes him, unconscious. Maybe, dead.

"I can understand you're scared," he says, placating. "But I did this for *you*. For us. If the blood test hadn't happened, we would have had a normal life together. I would have moved to Los Angeles. You never would have known I was Hansel. We could have—"

I stare at him. Remember August's still body. Her terrified scream. The pain and suffering he's caused. Esme's body, blood streaming in rivulets. Literal fucking breadcrumbs. And then he made it look as though Guy had kidnapped *him*, when really, he tore up the photo and left of his own accord, not a care in the world. It's all been one big game, first to amuse him, and then to get me.

"You told me you wanted this. Wanted *me*." He's waving his arms around, accentuating his points, *still* talking about how he did this for us. For me. He stands between me and my goal, and for a moment, I flash back to the hotel room. The dojang. The making out, the sex, the *catch- me-if-you-can*, and this is almost like that, and nausea rolls through me.

Did he get off on hunting me in that entirely other way? I swallow back the urge to vomit.

This time, it will end differently.

I wait until he throws his arms up again, and I dart in, land a jab-cross-jab, and he's on the ground, but he's mad and spitting blood. I try to slide around him, to wrap an arm around his throat, but he spins, comes up on one knee, shoots his own foot out and catches me in the knee.

Pain sears through me like lightning. I fall, and he's on me, but I've done this a thousand times—we roll. I get a leg lock on him, and squeeze, but he swivels out of it, and suddenly I'm pinned face down, but again, I throw him off. He hits the table, and his head smacks on its surface. A dazed look comes to his eyes, and that's all the opportunity I need.

I race for the door, take a quick glance around for the gun, but it's nowhere to be seen. I throw the lock, and he's already heaving himself to his feet. Footsteps stamp the ground behind me as he rushes to stop me. Cold air hits me before he can, and even with the stabbing sensation in my knee, I sprint into the darkness, find a tree to hide behind, and freeze.

I wait, breath harsh, in and out of my lungs.

Not just the anaerobic rush from fighting, from running, but the adrenaline, sizzling through my veins.

Leaves crunch behind me.

A curse. Then, "Norah! I don't want to hurt you. I just want to talk. I did this for *us*."

I stay where I am. Press my fingers to the phone in my pocket, but I can't use it, not yet. It would be like lighting a fire in the night—showing him my exact location. And there's a good chance he's found his gun.

The seconds tick by. My heart slows to a steady rhythm. Leaves rustle and somewhere far off, a coyote howls. I squeeze my eyes shut. It's like I'm living in a horror movie.

The worst part is this isn't over. I can't just escape. Can't just call for help. I can't let him disappear. I won't disappear into the woods to save myself. Not this time.

This time, I'm seeing it through to the end. Because I won't live another day knowing Hansel's out there, waiting for me.

EIGHTY-SIX

He has a flashlight. A big fucking flashlight.

And he's headed my way.

A thick forest surrounds the cabin. No noise from a road or highway, no lights shining through the trees, betraying other homes. A single cabin on a big lot, somewhere in Kansas. Or maybe, Missouri. He could have driven hours with me unconscious.

I cross my arms, the chill raising hairs over my skin. My jacket is long gone—left behind at Janie's. It's not as cold as it has been, maybe the low forties, but that's cold enough. I flex my hands, my toes in my shoes. Try to keep circulation moving well enough that numbness doesn't set in.

I peer around the giant tree I'm crouched behind—an obvious hiding spot. But he's looking right where I raced into the woods, a location I've managed to get at least thirty feet from. But it was slow going, every move I make is a risk a twig will snap beneath my sneakers.

Climbing the tree is an option. But he has a light. A gun. I'd be trapped if he saw me.

But the tree provides enough cover, and he's looking the other way, so I slide my phone out, start to dial 911.

But there are messages waiting. A lot of messages, coming through, vibrating the phone in my hand.

The first one is from Hansel, from seconds ago.

MMAddict: *I'm starting to think you tricked me. Again.*

And then another comes through.

MMAddict: *Bitch.*

And though I've harbored no doubts he would kill me in the right situation—he's a fucking serial killer—I grow even colder, reading this message. One more comes through.

MMAddict: *Wait until I find you. And when I'm done with you. What breadcrumbs should I use for you, Norah? Maybe—*

I close the message before reading the rest. Start to dial 911. But something occurs to me, and instead I open Maps. Find my location. Drop a pin. And message it to Janie, Chloe, Detective Cron, and Rob.

Then I add: *He's here. He has a gun. I'm trapped in the woods. There's a cabin.*

I wait, and somewhere behind me, a shot goes off. I jump. Slam my hand over my mouth, because for half a second, I almost screamed. Not because the noise scared me—*it did*—but because I expected a bullet to find me. To cut through me.

A chuckle that makes me think *evil villain* and then, "You're dead, Norah Silverton! Do you hear me? And Janie, and Chloe, and—" He stops. Snorts. I hug the tree, wanting to look, wanting to see what he's doing that has him so amused. Instead, I focus on survival. I grab a rock. Pitch it as hard as I can in the air, aiming to pull his attention away from me, here.

It hits a tree, thuds to the ground. I take a peek, and Hansel swivels, the gun in a two-handed position, aimed right where the noise was. He laughs. "Want to play games? Sure. I've got the best game of all."

I throw another rock, this time over the clearing, because he's not looking my way; there's no way he can tell where it came from. It hits more to his right, and he turns that way, gun still raised. And then there's *another* crunch, but from back toward the cabin.

He takes a long look around the woods, then points the gun where I threw the first rock, strolling slowly through the grassy clearing surrounding the cabin. "Back to games, Norah. How about we play a round of guess who?"

I tense. What does he mean by that?

"Want to know how this all got started? The first person I killed? The death that made me realize I could get away with it? Not get caught?"

My stomach goes fluttery, but whatever he says, it doesn't matter. He's going to die tonight. I glance down at my phone— five minutes have passed. *Why hasn't anyone messaged me back?*

"You listening, Norah?" he booms. "This is important. I think you'll want to hear this part."

I curse under my breath. Wish he would just *shut the fuck up* already. Wish I'd stayed in the cabin and fought him hand to hand, because maybe he'd be unconscious by now. Maybe I'd have the gun.

"My first victim," he says, "Was your mother."

It's like a literal punch to the gut. Breath escapes me. I cling to the rough wood of the tree, try my damnedest not to move, because everything inside me has me collapsing to the ground.

He *laughs*. That same haunting, villainous laugh.

"It was so easy. She was going to give me a shitty grade, Norah. Which would have caused hell at home. I was so mad. I asked her to change it, and—she wouldn't. So I took care of the problem the best way I knew how. Covered my tracks pretty well, too, with the ATM, the note. I hadn't planned on telling you, since we were planning a life together and all. Since—" He stops. Swears. A note of anguish fills his tone, "You tricked me, Norah. Twice."

I force myself to open my eyes. To breathe. To get my shit together. I leave my phone on the ground, because I want no obstructions, no distractions. I peer around the tree. I throw three rocks in quick succession, all in the opposite direction of where I am, and then, when he starts to stride off toward wherever the fuck he thinks I am, I move.

It's my turn to hunt him.

EIGHTY-SEVEN

A giant oak stands in the midst of the clearing, and it's my goal. I need to get there before Hansel can stop, survey his surroundings. I sprint for it, footsteps light and fast, and I make it, just in time. He comes to a halt, likely realizing the noises were mere distractions, just as I press my body against the rough bark hard enough it hurts.

I inhale. Exhale. Shut my eyes. Open them.

Battle to focus on the moment, and not the memory of my mother. A rewind and reset of the last decade. She hadn't left me. She hadn't left *us*. She'd been taken.

By Hansel.

"Noraaaaah." He stretches my name out, a haunting howl. But I wait, and the whisper of his boots over leaves comes, and I spare a thought for *how the fuck did I ever think he's the one I've been waiting for?* I squat. Check his position—he stands with his back to me, ten feet deep into the thicket of trees.

Here's the questionable move. Chase him down. Or bring him to me?

He has a gun, so there's only one answer.

More rocks. A heavy stick. I hurl them where I was minutes

ago, where I left my phone's screen bright, running a video so it won't dim itself. So it will attract his attention.

"Gotcha." His voice is soft, close. Hansel strides by the tree, and I circle it slowly, clinging to it, keeping the trunk between us, and he's walking *away* from me now. I see the moment he catches the white-light flicker of my phone because he begins jogging. And my heart almost explodes with satisfaction that he's fallen for my trick, but I try to tune it out like Rob taught me—try to home in on what I need to do to *win*.

It's just one more fight.

He's at the edge of the tree line, and I'm five feet behind him, matching my step for his step. Letting his movements cover the noise of mine, because silence in the windswept autumn lawn is simply impossible.

Hansel comes to a stop. I do, too.

I wait and hold my breath. Wonder if he can hear my heart, it's so loud in my ears.

His head swivels one way, then the other. Checking for a trap. Because he can see the phone, and I can see even from where I am that it's evident it sits on the forest floor—not in my hand.

"Norah," he calls. He lifts one foot as if to step forward, but then he does what he always does—he telegraphs. Starts to turn at the knee, the hip, to spin to face me, long before he actually does it.

And I don't wait. I leap on his back, and I wrap one arm in a V around his throat. I grab that wrist with my opposite hand, press my elbow down, using his own body to leverage the choke-out, and I feel his hand spasm against my arm as he grabs at it, tries desperately to free himself. It's a *blood* choke, which means he'll pass out in seconds instead of minutes, and I squeeze tighter, burying my face in his hair, using every ounce of energy I have. I hear something hit the ground with a thump—the gun? Adrenaline slams through me, and I welcome it, welcome the superhuman strength it supposedly will give me in a life-or-death situation. I've got him. I've got *Hansel,* and I'm not letting go until the life is gone from his body.

But I missed something.

I missed the knife he hid somewhere on his body, and with a grunt, he buries it in my leg with his free hand.

I scream in pain, in rage. But that means the gun is no longer in that hand, so I release him, let myself fall to the ground, let him think he's won.

Breathe, just keep breathing—

I ignore my aching knee, the shooting agony of the knife in my leg, but he didn't hit the artery. I sweep my hands through damp, musty leaves, searching for the damn gun. But nothing. Nothing but twigs and rotting leaves and—

"I warned you," he growls. Hansel yanks me up by the collar of my shirt, and that's just fine, because I still have one good leg, and I connect it with his groin. I yank the knife out, slash at him, and he shoves me to keep the weapon from connecting. I drop it. We both go down hard, but he's up again before I can recover, the knife in his hand. He jumps on top of me, swinging the blade, and he's yelling—

No, *someone* is yelling—

Hansel's head jerks up, and he looks behind him, toward the sound, and I take the distraction for the opportunity it is, landing a punch to his throat. He falls back, gasping. Hopefully, I collapsed his trachea. Hopefully, he'll die slowly in a pool of—

A deafeningly loud popping sound. It echoes through the trees, and I yank back, searching desperately for the source. It was a gun, but there isn't one in either of Hansel's hands.

And that's when I see his eyes—those dark, moody, serial killer eyes—wide. Shocked. Hands no longer going for his throat, where I hit him, but to his chest, where something dark spills out, like a faucet turned on.

A dark shadow appears behind him, hidden in the blackness

of night. I start to pull myself backward, to get away, to dash into the woods.

But the shadow says, "I hate guns. But for you, *Hansel*? I'll make an exception." And then Hansel collapses, and the shadow steps forward.

Janie.

EIGHTY-EIGHT

Janie rushes to my side, one hand pressing down over the wound in my leg, the other curling around my shoulders and pulling me to her.

"You're alive," she whispers, and I'm about to say something, but more forms appear around the edge of the house—Chloe, Detective Cron. More officers. The officers have their guns out, and they skirt the edge of the perimeter, but Detective Cron comes straight for us, gun still in her hands.

"You were supposed to wait!" she tells Janie. Her eyes skim to me, to Hansel, squinting at the hole in his chest. "What happened?"

"He was going to kill me." The words pour out without hesitation. "Janie saved my life." *And she did.*

"He was about to stab her," Janie murmurs, hands moving over me, checking me for wounds.

"I'm okay," I say. Janie's eyes narrow, and she brushes dark hair out of her face, and she gives me that look—*Don't you try to bullshit me.*

A lull in the conversation, as all eyes go to Hansel. Detective Cron has a flashlight, and she holsters her gun and turns it on him. Takes in the wild look frozen on his face. Touches his neck and mutters, "Dead." Snorts. Shoots me a look. "Twice now, Silverton. You've survived a serial killer *twice*." She sighs. "Janie, we'll have to get a full report from you for shooting him, but—" She waves a hand. "He's Hansel. We know he took her. I can't imagine anyone will try to press charges."

Janie doesn't answer, doesn't seem to care. She just hugs me, and I hug her back, but my eyes are still on him. On Hansel. The moments I spent with *Owen* flicker through my brain on repeat, try to realign and understand it all. And worst of all— "He killed my mother. He admitted to it."

Detective Cron blinks at me. Her gaze lowers to my leg. She holds her radio up to her mouth and murmurs something, and moments later, a medic arrives. The woman sets her kit down, turns on the headlamp strapped to her forehead, inspects the wound.

"I have to cut your pants," she says, but she's not asking permission. She finds shears and begins cutting, and I watch, adrenaline beginning to fade. In its wake is pain, and what people refer to as *shock*, though I've never really believed in shock until this moment. My eyes catch on Hansel again, and this time I remember the first night I saw him, and August was dead, but tonight, August's twin killed him. A fitting end the second time around.

I smile. A thin line of grim satisfaction. But then the medic splashes something over the wound, and it burns like acid, and I hiss. Janie comes closer, effectively holds me in her lap.

"What happened?" she asks. Detective Cron comes in closer, kneels, listens.

"Elaine emailed me lab results." I relay the moments up until now, voice slow, gritting my teeth through the pain of having the stab wound fixed up. Chloe comes to my other side and takes my hand. Janie rubs my back. The medic finally asks if I want pain medicine, and I nod, and then I remember my phone in the woods and that Rob hasn't been updated and Janie goes to find it.

"Where am I?" I ask Detective Cron.

Her face pinches. "Woods outside of Clinton Lake. Downtown Lawrence is—" She waves in a direction. "Somewhere over there."

"Lawrence?" I murmur. It's a college town, nearly an hour west of Kansas City.

"How did you get here so fast?" I ask. "I only sent my location maybe twenty minutes ago."

Detective Cron presses her lips together. "I told you I'd try to figure out where Janie was held from the lake photo. We thought it was near the cabin where you found her, but we were wrong. He must have moved her there so you could find her. We were able to narrow it down to Clinton Lake. So, we raced out here when you went missing. Been combing through the forest looking for anything resembling a cabin—" She sits down beside me on the damp ground. "Then, you sent us your location. We were only ten minutes away."

I stare at her a moment. So, she wasn't quite as bad at her job as I thought. In fact, her doing her job might have saved my life. Same as Elaine. I would have never guessed I'd feel the need to thank either of them—much less both.

"Thank you," I say. "You saved my life."

She waves at the body. "I'd say you saved yourself."

"Janie did," I reply instantly, remembering the gun in her hand. Hansel's own gun. I owe her a drink. *Several* drinks. Everything. God, what a badass friend I have.

Janie returns, and I call Rob.

"I'm alive," I say when he answers.

He chokes a sob over the phone. "Sorry, sorry. I just thought —hours passed, Norah, *hours*. Let me talk to Janie. I'm coming back to Kansas City."

"Rob, you don't have to—"

"You got stabbed, Norah. You're my friend, my family. I'm coming back."

I hand the phone over without further argument.

The medic takes my hand and says something about starting an IV, how the pain medicine may make me tired, and there's a tiny prick, and then pain medicine, and she helps me lie back on a blanket. Stars swirl overhead. The world grows dim. I close my eyes, and with Janie and Chloe here to watch over me, I sleep.

Janie found her dress. It's knee-length, sheer, in an ivory color that sets off her pale skin, her dark hair, her red-lipsticked smile. And smile, she does. Chloe stands across from her, in matching pants and tank top, and her smile positively glows from where I sit in the front row.

After the chaos in Kansas City, Janie and Chloe decided on a beach wedding in San Diego. It's sunset, blazing oranges and reds and purples smoothing over the horizon, the wink of the sun almost gone. Rob stands beside me, my "date," and we watch as they exchange vows, rings, kiss.

The reception is small, no more than twenty people, at a beachfront restaurant with torches lit and a dance floor, drinks flowing, laughter ringing through the night. This beach will be college-party-central in another month. But for right now, it's our own private place to make new memories.

I find Janie and hug her. Whisper, "You look amazing," and she smiles. Nods suggestively at Rob with her eyebrows raised.

"No!" I laugh. "We're just here as friends. He's *Rob*." And she sighs, forever on the hunt for my happily-ever-after, but I think I've found it for now.

Here, among my friends.

"Norah Silverton!" Janie's mother sweeps over, looking almost like an older sister instead of her mother, the main difference long, curly hair. "It's *so* good to see you! Why don't you come visit more often? Maybe we could—"

"Mooom," Janie groans, pulling her away.

Rob finds me, then. Takes my hand, leads me to the dance floor. I laugh, because we're in close contact for training every day, but dancing feels different. Intimate. But I wrap my arms around him anyway, and we sway like that for a while, both lost in our own thoughts. My eyes are still on the sunset, though the colors have faded to a distant orange, the sun long gone. Owen—Hansel—last held me like this, and I still think about him—*them*—all the time.

Sometimes, late at night, I wonder which one he really was underneath it all. But then I remember it doesn't matter. Because he was a murderer. He killed my friends. My father. My mother. A crime I'll likely never know the end of because he hadn't lived long enough to ask the important questions—What did you do? Where did you leave her body?—and there are even moments, I wonder if he was telling the truth, or if he just knew she disappeared one day, and he'd say anything, do anything, to throw me off my game.

But in the end, what matters is he was stopped. For good. He can't ever come back now.

And I survived.

Guy and Elaine waited only a week after it happened to come after me for the next story—the next book. But I've decided, at least for Guy, there's not much to write about. Because we won. The case is closed.

I'm ready to think about the future, ready to move past this, to buy in with Rob. Ready to call it quits on amateur fighting and focus on being a coach, because my battles are won.

"Rob?" I ask.

"Yes?"

I break away from his arms and pull him toward the beach, kick off my shoes, feel the cool grains of sand between my toes. Realize that as much as Kansas City is a part of me, it's in my past, and the West Coast is where I belong now. Forever.

"I'm ready to talk about being a partner in the gym if you haven't already found someone?"

He snorts. Smiles. Wraps an arm around me in a half hug. "I wouldn't give it to anyone else."

Janie and Chloe wander over. A photographer asks us to pose together, and snaps a photo, and then Janie's mother swings by for a goofy candid shot with an old-school Polaroid. Janie and Chloe are back on the dance floor in the next moment, a favorite song blaring through speakers, and Janie's mother hands me the photo.

It slowly develops, the four of us appearing in grainy, washed-out color. In my mind's eye, I can see who's missing—August and Esme. But it's a wedding, and the four of us are alive, and our job is to keep living. So instead of focusing on them, I put the photo in my purse and return to my friends.

A LETTER FROM JESSICA

Dear Reader,

The letter I get to write to you is one of my favorite after-the-book-has-been-written activities. I mean, honestly, it's genius. I wish more of my favorite books included the author writing a letter to the reader. This is my second book to go out into the world, and I've learned so much over the past year. What I've learned most of all is that readers are wonderful, kind people who want to love your character and lose themselves in your book. We exist in this reading and writing community together, and though we play slightly different roles, we cannot exist without one another.

So, dear reader, thank you. Thank you so much for taking the time to come play in my world for a while. And to everyone who has shared one of my books in some way—mentioned it to a friend or posted about it on social media—thank you. It's the lifeblood of how authors are discovered by new readers, and it makes a world of difference.

If you've enjoyed *The Lucky One*, be sure to sign up for updates about my upcoming releases.

www.bookouture.com/jessica-payne

My personal newsletter is another great way to stay up to date with my book releases. I send occasional emails about give-aways, bookish news, upcoming releases, and more.

So, let's chat a little bit about *The Lucky One*. This book was first inspired when I listened to a podcast about a woman who had survived a serial killer—she had effectively tricked him into letting her go. I always wondered about that woman. Who she'd been before she found the strength to face down her would-be murderer. Who she was after. Because I couldn't imagine someone would survive something that horrific without being utterly changed. Their outlook on the world completely transformed.

It got me thinking.

I also have always loved martial arts. I studied them as a child and teenager, and even taught them for a while in my twenties. I'd always wanted to pull them into a book somehow, and I decided maybe this was the right one. Norah emerged slowly. Who would a survivor be ten years later? How would she live her life? Well, I have a thing for strong, kickass women, so she of course learned to take care of herself.

There is also plenty of commentary on true crime here. I don't mean to pass judgment—more, raise the question. Remind us all that, though we love listening to these stories, these true crime podcasts and shows and books are real. They are telling the stories of people who lived and died. Who had mothers and fathers and children and hobbies they loved and futures they looked forward to. They are not mere entertainment, and I think it's important we remember and respect that.

If you've enjoyed reading *The Lucky One*, my first book is called *Make Me Disappear*, and is about a woman who arranges for her own kidnapping to escape her narcissistic, sociopath boyfriend—but nothing goes as planned. Please consider picking it up next.

And please consider leaving me a review on Amazon, Barnes & Noble, Goodreads, or any other place you frequent.

Also, I'd love to hear from you on Facebook, Instagram, Twitter, etc. Here are links to keep in touch with me:

Thank you again for reading *The Lucky One*!

Jessica

https://jessicapayne.net

facebook.com/authorjessicapayne

twitter.com/authorjesspayne

instagram.com/jessicapayne.writer

goodreads.com/authorjesspayne

tiktok.com/@authorjesspayne

ACKNOWLEDGMENTS

I want to say thank you to Kimberly Brower, my incredible literary agent. I started a list of all the things I wanted to thank you for, but it got quite long, so I'll simply say thank you for everything. I'm so glad we are partners on this journey.

Thank you to Joy Kozu, who continues to add perspective and ideas. I'm always glad to see you on a call.

Thank you to my editor, Kelsie Marsden. You have a talent for pulling out the most important threads, for identifying the things I haven't thought of, for making my books shine. I appreciate you.

Thank you to my publicist, Jess Readett, who has been so phenomenal at helping keep everything organized and getting the word out. You are so fantastic to work with.

Thank you to everyone at Bookouture. What a fantastic publishing team I get to work with!

To my work wife, Sara Read, you are the best—my day would not be complete without at least a hundred voice messages from you.

Hugs to Jaime Lynn Hendricks and Judge Judy, both of whom brighten my writing day. I'm *so* glad we randomly happened upon one another. I wouldn't be here without you.

Cheers, Evie Hughes. I so appreciate you, friend. You always have an interesting thought, perspective, random fact. I'm so glad we stumbled upon one another. Thank you for being with me since day one on this writing journey.

Thank you to Jeneva Rose and Mary Keliikoa. You both

provide the most helpful feedback, advice, and writerly wisdom.

All my love to Emma, the reason I wake up super early to write. You inspired me to start this journey.

Extra pets to Lilst Kitty, who continues to wake me up early and chirp at me to feed her and make coffee.

Thank you to each and every member of #MomsWritersClub. You all are amazing moms and writers, and I'm so glad we all found one another.

Thank you to the Porch Crew—Mikey, Sally, Alyssa, Marina, and Joy. You all are amazing, and I'll be right over for a "splash."

I've already mentioned you by name, but I am so thankful for the Uffish Writers' Retreat. Next time we'll figure out our signature cocktail!

To my Launch Group—you made debuting a dream. Thank you all for reading my book, getting the word out, and cheering me on. I'm so grateful to you all.

Thank you to bookstagrammers! Seriously, you all are a gift to authors. Thank you for the time you've dedicated to me, my books, getting the word out, making beautiful images, sharing my book, and more. I would especially like to thank Tonya and Stephanie. I had no idea how badass bookstagram was until I met you both. Thank you for this incredible introduction and all the support.

Thank you to Browsers Bookshop in Olympia, especially to Andrea.

And thank you to you, reader. You picked up my book. You read it. For an author, that means everything.